THE EXECUTOR

The Executor

BLAKE MORRISON

Chatto & Windus
LONDON

1 3 5 7 9 10 8 6 4 2

Chatto & Windus, an imprint of Vintage,
20 Vauxhall Bridge Road,
London SW1V 2SA

Chatto & Windus is part of the Penguin Random House group of companies whose
addresses can be found at global.penguinrandomhouse.com

Penguin
Random House
UK

First published by Chatto & Windus in 2018

penguin.co.uk/vintage

A CIP catalogue record for this book is available from the British Library

ISBN 9781784742140

Typeset in India by Integra Software Services Pvt. Ltd, Pondicherry

Printed and bound by Clays Ltd, St Ives plc

Penguin Random House is committed to a sustainable future for our
business, our readers and our planet. This book is made
from Forest Stewardship Council® certified paper.

For Kathy

It is commonly supposed that the uniformity of a studious life affords no matter for narration: but the truth is that of the most studious life a great part passes without study. An author partakes of the common condition of humanity; he is born and married like another man; he has hopes and fears, expectations and disappointments, griefs and joys, and friends and enemies, like a courtier or a statesman; nor can I conceive why his affairs should not excite curiosity as much as the whisper of a drawing room, or the factions of a camp.

Samuel Johnson, *The Idler* (29 March 1760)

I care not though I were to live but one day and one night if only my fame and deeds live after me.

Cúchulainn

1

'Wow,' I said. 'That's some ask.'

'It wouldn't be much work,' Rob said.

'I don't mind the work – it just feels so morbid.'

'Don't be soppy.'

We were eating at Archie's in Soho, a restaurant that's more like a club, very intimate, an upper room with a dozen tables and a small bar with high stools. The floorboards stretch from one end of the room to the other, and we were sitting near the door to the kitchen: every time one of the waiters walked past, the table wobbled. During our mains I'd slipped a table mat under one leg, without success. There was no way round it. We were on shaky ground.

'I know it's an imposition . . .' he said.

'I just hate the thought. You're my friend.'

'Which is why I'm asking.'

'Friend' was true. But our contact had dwindled to an annual lunch and occasional emails. The lunch was always timed for late November – just far ahead enough of Christmas to avoid groups of office workers wearing party hats and eating turkey. And the emails we exchanged were jokey, not like the serious stuff today.

'It's not that you're ill,' I said.

'Just thinking ahead. My dad died at sixty-one.'

'We're all living longer these days.'

'Except those with bad genes. Even if I add five years to his, my prospects aren't good.'

'Come on. You're only what . . .?'

'Fifty-nine.'

I knew that. Both our birthdays fell in May, his fourteen years before mine. But I didn't want him thinking of me as an acolyte. Christ, I hadn't even read his last collection.

'I'm surprised you think I'm qualified,' I said. If I was going to do this, I deserved to hear him spell it out.

'You've known me longer than anyone else.'

'That can't be true.'

'My parents are dead, my sister doesn't count, and no one from school has ever read me.'

'You must know other poets.'

'None I can trust not to fuck up.'

'Or Jill. How *is* Jill?'

'Jill's fine – but she won't want to do it.'

Fine is how Jill always was, or how he always said she was: steady, loyal, more mindful of his needs than of her own. Or perhaps none of those things, just not a subject for discussion.

'Dessert?'

'Nah. Just a coffee.'

'More wine?' he said, dangling the empty bottle by the neck.

'I shouldn't.'

'Just a glass then?'

'I've work to get back to.'

'Small or large?'

'Well, if we're going to bother at all . . .'

He waved to the waiter, who cleared our plates and went to fetch two glasses.

'No need to decide now, if you want to think about it. There won't be much you've not seen. The last collection cleaned me out.'

'But there'll be other stuff to come.'

'Little worth keeping gets written in old age.'

'Stop pretending to be geriatric.'

'I feel geriatric.'

'You don't look it.'

And he didn't. There was a boyish glint in his eye. I'd never quite understood what it signified — irony, mischief, an appreciation of life's little absurdities — but it shone as brightly as ever. His hair, despite a few grey hints, was exuberant: the Frizzy Guy I'd heard him being called in Brandon the year I'd gone there to study, or rather to write. I'd envied him then — for his knowledge, his energy, his independence. Despite his gloominess, I envied him still.

'OK, I'm not old, but I'm realistic. I peaked in my forties and now I'm past it. The reviewers of my last book said as much. Including the one on your pages.'

'He's always harsh,' I said.

'Pity you gave it to him, then.'

'Leonie commissions the poetry reviews.'

'I'm not complaining. He made some good points. Fuck, I *agreed* with him. That's the problem. Thanks, and could we have the bill, please?'

The waiter's arrival distracted him and allowed me to change the subject. I still remembered some of the adjectives the review had used — 'tired', 'hollow', 'pompous', 'antiquated', 'devoid of life and conviction'. I'd felt bad when we ran the piece, all the more so because Leonie had consulted me before sending the book out — was Marcus Downe the right reviewer? Why not? I'd said, half distracted by a picture caption I was writing, but

3

not so distracted that I couldn't foresee the possible outcome. At least Marcus's reviews were long and prominently displayed – that would be my defence if Rob brought it up again, along with the argument (diametrically opposed) that book reviews don't count for much these days. But reviews mattered to Rob, and it was no use pretending that to allocate 1,500 words to his new collection was a mark of respect when 1,200 of those words were devoted to demolishing him. I'd sent a warning email the day before the piece appeared; he didn't reply. That was six months ago. When he finally got in touch to suggest lunch ('the annual ritual', as he called it), I wondered if his purpose was to berate me. Well, I was right that he had an agenda. But not the one I'd been expecting. Far from banishing me to the wilderness, he wanted to anoint me as his disciple.

'Do I have to sign anything?' I said.

'I just nominate you.'

'And that's it?'

'As far as I know. My solicitor's dealing with the will.'

'You've made a will?'

'Haven't you? You've two kids, for Chrissake.'

'Three soon – Marie's four months pregnant.'

'Get a move on then. That's a lot of dependants. You don't want to leave them in the shit.'

He didn't offer congratulations and I didn't tell him that we knew it was a girl. The subject of children, like the subject of Jill, was one we usually skirted round. I can't recall him expressing a particular aversion to kids when we first met, in Brandon, no more so than was average for a determinedly single man, for whom the prospect of getting a woman pregnant was a routine terror, not to be assuaged by her whispering *Don't bother, I hate the feel of those things, I'm on the pill.* When he returned to England and married Jill in his early forties (the registry

4

office ceremony taking place on the day his second collection came out), I wondered if they might have children; she was younger than him, after all. But nothing happened. And went on not happening. A fertility problem? Or a decision jointly arrived at that a life without children suited them best, what with her career in the charity sector and his as a poet needing solitude? We never talked about it, but the latter seemed more likely, given how at ease with his life he seemed and how incurious about my kids, to the point of never remembering their gender or names. There are people who say they don't have dogs because they lack the time to look after them properly. I could imagine Rob making a similar case against kids, and Jill – loyal, selfless Jill – going along with it, whatever her true feelings.

'I'm serious, Matt. It's irresponsible otherwise. I hope you've taken out life insurance too. You never know. That's why I'm asking if you'll –'

'Can we talk about something else?'

'Last word, promise: if you die before me, I'll do the same for you.'

'What, get it all out there – the unpublished stories, the abandoned novels, the letters and diaries?'

'Exactly.'

'Don't be an idiot, Rob. No one gives a toss about my work. There's nothing to give a toss about.'

'If you say so,' he said, signalling a reminder to the waiter: where the fuck was our bill? It was touching if he really believed that despite my having a ten-to-six, five-day-a-week job to do, two small children to bring up, and an elderly parent to visit as often as could be managed, I still had the time and energy to write something worthwhile.

'My turn,' he said, as always, when the bill finally arrived, and 'Give it here, the paper will cover it,' I replied, as always, laying my credit card on the plate without even looking at the amount. In the early days, the paper *had* covered our lunches. Newspapers were more affluent then, and expense claims less closely monitored. Besides, Rob was a name, and wrote the odd review for us, so treating him to lunch seemed appropriate, all the more so since I received a monthly salary, and he, for all his renown, was a freelance writer, what's worse a poet, dependent for his living on the money he scraped together from readings, talks, bits of teaching and occasional book reviews. We never talked about it (pride would have prevented him from pleading penury), but these days he probably earned less than ever. If he'd known it was me paying, not the paper, he'd have felt humiliated. But I doubt it occurred to him. The fact that our circulation was in freefall, that twenty-odd members of staff had just been laid off, and that those of us remaining had been forced to take a salary cut – none of this would have reached his ears, or his eyrie, despite it being widely reported, or if it had, would not have struck him as having any connection with our lunch.

'You must write something for us,' I said, punching in the code for my credit card, as the waiter stood there with a smile he probably hoped would bring a tip, despite the 12.5 per cent service charge already added to the bill.

'Last time you were probably the only person who looked at the piece.'

'Rubbish. There's a team who monitor page traffic. OK, it's not like we're the news pages, but people do read reviews.'

'The online stuff, maybe – for the comments by groupies or trolls. At least your guy had some discrimination.'

'My guy?'

'The one who pissed on my book. He meant what he said and he put his name to it. Fair enough.'

6

We were back to that review. It had hurt him even more than I thought.

'It's the assassins hiding behind pseudonyms I object to. They stick the knife in, then disappear into the night. That's why I avoid the Internet. It's a haven for cowards and thugs.'

I took the receipt from the waiter and stuck it in my wallet. Had he been listening? Did he realise Rob was a well-known poet? Or did he see him as just another grumpy old man? Even I felt embarrassed hearing him bang on.

'I'm not blaming anyone,' Rob said, seeing my expression. 'I had my moment. No one wants to hear poems by white, middle-aged, middle-class Englishmen any more. We're dinosaurs. Doubly disadvantaged — male and pale. Quite right too. We ruled the roost for too long. *I* wouldn't listen to someone like me either. You have to have *content* — a story — and I don't.'

'Everyone has a story,' I said.

'Maybe. But the point of a poem is to hold back, not spill the beans, so readers keep finding more. Freedom of expression includes the right not to reveal anything ... Sorry, I'm boring you, we need to go.'

'Nice scarf,' I said, as we retrieved our coats from the cloakroom halfway down the stairs.

It was navy blue, with small red foxes across it.

'I've had it for years. Treated myself. It was either foxes or squirrels. A small shop in one of those arcades off Piccadilly used to sell them. I came across it by chance. Old Italian guy. He had a photo of Princess Di in his window. She once bought a tie there. For Charles, I suppose.'

'Or Dodi Fayed. Silk's more for a lover than a husband, wouldn't you say?'

He shrugged and led the way downstairs.

'So, how are you spending Christmas?' I said.

'Quietly, at home. Sounds like someone's death notice, doesn't it?'

'No family coming?'

'We might see Jill's brother at some point. But we don't really get on.'

Certainly, Rob didn't. I could remember him describing Jill's brother as an orang-utan.

'At least he's sane,' he said. 'Unlike my sister.'

'She's no better, then?'

'The last I heard she was living in Sydney. On the streets, probably. Who the fuck are all these people? London gets more crowded every time I come in. Which way are you going?'

The air was cold. He tied his scarf tighter. Since his sudden move to Hadingfield ten years ago, he'd adopted the pose of a baffled provincial, unable to keep up.

'I go right, you go left,' I said, hugging him. 'Same place next year?'

'If I'm still here.'

'Yeah, yeah. Better meet sooner, then. Let's fix a date once the Christmas madness is over.'

'Absolutely,' he said, and probably meant it, just as I meant it. But we both immediately forgot about it. At any rate I did.

*

'Being an editor's like being a Sherpa,' my about-to-be boss Leonie said during my job interview eight years ago, 'we do all the work and they get all the glory.' By 'they' she meant reviewers, though in relation to the authors whose books they appraise, most of them feel like Sherpas too. Still, I'd had some experience of editing by then and took the point. There's a lot of baggage to carry and a lot of dull slog. And at the end, we're anonymous, backroom girls and boys known to those in the business – authors, agents, publishers, fellow journos – but not to the world beyond. The only byline is the reviewer's, even if, as often happens, we've virtually written the piece ourselves. It was a shock to discover how sloppily some writers write, not least famous ones. No doubt they're too busy getting on with their own stuff to think a mere book review or arts feature is worth losing sleep over, though I've heard publishers' editors complain that even with novels and memoirs it's left to them to tidy the prose. For us it can be more like building a new house than tidying. Only a few writers send in good copy – and say what you like about Rob, he was one of them.

I was still thinking about him when I got back to the office. It was 3.15, absurdly late by my standards (on most days I buy a sandwich from round the corner and eat it at my desk), but we'd put the pages to bed the day before: the annual stunt whereby celebrity names (including the odd author) recommend their favourite titles had kept us there till after ten at night. Now the pressure was off, and with Leonie also out for lunch I'd not needed to rush from mine. Indeed, she still wasn't back when I sat down at my screen and logged on. There were no interesting emails, just the usual stuff – an editor wondering why a 'glitteringly authentic' first novel she'd published in August hadn't yet been reviewed by us (or anyone else, probably); a poet submitting three new odes (his word) from his Cornish Megalith sequence; a twitcher from Chipping Norton objecting to a passing reference to Manx shearwaters in a book review the previous week ('everyone knows they migrate to the South Atlantic in winter'). It was too early to start laying out next week's pages – none of the copy had come in. I spent an hour in the book cupboard instead.

It's more a glass cubicle than a cupboard, but the floor-to-ceiling shelves close it off from the rest of the office and if you shut the door, which has frosted glass, you're invisible from

9

outside. The rest of the office is open-plan, which makes the cupboard an object of envy and nudge-nudge comment. To my knowledge, no sexual activity has ever occurred in there, but colleagues have sometimes slipped in clutching a handkerchief or asked to borrow it for clandestine phone calls. We've taken to locking the door when we leave, but during the day it stays open, and there are always journalists who drift in, 'for a browse', which Leonie finds annoying ('we're not a fucking bookshop'), all the more so when, as invariably happens, the browser emerges with a review copy and offers to write a piece, an offer she'll politely decline ('ah, sorry, we've already commissioned someone'), then ridicule when they've departed ('why the fuck does the fucking environment correspondent think he's qualified to review the new Rushdie?'), unless the book is chick lit or military history, in which case she'll say no thank, but they're welcome to keep it. I'm easier-going than Leonie, but I didn't want to be intruded on that afternoon and made a point of closing the door behind me.

I love it in the book cupboard – the half-light, the monkish silence, the smell of freshly printed pages – but it's hard not to feel chastened. You pick up a novel, say, and think of where it began, with a man or woman sitting alone in a room, and of the work that's gone into it since (the agenting, copy-editing, proof-reading, designing and printing), and of the work still to come putting the word out and getting copies into bookshops, and of how any review you run, however brief, will matter hugely to the author, regardless of sales, which ought to weigh heavily on you, except that several dozen other novels are also coming out the same week, all of them in front of you in the cupboard, and if a glance at the dust jacket, or rapid sampling of the first page, suggests it's not a book worth bothering with, you put it in the reject pile without even a twinge of conscience. Does that sound cynical? Maybe. But we've space to cover only a tiny fraction of the books published each year. And those we do cover have to be worthwhile journalistically, with either the author or the subject matter sparking an interesting review.

That afternoon, in the space of ten minutes, I put forty-three books in the reject crate, seasonal tosh mostly, or books that shouldn't have been sent to us in the first place, since anyone familiar with our pages knows that we don't review books on DIY, pet care, yoga, self-help and how to make your first million. That left only five books worth commissioning reviews on, all due out in January, one by a contemporary of mine at Bristol, Ed McKeane, whose last novel had been longlisted for the Booker and whom Leonie rated highly, as I might have too and indeed briefly did, since he seemed a good guy despite his public-school patina, someone who might become a friend, I thought, until he humiliated me in a first-year seminar for my pronunciation of the word 'rhetoric' – I knew what it meant, but I'd never heard it said aloud and put the stress on the second syllable, an error which Ed highlighted by leaping into the class discussion straight after me and repeating the word, with a stress on the first syllable and a smirk across the table. Now he was smirking at me again, from a dust jacket, twenty-odd years older but with his sheen and cleverness undimmed. I'd have loved to dump him in the reject crate, but Leonie had already set up a reviewer and I'd a duty to send it out.

'*There* you are,' Leonie said, pushing the door open as I stapled the Jiffy bag with Ed's novel in it. With her black hair and dark brown eyes, she can look eerily pallid, but for once her cheeks were pink. 'Good lunch?' she asked before I could.

'Yes. Not long back. I was seeing Robert Pope.'

'God, Robert Pope. I'd forgotten about him. You should get him to do something for us. He's not a bad writer, for a poet.'

'He's rather picky,' I said. 'And less keen on us since we trashed his last collection.'

'*We?*'

'Marcus Downe.'

'Remind me.'

'Long piece back in the spring. Even by Marcus's standards it was harsh.'

'What's he expect, veneration?'

'Pretty much.'

'He'll get over it. We should bung him something and offer lots of space. What's in the Jiffy bag?' she said, narrowing her eyes.

'The new Ed McKeane. For Daphne.'

'Sorry. Change of plan. Daphne read the proof and hated it. I've asked Bridget instead.'

'I thought Bridget did his last one.' I *knew* Bridget had done his last one. She'd called Ed the new Graham Greene. We try to avoid reviewers covering the same author twice, especially if they've been fulsome the first time. Bridget was like a Labrador pup: whoever the author, she jumped up and licked them all over.

'Everyone else is too busy or already reviewing it,' Leonie said. 'What else has come in?'

'Rubbish time of year. But I've found a few things. There's the new —'

'Actually, I've a couple of calls to make. Can we leave it till later?'

'Sure.'

'Or tomorrow, definitely.'

Leonie's not a procrastinator, but she likes to do things on her terms. By tomorrow, she'd have looked at the books I'd saved from the reject crate and decided who should review them – she wouldn't send them out before consulting me, but any discussion would be token. I'm not complaining. She's the one responsible for the books pages. And they're good pages, sharper and livelier than our rivals'. But if I were ambitious, I'd feel frustrated by how little commissioning I get to do. And if I were thinner-skinned, I'd feel slighted by her lack of regard for any suggestions I make.

The upside is that she has children and – unlike the other (mostly male) department heads – doesn't believe in us working after six unless we have to. It's a mixed blessing to be home before the children go to bed. But I usually manage it.

*

'What a narcissist,' Marie said.

We'd finally got Jack and Noah off, though with Noah you couldn't be sure about the finally: he was two now and capable of sleeping through, but as often as not he'd wake about an hour after we'd put him down and demand that one of us sit with him till he went off again, so dinner tended to be a quick affair, timed so that we'd just about digested whatever it was (tonight, tortellini with pesto and parmesan, plus green salad), before whoever's turn it was to deal with him disappeared upstairs, often never to return, since there's nothing like lying in bed with your infant son after a meal and glass of wine to send you to sleep, even if it's not yet ten o'clock and even if, since Marie became pregnant again, we'd given up the wine, she for health reasons and me out of solidarity.

'I took it as a compliment,' I said.

'I'm sure you did. But it's some creepy power thing. He wants to keep a hold over you when he's gone.'

'He trusts me to look after his interests.'

'Which are what? He'll be dead.'

13

'He's his reputation to think of.'

'It's all he ever does think of. Himself and all things pertaining to. Never Jill.'

Marie had met Jill only once, at a small dinner for the launch of Rob's fourth collection. She wasn't much more acquainted with Rob – my relationship with her goes back only a decade, by which point I was seeing less of him. But that dinner was enough to convince her that she'd got the dynamic of their marriage sussed. And that Rob was even more vain, pretentious and misogynistic than she'd feared. She might have forgiven him for that, up to a point, since several other male writers she'd come across were no better. But she couldn't forgive him for neglecting Jill, who, as Marie saw it, he'd left on her own that evening, at the far end of the table from him, and who looked lost, miserable and bored until Marie swapped places with someone and came to her rescue. It wasn't that she especially warmed to Jill. Their lives and careers had little in common. Marie works with children who have speech problems and she spent the evening struggling to coax words out of Jill. None of which she held against her. It was all Rob's fault, for being a selfish bastard.

'I know you've reservations about Rob . . .' I said.

'Reservations!'

'He's an old friend. I couldn't say no.'

'It's your funeral.'

'All I'll have to do is keep him in print. And see that any royalties go to Jill.'

'Jill won't have crossed his mind. He treats her as if she's of no account.'

'Of no account but an accountant – I like that.'

Rob used to joke about being the only poet in history married to an accountant ('Other poets have muses or mistresses, I have a mathematician'). The word wasn't quite accurate. At university Jill had read geography, and her job as CFO to an environmental charity was more about managing people than managing money. But she'd a talent for numbers: that much was true.

'Whatever else,' Marie said, helping herself to the last soggy parcel of tortellini, 'I know you love me. Jill's never had that reassurance from Rob.'

'You don't know what goes on in bed.'

'Does anything go on in bed? They've not had kids.'

'I don't think they wanted kids.'

'Jill did.'

'Is that what she told you?'

'She didn't need to. I could tell.'

Marie sees the world in black and white, whereas I like to think I'm more nuanced, even if that doesn't impress her ('Nuance is for people too chicken to say what they think'). She's quick to pass judgement and never fails to overstate the case. But she's also rarely wrong. If her instincts tell her something, there's no dislodging it, and invariably subsequent events will prove her right: that teenage boy whose inertia everyone attributed to adolescent torpor *was* addicted to skunk; the husband who she noticed playing with his wedding ring over dinner *was* having an affair; that babysitter she wouldn't use despite all the friends who swore by her *was* stealing from them. Maybe that's why I needed Marie, to give me a handle on life. She knew next to nothing about the world I moved in, but when something was bothering me (one of the subs being uppity, say, or the editor leaning on me, while Leonie was on holiday, to get a book by a friend of his reviewed), she'd help me see my way round it and encourage me to make a stand. Perhaps that's what marriage is about, once kids come along and there's no time for sex or not the kind of sex you had at the beginning (a languorous run of repeats rather than *coitus interruptus*). I was no less attracted to Marie than I'd ever been: if she'd lines on her forehead and shadows under her eyes, so what? She was still Marie. Her belief in me helped me to believe in myself. And made me tougher and more resolute. Well named, she used to say about me: Matt as in doormat. These days I was less of a pushover.

Still, as far as Rob's request went – his 'demand', as Marie put it – she thought I'd given in too easily.

'He's always been brutal about looking after himself. And when he's dead, he'll expect you to be brutal on his behalf.'

'That could be thirty years from now.'

'But it'll be hanging over you.'

'It might be fun.'

'If sorting through his stuff is how you want to spend what little spare time you have, then fine. My only point is: you don't owe him a thing. He wouldn't do it for you.'

'Actually, he said he would.'

'And you believed him?'

'Why not?'

Why not? Except that on the one occasion Rob had been asked to help me, when my first and only novel came out, he had let me down. Officially, it was my publishers who asked him, when they sent a proof copy which they hoped he'd 'endorse' with a quote for the dust jacket. But he must have known it was me who suggested him. Rob's reply, which my editor passed on to me with an accompanying '!!!', was a lesson in how not to decline an invitation. He would like to help, it went, since I was 'in effect' an old student of his and we were good friends, but he doubted that praise from him would cut much ice, since he was a poet not a novelist, besides which he had an urgent deadline to meet (do poets have deadlines?), and since the events of the previous year (9/11) he had lost faith in the power of literature, on top of which he'd begun a set of onerous dental appointments for root canal work, all of which meant he wouldn't be able to read the novel before it came out, so with regret he must decline. As Marie says, if you're going to decline an invitation, give one excuse, not a hatful. A sentence was all we were after, which – since he'd seen parts of the novel in draft – would have taken far less time than the paragraph he'd written explaining why he couldn't write it. But for the fact that two novelists from the same publishing house (close friends of the editor) had come up with puffs as good or better than anything Rob would have written, I might have been seriously offended. But in my virginal euphoria at getting a book published, I let it go, and felt right to have done so when, after a couple of lukewarm reviews appeared, Rob wrote a long letter to say how much he liked the book, which he'd now read twice, and proceeded to give a breakdown of what was good about it – ending the letter with a PS that read 'By the way, your publishers asked me to give a quote, but I was suffering from depression at the time: apologies, now I'm feeling better of course I wish I had.' Had he been suffering from depression? Marie would have dismissed that as bullshit. But I'd never told Marie about the episode, because it predated her, and I certainly wasn't going to tell her now.

'Any pud?' I said, rearranging the dishwasher before sticking our plates in – Marie might be wise about most things, but when it comes to stacking crockery and glassware so there's an outside chance of it getting clean or remaining intact, she hasn't a clue.

'Since when do we have pud during the week?'

'It's been known.'

'You had lunch out.'

'I still feel hungry.'

'There's cheese. And a few grapes.'

'Want some?'

'A peppermint tea will do me.' A cry floated down: Noah, bang on time. 'I'll have it upstairs.'

'You don't want me to see to him?'

'I'd rather you cleared up.'

She kissed me on the cheek as she passed, and I watched her kick a balloon aside in the doorway. It was Jack's latest fetish, since his fifth-birthday party three weeks previously: five balloons were to remain inflated at all times; if one of them burst or began to sag, another must take its place. The balloons added to the general clutter in our basement kitchen, which had seemed so spacious when we moved in. Everything seemed spacious after the Hackney flat, and though buying a house meant moving further out, to Wood Green, because no property nearer in was affordable, we revelled in the freedom: four storeys, three bedrooms and a forty-foot rear garden was more than we'd dared to hope for when we started looking, London property prices being what they are or have become. Luckily, the flat sold for more than we'd expected (Hackney was cool), and Marie's parents met the shortfall on the mortgage with a £30,000 loan, one they didn't seriously expect us to repay. We felt to be living in Arcadia – 41 Arcadian Gardens to be precise – and, with Jack just a baby, the house was far bigger than we needed. When Noah came along he slept with us at first, then moved in with Jack, which left the spare bedroom free to double as an office. But with a third child it would become the nursery, and any work Marie or I brought home would have to be done at the kitchen table. We'd cope – of course we'd cope. We loved living where we did, in a street whose inhabitants were so proud, old-fashioned or impoverished as to do their cleaning, gardening, childcare and dog-walking themselves, rather than hiring others to do it for them. But any space in the house was shrinking, and the clutter in the basement kitchen, which doubled as a playroom, shrunk it even more. Pre-children, clearing up meant little more than a quick wipe of the table and worktops. Now, to take a small sample of the tasks I found myself performing while the tea brewed and Marie quieted Noah upstairs, it meant picking up stray pieces of jigsaw puzzle and finding the right box to put them in; stowing the Lego back in the red crate and the alphabet cards in a transparent plastic bag; detaching Play-Doh from chair legs, and swabbing juice stains from seats; herding Jack's five coloured balloons into a corner, while resisting the temptation to burst them, since bursting them might wake him and even if it didn't would require that I blew up five more; and – because I was feeling especially virtuous or malicious, I'm not sure which – wiping the blackboard clear of the chalky purple giant depicted there, with the twiggy arms that came out of his ears and the nine toes on each of his feet.

The kids are too young to tidy up, Marie said, if I complained, adding, on one occasion, 'If *you* were younger, you'd not make such a fuss about it.' She had a migraine at the time and later apologised, saying she hadn't really meant it. But I knew she did mean it, the ten-year gap in our ages being a topic I was touchy about, and which Marie had learned to avoid, though the fact was always screamingly present to me, not so much because the statistics suggested I might pre-decease her by as much as twenty years (that was too distant a prospect to worry about), but because it reminded me of other gaps between us, some of them minor (like the lack of overlap between the television programmes we watched as kids or the music we listened to as teenagers), others weightier but get-roundable, like the dispar-ity in our upbringing and education, yet a few that caused us more grief, like the reality of Marie having friends who were still in their mid-thirties and, as she put it, *up for doing stuff*, whether clubbing, weekends in Barcelona or trips to health farms, whereas my friends were people like Rob, who'd never done stuff in the first place or weren't about to start now.

Being fourteen years younger than Rob and ten years older than Marie put me in the middle, more or less, just as having parents (a mother, anyway) as well as kids put me in the middle. My job put me in the middle, too – between my colleagues on one side and authors, agents and publishers on the other. And I was middle-aged – forty-five – and middling in height (five foot ten), weight (eleven and a half stone) and appearance (brown-black hair, hazel-green eyes, ochre-white skin). I thought about my middlingness a lot. On good days, I took heart: there I was, look, a centred kind of guy living at the heart of things. On bad, I despised myself as grey, compromised, Matt the middleman. Becoming Rob's executor would mean more of the same, as I mediated between his manuscripts and the public, a task I hoped wouldn't arise for some time, but if it did would have to be fitted in between obligations to the paper, Marie, the kids, my mother and my increasingly neglected ambitions as a novelist. He'd left it open to me to decline, but I couldn't. Increasingly melancholy in recent years, he had seemed bleaker than ever at lunch – bitter, too, that the world, or his muse, had abandoned him. To refuse him would have been cruel. As my dad used to say, never kick a man when he's down.

Marie's peppermint tea had brewed too long; I poured half away and topped it up with boiling water. Jack's wind-up woolly dog lay waiting to trip me at the bottom of the stairs. When I nudged it aside with my foot, its tail wagged and it let out noisy yaps. Setting down the mug of tea, I removed the A4 batteries housed in the underbelly hatch and left it lying stiffly on its side.

2

Rob and I met at Brandon, Massachusetts, in the early nineties. I was twenty-four and had been awarded a scholarship on the MFA Fiction program on the basis of a good degree and a couple of Carveresque short stories. I was immensely chuffed and couldn't have afforded it otherwise, but (unlike Iowa's, say) the creative writing program at Brandon was far from prestigious, as I soon found out. Rob didn't teach creative writing. Throughout his twenties he'd been working towards a PhD on Keats. The PhD was never completed, but he succeeded in placing a chapter from it in an American scholarly journal, and on the back of that, against all odds, was appointed to a lectureship in Tennessee ('a hotbed of Keatsians', he said), where he taught for several years before moving to Brandon. As an authority on Romanticism, he was put in charge of the fresher course on Byron, Keats and Shelley, a course students flocked to 'because of the James Dean Marilyn Monroe Keith Moon Mama Cass all-the-good-die-young factor, which I do my best to dissuade them of'. He preferred the postgraduate seminar he ran, on the Augustan period ('I'm a Pope by name and nature'), because the students were fewer in number and sometimes went so far as to read the texts. It was through the seminar that we met, not because I was enrolled for it, but because Kirsten, a girl I knew on the fiction course, had taken it the previous year and described Rob as a genius – a tortured one, she added, which I took to be a reference to how he looked and spoke in class, not to the fact that (so I found out later) he'd failed to respond when she flirted with him, something so unfathomable to her (Kirsten *was* a very beautiful girl) that only the word 'tortured' could explain it, though it's true that after a second, more decisive rejection, at which I was present, she did use several other words, including 'weird', 'repressed' and 'fucked up'.

'You're both Brits,' she said, 'you should meet.'

'Sure.'

I'd left the country to get away from them. But anything to please Kirsten.

'There's a bar he goes to on Thursdays after class. We could hang out there.'

The bar was mock Western: swing doors, wooden floor with sawdust, lassos and cowboy hats festooning the walls. The last place I'd associate with Rob. But he was different back then – less fixed in his ways.

He was alone at a table in the corner, with a beer, the *New York Review of Books* and the air of someone who doesn't want to be disturbed. With his T-shirt, jeans, mass of hair and bushy forearms, he looked more like a construction worker than an academic. The only pedagogic touch was his beard, with its premature dabs of grey.

Kirsten ploughed in. 'Hey, Professor Pope, can we get you a beer?'

'Um, not really,' he mumbled, which I took to be a refusal of the beer, rather than a protest at the title – he wasn't a professor, but every lecturer at Brandon, however lowly, got called that. He didn't look as if he recognised Kirsten, let alone knew her name.

'This is Matt,' she said, undeterred. 'From London.'

'From Norwich, actually,' I said, thrusting my hand at him.

'What brings you here?' he said, reluctantly shaking it.

'The Fiction course.'

'You could have stayed home. What's wrong with UEA?'

'Brandon offered me a scholarship.'

'Well, good luck. I don't believe creative writing can be taught. Certainly none of the poets here should be teaching poetry.'

'I'm enjoying myself so far.'

'It's only October,' he said. 'You wait.'

'Are you sure you won't have a beer, Professor Pope?' Kirsten said, oblivious to how badly things were going.

'Robert, please,' he said. 'Go on, then.'

'I'll get them, Kirsten,' I said, helping him out with the name.

'I insist – you guys sit there and catch up on the old country.'

'Sorry if we're intruding,' I said, once I'd sat down.

'I'm only reading this shit. Ten thousand words on John Ashbery. Christ, he's not even any good.'

Not having read Ashbery, I was stuck for something to say. Rob didn't seem to mind. He spent the next five minutes telling me – and once Kirsten had returned with the drinks, the half-hour after that telling both of us – why Ashbery was no good, and Wallace Stevens not much better, and that the whole American literary-critical 'circus' were either stooges of the CIA or dimwits who couldn't tell a Hardy from a Heaney. I could follow barely half of what he was saying, but I enjoyed the spleen. He waved his arms around a lot. The word 'repressed' seemed way off the mark.

The incident that made Kirsten use it of him was yet to occur. And there was no reason to see it coming. Both of us were equally wide-eyed, would-be novelists whose opinions on what constituted good writing were still at the infant stage and who couldn't imagine ever becoming as knowledgeable as Rob. Far from resenting our presence, he seemed to enjoy having an audience, one that wasn't there by compulsion (as his undergraduates were) and wouldn't argue back or cut him off (as his fellow profs doubtless did). A bar, rather than a lecture theatre, seemed to be his natural habitat. From time to time, I glanced across at Kirsten. 'Open-mouthed' is the cliché for awestruck listeners, but she was tautly attentive rather than slack-jawed, smiling and nodding as if she too thought 'Self-Portrait in a Convex Mirror' the least fatuous of Ashbery's poems, even if horribly flawed.

'I love poetry,' Kirsten said. 'Expressing your feelings – that's so creative.'

'Is it?' Rob said.

'When something's come from inside you and you share it.'

'Piss and shit come from inside you – you wouldn't share them.'

'Poets are so physical,' Kirsten said, undeterred, 'so intimate, so erotic, it's what I'm aiming for in my own writing. I just love Whitman's "Song of Myself".'

'Terrible title, terrible poem. "Every atom belonging to me as good belongs to you" – what bollocks.'

'What about British poets?' I said, to spare Kirsten from Rob's harangue. More vituperation followed. I wish I could remember all the epithets he used, and though I did later write a few of them down, Boswell-fashion, they seemed lame without hearing his voice, or rather the voices of the poets he was taking off. He'd a gift for mimicking regional accents, Northern Irish as well as Liverpudlian, that Kirsten couldn't have appreciated, though she laughed as if she did.

'So it's not just American poets you hate?' I said.

'I love America,' he said, which wasn't an answer, but prompted another riff, non-literary this time, on how he'd always wanted to come to the US, his great-grandfather having emigrated to Michigan as a young man to work for Chrysler, which he did for twenty years before returning to the UK with his family and, armed with advanced mechanical know-how, setting up a garage business, which had prospered so well that the Pope family was still reaping the benefits, long after they'd sold the business. He'd been told that his great-grandfather once killed a man, a no-good negro ('his phrase, not mine', Rob said) who used to lie in wait each Friday as the workers came out of the Chrysler factory with their pay packets, until he, the great-grandfather, bought a gun and shot him dead – perhaps in collaboration with others, Rob said, since they carried the man back inside the factory and laid him out on a workbench and left him there, rightly guessing that the corpse would be gone by Monday morning, no questions asked. 'Probably apocryphal,' Rob said, 'and deeply shameful if true,' but to a young boy the story made America seem an exciting place, and so it had proved. He'd no intention of going back to the UK in the immediate future, though to get his poems published he would have to; the stuff he wrote, such as it was, had no appeal to Ashberyites, about whom – apologies if he'd bored us with his rant – he'd said more than enough already.

Rob was impressive. And I was lonely, new to the US and in need of a new mentor. My dad had been first; then Mr Haigh, our English teacher at school (who came into his own, or helped me to come into mine, in the sixth form); then Diarmid Shannon, convener of the Modernist module at Bristol. I'd left them behind, in the UK, opening a space for Rob to fill. Even as I sat there, having only just met him, the familiar sensations passed through me – deference, admiration, the wish to learn.

The incident that made Kirsten call him 'repressed' occurred as I brought the third or fourth round of beers back to our table, though I caught only the tail end, which consisted of Rob saying 'No offence' and Kirsten looking highly offended. She had proposed, so she reported to me later, that we all have dinner afterwards, and he'd replied that it would be inappropriate. 'Man,' she said, 'he might be a genius, but he's so fucking weird and repressed. I mean, what's inappropriate about a prof having dinner with two grad students? It's not like we're even taking his course. How fucked up is that?'

'Yes, seriously fucked up,' I concurred, not because I believed it (didn't genius and fucked-up-ness go together?) but in the hope that concurrence would allow me to make a move on Kirsten, with whom I was by then drinking tequila over an oilcloth-covered table at her place. We'd left the bar pretty swiftly after Rob's refusal, she having fallen silent in its wake. She'd remained more or less silent as I walked her home, and her 'Wanna come up?' took me by surprise. Up was the fifth floor of an old tenement building, now occupied by students. She shared the flat with three other girls, all currently across town at a gig, she told me, which seemed a good omen, as did the offer of tequila rather than coffee. Most encouraging of all was her dissing of Rob, his genius status now forfeited by his fucked-up-ness. Beyond the oilcloth-covered table was a sofa, and beyond that a couple of doors, one of which surely opened to her bedroom. American courting etiquette can't be so different from British, can it? I reflected, as Kirsten, excusing herself, disappeared to what she called 'the ladies' room', a term I associated with pubs and restaurants not domestic spaces, and anyway every room in the flat was a ladies' room or lady's room. Would Kirsten return wearing 'something more comfortable', as women did in Hollywood films, having changed into a flimsy nightdress, hair unpinned for good measure? Undeterred when she didn't, I stood up with the intention of taking her in my arms ('sweeping her up' was the phrase in the film scenario still running in my head), till she cleverly sidestepped me, like someone shrinking back from a shower because the water has run cold.

'You're so sweet, Matt,' she said, 'but I'm not ready for a relationship.'

'Sure, sorry, I didn't mean to rush you,' I said, though that's exactly what I had meant. I was used to rejection and understood that my Englishness appealed to her only up to a point, one that stopped short of a kiss, let alone bed.

I didn't stay long or try my luck again. By next morning I'd succeeded in persuading myself that what had happened, or not happened, was for the best: sitting in class with Kirsten would have been awkward otherwise. My heart lurched a little when I saw her, but I smiled, in a no-hard-feelings, business-as-usual kind of way, which seemed to work, because we went for coffee after class, and talked some more about the text we'd been discussing, a D. H. Lawrence story that I liked and she didn't, her objections to it being (I couldn't help but feel) more than a little predictable, focusing as they did on Lawrence himself, or a received feminist caricature of him, rather than the text. Now I'd no reason to hold back, I let her know what I thought of her argument, even using the word 'lightweight' at one point, which I suppose was vindictive: literary criticism as sexual revenge. She took it well, but we were cooler with each other after that and I put the humiliation in her flat behind me.

I didn't give much thought to the early part of the evening, either, till I bumped into Rob on the steps of the college library the following week. He was on his way in, with a clutch of slim volumes, and to my surprise he recognised me. After disowning

27

the volumes – 'all horseshit, it turns out, I don't know why I bother' – he asked if I'd wait a second while he returned them, then maybe we could grab a coffee. I know he said 'grab', because it seemed too American a usage for him, as did 'horseshit', and I remember reflecting that if someone as resolutely English as Rob could resort to US idiom then the same thing would eventually happen to me, which hardened my resolve to leave once the course was over, not because I disliked the place, or the language, but because I missed England and even more so (embarrassing to admit at twenty-four) my parents.

'Let's skip the coffee and have a walk,' Rob said, when he emerged.

The walk took us from the library, past the Medical Center and Science Block, out on a path that meandered through halls of residence down to and round the campus lake then up again through a small wood bisected by cycle paths to the Arts Building. Rob walked as quickly as he talked; I struggled to keep pace with him in both regards. Many of our best conversations that year – soliloquies from him underscored by occasional footnotes from me – took place while we were walking round the campus, or in town, or even, once, round his local supermarket, where Rob was so preoccupied discussing T. S. Eliot (was he or wasn't he anti-Semitic?) that he took an hour to fill his shopping trolley.

I didn't feel he was trying to impress me or flaunt his knowledge. He just lived in a world where the latest book (or review, or article) he'd read was all that existed, and from which he couldn't move on till he'd articulated what he felt about it. That day of our walk the subject was Larkin: the biography and letters had recently come out and, in the light of what they showed about Larkin (as misanthrope, misogynist, racist and porn addict), Rob had been rereading the poems. His position was clear even then, and hardened over subsequent years: the life was one thing, the work another; a nasty man might still be a great poet. The argument was more complex, of course, but that's what it came down to, and it was just as *we* came down to the lake, the eastern end of it, where the sludgy reedbeds opened out to deeper water, that he reached a conclusion, with a phrase that still resonates: 'The life's irrelevant. Being alive on the page is all that counts.'

I'd been told that there were beavers in the lake, and was looking out at what might have been a beaver's dam when Rob said:

'That girl you were with the other night.'

'Kirsten.'

'She's not your girlfriend, is she?'

'No.'

'Good.'

In the two hours we'd spent together at the pub, and the half-hour walk till then, literature had been Rob's only subject. The switch to Kirsten came as a surprise. As a relief too – I'd begun to feel bombarded.

'When you were at the bar, she asked me to have dinner,' he said.

'She told me. And you said that having dinner with us would be inappropriate.'

'You weren't included.'

According to his version – which seemed altogether possible, rather than some self-aggrandising fiction – while I'd gone to buy drinks, she'd suggested that the two of them go on to a bistro near her flat, 'and maybe coffee at my place afterwards'. When she'd come on to him before, he'd pretended not to notice. But this was blatant, and though he was no longer teaching her, which would have made it OK, just about, to accept her invitation, he didn't fancy it. Unable to say so, he'd used the excuse of inappropriateness instead, 'a coward's way out', he added, 'but she's probably nice underneath the pushiness and I didn't want to upset her'.

'She thinks you said no because you're repressed.'

He laughed. 'It worked then. Her self-esteem's intact.'

'I doubt it. Kirsten's used to men wanting to fuck her. You disappointed her.'

'And you? Do you want to fuck her?'

'I did.'

'Good for you.'

'I mean I *wanted* to, but she wasn't having it.'

'She'd have been the same with me.'

'No, she thinks you're a genius.'

'More fool her.'

'Plus, you're a prof.'

'Ah yes, the teacher–pupil dynamic. The exchange of old minds and young bodies. It's the first rule: don't fuck your students. I learned the hard way.'

He didn't elaborate and I didn't push him. We walked on a few yards in silence, till a ball came bouncing past us, then a dog bounding after it into the lake, then a woman striding quickly who smiled and said 'Silly animal' as she passed us, though it was said with pride, and once the dog had retrieved the ball, and shook itself dry on the shore, and dropped the ball in front of her, she threw it straight back in the lake, fifty yards further ahead.

'*I will arise and go now, for always night and day I hear lake water lapping with low sounds by the shore,*' Rob said. 'Pure crap. If I have to read another fresher essay on how the alliterative "l"s in Yeats's poem mimic the sound of water I'll kill myself.'

We walked on past the lake towards the little maple forest at the edge of campus.

'*Whose woods these are I think I know,*' he said. 'Now that *is* writing. By one of my namesakes – Robert, I mean, not Pope. There are quite a few of us – Frost, Burns, Browning, Lowell, Zimmerman. But to friends I'm Rob, OK? How's yours by the way?'

'My what?'

'Your writing – how's it going?'

'Badly,' I said, an answer I'd not have given my classmates, all of whom were relentlessly upbeat about their progress, as were our tutors, who'd drummed it into us in the first week that we had to be 'sensitive' to each other's efforts, and who led the way by tempering the mildest hint of criticism with bucketloads of praise, so that when Kirsten, for example, submitted a Magical Realist fable about a woman giving birth to seventeen giant yellow chipmunks, the suggestion that she might be over-indebted to García Márquez or Angela Carter was swiftly passed over in order that we focus on the 'verisimilitude' with which she'd depicted the chipmunks. My own fiction had been treated as respectfully as everyone else's, perhaps more respectfully because of my status as a foreigner. But I wasn't happy with it and needed to understand where I was going wrong.

'Now you see why I prefer teaching Swift and Pope,' Rob said. 'They understand you've got to be savage. All this happy-clappy stuff will get you nowhere. Writers need constant discouragement. You should study *The Dunciad*. Come to my seminar. We're discussing it next week.'

'I'm not really into poetry.'

'Well, come the week after. Thursday afternoon. We're discussing *Rasselas*.'

'I'll try.'

'Try? I expect to see you there. You *have* read *Rasselas*?'

I hadn't read it, but after we parted, outside the Arts Building, I walked back to the library and found a copy, one of seven sitting on a shelf marked 824.63, all in pristine condition and only a couple of them previously taken out, which I found odd, given that Rob's seminar group consisted, so he'd told me, of twelve students ('which with me makes thirteen, though I've never been unlucky enough for everyone to be present at the same time'). But even with postgraduate teaching there was a pressure on staff to stick to texts in the *Norton Anthology*, so perhaps it wasn't so strange.

Rasselas made a deep impression on me. I'd never have admitted as much to my creative writing tutors, for whom only texts published since 1960, and ideally 1980, could serve as models. Not that they were ill-read. Both of them had studied Eng Lit. And from the little I'd read of their work (Seth Erden was a bearded short-story writer in his thirties, and Henry Glisson a novelist in his late fifties), both were more old-school than their professed classroom embrace of postmodernity would suggest. If I'd alluded to *Rasselas*, metafictionally, they'd have been respectful – but not if I'd said I planned to use it as a model for my own work. Even I knew that sounded daft. But the moment I read it – or rather, from the day I sat in on Rob's class and heard him talk about it – the thing seemed unavoidable. I fell under Dr Johnson's spell by falling under Rob's.

I felt nervous turning up. I'd not seen him since our walk and wondered how serious the invitation had been. Because the departmental noticeboard offered no clue as to where the seminar was taking place, I had to ask the office administrator, who gave me the room number, but then became suspicious and more or less told me I couldn't attend: it was too late to enrol – as a creative writing student I wasn't entitled to enrol – and sitting in on classes unless you were enrolled was contrary to college policy; even if it was true, as I claimed, that Professor Pope had invited me, he would need to seek permission from the head of department, Professor Jacobs, and as far as she knew, in her capacity as his assistant, a post which placed herself and Professor Jacobs in daily liaison (I tried not to smile at the word), such permission had been neither sought nor granted.

'Fuck all that,' Rob said, when I filled him in while hovering nervously outside Room B64. 'You passed the test. You made it. Come and meet the zombies.'

They weren't zombies, just painfully earnest, their contributions framed either in the structuralist discourse of the day or in a quasi-Christian idiom that probed the moral standing (saint? sinner? both?) of each character. Rob's approach gave neither sect any comfort. He was brisk, rude and interested only in Johnson's language, to the exclusion of any discussion of character, structure, narrative, symbol, etc. The students might not have taken it from a fellow American. But Rob's Englishness let him off the hook. In the midst of denunciation his voice would soften as he paused on a phrase, whether Johnson's or an unconnected-yet-pertinent writer's, and said it over, lovingly, two or three times. *Lovingly*: that's the point. It was his love of great literature that made him intolerant of writers who fell short. Even the slowest in the class could see that.

He'd introduced me as 'an interloper from the creative writing school – let's see if we can teach him a thing or two'. I sat in a chair to his left. Only once, when asked, did I speak, or rather mumble. But at the end, he suggested we go for a drink. Most of the students were still there, gathering up their stuff, and I wondered what they made of us. Did they think we were gay? It occurred to me that I'd missed the point about Rob's rejection of Kirsten; maybe he *was* gay.

Outside the big cities, most Americans eat dinner absurdly early, and after a couple of Happy Hour drinks in a pub just off campus Rob and I did the same. Maybe he'd talked enough about books for one day. Or the cocktails made him indiscreet. Or he felt I was someone he could trust. Whatever the reason, he got on to sex.

'It's nothing to boast of, but I was a virgin when I went to university,' he said. 'I'd grown up in a tiny village and been to a single-sex school. The idea that a girl might talk to me, let alone allow me to touch her, was extraordinary. After three years in London doing my degree, then three more not getting on with my doctorate, I could still count my sexual experiences on one hand. My main memory is how awkward it was waking up with someone next morning: she'd make you tea, or you'd make her tea, and you'd find a way past the embarrassment and maybe have sex again, but when you next met up the spark would be gone, for her if not for you, and you'd wonder what the point had been, which was sad if not a dagger through the heart. I guess we were learning the difference between love and sex. I tried to write about it at the time, but the poems were no good.'

'And now?'

'I'm writing a different kind of poetry.'

'I meant . . .'

'Oh, my love life. It isn't hard to meet women in a place like this. I've had a few relationships. But nothing serious. And I don't go anywhere near the students. It's the first rule, as I say: don't fuck students – unless you're a student. When I was in Tennessee . . . no, it's too long a story, I'll tell you another time. Shall we get the check?'

I'm sure he said 'check' rather than 'bill', and that he paid for us both, not only that night but on all the others in Brandon. When, years later, we began our habit of having lunch once a year in Soho, I didn't begrudge doing the same: not only was I the higher earner, I owed him. Intellectually as well as

34

financially: I learned far more from Rob than from my writing tutors. I even said as much, in the solitary interview I gave, for the *Eastern Daily Press*, when my novel came out. Rob wouldn't have seen it, but he knew. And I like to think I didn't disappoint him when I later started working as a literary journalist. Though he affected to despise the press, he depended on it. And though I never felt used, I played my part in giving him work and keeping him visible at a time, in his fifties, when he thought he was slipping from view.

3

Leonie sends her kids to private school, which, as she says, means paying a fortune for them to have longer holidays. She likes to get away in early July, before the state schools break up. Others on the paper (not only those who are parents) do the same. It's a quieter time at the office. You feel the change in various ways – the empty desks, the lack of queues in nearby sandwich bars, the appearance of features that would normally be deemed too slight or whimsical to publish. But it's a busy period for those of us left behind, especially me, with many publishers bringing out their lead fiction titles. I ought to enjoy the added responsibility. But I don't like feeling under pressure. And with the fallout from Mabel, the new baby – broken nights, visits to the doctor, extra school runs, Marie feeling tired and crotchety – I felt it especially that summer. We'd booked to go to Majorca for two weeks, along with my mother. When Leonie returned for what she called 'the handover', on the Thursday before our Saturday flight from Stansted, it came as a huge relief.

'Don't ever have teenagers,' she said.

'Jack already behaves like one,' I said.

'Well, don't ever take them to Italy. *Not another boring church, Mum. Actually, this is the Sistine Chapel, sweetie, famous for the artwork on its ceiling by Michelangelo, the greatest artist of the Renaissance.*

Whatever. Both of them are doing art GCSE. You'd think they'd be interested. But all the ice creams and pizzas in the world weren't enough to get them onside. *I hate you, Mum*, Carmel told me every morning. At least her resentment took the form of words. Douglas just grunted. Heigh-ho, how's it been here?'

I showed her that week's pages, already put to bed, and updated her on the next: most of the reviews had come in, with several more held over through lack of space, so she wouldn't be short of copy. I hoped she might tell me to take the Friday off, and perhaps she would have done, but she was rushing to the morning conference. I'd found the obligation to attend it – when nothing of relevance to Books came up and the pages were waiting to be worked on – the worst aspect of deputising for her. But Leonie enjoyed going. It made her feel part of the team. And, she claimed, helped prevent Books from becoming a backwater.

She emerged round 12.30, just as I was nipping out to buy a sandwich.

'Anything new?'

'Nah, it's like I've never been away. The migrant crisis. There's no other story. Sad to hear your friend popped it, though.'

'What?'

'Robert Pope. Surely you heard.'

'Rob's dead?'

'I'm sorry. I thought you were friends.'

'We are . . . we were. What happened?'

'No idea. Talk to Tony. He asked me were we doing anything. Maybe you'd like to.'

Rob dead? I got up and headed to the Gents. It was only ten yards away but took forever, as though I were wading against a fast-flowing stream. Rob dead? A large mirror hung over the washbasins. I studied my face to see what I was feeling. It gave nothing back. I wasn't conscious of feeling *anything*. But my hands gripped the side of the basin and I stood there for several minutes before heading back outside.

Tony is our obits editor, formerly foreign editor till they appointed someone younger. Obits was considered a demotion, almost as bad as redundancy, but Tony loves the job and has brought a new gravitas to the pages.

'Do you have a moment?' I said.

He must have noticed how shaky I looked, because he stood up and ushered me into the lobby by the lifts, away from his colleagues at their keyboards.

'Yes, Leonie said you knew him well,' he said, when I explained.

'What happened?'

'Heart attack, I believe.'

'Right. Good. Not good, obviously, but with it being so sudden I wondered if . . .'

'Definitely not suicide. The chap who called me was keen to emphasise that. Louis someone.'

'Louis de Vries. He's Rob's agent.'

'He died on Tuesday, apparently, but his wife didn't call till last night. It often happens that way when it's unexpected. The relatives are in shock and need a day by themselves, as a family, till they make it public.'

'Rob didn't have family. Just his wife. No kids.'

'This Louis chap mentioned a sister. They're trying to track her down.'

'She lives in Australia. She and Rob didn't get on.'

'We have an obit on the stocks,' Tony said. 'Might need refreshing. I'll send it over. Leonie thought you might want to do something on the books pages.'

'This week's have already gone to bed. It'd have to wait till Saturday week.'

'Speak to Rachel, then.' Rachel is, or was, our features editor. 'She might let you write something for Saturday.'

'Me?'

'As a friend.'

Not just as a friend, as his literary executor. But I wasn't getting into that.

'It might be better to get a poet,' I said.

'Well, see what she says,' he said and touched me on the arm. 'My condolences. He obviously meant a lot to you.'

Though it was surprising to hear an obits editor offer consolatory platitudes, I felt better for his touch. I left the building, rather than return to my desk, and bought a crayfish-and-rocket wrap from the nearest sandwich bar, and took it to the park, where I sat on the bench and thought about Rob, and of times I'd spent with him. It was a sunny July day. Tuesday had been sunny, too, not the sort of day for someone to die on, least of all Rob, who had liked the sun – the open air anyway – when we were in Brandon. I remembered walking with him through woods, along riverbanks, on ridge-trails, him talking and me listening, master–pupil, each with our literary ambitions, still years from achieving them, but with him leading the way. He was hard to keep up with: I was always one step behind. Latterly, he'd seemed less fit, with a sedentary paunch. In fact, when we came back to England (with me, for once, leading the way) the walking had ceased. The furthest we went was to a pub or restaurant, where his only exercise would be waving his arms while he talked. Still, he always looked well, not a man heading for a coronary. *Heading for*: it was impossible not to think that way; not to survey the past for signs of why he'd ended where he had, short of a future.

I called Marie, at home, but her phone went straight to voice-mail; she'd be at the toddler group. I didn't leave a message. In retrospect, I felt relieved she hadn't picked up. She'd disliked Rob, not just for who he was but for belonging to a time before I knew her. Any sympathy she offered would fall short. Only an acknowledgement of his greatness and of my privilege in knowing him would suffice. I was feeling hagiographical as well as grief-struck.

A young couple carrying Harrods bags asked in broken English if the bench was free and I shuffled up to make room. I could have moved to the grass, where office workers lay sun-bathing in the heat or sat gossiping in the shade. But a bench seemed more dignified and if I sat upright I wouldn't collapse. *No one died* was a mantra I used to calm myself with in the middle of crises. A shunt in the car, a flood bringing down a ceiling, the childminder crying off at the last minute: so be it, I'll cope, *no one died*. The mantra didn't work this time. Someone had.

I thought back to my last meeting with Rob, at the end of the previous year. The subject matter had been sombre: given the executor business, how could it not be? But he didn't look ill and there'd been room for banter. What of the time before that, same venue, same time of year? He'd brought a proof copy of his new collection – his final collection, as it turned out – and pressed it on me: 'Read it, no one else will.' Self-disparagement was a trait of his, always (as Marie said) with a touch of vanity: he did himself down in order for his listeners to praise him. Which I did, of course, albeit joshingly. 'As long as posterity reads you.' 'Posterity!' he snarled. 'What has posterity ever done for the living?' But he was anxious that his work survive him. Why else appoint an executor?

That job was now down to me. Was writing a piece for the paper a good way to start? Rachel might propose it when I saw her. And Leonie would certainly encourage it: she was always pushing for books-related articles to go on the feature pages. I was in shock. But if I didn't write something, who would? There were no poets I could think of who'd been close to him. Didn't I owe it to Rob?

Then again, was a piece written in haste any way to pay tribute? There'd surely be better opportunities for me to honour his memory.

I'd two excuses if Rachel asked: lack of time (I was about to go away on holiday) and surfeit of distress. But the former would sound lazy ('we're only looking for eight hundred words, Matt'), the latter wimpish, and both of them unprofessional coming from someone employed on a newspaper.

I'm not sure how long I sat there. But by the time I returned to the office, I'd reached a compromise: I wouldn't volunteer, but if Rachel or Leonie pressed me to write something, then fine. I sat at my screen reading the obit Tony had sent. He'd omitted to include the byline, but it read like the work of an academic, perhaps Aaron Fortune, the Australian who'd devoted a chapter to Rob in a survey of contemporary British poetry. I remembered Rob complaining that though the account was appreciative, he hated the chapter heading, 'The Return to Formalism'. 'That's what they'll put on my fucking headstone: Robert Pope, formalist.' A reference to Rob's 'famously formalistic verse' came up in the first para of the obit, so I changed it to 'famously measured but quietly passionate'. Was his poetry passionate? Critics called him cerebral, but he denied it: 'the deeper you feel, the harder it is to speak', he used to say, quoting Orlando in *As You Like It*: 'What passion hangs these weights upon my tongue?' Certainly *he* had been passionate when I first knew him. His years in the US had only a brief mention in the piece, because they predated his first book, but I added a sentence about the influence they had, 'both in generating ideas about poetry and in creating lasting friendships'. I sent the piece back to Tony with one important factual correction (it was Sussex not Surrey where Rob had grown up) and one further change ('his last collection disappointed most critics' became 'his last collection received mixed reviews'). The best photo of Rob, I told Tony, was the one of him smiling when his third collection won an award; we'd used it before, so I knew the paper had it on file.

The obit didn't do Rob justice: how could it in two thousand words? Eight hundred words on the op-ed page would be inadequate, too, but as the afternoon wore on the idea of writing them became increasingly appealing. I sent a short email to Rachel, whose reply came back instantly: 'Yes, Leonie told me you were friends with him, and it would have been great, but we've just decided to go big with a refugee feature on Saturday, so there's no space.' She'd copied in Leonie, who sent me an email: 'Pity but with another 50 drowned in the Med I see her point. Why not take tomorrow off?' She meant to temper my disappointment, but another part of me was relieved. I raised my head from the screen to find her looking at me. I smiled and mouthed 'Are you sure?' 'Go now,' she mouthed back, waving her thumb towards the exit.

On the way to the Tube I stopped off in the park to phone Jill. I'd have felt inhibited calling from the office and, once home, I'd be mobbed. The bench I sat on earlier was occupied. I stood in the shade of an elm. What to say? My mind ran with clichés: *shock and sorrow, no words can suffice, deepest condolences, so terrible when he still had so much to live for* . . . What I really wanted was the detail: where? when? how? etc. But that could come later. What she needed was sympathy – from me, from friends, from anyone who'd known him.

I'd two numbers for him. Rob/Mobile was the one I normally used. But this wasn't normal. I called Rob/Home.

Eight rings, then *Sorry we're not here: please leave a message.* His voice, not hers. My eyes filled, hearing it. I hung up. *Not here.* Not anywhere.

Leaves rustled over my head. Not the wind passing through them, but a squirrel sliding up a branch. I composed myself and called again, half expecting her to answer this time, but ready with a message when she didn't. *I'm so terribly sorry, you must be devastated, please let me know if I can do anything* was the gist. I left my number in case she didn't have it.

The Tube carriage was half empty. Two men and a woman sat opposite, grey-haired, wrinkled, seventy-plus. It wasn't fair to hate them for being alive, but I did.

Walking home from the Tube felt strange, as if I were wading against strong currents again. The Severn bore or a line of breakers. Green water, crested with white.

'Daddy, Daddy,' the boys shouted, surprised to see me home so early. They were still finishing their tea. I kissed Marie, who was breastfeeding Mabel. She could tell something was wrong.

'What is it?'

'Rob's dead,' I whispered.

'What?'

'Rob – he died.'

'What died?' said Noah, who never misses a thing.

'A robin died,' said Jack.

'Not a robin, sweetie,' Marie said. 'A man called Rob, who's a friend of Daddy.'

'Poor Rob,' Jack said.

'Poor Daddy,' Marie said.

'What's died mean?' said Noah, to whom we had tried explaining the meaning of death only recently, while burying Jack's hamster, and who had been preoccupied with it ever since.

'It's when a person or an animal goes away and doesn't come back,' Marie said.

'Or a bird,' I said.

'They go to heaven,' Jack said.

'Maybe,' I said.

'They do. Mrs Binns told us.'

'What's heaven?' Noah said.

'Mummy will explain,' I said, 'I'm going to change out of these clothes.'

'Can we play football?' Jack said.

'Give Daddy a minute,' Marie said. 'He's upset.'

'But can we, Daddy?'

'Of course,' I said, close to tears, not from grief but gratitude. The kids had their priorities right. They wanted to kick a ball with their dad.

We played in the back garden while Marie put Mabel down. Then I read to the boys while she made supper. She'd opened a bottle of red by the time I came downstairs – an expensive bottle I'd been saving for a special occasion.

'Sorry,' she said, when I pointed that out.

'No, that's fine. It *is* special. It's not every day your best friend dies.'

'Best friend? Really?' she said, dipping celery in the hummus while the potatoes boiled. 'It's not as if you saw him that often.'

'We go right back. *Went* right back. What other friends do I have?'

'Come on, love. I know you're grieving, but ... There are plenty of people you get on with. You were saying how much you like Mark.'

'We get on because our boys do things together. It doesn't go deep.'

'And you've friends from your job.'

'Colleagues.'

'And the guys at the squash club.'

'*Opponents.* That's all. And I don't play that often. You're the one with friends.'

Unable to deny it, she stood up to check on the potatoes. It was the same with most women: they met for coffee, talked on the phone, Skyped, texted, emailed, shopped together, socialised. Whereas the men only mixed through work or sport.

'Rob and I talked about writing. I don't do that with anyone else.'

'Not with Leonie? Or what's-his-name who helps with the pages?'

'Chris. No. We only talk about subbing copy. It's not the same.'

'You'll miss him, I understand that,' she said, bringing the food to the table, the kind we like on summer evenings: smoked fish, new potatoes, green salad. 'All I'm saying is, you do have other friends.'

She passed the bowl and I scooped out a heap of mixed leaves with the tongs.

'When's the funeral?' she said.

'No idea,' I said, shaking my head. I'd not even thought about it. Would Jill have made the arrangements by now or was it too soon? When my dad died, my mum took care of nearly everything. I was a child in these matters.

'I daresay it'll happen when we're in Majorca,' Marie said.

'Christ,' I said, 'you're right. I'll have to come back.'

'You're joking.'

'Majorca's not far. Two hours by plane. I'll get there and back in a day.'

'Fuck that. It's our first holiday in ages. We have a tiny baby. And your mum will be with us. It's not fair on her. It's not fair on me. There'll be other ways to pay your respects.'

'I can't not go. I'm his literary executor.'

'You're a parent to three small kids. People will understand.'

'Rob wasn't a parent. I don't think he would.'

'Jill will understand.'

'Makes no odds. I'll have to do it.'

'Don't bother to come back, then. In fact, don't bother coming in the first place. Rob's obviously more of a priority to you than we are.'

'You know that's not true.'

'Do I?'

I backed off. We weren't going to agree. But there was no point arguing about it till I heard from Jill. When my phone went at 9.15 I thought, Good, that'll be her. But it was my mother, calling about the arrangements for the next day. It wasn't the first time we'd been through them, but I suppressed any impatience: yes, I knew she'd ordered a taxi to Norwich Station; yes, I'd be waiting at Liverpool Street when the train got in at 6 p.m.; yes, I'd checked us all in for the flight and she'd be sitting with us, in the same row. She wasn't forgetful, just anxious. Since my dad died five years before, she'd become increasingly dependent. That her mind was still sharp made things only tougher for her: with dementia she'd have been less conscious of how alone she felt and how hampered by her lack of mobility. I was tempted to tell her about Rob; she'd heard me mention him many times and would know what I was going through. But our experiences didn't compare. She was widowed, lived alone, had no children to distract her from her grief, just me, her only son, whose voice and mannerisms (so she said) reminded her of my dad's. Death wasn't a subject we could share.

The phone rang again after we'd hung up: it was Alec, from squash, looking for a game next week, when I'd be away. I'd opened a second bottle by then, cheaper than the first. By eleven, half pissed, I gave up and went to bed. Marie was already there but still awake. We'd not made love since Mabel was born, but we did that night, she (I suspect) out of pity, me seething with sorrow and this-is-what-life-amounts-to desire.

I called Jill again next morning, going straight to voicemail again and repeating my condolences: could she please call me if she felt up to it, I added, since I'd be going away on the Saturday. It was the last day at school and nursery for the boys, morning only. After walking them there I looked after Mabel, while Marie organised the packing. Mabel had so far been a placid baby, but today she kept grizzling, which added to Marie's stress: 'Can't you even manage her for one hour, Matt? For fuck's sake, take her out in the pram or something.' Mabel was screaming when we left the house, but dropped off by the end of the road. This would be a good time for Jill to call, I thought, just as she did.

'Thanks for the message,' she said. 'Everyone's been so kind.'

Her voice sounded upbeat rather than flat. (It's the second grieving stage, Marie said later: after the shock and disbelief comes the phoning round and organising stuff. The flatness comes later.) When I began offering my sympathies again, she cut me off.

'You know what happened?' she said.

'No,' I said. So she told me. (Of course she told you, Marie said. Only by telling it repeatedly will she come to accept it's true.)

47

He'd been off-colour for a few days, she said. And when he woke on Tuesday morning, he complained of stomach pains. He got up, nevertheless; it took a lot to keep him from his study, even on days (and there'd been more and more of those) when he didn't feel like writing. She suggested porridge; maybe that would calm his stomach. He agreed to give it a go and sat at the table while she filled a Pyrex dish with water and oats. I'll be late for work, she thought, as she stuck it in the microwave, but if need be I'll cancel my first appointment. While the Pyrex dish circled round, he complained the pain was worse. All the more reason to try this, she said, lifting the dish out with her oven gloves and turning to see him topple from the chair and slump to the floor. She crouched beside him, putting her ear to his mouth, then his chest. Thank God, he was breathing, but his eyes were thick and as watery as the porridge. She called an ambulance. He was still alive when it arrived seven minutes later, but by the time they reached the hospital – she sitting in the back with a paramedic – he'd gone. They showed her to a waiting room while they tried resuscitation. Twenty minutes later they came through. If she hadn't known already, she'd have guessed from their faces. I'm sorry, Mrs Pope, we did all we could.

'They think it was an aneurysm of his abdominal aorta, not a coronary,' she said. 'And that he died of internal bleeding. The post-mortem results haven't come through yet, but that's what they're saying.'

Internal bleeding. Rob had always been so out there. It didn't sound like his kind of death.

'You're probably wondering about the funeral,' she said. 'If he'd seen a doctor in the past month, it'd be easy, but a sudden death means a post-mortem, which complicates everything. Till the coroner signs the death certificate, there's nothing I can do.

You'll be able to see his body at the undertakers, but I don't know when that will be. You said something about going on holiday.'

'Yes, tomorrow, to Majorca, for two weeks. But I'll have this mobile with me. You can let me know about the funeral.'

'Burial's what Robbie wanted, not cremation. That may delay things, too.'

'I'll come back whenever it is.'

'There's really no need. It wouldn't be fair on Marie and the children. All that way just for a short ceremony.'

'It's fine,' I said. 'I want to be there. You know he asked me to be his literary executor?'

'I know he left a will with his solicitor, but I've no idea what's in it. Until the funeral's over I can't even think about it.'

'Of course. The executor thing is neither here nor there.'

'A plain religious service is what I have in mind.'

Whatever Rob thought about his funeral being held in a church, he'd surely have wanted one of his poems to be read. Some kind of eulogy would be in order too. Which someone would have to deliver. All this was running in my head. But I kept my mouth shut. It wasn't the moment. He'd only been dead for three days.

I took my time wheeling Mabel back (she could do with a nice long sleep), worrying I'd struck the wrong note with Jill and recalling three things in particular: first, that she'd remembered Marie's name, though they'd spent very little time together; second, that she called her husband Robbie, when everyone else knew him as Rob; third that she assumed I'd want to see his body. Would I? There'd be no chance to now I was going away, but even if there had been I didn't think I would. I'd never seen a dead body. And I didn't want Rob's to be the first.

49

4

In late April, halfway through my first year at Brandon, I rented a lakeside cabin for a week, partly because I'd barely left the campus since arriving, partly to get some writing done. When I mentioned it to Rob, he ridiculed the idea ('Why would being next to a lake help anyone write?'), then invited himself along. I felt too flattered to turn him down. Despite the many hours we'd spent together by then, I couldn't forget the gap between us – in age as well as status.

The lakeside cabin was a two-hour bus ride from Brandon, then half an hour by bike. Our Walden week, Rob called it, who spent the bus journey mocking Thoreau ('Total fake. His cabin was next to a busy commuter route. In twenty minutes he could be home eating his mother's biscuits, and usually was'), before surprising me with his appetite for outdoor life. Little writing got done, but every day we'd swim from the jetty or take out canoes or hike through the woods or cycle by moon-light to the diner on the distant highway. His boyish enthusiasm was matched by a Boy Scoutish expertise, which included bar-becuing chicken over a fire built from driftwood and twigs.

He also surprised me with a love of pranks. The cycle-hire place in town was small and only one suitable trail-bike was avail-able – Rob settled for a lumbering old ladies' bike with a basket at the front and a child-seat behind. He didn't seem to mind. One afternoon we were cycling through the forest and came out in a glade overlooking the lake, where several families were having picnics, each sitting apart at its own table. 'Watch this,' Rob said, pulling up with a screech of brakes and looking round at the empty child-seat. 'Oh, my God,' he shouted. 'The baby! The baby's fallen out!' He swung round and pedalled off in the direction we'd come from, leaving me to watch the expressions on the picnickers' faces. What did they look like, he wanted to know when I caught him up: horrified, bemused or merely curious? I accused him of ruining their day. Not at all, he said, he'd given them something to talk about: 'Intriguing your audience, it's called: grabbing their attention and then tantalising them – don't they teach you that in creative writing classes?'

Little writing got done at the cabin, as I say, but there was a lot of talk about how to go about it and (Rob's speciality) how not to. 'I'm here to save you from all the crap you're being fed on the MFA,' he said. '*Show don't tell.* Don't do either. Be ambiguous and evasive: hide, camouflage, disguise. *Write about what you know.* No, write about what you'd like to find out. *All the best stories are true.* All the best stories are made up. *Kill your darlings.* God no, why the fuck do that?' Having him around stopped me from getting on. But as he saw it, that was a mercy. Better to listen to him than to my tutors.

On the last night, a Friday, after burger, fries and beers at the diner, we sat on the cabin porch, a row of citronella tealights on the wooden rail in front of us (the mosquitoes were terrible) and a bottle of Jack Daniel's between us.

'Here's to exile,' he said, chinking glasses.

'It's hardly exile,' I said. 'We could go back home any time.'

'To England, yes. And I will one day. But Tennessee, no, I can't go back there.'

'Why not?'

'Old story: man lets his guard drop, offends the authorities and is sent away. You don't want to know.'

'I do.'

He went off at a tangent and talked about Joyce, Mandelstam, Ovid and how exile could benefit a writer ('you have to leave home in order to know it'), whatever the personal cost. It was typical Rob – evasive literary table talk. He could see I was bored.

'Fuck it, I might as well tell you,' he said. 'Every fucker in Tennessee knows. It's hardly a secret.'

'My Corinne', he called her: whether that was her real name or one he invented, I never found out.

*

He'd been teaching in Tennessee for two years, 'long enough to know the ropes', when she appeared in his class, instantly conspicuous because she looked, and was, ten years older than all the other students, more or less Rob's age in fact. She'd married young, had a child, divorced, worked in a bar and saved enough money to go back to school. The child, a girl, was still only seven, which made it tough to get to every class. My girl's been sick, she told Rob, appearing in his office one morning to plead for an extension to an essay deadline. He was used to such pleas, but not to them coming from parents, let alone a parent as striking as Corinne – striking in appearance (diminutive stature, big head of red hair) and striking in her will to succeed. There were strict departmental rules about deadlines, but Rob marked all his own essays, so no one but the two of them would know. Sure, he said, assuming that would satisfy her and she'd go. Instead, she took it as a cue to sit down and started to discuss the essay she had in mind, asking if he thought her ideas would stand up, supposing she could express them in writing – writing was something she found hard, she said, essay-writing anyway, which she hadn't done since school and a lack of practice at which put her at a disadvantage to all the other students. It would be absurd to say that he fell in love with her there and then, as she sat three feet away on the other side of his desk, small, vulnerable, wringing her hands. Absurd but probably true. Why else would he have kept her there, reassuring her that her ideas weren't stupid, suggesting a structure that would help them emerge, passing on tips for further reading, even plucking a critical book from his shelf and letting her borrow it (something he never did with undergraduates after one of them dropped out and failed to return his Collected Tennyson)? Why else would he have noticed the silvery scar of a recent pan-burn on her left wrist? Why else would he have closed the window, despite the heat, so that her perfume hung around long after she'd left the room? Why else, when her essay came in — misspelled, ungrammatical, poorly argued — did he give it a grade higher than it deserved?

She herself asked him that question, appearing in his office again a week or so after he'd handed it back. He'd made so many corrections in red pen — far more than she was used to from other tutors — that she knew his mark had been too generous, she said, and would like him to explain some of his marginal comments. She was wearing jeans with a black belt and a red-and-blue check shirt with the top two buttons undone. Unlike his colleagues, he always made marginal comments on student work, but it was true that he'd made more than usual on Corinne's paper, not because it was especially bad but because he felt she had potential and needed encouragement, and perhaps, too, hard though it was to admit to himself, because he secretly hoped that the more oblique of the comments would produce exactly this result: the chance to see her again, one to one. They spent an hour going over the essay – forty-five minutes longer than he'd ever given any other student, and fifty-five above the recommended departmental limit for undergraduates. She's a special case, he told himself, a single parent struggling to cope but driven by her desire for knowledge. His own desire didn't come into it. The collarbone showing above her undone buttons; the anxious, am-I-good-enough smile; the dark green eyes (the same shade as Virago book jackets, he decided): he pretended not to see them, that they didn't exist.

It became a pattern. She'd come to his office to discuss forthcoming assignments – to start with just those on his course, but soon enough those on other courses too. And after she'd done the assignments and had them back, she'd come again for clarification about his comments or, where the essay wasn't for him, about the mark she'd been given. Over time, the marks improved. Her essays hadn't been bad in the first place, just lacking in discipline. Now she was getting good grades, and not only from him. She challenged him over the justice of that. He had heard of students disputing their grades, but not when they'd been given As. He told her that. They joked about it. He loved it when she laughed.

She was a one-off. Which is why he longed to see her repeatedly. And did, platonically, for over two years.

The turning point came at the end of her third year. Exams were over, he'd done all his marking and she'd got her grades (all As and achieved on papers assessed by other colleagues, not him). It should have been a time to celebrate. She was wearing denim shorts and a pink gingham shirt, a relaxed, summery, end-of-term look. Yet she seemed more than usually stressed, fretting about which modules to take in her final year, and was no calmer by the time the hour was up (it was always an hour – 'my shrink session', she called it). Was anything wrong?

he asked, at the end, seeing her reluctance to leave. Anything beyond the modules, all of which she'd be fine at, whichever she chose? She'd not been sleeping well, she said, the neighbour's dog had been keeping her awake and she worried about her daughter, who was being bullied at school. On top of which, she was behind with the rent, her asshole ex having stopped his maintenance cheques after quitting his job and moving on without saying where – that's how he was, a drifter, last heard of in Lexington, but that was months ago, he could be dead for all anyone knew and maybe it'd be better if he were, the way he was living he soon would be, crystal meth, crack, heroin, you name it, he'd been on it ... While she talked he noticed something glistening on her left wrist, not the silvery pan-burn, which had long since cleared up, but a teardrop. And now another. And her eyes filling. And her droopy-shoulder helplessness. He stepped out from behind the safety barrier of his desk and pulled her to her feet, into a hug, so she could sob into his chest and he wouldn't have to look at her looking at him looking at her, which had been adding to her distress. Her hair tickled the underside of his chin and he moved a hand to stroke it, and slid his knuckles gently up and down her cheek, the sort of comforting gesture he might have offered to anyone, but Corinne wasn't anyone and holding her at all, let alone so tightly, with his hand on her cheek and her hair under his chin, was breaking the No Touching rule that was sacrosanct to the university, *all* universities, as he knew, as she surely knew too, but she'd the excuse of being distressed and disoriented, whereas he, as her teacher, in a position of authority ... She was in his arms, quietly shaking, and he looking over her head at his poetry shelves wondering if any poet had ever described a situation of this kind, where a man flouts officialdom for the higher cause of consoling a creature in distress. What was he meant to do: stand aloof and send her off to Student Counselling? It was too late for that, and he went on stroking her cheek till she shifted her head slightly and brushed his knuckles with her lips, hardly a kiss – if all his senses hadn't been so charged he might not have felt it – but the second time it was a kiss, moist, unmistakeable, and she began to kiss the tips of his fingers, and how could any man resist doing the next thing and pressing his mouth to her lips? And after that there was no stopping – they'd been denying themselves for so long, that was clear now, holding themselves at bay on opposite sides of the desk. But the desk was behind him now, literally, his coccyx hard up against the wood as they kissed and swayed, with all the months of Shakespeare, Byron, Keats, Woolf, Faulkner and Toni Morrison packed into their embrace, and there was no more talk from her about failing, and no more Beckett comeback from him about failing better, because their bodies had taken over and they'd dropped to the floor, and the thing they'd wanted but not intended was about to happen, and did happen, in his office, on the rough blue carpet, both half dressed still but fully exposed – no secrets any more, no pretending, the only mystery was why it had taken so long.

Lying there, with his desk behind him, he suddenly laughed. What? she said, as though afraid he was mocking her. I won't be teaching you next year, he said. You mean you won't see me any more? she said, sitting up and buttoning her shirt. The opposite, he said, pulling her down again. I don't teach on any of your options and I won't be marking any of your work – we're in the clear. How? To see each other, he said. If that's what you want, she said, kissing him again, but then standing and pulling up her shorts and reaching for a tissue from her bag and readying herself to leave. Thank God one of them was being prudent, he thought, climbing to his feet and adjusting his clothes – most of his colleagues were already on vacation and the department was deserted, but you never knew who might choose to drop by.

In the clear. So they were, for the rest of the summer. They met in his office; at a motel on the other side of town; and when Rob's landlord (a physics professor) and his wife were on holiday, at the house where he had lodgings. He went to her place once, too, the 'scummy apartment' (her phrase) she lived in with her daughter Maya. Introduced as 'Mommy's literature professor', he entertained Maya with card games while Corinne cooked supper, not that playing rummy could be much fun for an eight-year-old American girl, but as Corinne said at least it stopped her watching TV. The three of them went swimming at a lake one day, and on another, in baking heat, took refuge in a cinema, where *Home Alone* was playing. Their time was necessarily limited (Corinne had Maya to look after and in August Rob spent two weeks back in England), but they'd have more once school resumed. Discretion was important, of course. But Rob felt he could handle that. It was only a year and then – who knows, if both of them still felt as they did – maybe they could move in together.

She was his age, or older, not a twenty-year-old. A parent and divorcee. Intellectually his equal, if not as well read. And he wouldn't be teaching her or assessing her work.

In the clear. So they might have been, and should have been. But for a chance episode or chain of events. They were having coffee one afternoon, off campus (they always met off campus now; she no longer visited his room), when a young man came by, wheeling a bike and talking to another young man, only for one of them to drop a folder, right by the table where Rob and Corinne were sitting. Rob bent down and helped them retrieve the papers that had scattered from it, graphs and tables mostly. The two of them must be science students, he thought – neither looked familiar and though he noticed the boy with the bike stealing looks at Corinne that wasn't uncommon, she was a striking woman after all.

He thought no more of it. The autumn semester was his busiest. And he'd been landed with an extra course that year, on Victorian literature, little of which he'd read (his expertise stopped round 1824, when Byron died). It meant a lot of extra reading, and midnight oil, and less time for Corinne, but she was busy too and they took their chances when they could. (If he'd had his wits about him, he'd have moved from the house of the physics professor and his wife and found a flat somewhere, but he'd committed himself to another year and didn't want to upset them.) In late October the first batch of essays came in for the new course, a comparison of Tennyson and Browning. He marked them leniently by his standards, allowing for his own lack of expertise as well as that of the students, not all of whom were majoring in English. The only C he gave was to a student called Lisa Harding – the first couple of pages were largely plagiarised from a monograph he'd happened to read during his crash course on Victorianism, while the rest was a hotchpotch of misquotations. The girl came to see him after getting her grade. With her pigtails and dungarees – the sharecropper look, as he thought of it – she seemed an innocent, simply baffled to have done so badly and eager to learn how she might have done better. He took her through the essay, trying to explain and amplifying the marginal comments he'd made in red pen, some of them, in truth, not so much comments as exclamations – ! was a punctuation mark he used liberally. He interpreted her silence as proof that she was listening. At the end, though, she asked if he'd regrade her: she understood the essay wasn't top-rank, she said, but a C was really harsh. No, the grade had already been registered, he said, but she shouldn't worry too much, it counted for only a fifth of the course, if she concentrated she'd surely do better on the second essay and in the end-of-year exams. Yes, but where a student disputed a grade, an essay could be second-marked, she said: she'd read that in the student handbook. He had no experience of that, he said, no student he'd graded had ever asked to be reassessed before; from what he understood, it was a cumbersome process and the original grade was usually upheld – did she really want to bother, when the essay counted for such a small part of her final grade on the course, and the course such a small part of her overall degree? She certainly did want to bother, she said, her college career was important not just to her but to her parents, who'd borrowed money in order to subsidise it and had invested hope as well as dollars in her, and so far she'd repaid those hopes with As and high Bs. Well, if that's what she wanted to do, he couldn't stop her but ... No, he couldn't stop her, and she trusted he wouldn't try to, since from what she understood he was pretty new to the American system – *No offence, professor, but we've a different way of conducting ourselves here.*

The phrase might have told him that there was more to this than a below-average student wanting to graduate with an above-average degree. But though he brooded about the exchange and how badly it had gone, and how her downtrodden sharecropper look had made him underestimate her, he didn't think he'd underestimated the essay, which he'd read enough of again while taking her through it to be reminded of its inadequacy, to the point of wondering whether a D wouldn't have been more apt, even if Ds, in the US, were unheard of. She took her essay away with a defiance he almost admired, but expected nothing to come of her appeal. Even when a message came from the head of department, Prof Cutler – 'Chuck' to all the staff – to 'drop by' for a meeting at 7.30 next morning, which since Rob had never been summoned in that way before, let alone at such an ungodly hour, he knew must be to discuss Lisa's appeal, he wasn't especially worried.

'Sit down, Richard,' Chuck said. He was a tall, barrel-chested, long-sideburned Texan in his fifties, who looked as if he ought to be out on the range or inspecting oil rigs in a Stetson, rather than sitting at a large desk heaped high with monographs about Christopher Marlowe.

'Robert, actually.'

'This Harding student – lousy essay, uh? Read it myself. Starts off OK –'

'Though that part's largely plagiarised.'

'I see why you didn't much go for it. Kid's pretty angry with her C, though.'

'She's disappointed, naturally. I tried to show her where she fell short.'

'Sure. All these exclamation marks, though . . .' He held the essay up and chuckled. 'You didn't hold back, eh? Course, I see what you meant by them. But a kid like her, sensitive and all, well, what she sees is you calling her an idiot.'

'I explained what was meant by them when she came to see me.'

'But the damage was done. Look, it's not the main issue here. I'm just saying – go easy on the exclamation marks, Robin!'

'The main issue being whether to upgrade her, right?'

'Yes and no. I had Prof Cartwright look at the essay. He once wrote a paper on Browning. Good man. He kind of agreed with you. But all things considered – to draw a line under it – given other matters – I'm gonna uphold the appeal and let the girl have a B.'

'When you say other matters . . .?'

'Well, now, this is damn awkward. See, the girl wrote me a letter as well. Questioning your objectivity in awarding grades is what it came down to. Alleging preferential treatment given in at least one case for reasons not based on academic ability but because of a personal connection. Here, you'd better read her letter.'

It was written in ghoulish green ink and in an odd mix of babyish sanctimoniousness and legalistic abstraction. He felt a strange disgust as he read it, not at Lisa so much but at his relationship with Corinne as seen through her eyes. It was well known around campus that he'd had – and was still having – a sexually intimate relationship with one of his students, it said. Lisa's own boyfriend had seen them behaving in a flagrantly inappropriate manner, in a café often patronised by students. The student in question had boasted to friends of getting extra coaching from him as well as A grades she didn't deserve. She, Lisa, wasn't fully acquainted with college regulations and would prefer to let the issue be dealt with by the department, but she felt it her moral duty to draw attention to Prof Pope's behaviour, especially in the light of the unfair mark he had given her, which they now had the opportunity to 'reassess'.

'It's blackmail,' Rob said, handing back the letter.

'But is it true?'

'It's true that I'm in a relationship with a mature student. But I don't currently teach her or grade her work.'

'But she's a literature major.'

'Yes.'

'And you've taught her in the past.'

'She was in my Romantic seminar in her freshman year.'

'And the extra coaching?'

'She came back to university after ten years out of school. She was struggling and I tried to help.'

'You've never graded her work, you say?'

'I marked a few essays in her freshman year, but in a four-year degree they don't count for much overall.'

'I'm well aware of that,' Chuck said, suddenly angry, at Rob's composure if nothing else. 'I run the department, in case you hadn't noticed.'

'I'm sorry if I've caused any trouble.'

'*If.* Damn right this is trouble, and unless we play our cards right there could be a heap more. Look, Ronald –'

'Robert.'

'– we're all human. Those girls sit there in the front of the lecture theatre with their big eyes and their short skirts and they think you're a god because you can quote Shakespeare, and they hang back after class or come to your office to ask if there's any extra reading you can suggest, because they really want to do well on the course and your lectures are so inspiring, and so forth, there they are with pouts and their eyes and their low-cut tops. We've all been there. But when they come on like that it's our duty to resist.'

'Corinne is thirty. She has a daughter. She's had a life. She isn't naïve.'

'She's a student in the department where you teach. As far as the college is concerned, that's all there is to it and you're way out of line. With any luck, we can keep the lid on this. The Harding girl will get her B and not make any more trouble. God knows, you're not the first. Still, if you've any sense you'll break it off with this student at once. So long as there's nothing ongoing, it'll stop the gossip; the college authorities won't get to hear and we'll avoid having to instigate disciplinary proceedings against you. Sound fair? Hope so. I'd better get on. Damn timetable to draw up for next year. Don't ever be a head of department, Ricky, it's a nightmare.'

Rob came away shaken. He'd classes to teach, but even they couldn't distract him. The business about changing the grade was undermining and he hated the idea of Lisa gloating over her victory. But the bigger issue was Corinne: to break it off seemed unthinkable; this was love between two adults, not a squalid teacher–student affair. On the other hand ... no, there was no other hand, he mustn't weaken; to compromise over the grade was one thing (in effect, he'd had no choice), but to give in to blackmail, inapplicable codes of conduct and outdated Christian morality was another. Only ... was it true that Corinne had 'boasted to friends' about him giving her extra lessons and upping her grades? It didn't sound like her. But how well did he know her? Intimately, he'd thought, mind and body. Now he wasn't sure.

He hadn't learned to drive (never did learn), but cycled across town that night, in the luminous dark, with his head buried under a hood, paranoid about everyone he passed. 'It's Rob, can I come up?' he buzzed from below, and left his bike in the stair-well while he climbed to the third. From the brevity of his kiss if nothing else, Corinne could tell how agitated he was. 'Bud?' she said and opened two beers. As he'd hoped, Maya was in bed asleep. They sat on opposite sides of her kitchen table (just as they used to at his desk), she in pyjamas, PJs as she called them, an abbreviation he hated for its tweeness, but, given how young she looked in them – like a child, the pale blue sleeves with little red kites on them riding up her arms – PJs seemed right. He came straight to the point: Lisa's grade, Lisa's boyfriend, the gossip, the meeting with Prof Cutler, the ultimatum.

'I never boast,' she said. 'I've nothing to boast *about*.'

'But you told people you were having extra lessons with me.'

'Not at the time. Later, afterwards. And not people – only my friend Julie.'

'Julie?'

'You'd probably recognise her. She's in my poetry group.'

'I didn't know you were in a poetry group.'

'Informally, just a few of us. From my year. We get together now and then to discuss our poems.'

'You've never shown them to me.'

'They're terrible. I'd be ashamed to. But hey, we try.'

'So that's where the rumours started. With Julie.'

'She's not the sort to talk. And I didn't say you upped my grades, only that I'd done better than I thought. You know me. It's what I always say. I've no confidence.'

'Confidence. That's the thing. You took Julie into your confidence and word got out about us.'

'I never said we were –'

'She inferred it.'

'And now you're going to dump me.'

'Did I say that?'

'But you are. Just like that. Because a bunch of kids are gossiping.'

'Maybe you don't mind the gossip,' Rob said.

'Fuck you. Why would being associated with some assistant lecturer who all the students think is a dork make me look special? The guy who wears leather shoes and woollen shirts even when the temperature's in the nineties? Who crosses the word *gotten* out every time some kid writes it in an essay, even though *gotten* is normal usage here.'

'Do all the students think I'm a dork?'

'I'm just saying: you're not some fucking Adonis.'

Their beers were empty, but if she'd more in the fridge she wasn't offering. He hadn't meant it to go like this. He'd come to reassure himself that she'd not been flaunting their relationship, and, having established that, to discuss what to do next, how to 'put a lid on' and 'draw a line under' their relationship, but only in appearance, to satisfy the authorities and quash the malice, not to end things or sacrifice what they felt for each other, the passion and desire he felt even now, in the middle of the worst argument they'd ever had, as she sat there opposite him, the lovely V between her breasts showing above the top button of her PJs, the sun-bleached hairs faint on her arms, the Virago-book-jacket-green eyes. He reached for her hand. She snatched it away.

'I didn't come here to dump you,' he said.

'What, then?'

'It'll be difficult still seeing each other, but —'

'It's impossible.'

'I'll be risking my job, but —'

'It's not just about you. Do you think I'll be graded fairly, now the whole department knows? You've no idea what this place is like. They'll want to penalise me, to make an example; they pretend to want older students like me, but they don't; we unsettle the younger ones; we're needy and we over-think things and we don't know how to behave. I'm proof of that. I went and seduced the nice young Englishman. That's how they'll see it. If I'd been twenty it would have been his fault, but I'm thirty, a divorcee, from the wrong side of town, so it'll be mine, and for that I won't get my As, even if I do finally deserve them.'

'Getting As isn't everything.'

'Easy for you to say. Your education was paid for, you just waltzed through. For me it's been a fight. I might train as a teacher next and I need the grades for that. Or I might stay on and do a master's and get to be a prof one day. Don't look at me like that.'

'I wasn't looking like anything,' he said, but to imagine her as a literature professor was a stretch, and the stretch must have shown in his face.

'The world's changing, not all profs are like you.'

'I agree.'

'Well, that's why the As matter. Or did. I'm fucked now, whatever.'

'Of course you're not,' he said, reaching for her hand again, which this time she let him take. They sat there for an hour, pulling back from the brink, making up, pretending certain bitter words hadn't been spoken or hadn't been meant. They were, they agreed, in shock – best get some sleep and by morning things might not look so bleak. There must be a way they could see each other without his job being risked and her grades being affected and the two of them being the subject of gossip. They held each other by the door, before he left. There was no question of them making love, but the hug was a promise to each other: *We'll find a way, this will go on.*

Cycling back, though, he felt upset again, and upset in different ways: the interview with Prof Cutler had been bad enough, but Corinne's reaction had made it worse. Did his students really see him as a dork? Not the bright ones, surely, the kind that Corinne mixed with in her poetry group. Why had she never mentioned the group before? Shyness probably, but the fact of her being in a group and of her having friends – one of whom, Julie, she felt close enough to confide in about the so-called extra coaching – that had shocked him, still shocked him, because it didn't fit with the image he had of a woman who felt isolated, adrift, uncertain, for whom college was an alien place, her real life, her *established* life, lying elsewhere, in a flat with her daughter, on the other side of town. And her ambition! That obsession with As. He'd come expecting her to sympathise with his dilemma as a young lecturer in his first job who now risked falling foul of the university authorities, and even of losing his job, and all because of her – not that he'd uttered a single word of blame, it wasn't her fault he'd fallen in love with her, but still he hoped she'd understand and comfort him. Instead of which, her response had been all about her and the risk she now ran of being ostracised by the department, penalised in her grades and thwarted in the career she'd set her heart on. He didn't believe for a moment that she would be penalised. But even allowing for her shock and panic – hysteria even – it was striking that what she most feared wasn't the loss of their relationship but missing out on a good degree.

You have to admire her ambition, he thought, leaving his bike in the garage and creeping up the stairs (it was past midnight and the physics professor and his wife would be asleep), but she doesn't understand how universities work; she has a weird take on things; you could even say that for all her As she's actually a little bit stupid.

He didn't see her for two weeks. Before that intense we-still-have-a-future hug, they'd agreed a pause would be best. He phoned her one night, but the conversation was perfunctory: she'd an essay to get in the next morning and hadn't been sleep-ing well; Maya was being bullied at school again. He phoned another night and asked if she could get a babysitter the follow-ing Saturday so they could meet at The Day's Inn: it was on the edge of town, he'd cycle there and get a room, and she arrive separately. She took some persuading, but agreed. The room was grim but their lovemaking made up for it: so much need had built up. Afterwards, lying there – he with a Bud, she with a cigarette (post-coitally was the only time she smoked) – he tried to soothe her worries. It was nonsense to think she'd be penal-ised, he said. His colleagues were above such pettiness. Their duty was to be objective.

'You're not the only prof to give me extra time,' she said, unconvinced. 'You gave me the most, sure. But I couldn't expect you to know everything about the whole of literature.'

'Who else did you see?'

'Doesn't matter.'

'But male?'

'What else? The whole fucking department's male. Nothing went on, if that's what you're thinking. Though I kind of sensed an interest from one guy. And when he and the others I saw hear about us, they'll sure as hell punish me. You think I'm being paranoid. But I've had this kind of thing in my jobs. With my ex, too. It's human nature – with men especially.'

Of course she'd consulted other profs. She was that kind of student. It was odd that he'd never thought of it. But even odder that she'd never mentioned it. Had she guessed he'd be jealous? He was now, at the thought of the *interest* she'd sensed from a nameless colleague. What form did it take? If she'd not been involved with him, Rob, might she have responded? Lying there in the half-light of the room, two dead bulbs in the matching wall lights and a Gideon's Bible in the drawer, he no longer felt exclusive. Till then he'd seen her as an ingénue, more of one than students ten years younger. But she'd surely been sly not to mention the sessions with his colleagues.

Their lovemaking was usually tender. When they made love again that Saturday, ten minutes before she was due to leave, he was rougher. The roughness included a bite on her neck. He was angry and wanted to leave his mark on her.

He spotted her in the campus café a few days later. She was with a group of female students, laughing together, one of the crowd. She stopped laughing the moment she saw him. He'd never seen her in a polo-neck sweater before. The love bite must be underneath, dark purple, hidden out of discretion or shame. He bought a latte-to-go from the counter and nodded as he passed, a general nod, to the group, avoiding eye contact with her.

For the next three weeks they avoided *any* contact.

He'd booked a flight to spend Christmas at home. A ten-day trip only, but in his mind it was a watershed, a crisis point, do-or-die: he couldn't not see her before he went.

'Maya's out with her dad,' she said, when he phoned. 'You could come round now.'

Out, she said, not *away*: was he back in town, then?

'Sure is,' she said, when he arrived. 'He's got a job with the electric company.'

'I thought you were divorced.'

'Separated. Same thing. He's not living here. I won't have him fucking up my life again. Bud? Don't worry, they won't be back for a while and he won't come in when he drops her off.'

They drank their beers at the table – the last time, just a few weeks back, seemed a century ago. He told her he was going home for Christmas, omitting to mention that he'd once had thoughts (at the high point of their summer) of spending it here, with her, the lights blinking on the tree, and the presents under it, including his to her, a necklace he'd seen in town, curled up on the purple velvet slope of the jewellery-shop window, still there probably – he could go tomorrow to buy it and bring it to her as a token of his love. But love seemed out of the question now. Or in question. Hers for him, that was. He knew about his for her.

The last time he sat there he'd been quick to get to the point. This time he was slower, and the point a different one, but he got there eventually, fearful that putting the question would mean the end, but doing so anyway, because he couldn't endure the sense of limbo. Did they have a future was what it came down to, but either he put it badly or she chose to misunderstand.

'I sure hope I've a future,' she said. 'I've a kid to bring up and a degree to get. I'm not planning on pegging out just yet.'

'Do we? Together?'

'Now, honey,' she said, an endearment she'd never used before, one which made him feel like a child being addressed by his grandmother, 'we've been through this.'

'Have we?'

'You can't see me and I can't see you. OK, we've tried. But sneaking around's not right. The last time, at the motel, was terrible. I came home and cried all night long, then missed school half the next week. I don't know how I got through. But then Jim turned up and though he's nothing to do with this I finally realised how wrong it is, how much damage it's doing. You only see me when I'm OK. I've never let you see the other me, the emotional wreck I am the rest of the time. I'm barely holding myself together, and I have to, for Maya, and for my studies, I can't afford to fail.'

'But after next summer? When you've finished.'

'It'll never work. All the rumours, people spying on us, the warning you had from your prof – they've poisoned everything. Not for you maybe, but for me. I hate saying this. It breaks my heart. But we have to stop, sweetie. No more mess. No looking back. Scorched earth policy. That's how I am. I've done my grieving already. Now you have to.'

Though he hated what she was saying, he loved her forthrightness. She seemed so worldly, so mature, so good at endings. Perhaps she'd had practice at them: the ex, the death of her mother (which she'd once described to him in grisly detail), the move from Oregon to Tennessee. What could he say? She had left him no room to argue. His whole body hurt, but that was good, authentic, necessary.

He finished the beer and left. In time, they agreed, it'd be fine to have a coffee together, after graduation maybe, for old times' sake.

It didn't happen. It would have been too painful. Back in Sussex over Christmas he hunted for jobs in the *THES*. There were none he fancied and without a PhD, despite that article he'd published on Keats, no reputable university would have him. Back at college, he spent as little time on campus as possible. And when he marked essays did so quickly, perfunctorily, with a minimum of marginal comment and no exclamation marks. One day he overheard some students talking about a friend who'd 'taken that jerk of a husband back, the one she had her kid by'. Could that have been Corinne? He didn't want to think about it.

It was a bleak few months. But he began writing poetry again, seriously this time, having only played with it in the past. And when he wasn't writing poems he was writing job applications. In April, after several shortlistings and failed interviews, he got the post in Brandon, to begin in the autumn. His elation lasted only till the phone call came a few days later, to say his father had died: suddenly, of a heart attack, at sixty-one. He was given compassionate leave to stay on in Sussex after the funeral, rather than returning to Tennessee; teaching had finished by then anyway, and he knew Prof Cutler, 'Chuck', would be glad to see the back of him. He made no attempt to say goodbye to Corinne and never found out how she fared in her exams. His books and clothes were sent on to Brandon in a trunk.

*

'So that's my story,' he said, the near-empty bottle of Jack Daniel's between us on the porch of the lakeside cabin, moths fluffing against the lit window, a bridal train of moon across the water. 'The only one I have. Not to be repeated.'

'You can trust me.'

'Not to be repeated by me, I mean. No more falling in love with students. No more falling in love, period. My first experience and my last. It cost too much. Took years off my life and left me with nothing. Love's the ruin of people.'

'Come on, you can't –'

'Survive without love? I did before and I will again.'

'One day you'll meet someone.'

'And marry? Not from love. It's too consuming. You lose all perspective. I went crazy for a while. Writing's been the one consolation.'

'Do you write about Corinne?'

'What other subject is there? But no, I don't. I might write *to* her one day. Who knows? Here, have some more.' He aimed the bottle towards me.

'I'm done,' I said, covering my glass.

'You're right. Early-morning swim?'

'Sure.'

But both of us slept in till lunchtime and by two we were heading off. He didn't speak of Corinne again.

5

It had the decency to rain at the funeral. There was a wind, too, and had been for several days, bringing leaves and twigs down, as though autumn had already arrived. Unlike the strip of AstroTurf draped across the newly dug hole, the grass in the graveyard was long. I got there early, having driven down, and wandered between the headstones, killing time. A line from Rob's work came back to me: 'the grassy mounds and lichened headstones of forgotten ...' What? Serfs, yeomen, peasants, something like that. An umbrella kept my head dry, but not my feet. Inside, as the vicar led us through the ceremony, I was conscious that my socks were wet, and, head bowed, noticed the drops stippling my polished shoes. Like tears, I thought, then thought again – Rob hated corny similes.

Ashes to ashes, dust to dust. But I was drenched.

I'd read most of the press about Rob on my iPad, in Soller. There'd not been much apart from the obits, just a paragraph on the BBC website and a brief news story in the *Telegraph*: 'Author of the *Martello Sonnets* dies at sixty'. I probably missed other pieces, but thanks to the delay Jill had talked about I didn't miss the funeral, which took place not in Hadingfield but in Carforth, the village where Rob had grown up. He'd told Jill he wanted to be buried and, according to Louis de Vries, who I sat next to in the church, none of the places local to her offered burials. To begin with, the local authority in Sussex wasn't helpful either. But Jill was insistent: not only was it Rob's birthplace but his mother had spent her last years in a nursing home just up the road. It turned out that the Carforth vicar – triple-chinned, balding, sixtyish – was a fan of Rob's poetry and as he said at the start of the service welcomed giving him 'a place among the honoured dead of this parish' (adding that he, too, had been 'known to scribble the odd verse').

Jill had warned me the service would be religious and it was. We even knelt for prayers, the dusty psalter making my nose itch. She was in the front pew, under a black veil, supported by a man whom I took to be her brother (the orang-utan, Rob had called him, though nothing in his appearance suggested it, and Rob – in the coffin on its stand in front of the altar – was in no position to explain). There was no sign of Rob's sister, though there'd been ample time for her to come back from Australia; either Jill had failed to contact her or she was too ill to travel. As for the rest of us, about sixty in all, half were literary acquaintances of Rob, mostly poets, and half (I assumed) neighbours or friends of Jill. She held up well till the last part of the service – a recording of Rob reading one of his best-known poems, 'Pond', which described his childhood fascination with murky water and unknown depths. The hissing tannoy added to the effect. I kept my head down, for fear of blubbing. 'For those of you who care to visit,' the vicar said, to lighten the mood, 'the pond in question is just fifty yards from here, next to the pub.'

Then the exit to the grave began – with the vicar, the six pall-bearers, Jill and her brother, and Alexis Speke (Rob's editor) leading the way. The rain had eased. While the coffin rested beside the AstroTurf, Alexis – Lexy to those who knew her – read a poem from Rob's first collection, *Homeboy*, a celebration of the nearby countryside (one of the obits had singled it out as 'an eco-poem ahead of its time'). What would Rob have thought of the local emphasis? He used to tell me how bored he'd been growing up here and what a relief it was to come to London as a student; his later collections had strenuously rejected the provincialism of the first. Even Lexy seemed hesitant in her reading, though that might just have been nerves; she was younger by several decades than most of the mourners. Perhaps the poems had been chosen by the vicar, as a trade-off for the privilege of a burial.

It was he who had the last word, blessing the coffin while the pall-bearers raised it with ropes and dangled it over the grave. As they lowered it into the ground, the AstroTurf slipped down with it, and when both coffin and AstroTurf were out of sight and the ropes retrieved, two of the bearers shovelled earth on top. Jill's brother tightened his grip on her shoulder. In films I'd seen, the relatives throw handfuls of earth on to the coffin lid, but Jill didn't do this, nor (another movie cliché) did she have to be restrained from hurling herself down to join her spouse. I became fixated on the shovels: with all the rain, the earth had turned to mud and to unclag it from their shovels the two bearers had to bash them on the ground. They stepped aside once a few token spadefuls had plopped down. Evidently a gravedigger would be along later to finish the job.

As we left by the wooden lychgate, I fell in beside Connor Buckhurst, who reviews poetry for our pages. Conversation with him was always awkward, not because he's shy but because of his mouth, a blockish, oblong slit that opens and closes like a puppet's, with a clumsy mechanical parting of the lips. At least walking alongside I didn't have to face him.

'What did you think of Lexy's reading?' I asked. Though personally not the least miffed that she'd been given the job

(I hate speaking in public), I wondered if others might be, including Connor.

'Not bad,' he said, 'for a non-poet. She got the stresses in the last line completely wrong: it's "where the *buds* break from the prison of ice", not "where the buds *break* from the prison of ice". Of course, Lexy only inherited Rob. It was Charles who discovered him. She hasn't the same investment.'

Like Rob, Charles Durrant had died young, in his sixties, taking early retirement from the publishing company after bowel cancer was diagnosed and succumbing to it within a year.

'She published Rob's last collection, didn't she?'

'Saw it through. Perfunctorily. He wasn't one of hers. She's only interested in poets her age. Still, that's more than you can say for Jill. She's not interested in poetry at all. That's why she held the funeral down here: it's an awkward place to get to and she hoped no poets would come.'

'Come on, Connor. Rob asked to be buried. And there aren't many places you can be buried these days.'

'It's an excuse. Jill always wanted him for herself. Ideally there'd have been no one at the funeral except her.'

'Give her a break,' I said. 'She's devastated.'

'Of course. And he can't have been easy to live with. Always so full of himself. I bet he was hoping Highgate Cemetery would have him: Karl Marx, George Eliot, Robert Pope . . .'

'Is this why people come to funerals?' I said. 'To slag off the deceased?'

'Lighten up, Matt. I admired him. If you'd sent me his last collection, I'd have given it a good review instead of that hatchet job you printed. No, the reason people come to funerals is to spot the mystery mourner. That woman ahead of us, for instance, in the blue coat.'

'I overheard her talking earlier. She's one of his neighbours.'

'Pity. No scandal there, then. But what about the woman with the long hair who sat at the back of the church, then disappeared before the burial. Now she *was* intriguing.'

We'd reached the pub by then, the one overlooking the pond, where Jill had booked a side room and laid on sandwiches. Connor wandered off for a glass of wine; I'd driven down, because the train journey seemed complicated, and had to stick to orange juice. I chatted to several neighbours of Rob's from Hadingfield, none of whom I knew any more than I knew why he'd moved there in the first place. They stood in a cluster, rehearsing tales of the time Rob did this or Rob did that – burnt the meat so black when barbecuing that Jill had to send out for a takeaway; talked to himself, 'intoning verses', while walking up and down the garden; failed to recognise people when he passed them in the street; turned up late for appointments, notably for his one appearance at the local Literary Society, when he claimed he'd 'got lost', though the venue was only a quarter-mile from his house. The Rob I knew was not the eccentric they knew: he'd never been late when meeting me or meeting deadlines; he even knew how to barbecue. But if you were a poet living in the sticks, perhaps the caricature was inevitable. People saw what they wanted to see, in technicolour.

Half an hour crawled by. Though I'd watched her receiving handshakes and murmurs of sympathy, I hadn't yet spoken to Jill. And if I'd not been near the door as she headed towards it, intent on leaving, I would have missed her altogether. No longer veiled, she was wearing a grey suit, with a purple silk neck scarf, and looked a decade older than when I'd last seen her – which, come to think of it, maybe she was. We hugged a moment, not closely, while I offered my sympathies.

'I'll be in touch,' I said, seeing how eager she was to be gone. 'Thank you for coming.'

'There'll be the executor business to talk about.'

'All in good time.'

'I want to do my best by Rob. So that his work lives on. Hearing his voice today reading that poem . . .'

'Yes,' she said, and turned to her brother, who nodded at me, unsmiling, and led her away.

The noise levels rose with her departure. Most of the mourners were on to their second glass of wine. Had Jill been too consumed by grief to speak? Was she as abrupt with everyone? As I stood there brooding, Lexy came up.

'Hi, Matt, I didn't expect to see you here.'

'I got back from holiday last week.'

'I didn't realise you and Rob were friends, I mean. It's mostly poets here.'

'We met when I was in my early twenties,' I said. 'And stayed in touch. He did some reviewing for me.'

'Really? I thought you trashed his last collection.'

'Not me personally.'

'On your pages.'

'These things happen. Rob got over it.'

'Sure. I wasn't implying he'd not forgiven you.'

'Tricky' was how I'd sometimes heard Lexy described, a word Marie had banned as sexist ('Have you ever heard a man being called *tricky*? With them it's *subtle, independent-minded, complex, challenging, highly intelligent*'). I took the point, but even Marie might have found Lexy difficult. Slightly built, plain-looking, in her early thirties, she wasn't someone you noticed in a crowd; even when she'd stood reading the poem by the grave, you could have missed her. But the Jane Eyre-ishness was deceptive. Conversation with her (at parties, at prize ceremonies or over the phone) always left me exhausted. She'd a gift for putting you in the wrong or adding to your insecurities.

'Nice reading, by the way.'

'Thanks,' she said. 'I thought there might be other people closer to Rob, but Jill insisted.'

'He didn't mix much with other writers.'

'Least of all younger ones,' she said. 'The poets I know don't seem to read him.'

'Did Jill tell you he asked me to be his literary executor?'

'No. First I've heard of it.'

'Well, she's other things on her mind.'

'Oh, she did say something. About Louis doing it, was it? Excuse me a second – there's Connor Buckhurst.'

Jill's knowledge of the literary world was slight. She must have assumed that because Louis was Rob's agent he would automatically become his executor. A simple mistake. Unless for some reason she had blocked my appointment. It didn't seem likely. Still, I'd yet to be told officially or see written proof. Louis would know the answer. When we'd whispered to each other in the pews, we'd avoided any mention of Rob's will. Now would be a better time.

I saw him nipping out for a smoke and followed. Handsome, fiftyish, an elegant dresser with a patrician air, he could be tough when doing deals, as Leonie (who sometimes bought features from him) often complained. But no one was more widely read. He'd done a PhD and been a junior lecturer, before escaping academe (as Rob had done) and joining a literary agency. There were no bad authors on his list. Some wrote for film and television, which was where he made his money. But Rob wasn't the only one to have earned him next to nothing. However poor their royalties, he stuck with writers he admired. No wonder people looked up to Louis – literally as well as metaphorically, since he was six foot four.

The rain had stopped. I shook my head when he offered a cigarette. We stood overlooking the pond.

'Snakepit in there,' he said. 'It always is when a writer dies. I knew him better than you did, na-na-na-na-na-na. With a bit of backstabbing thrown in: great man, great man, pity he didn't fulfil his promise. Unlike themselves, they mean. Poets are the worst. When Robert Frost died, all Lowell and Berryman could think about was where it left them in the pecking order – which of us is Number One, Cal? Piranhas, all of them. Rob's the only poet I ever took on.'

'I've always wondered why you did. Most poets don't even have agents.'

'I read an article of his and thought, bright chap, worth signing up, he could do a book of essays one day or even a novel. Ten, fifteen years ago I could have got him a decent advance. But he wasn't interested. Poems were all he cared about.'

'Any plans for a Selected?' I said. Only three weeks had passed since his death. But agents sometimes move quickly.

'Depends on Lexy. And if there's any new stuff.'

'Did he ever talk to you about appointing a literary executor?' I said.

'Yes, he asked me if I would.'

'Appoint someone?'

'Do the job. "You're my agent," he said, "why not?"'

'When was this?'

'A few months ago.'

'He asked me as well. Late last year.'

'Did you turn him down, then?' Louis laughed, making light of it.

'No. I said I'd be happy to.'

'Strange – he never mentioned it.'

'What the fuck was he up to?'

'Search me,' Louis said. 'We'll have to see what his solicitor says.'

'Is he here?'

'She. Nah, she's on holiday. I'll give her a bell next week.'

*

It wasn't antipathy to Rob that stopped Marie coming to Sussex. If pushed, she'd have joined me. But we'd have had to bring Mabel and the prospect of a crying baby in church put us off. She'd written a letter to Jill instead. 'When you're feeling up to it, Matt and I would like to take you out to dinner,' it ended, 'or for a walk, to see a play, anything you fancy really. Matt's full of regret that he didn't see more of you both.'

The last part was only half true; it was Rob I wished I'd seen more of. And after the conversation with Louis, I'd no desire to see Jill at all. Not that I blamed her for Rob's change of heart. And not that I'd any right to expect her to be friendly when her husband's coffin had just been lowered in the earth. But she obviously knew what he'd decided; it explained her offhand manner with me. 'All in good time,' she'd said, unable to tell me herself. Fuck, it's not as if I need the work, I thought, as I meandered through B-roads to join the M23 and, beyond, at a snail's pace, headed north-east round the M25. It had rained again, and there'd been several minor collisions. It took me two hours to travel ten miles. The others at the wake – Louis, Lexy, the poets and neighbours – had come by train. I'd left in a rush long before them, straight after the chat with Louis. But they were probably back home long before me.

I found a parking place in the next street (there were none left in ours) and hung my sodden coat on the pegs inside the front door. The kids were upstairs, asleep. Upset by the conversation with Louis, I looked to Marie for support, but after a bad day with Mabel ('a funeral would have been a doddle in comparison') she was in no mood to give it. To cheer her up, and reward myself for my earlier abstinence, I poured us two large whiskies. We sat in the conservatory, or rather I did: she was growing six tomato plants in large pots, and as we talked she watered them.

'Rob obviously decided Louis is more suitable,' I said.

'Nah. He loved manipulating people. Here he is, still doing it, from the grave.'

'Perhaps I didn't sound enthusiastic enough. I should have made it clearer.'

'What were you supposed to do, dance up and down on the table?'

'He may have thought he was sparing me, what with the kids and the job and everything.'

'He didn't give a fuck about that. He wanted a poodle to fetch his sticks for him when he threw them. You're well out of it. But he could at least have told you.'

'I'm sure he would have. He wasn't expecting to die.'

'I don't know why you're sticking up for him,' Marie said, putting down the watering can and joining me on the wicker two-seater. She smelled of compost and vine. 'He betrayed you.'

'It's too strong a word.'

'OK, he upset you. And I hate seeing you upset.' She kissed me on the cheek. 'How was the drive? I expected you earlier.'

'Crap. Ten miles an hour round the M25.'

'No points for speeding, then.'

'Not on the motorway. But once I came off I put my foot down. I knew you'd approve.'

'Just watch it,' she said, picking up the watering can and pointing the spout at me – then snuggling up for the hug my allusion invited.

*

I should explain. Marie and I didn't meet in the usual way, at work or through friends, or in a pub or club or on a dating site. We met on a speed awareness course in Brentwood. Breaking the law is what brought us together.

The course was a pilot scheme for the one that now operates throughout the country. I'd been stopped by a patrol car in Essex, doing eighty on a dual carriageway, on the way to see my parents; Marie was caught by a speed camera in Leyton, on the way to work, doing thirty-six in a built-up area. We were offered the course instead of being docked three points on our licences. Marie chose Brentwood because it was nearer than Ealing, the only London venue offering the course on a Friday afternoon. I chose Brentwood because it was en route to Southwold, where I'd been due to spend the weekend with an old schoolfriend till he cancelled the day before. Call it what you will – serendipity, destiny, criminality – that cancellation, and those three hours of being lectured to by a pair of ex-police officers, changed our lives, if not my driving habits.

I noticed her in the lobby of the hotel even before we were escorted to the meeting room. There were twenty of us offenders, four women and sixteen men, of whom two stood out: Marie, with her dark hair, olive skin and intended-to-be-sensible-but-really-rather sexy pencil skirt; and a man in a purple fleece who glowered at us all so angrily that I took him to be one of the instructors. I was wrong about that. Once in the room he took a seat, like the rest of us. And whereas he continued glowering, as though disgusted to be in the company of dangerous speed merchants, the two instructors standing at the front were all smiles: they weren't there to punish or guilt-trip but to jolly us along. In appearance and idiom, the smaller guy was a dead ringer for David Brent in *The Office*. The taller one talked as though he'd recently completed a degree in evolution theory, likening car drivers to hunter-gatherers with spears. We were seated at semicircular tables of four; when I'd spotted the empty chair next to Marie, I'd been quick to grab it. We were given sticky white labels with our names on – GEORGE, DAVE, MATT, MARIE our table read left to right. After half an hour of easing us in, the instructors turned to the screen and flashed up a series of statistics – the number of deaths and serious injuries each year of drivers, motorcyclists, pedal cyclists and pedestrians – and asked for comments. The glowering man was first to speak: he was a lorry driver, he said, and resented lorry drivers being blamed for killing cyclists when it was usually the cyclists' fault, especially in London, where cyclists were crazy, ignoring and jumping red lights all the time, yet it was lorry drivers who had their licences taken away, whereas the cyclists got off scot-free. The instructors gently queried his opinions and moved on to a discussion of braking speeds, in particular the fatal difference between hitting pedestrians at 30 mph and hitting them at 40. The lorry driver spoke up again: why should he get the blame if a kid ran out in front of his vehicle? If the kid got killed that was the kid's fault or the kid's parents' fault, not his. Yet he'd be the one to go to jail; the law had it in for lorry drivers; it was always them that got prosecuted. Any comments? the instructors asked. Silence. We studied our laps, too embarrassed or afraid to speak. Then Marie stood up. I don't understand why you're talking about blame, she said, in an accent I mistook for Scottish at first, not Northern Irish. This isn't about blame, it's about avoiding tragedies, we've just

84

seen the statistics, if a child runs out in the road and you're exceeding the speed limit in a car, there's a greater risk the child will die, and if you hit a child while exceeding the speed limit in a lorry, the child will certainly die and you'll have it on your conscience for life. OK, I hold my hands up, I was caught speeding in a built-up area, I was late for a meeting and rushing, we all do it, but what an idiot, just think if I'd hit a child that day, I wouldn't be here, I'd be in prison or else so traumatised I couldn't sleep or go to work, let alone drive, all I'd be thinking of was that child, and of its parents – if and when I become a parent, I want my kids to be safe from speeding vehicles, especially lorries, which shouldn't be allowed to do 30 in built-up areas, 20 would make more sense in my view, I don't know what other people think.

People nodded and grunted assent. I want this woman to have my babies, I thought.

Yes, but when it's not the lorry driver's fault, the lorry driver said, at which point the taller of the instructors invited him to step outside 'for a quiet word', while his colleague moved on to the next stage of the course.

This sometimes happens, the other instructor said after they'd left the room: an individual can hijack the course, we do our best to stop that happening, but it's an interactive session and we need you to participate too – thank you, Marie, for speaking up.

Now it was Marie who looked embarrassed.

The lorry driver didn't return.

There was a break halfway through the afternoon – tea and biscuits. I stepped outside to get some air. Marie was standing there with her mobile, listening for messages. I took out my mobile and did the same. There were no messages, but I kept the phone pressed to my ear, pretending to listen, staring over the car park with its diagonal white lines, till she snapped her phone shut and put it in her handbag.

'You were great in there,' I said.

'I didn't mean to bang on, but that guy . . .'

'The Neanderthal.'

'I must have sounded awful: Miss Prim, the teacher's pet.'

'You said the right thing. Everyone thought so.'

'Someone just asked me if it was a set-up – he thought the lorry driver and me were plants.'

'But you're not.'

'No. I'm an offender. Same as you. We'd better go back in or they'll fail us.'

'The Holiday Inn, Brentwood,' I said, as we entered the lobby. 'Has anyone ever had a holiday in Brentwood?'

The instructors switched us round to work in groups. Marie's was the noisiest table; there were only three on mine (the departing lorry driver left the numbers short). We were asked to study photos and assess potential risks; my parents say that I've always been bad at anticipating danger and they're probably right; certainly, I was rubbish at the exercise – I kept glancing across at Marie and the man next to her, with whom she seemed to have hit it off. Then came a short film, which ran three times: the driver of a car at a T-junction briefly looked right, then left, then pulled out. The camera pointed down the road so that we saw what he saw. I too missed the motorbike approaching from the right. The noise of it crashing into the car still made me jump third time round. To finish off, we were asked to write how we might drive in future. *More carefully* I put, the same answer everyone gave.

I'd been sitting at the back of the room, Marie at the front, and with all the handshakes and thank yous to be said as we filed out I lost her. Outside I scanned the vehicles leaving the car park; if nothing else, I might get a wave. After five minutes, I gave up and went back inside to use the Gents – and there she was, in the lobby, sitting on a low leather sofa, a tall glass with a slice of lemon in front of her.

'Fizzy water, I trust,' I said.

'G and T. That film shook me up.'

'So the teacher's pet thinks it's OK to drink and drive.'

'I came by train. The station's a twenty-minute walk. I'm fortifying myself for the hike.'

'Can I get you another?'

'No, I'm fine.'

The bartender was quick, but even the sixty seconds he took felt too slow.

'So you're not driving either?' she said, nodding at my glass.

'It's fizzy water. Have you far to go?'

'Hackney.'

'You're joking. I live there too. I'll give you a lift.'

'I bought a return ticket.'

'I'll get you there quicker than the train will.'

'Have you learned nothing?'

I laughed. 'Without speeding.'

'Promise?'

'Promise.'

On the drive she told me about her childhood (in Belfast), her degree (at Southampton) and her job as a speech therapist (in Haringey) – NHS work mostly, though she also had a few private clients. At best it was hugely rewarding: to see a five-year-old who refused to speak at all during the first session, who struggled with the simplest words ('book', say, which came out as 'bot', or 'milk', which came out as 'malt'), who'd been teased and made to feel stupid at infant school, who screamed and kicked and head-banged in frustration when the words came out wrong, whose hostility kept breaking through no matter how patient you were and how careful to encourage – to see that child persevere, and its vocabulary increase, and its speech become intelligible, and its confidence and self-esteem flourish, was a wonderful thing, a gift, the best feeling she knew, all the more so when the child was a recent immigrant for whom English was a second language. Though for every case like that, it had to be said, there were several where you made no headway because the child's speech problems were the tip of the iceberg, the source of them lying in parental issues (violence, sexual abuse, poverty, neglect, alcoholism, drug addiction, depression, mental breakdown) that were beyond your remit and which the specialists you liaised with, the social workers and child psychiatrists, also lacked the time, skill or resources to remedy, however hard they tried.

'What about you?' Marie said, as we dropped down from the North Circular. I'd kept her talking till then, not just because I wanted to know all about her but because my work seemed trivial in comparison.

'I'm a writer.'

'Cool.'

'Not that cool. I'm a freelance journalist.'

'So you publish stuff in newspapers?'

'Occasionally. Mostly book reviews and arts features.'

'How did you get into that?'

'With difficulty. Are you hungry? There's a nice Greek place coming up here on the right.'

'Odysseus! I love it there.'

She ordered shish kebab, I had kleftiko, and with home just a short walk for us both ('I'll leave the car and collect it in the morning,' I said), we shared a bottle of retsina. In the course of explaining what I did, I mentioned my novel, which had come out a couple of years before.

'Should I have heard of you?'

'Christ, no,' I said.

'What's it called?'

'*The Return of Rasselas.*'

'Rasta-who?'

'Rasselas – a character created by Samuel Johnson in the eighteenth century,' I said, careful not to suggest she should have known. (She wasn't the first person to think that the name had something to do with Rastafarianism.)

'So why did you bring him back?'

'Good question.'

I smiled and drained my glass.

'Which deserves an answer.'

'Let me walk you home and I'll tell you,' I said. 'Shall we get the bill?'

We kissed goodnight outside her door, by which time the conversation had moved on from Rasselas and why I'd revived him to the desirability of the neighbourhood, which till then I'd felt little affection for, but now, thanks to Marie, seemed the perfect place to live. We talked of meeting up again soon. To phone her next day would have looked desperate, I decided, so I left it till the Sunday. 'What kept you?' she said, when I did.

I moved in with her three months later. Neither of us was young. She'd lived with a boyfriend, Tom, for five years in her early twenties; I'd had a series of relationships, three months here, eight months there, none of which had worked out. Both of us were ready for children. Both of us *wanted* children. And we conceived a child on our wedding night, at home, after the registry office and a party for friends – a good old-fashioned thing to do, except that the child was our second: we'd married as a present to ourselves for surviving two years of nappies and sleeplessness, though the real present was Noah, born forty weeks later after a two-hour labour (which was twenty-seven hours fewer than Jack had taken).

Would we have stayed together if we hadn't had children? Suppose one of us hadn't wanted them – what then? It's a debate we've sometimes had, with the childlessness of others – not least Rob and Jill – brought in. I say debate, but it's a sensitive issue for us both. I once upset Marie by telling her that I couldn't imagine a life without children (Jack was six months old at the time). 'Oh, right, but you can imagine one without me, if I'd not been fertile you'd have left me by now, thanks a lot,' she said. It wasn't what I meant, but she was feeling miserable, after a bout of mastitis. On another occasion she complained that she'd started having children too late: women's bodies were better adapted for having them in their early twenties, she said. In your early twenties you were with Tom, I said, not me. True, she said, but Tom wasn't parent material. But if you'd got pregnant? I said. I thought I was once, she said, and when my period came I felt disappointed. So if life had panned out differently, another man would have fathered your children and you'd have been happy with that, I said. Every child's a gift, she said. That's not an answer, I said. Who knows if I'd have been happy, she said, it's irrelevant, what matters is whether I'm happy with you. And? I said. You know I am, she said, except when you get jealous like this.

We've each had our touchy moments. But love overrides them. Solid, friends call us. I've never doubted our three children are mine and Marie knows that I've not looked at another woman since the day of the speed awareness course.

Why would I? More than parents, teachers, friends and all the books I've read, it's she who helped me grow up.

*

I got the call at the office a couple of weeks after the funeral. Only Marie phones my extension – everyone else emails – so it took me a moment to grasp who the caller was.

'What do you mean, both of us?' I said.

'It's common enough,' Louis said. 'After we talked at the wake, I realised that's what he'd probably done. I tried to find you to say so, but you'd rushed off. I spoke to his solicitor yesterday. The will was straightforward: he left everything to Jill. The codicil concerns his literary remains. Nice phrase, eh? He named us as joint executors. Officially I'm general executor and you're literary executor. But in effect we'll be acting together.'

'Right.'

'You sound dubious.'

'Just surprised. I assumed he'd dropped me.'

'I'm glad he didn't. My role's to sell his work. I've not the expertise to sort through the manuscripts.'

'I'm no scholar, either.'

'But he trusted you. He knew you'd do it well.'

'There might not be much *to* do. He told me he'd written nothing since his last collection.'

'Let's hope he had a late burst. Sorry, unfortunate metaphor ... The solicitor says he'll put a copy of the relevant document in the post. Then we'll see exactly what Rob said.'

'Before you go,' I said. 'Do you think he somehow *knew*?'

'What?'

'That he was dying. It makes no sense medically. I've researched it – there are no symptoms for ruptured abdominal aortas. All the same. Normal life expectancy for a man is around eighty these days. So why the sudden urge to appoint us?'

'It's no great mystery,' he said, worldly-wise. 'I've had it with other writers: once they hit sixty, they can smell their mortality. And Rob was obsessive about his reputation. As was his namesake. "Pope may be said to write always with his reputation in his head." Dr Johnson said that – somebody quoted it in one of Rob's obituaries.'

'Even so. Maybe some gut instinct was telling him. Sorry, another bad metaphor.'

'Did he keep a journal?'

'I don't know. We'll have to see.'

'*You'll* have to see, Matt. Give me a call when you start.'

'Jill might find it difficult – me going through his papers. I'll probably wait a while.'

'Don't leave it too long. Writers' reputations rise after their death. But only briefly. Then they dip. We don't want to miss the boat. Rob would never forgive us.'

'Interesting-sounding call,' Leonie said when I hung up. No phone calls are private in our office. Usually it's me overhearing hers.

'It was Louis de Vries. Robert Pope has made us joint literary executors. My role's to sort through the manuscripts.'

'What about your novel? Won't the executor stuff get in the way?'

'You sound like my wife.'

'Hah. If you turn up something interesting, tell me. Then we'll splash it.'

*

The addendum to Rob's will arrived in the post two days later, along with a short covering letter from the solicitor inviting me to contact her if there was anything I didn't understand. It was dated 26 March, three months to the day – so I found when I checked my old office diary – from the lunch we'd had.

I hereby appoint my literary agent Louis de Vries and my friend Matthew Holmes as general and literary executor respectively of my estate. They are entrusted with the tasks of

a) *collecting and cataloguing all materials consisting of or related to my published work, with a view to depositing them, at a price to be negotiated, in a suitable archive, preferably in a university environment where students – postgraduates only – can consult them*

b) *assisting in the dissemination – initially in journals and then, if a sufficient number exist, in a collection – of any poems completed but not published during my lifetime*

c) *ensuring the destruction of any remaining work not encompassed in a) and b) above, namely journals, notebooks, letters and unfinished drafts,*

these three tasks being pursuant of a single purpose, namely to sustain and enhance my posthumous reputation.

In recognition of these duties, the trustees are to receive 15 per cent of any monetary proceeds from the estate, to be divided equally between them.

Any remaining monies, as heretofore specified in my will, are to go to my wife Jill.

It looked simple enough, if not the kind of prose (*pursuant, heretofore*) Rob would have come up with himself. But to be asked to destroy *any remaining work* got me wondering about the form such destruction would take (shredding, burning, destruction of a hard drive?) and whether the parameters would be obvious: he specified 'journals, notebooks, letters and unfinished drafts', but if b) happened, and a new collection of poems was published, then the requirements of c) would arguably be superseded by those of a), in which case we'd have a duty to preserve those materials (supposing they threw light on his work), rather than destroy them. If it was true that Rob had stopped writing, then we'd be spared such dilemmas. Which would be sad for any admirers, but would make my role straightforward.

'It doesn't sound straightforward to me,' Marie said, when I read her the document.

'Give Rob his due. He's left most of his royalties to Jill.'

'And left you with muddled instructions. I warned you: where there's a will, there's woe.'

'You're always so hard on him.'

'He was a difficult man.'

'But now he's dead.'

'Now he's dead, he'll be even more difficult. Wait and see.'

6

'He called it his study,' Jill said, opening the door. 'He hated the word office. An office means colleagues. He didn't have any. Only books.'

They lined all four walls, narrowing the doorway, crowding the window, forming an arch over the cupboard on the left. The deeper shelves were double-stacked, the paperbacks in front of the hardbacks, like children in family photos posed with the adults behind.

'The people before had it as a children's bedroom. The wallpaper was light yellow, with pink dolls and blue teddy bears. Robbie spent our first weekend here stripping it with a metal scraper. I can't work in an effing kindergarten, he said.' She laughed. 'I took the next week off to get the house in order. With instructions not to disturb him, now he was back at work. He'd emerge every so often to make tea. And cook for us both every evening. But he locked himself away from nine till five. Routine, routine, I need my routine, he'd say. When we moved here he was terrified he wouldn't write another word.'

A wide rosewood desk stood in front of the window, its surface clear except for a pile of books to the left and an old Olivetti typewriter in the middle. Two large blinds covered the window.

'It's strange to see a desk without a computer,' I said.

'You know Robbie. He hated them – he'd type up poems when they were finished, but he wrote almost everything by hand.'

Writers who used word processors were sloppy, he once told me (this was after I bought an Amstrad in the 1990s): they dashed down their first thoughts, knowing they could revise them later, but then skimped on revision – whereas with a typewriter you made sure what you were writing was a final draft, or as near as could be, to avoid the effort of retyping. I couldn't understand the logic: what was so onerous about retyping a poem that took up less than a page? Without my Amstrad, then a succession of Macs, I wouldn't have completed my novel. Still, pen and typewriter had worked for him.

'Everything he wrote will be here, then?'

'Should be. He was very organised. I'll pull these blinds up so you have more light,' she said, tugging the cord. 'There's a good view of the garden,' she added, encouraging me to peer out. But it was the suddenly spotlit desk I stared at, or rather the chair in front of the desk, a black, fake-leather orthopaedic chair, bare of cushions – the chair he'd sat at when writing his last two collections, which I'd been rereading, along with his earlier ones, in preparation for my role. I imagined him in the chair, his back to the room, his head tilted downwards to where his hand held a pen or was pressing keys or lay loosely on the desk. The vision passed. He'd been here and now he was nowhere. But his smell still lingered in the room – an apple-and-woodsmoke musk I'd first noticed on one of our walks around the Brandon campus lake and which I associated, for no good reason, with beavers. Was it a certain brand of deodorant? I'd never asked him and wasn't about to ask Jill.

I moved next to her and looked out the window.

'The garden's south-facing,' she said. 'By midday the sun shines straight in, so he always kept the blinds down. I suggested he move the desk to the side, then the blinds could stay up and he'd have a view, but he refused. If I look out, I'll never get any work done, he said.'

Flowerbeds ran down either side of the long lawn. There was a small terrace outside the kitchen diner, with a metal table and two chairs, and a small fishpond below. An empty bird feeder stood next to it. Fruit trees, rose bushes and privet hedging added some shade and privacy. Brick walls separated the gardens either side. At the far end, in front of a wooden fence, was a vegetable patch.

'Too suburban a view for him, eh?'

'Sorry?' she said, though I could tell from her tone that she'd heard.

'He might have thought it too, you know, cosy and bourgeois, for a poet ... I could be wrong.'

'Robbie didn't think like that at all,' she said, turning away from the window. 'Any papers will be in his desk. Or in the filing cabinet. Or in the cupboard behind you. I'll let you get on. I'll fetch a coffee up later.'

The offer of coffee felt more like punishment than hospitality. I'd have to tread more carefully in future.

*

I'd waited over six months to contact Jill – from August to March. Spring will be a good time, I thought: longer days, the easing of grief, a fresh start. I wrote her a letter. Then when a fortnight went by without her replying, I phoned. She'd been in Australia, she explained, in part for a holiday, in part to see Rob's sister (who was doing better since being moved from a psychiatric unit to sheltered housing). Though she apologised for the delay, she put me off coming to see her for a fortnight, then cancelled and put me off for another week. Saturdays and Sundays were no good, she said: she was busy at her office all week and needed the weekends to recover – besides, I had my family. It occurred to me that she was reading Rob's stuff, to pre-empt me. Or tidying his papers, to make my task easier. Or making a bonfire of them, as widows have been known to do. I arranged with Leonie to take a Friday off. It was mid-April before I finally visited the house.

'Be gentle with her,' Marie said, as I left home. 'I wouldn't want someone coming here and looking through your stuff.'

Jill had asked me to arrive at eleven. I allowed extra time for the journey (Tube to Charing Cross, hour-long train ride, fifteen-minute walk) and, having arrived too early, walked past the house, number 93, and continued to the end of the street. Rob and I had always met in town – in Soho pubs, Covent Garden restaurants or at launch parties in publishers' board-rooms, never here. 'I'm going into exile again,' he'd announced over lunch one day back in the early 2000s. 'Where?' 'You'll not have heard of it. A place in Kent called Hadingfield.' He was disparaging – of the town, the house they'd found, himself for 'copping out'. It was madness, he said, they might as well have stuck a pin in the map at random for all the sense it made. Jill would have to spend an extra hour a day commuting. He'd have no friends nearby. The town had no university, no culture, nothing to recommend it. Living there would be the death of his art, for sure. Livelier than I'd seen him in a while, he enjoyed listing the negatives. Only when pressed did he admit that he and Jill would have more space, a garden, some peace and quiet. That there'd been increasing problems where they lived in Parsons Green ('drum-and-bass all night from the flat below, herds of stampeding children in the one above'). That from Kent it wouldn't be as far to visit his mother in her nursing home in Sussex. That a change might be good for his poetry ... Then the sad-clown mask went back on and he moaned about being 'driven out', 'neutered', 'sent back to the suburbs where I began, God help me' – Semi-Land, he called it, 'because everyone's half dead'. It wasn't the first time he'd upped sticks. Even so, I couldn't help wondering if there was more to it. However jokey, 'exile' was a strong word.

Duly warned, I shouldn't have found the neighbourhood surprising, but its blandness shocked me all the same: the net curtains, toytown roof tiles, neat front gardens, glossy front doors. VOTE CONSERVATIVE posters decorated a couple of bow windows, whether as gloating reminders of the last general election result or as early campaigning for next month's local council elections. Towards the end of the street a woman emerged from her house, an automatic smile on her face as she went through her exit sequence: the five beeps on the alarm keypad in her hallway; the slam of the front door; the click of her heels down the garden path; the clack of the gate latch; the *uck-thuck* of the car doors unlocking as she thumbed her ignition key from ten feet away; the leather squeak as she climbed in; the metal door thudding as she closed it; the engine whinnying into life; the tyre scrunch as she reversed two feet, then the slither as she pulled away. These were the sounds Rob had lived among – not silent fields punctuated by tractor-grind or bass-thuds from an inner-city flat, but a suburban in-between.

The door to number 93 was black, with stained glass. Jill was quick to answer when I rang the bell. She looked better than she had at the funeral – less grey, less lined, with a smile that was faint (a faintness mirrored or enhanced by her pale orange lipstick), but which didn't seem forced. She was wearing a black skirt and maroon blouse, as though dressed for work, which made me, in my jeans and jumper, feel too casual. Of course, this *was* work, but I'd assumed we could approach it informally, since we were meeting not as business associates but as two people who'd loved Rob. My emotions were running high, with the fact of Rob's death newly borne in on me because of where I was, in the doorway of his house (a house I'd never visited, but often imagined), with his wife, now widow, standing three feet away. Of course, I'd thought about him many times over the past months, but intermittently, between doing my job, looking after the kids, eating supper with Marie, going to see my mother – whereas for Jill he was an ever-present absence. Perhaps that's why when I stepped forward with the intention of kissing or even hugging her she took a step backwards, not flinching so much as straightening up, and why she held the palm of her right hand open and her arm outstretched as though to wave me through, like a butler or maidservant directing the new arrival to join the other guests in the drawing room. She wasn't being cold or discourteous; nor did I take it as a reproach. But whether instinctively or by design, she was refusing the equivalence that a kiss or hug would have signified. We both loved him, yes, but it was she with whom he'd shared his life.

That's how I read Jill's go-on-through gesture as I stepped past her – not as an attempt to put me in my place as a grubbing acolyte, but as a reminder of our different status. I was there on sufferance. I'd been his friend. But I wasn't hers.

Be gentle with her, Marie had said.

Stained-glass diamonds lit the floor in front of me. 'Go on through,' Jill said, in words this time, as I hesitated at the end of the narrow hall.

'Through' meant an arched doorway, beyond which lay the kitchen diner, a large airy room which once must have been two, with the fridge, stove, washing machine and dishwasher to the right, and a table and chairs to the left. The work surfaces gleamed. The tiled floor, too – 'You could eat your dinner off it,' my mum would have said.

'Coffee?'

'That'd be great.'

She'd made it already, trusting I'd be punctual. I felt reassured by that. She knew I was serious about the task ahead.

She put a tray on the table, with the cafetière and two cups – antique bone china cups, with fluted edges and floral patterns, not the chunky Ikea mugs Marie and I use.

'Milk? Sugar?'

'Just black, please.'

She asked after Marie and the children, remembering their names.

I asked about the Australia trip ('exhausting') and Rob's sister Angela ('sad case') and work ('busier than ever').

'Which I suppose is good,' she added, opening up a little. 'Stops me from maundering. I'd talked to Robbie about retiring early – maybe this year, maybe next. Now I plan to carry on as long as they'll have me. The weekends are worst. Not that friends haven't been kind. I'm doing OK.'

'Good,' I said, guilty that Marie and I still hadn't got round to taking her out somewhere. Perhaps if we'd tried, instead of agreeing to wait till after today, she might have been less stand-offish. Was she being stand-offish? Or was it me being paranoid? I didn't know her well enough to know.

I noticed an empty dog basket next to the fridge. She caught me looking at it.

'Rilke's,' she said. 'Our Labrador. I had to have him put down last month. He was fifteen and couldn't walk any more. I'm glad Robbie wasn't around to see it.'

'He never mentioned having a dog.'

'Really? We bought him the minute we moved here. But for Rilke he'd not have left the house. Long walks, morning and evening: that was his daily routine. More coffee?'

'No thanks.'

'Well, then,' she said, putting the cups and saucers back on the tray, and pushing it to one side with a determined, down-to-business look, like a general laying out a battle plan. The table between us was clear. She stared across, hands clasped, elbows on the table, right forefinger resting under her chin. Her face was round – when I first saw it, I'd thought of a white dinner plate – and her eyes a steely blue.

'I thought we should lay out some ground rules,' she said. 'How long do you think you'll need?'

'Until I see what's there, I can't say. A few visits, certainly.'

'Fridays are best for me – I try to take them off every couple of weeks. This afternoon I'm going out at two, but you're welcome to have till then to take a preliminary look. If you find anything worth keeping, leave it for me and I'll make a copy. But any originals should stay here.'

'That's fine,' I said. 'It's chaotic in my house. I wouldn't want to remove anything.'

'I haven't looked in his desk. Can't bear to. Can hardly bear to go in the room, to be honest. And I wouldn't know what I was looking for if I did. I liked his poems. But that's probably because I loved him. Poetry isn't really my thing.'

*

The desk had seven drawers: three to the right, three to the left and a wide shallow one across the middle. The top right-hand drawer was locked; I'd have to ask Jill about a key. I couldn't open the filing cabinet, either, an ugly, grey, badly scratched upright chest with two bulky drawers; it too would need a key. But that could wait. I'd six drawers and a cupboard to explore – plenty to be getting on with.

I sat in the chair, determined not to feel spooked or sentimental: yes, this was Rob's desk and this his typewriter and these the books he'd been reading in his last days (editions of Catullus, Ovid, Petrarch, Dante and Hardy), but in themselves, as objects, they were nothing out of the ordinary, and I had a job to get on with, one that would be best achieved by avoiding thoughts of him sitting there, mid-composition. Though he'd told me his last collection had cleaned him out, I'd hopes of finding unpublished poems. There might be diaries and journals, too. According to his will, I'd have to destroy them. But what if they were masterpieces, like Pepys's or John Cheever's? Kafka had asked Max Brod to destroy all his work. But Brod knew better than to do so. And literature was the richer for his betrayal.

I pulled open the top left-hand drawer. It was where Rob kept his pens, pencils, paperclips, rubbers, ink cartridges. The next drawer down was full of paper: typing paper (A4), letters with his address at the top (A5), notepads, index cards, Post-its, scrap paper, all of it blank. The bottom left-hand drawer looked more promising: inside were notebooks of different sizes and textures, some with thin metal ring binding, some with calfskin covers, one with the name of a literary festival on it. I thumbed through, in search of drafts, diary entries, whatever jottings I could find, but there were none – whether lined or unlined every notebook was empty.

The wide shallow drawer contained bank statements and cheque books. The last statement was dated 2012 and, according to the stub, the last cheque he'd written, the following year, was £129.94 to Majestic Wine. After that he must have relied on credit cards and internet banking, like everyone else, though some of the entries in his paying-in book were more recent: in the six months before he'd died, he'd deposited cheques from the BBC and the Cambridge Literature Festival, neither large enough to have sustained him for more than a week, but testament to his reputation: he'd never earned much, even at the height of his fame, and he made fewer appearances in his last decade, but he and his work were still in demand.

I bent down to open the bottom right-hand drawer. In a large, battered Jiffy bag I found various photos of Rob – publicity shots – from different phases of his career. There were also two scrapbooks: one from childhood, the other dating from the publication of his first collection. I set them aside, to look at later, and pulled out the bulky yellow folder underneath, marked LETTERS: RECEIVED. There were dozens of them, shoved in at random, it seemed, rather than sorted and dated, a few – so my sampling suggested – from fellow poets, the rest from readers, all congratulating him in one way or another: for this image or that line, this use of rhythm or that insight into nature. At the top of each, Rob had put a tick and scribbled 'Replied'.

The six folders in the middle right-hand drawer had the titles of Rob's collections written across them. At last, some original manuscripts, I thought, but the folders contained only cuttings: reviews of Rob, interviews with Rob, essays about Rob, Books of the Year recommendations of Rob's latest volume. I smiled at the thought of Marie flicking through them and snarling 'egomaniac' as she did. But the bad reviews were there along with the good, Marcus Downe's included.

The only other storage space in the room was the cupboard in the corner, which jutted out from the bookshelves that occupied the rest of the wall space. It had once been a built-in wardrobe (a metal clothes rail still ran across the top), but was now a mini-warehouse for plastic crates. There were six of them, clearly labelled, one for each of Rob's collections. I lifted down the top one and removed the lid. Here were all the materials from his first book, *Homeboy* – notebooks, scraps of loose paper, handwritten first drafts, revised drafts, typed-out final drafts, torn-out pages from the magazine in which each poem first appeared, uncorrected page proofs, corrected page proofs, jacket cover proofs, plus all the matter filling the gap between composition and publication – adds and deletes, marginalia, instructions to printers. They weren't what I was looking for, but I re-experienced some of the fascination I'd felt during my MFA, when I'd spent days in the manuscripts collection at Brandon, hoping to learn from the processes of a William Faulkner or Nathanael West. The book I eventually did publish, ten years later, was written straight on to a computer. Like most writers of my generation, I'm post-archival. But I respected Rob and the way he'd worked. Already I'd found something that would interest scholars. The only pity was the lack of a seventh crate full of unpublished work.

I went back to the scrapbooks, picked them up and took them over to the chaise longue spanning the biography shelves down one side of the room. Chaise longue? Couch? Or do I mean daybed? It was like the one in the Pre-Raphaelite painting of the death of Chatterton. I sprawled there for the next hour, looking through the scrapbooks. The later one had cuttings and photographs that, for whatever reason, had interested Rob. I could see no obvious connection with his work, but an academic might make something of them. The childhood scrapbook was more fun. He'd begun it at the age of six and continued with it into his teens, and it showed his different preoccupations during that time: birds, cowboys, stamps, dogs, cars, astronauts, guns, atomic bombs, Auschwitz, football, pop music and films, especially films in which pretty women appeared, the last few pages of the scrapbook being a gallery of starlets, none of them naked, but all in poses that a thirteen-year-old would have found sexy and each with some defining feature – high cheekbones, flamingo legs, conical bosom – that he must have looked for in girls and either found or grew tired of by the age of fifteen, since that's when the scrapbook ended, with a last cutting from 1971, leaving several blank pages at the end.

'Having fun?' Jill said from the doorway in a tone that suggested I shouldn't be: to loll about with a teenage scrapbook full of glamour pics was a clear dereliction of duty. 'I wondered if you'd like a sandwich. It's nearly one o'clock.'

'Already?' I said, closing the scrapbook. 'I lost track.'

'Ham and cheese sound OK?'

'Please don't go to any trouble.'

'I've made them already. Come on down.'

It was less an invitation than an order: she was banishing me from the room as a punishment for suspected frivolity.

We sat at the kitchen table, two tall glasses of water in front of us. She'd sliced the sandwiches diagonally and set them on an oval plate, with cucumber and tomatoes round the side.

'I love granary bread,' I said.

'It's wholemeal. How are you getting on?'

'Early days, but yes, it's going well. All the drafts and workbooks for his collections are there. They ought to be worth a bit.'

'An American university once approached him. It'd be like selling your children, he said. He wouldn't consider it.'

'But you might?'

'Me?'

'Or Louis and I, as executors, on your behalf. His will instructs us to sell his manuscripts to a suitable archive. Any proceeds from his literary estate will go to you.'

'I have my job. I'm not short of money.'

'But if academics studying him could look at his papers and see how his work evolved –'

'It depends what's there.'

'We retain copyright. Nothing of his could be quoted without our permission.'

I explained how copyright works. And permission fees. And the prestige attached to an archive. Her lips moved as I spoke, silently repeating each word. I remembered how she had done that the first time we met, and how I'd taken it for slowness or even stupidity. Now it struck me that the mouthing was for my benefit not hers – as though without her help I'd be blind to the import of what I was saying. I felt self-conscious, under contract to be as earnest as she was.

'Another sandwich?' she said, holding out the plate.

'I'd better get back to work. You're going out soon, aren't you?'

'In half an hour . . . I understand what you're saying about an archive, but I'm not sure about letting his papers go.'

'Of course. I don't mean to push you.'

'He liked to keep everything beside him.'

'All I'm doing is establishing what's there – I'll draw up an inventory before we decide. Incidentally, I can't open the filing cabinet or the top drawer of his desk – do you have keys?'

'For the filing cabinet. Not for the desk. I know the drawer you mean. It's always been jammed.'

She stood up and went to the Welsh dresser, a gloomy old antique ('monstrosity' would have been Marie's word), the top and bottom of which didn't match, the lower half an oak cupboard with two doors, the upper a shelf unit in lighter wood, with china cups dangling from hooks, commemorative plates standing upright and a small drawer underneath, from which Jill pulled a looped cluster of keys.

'Try these. The filing cabinet came from the insurance office where his father worked. It's a horrible old thing, but when he heard they were chucking it out he asked to have it. I've always wanted to get rid of it. If there's nothing in it, maybe I will.'

The first challenge was to locate the right key: the lock had a wide slit, seemingly made for one of the dozen or so large keys on the loose metal ring, but it was a smaller one, the smallest of all, in fact, which fitted. I felt excited, sliding the heavy bottom drawer open, all the more so on seeing the metal dividers, each of them carefully labelled. But the labels were the insurance company's, not Rob's. And almost all the compartments were empty. The three that weren't contained 1) his own birth, degree and marriage certificates, along with his parents' death certificates, 2) publishing contracts, and 3) freelance earning slips, tax returns and letters from his accountant. Admin and finance, in other words. Of marginal interest to a biographer, perhaps, but not to me. Still, at least the bottom drawer had something in it. Unlike the top, which slid open to reveal grey metal and empty space.

As Jill had told me, though I couldn't resist trying, none of the keys fitted the desk. And if the top drawer had always been jammed, there was no point trying to force it. I went back to the first crate, intending to itemise the contents. But it was already almost two o'clock, when Jill would be going out, and it didn't seem worth starting. Leaving the room as I'd found it – desk drawers closed, cupboard door shut, cushions on the daybed uncrumpled – I made my way downstairs.

*

'You didn't upset her, I hope?' Marie said, in bed that night.

'No, but she was prickly.'

'I'd be the same.'

'As though his room's a shrine. She won't let me remove anything.'

'Good. There's enough clutter here as it is.'

'I had to bite my tongue when she said she's not ready to sell his papers. It's not up to her.'

'She feels vulnerable. You're probably the first person to go in that room since he died. And she doesn't even know you that well. We should take her out.'

'I vaguely mentioned it as I was leaving. She either didn't hear – or pretended not to.'

'It's no good being vague. We have to call her up and suggest a date.'

'An evening with the Ice Maiden – I can't think of anything worse.'

'Sunday lunch, then. Here. With the kids.'

'She hates kids.'

'Rob hated kids. Jill doesn't.'

'How do you know?'

'Trust me. When are you next going over?'

'Two weeks today. If she doesn't cancel.'

'Let's ask her before then. For Sunday week, say. We're not doing anything.'

'You ask her. She doesn't like me.'

'Don't be stupid. She needs to learn to trust you, that's all.'

*

Marie was right. She always is, except when's she wrong and I've never heard her own up to being wrong, not even after losing the five-pound bet she'd made with me that Jack would be walking by thirteen months, a figure she arrived at on the grounds that she had taken her first steps at eleven months, and I (according to my mother) had taken mine at twelve, which meant that even allowing for slower development in our first-born, genetically he was bound to, it stood to reason ('Hah, stood,' I said). At a year, Jack was still shuffling round on his bottom and showed not the slightest interest in pulling himself up by grabbing a chair leg or low table, let alone in moving his feet forward when one or other of us held him steady with his arms aloft, so I felt pretty confident about winning the fiver, inexperienced as I was compared with Marie in the area of child development, though admittedly it's talking not walking she specialises in. He finally walked at fourteen months, gigglingly traversing the three feet of laminate flooring between Marie, kneeling by the fridge, and me, in the middle of the room, both of us ready to catch him. I won the bet, I said, whooping with delight not at winning but because the moment when a child takes its first steps is such a relief (as I've experienced again with my other two), laying to rest at least one of the fears parents are afflicted by – that the helplessness they saw when their child was born will remain and he/she will never walk, talk, sleep through the night, run, catch a ball, swim, ride a bike, eat with a knife and fork, learn to read, learn to count, make friends, etc. – in short, grow up. I won the bet, I said again, you owe me a fiver, but Marie said I must have mis-remembered, that I'd predicted he wouldn't walk till sixteen months, which meant her prediction of thirteen was closer, and that in any case we'd not shaken hands on it, let alone made a bet for money, and, though, yes, we'd had conversations about when Jack might walk and *I* might have thought I'd made a bet, she disapproved of betting, so it was most unlikely *she* had.

Marie is always right, as I say. At any rate she was right about Jill, whom she phoned the next day and invited to lunch, an invitation Jill was pleased to accept and didn't back out of, though I'd warned Marie, as we were buying a shoulder of lamb at the butcher's, that the chances of her coming were 50/50 at best. She came, she smiled, she drank two glasses of prosecco before the meal, she ate a surprisingly large portion of lamb and an equally large helping of summer pudding, and when we suggested a walk in the park afterwards, the ideal opportunity to slip away if she wasn't enjoying herself, she not only agreed to come along, linking arms with Marie en route and walking ahead, while I pushed the buggy and chatted to the boys, but when we reached our favourite spot, the oblong of grass by the bandstand, at which point Mabel threw such a wobbly that the combined forces of Marie and me were required to calm her down, she, Jill, played football with the boys, revealing skills I'd never have expected (including headers, volleys, dummies and nutmegs) and of which her late husband, energetic though he'd been when I first met him, would not have been capable. Her cheeks glowed pink. Her laughter was infectious. She'd the turn of pace of a twenty-year-old. The boys loved her.

Back at the house, she stayed for tea, joined Marie in giving Mabel a bath, and read stories to Jack and Noah as they perched on the arms of her armchair. I began to think we'd never get rid of her. 'Thank you, I've had such a lovely time,' she said, when she finally left, round nine, undeterred by the prospect of reaching home in the dark after a trek across town and a limited Sunday train service from Charing Cross. She said it again in the floral thank-you notelet that arrived on Tuesday morning, signing off 'Love, Jill', with three xxxs underneath.

'I told you she loved kids,' Marie said.

'You told me she didn't hate them.'

'Same thing.'

'Did she talk about Rob with you?'

'A bit.'

'And?'

'She's lonely. They used to sit for hours without speaking, she says, but now the silence is different.'

'Did she say anything about my visit?'

'Just that she found it hard. You going through his stuff. You talking of selling it off. As long as it's there, he's there too; once it goes, he'll be gone. That's how she thinks.'

'I'm trying to keep him alive.'

'His work, not him. And for people who read his poetry, not for her. You've got to be sensitive.'

'I am. I was.'

'It'll be better now she's been to see us.'

'I certainly hope so.'

*

That hope was soon dashed. It was Groundhog Day the follow-ing Friday. I rang the bell. She answered. I stepped forward to kiss her on the cheek. She backed away and waved me down the hall: 'Go on through.' I'd come at ten, to give myself a full day, but as we stood in the kitchen – 'Coffee?' 'If that's not a nuisance', 'I've made some already' – she said she had a dental check-up at 2.30 and, with apologies for having forgotten about it, that she'd have to leave the house by 2.15. 'No worries,' I said, hiding my suspicion that the appointment was an inven-tion. Why denying me an extra couple of hours should make such a difference I couldn't understand, but I knew better than to ask about staying on without her, though that would have been the obvious solution – I could even offer to have a pot of tea ready for her return. Be patient, I told myself. Four hours was a good stretch. Make sure to use them. When she offers sandwiches at lunchtime, say you're not hungry.

'It was good to have you round last weekend,' I said, coffee in hand, hoping to trigger *that* Jill, not the solemn gatekeeper across the table.

'It was so nice to come.'

'We had a great time,' I said and she smiled at me warmly, as though reunited with the father and husband she'd spent her Sunday with: *that* Matt. 'The boys especially.'

'I enjoyed myself,' she said, before the wariness returned – enjoyment wasn't allowed, not now, not here.

'Right then. I'd better get on.'

'I'll be in the garden if you need anything.'

'I'll be fine,' I said, replacing my cup in its saucer and more or less bounding upstairs.

*

I'd all the stuff to look at in the plastic crates. For a university to consider buying Rob's papers, they'd want a description of what was there. It needn't be exhaustive, just enough to whet their appetite – at which point they'd send their own expert. Not an onerous task. Rob had left things in order. Still, I did need to sift through the crates.

I went as far as taking one down, removing the lid, skimming through and making notes. But it was laborious work and for long periods I just sat in his chair, listening to jays squabble in the garden or watching clouds drift by like fluffy duvets. It was a rotating chair, and for minutes on end I'd slowly circle in it, like an LP on a turntable, pushing down with my right foot to keep up the slow momentum and picking out the titles on the shelves as I revolved: Auden, Dante, Gunn, Larkin, Pope, Tennyson, Wordsworth. I felt guilty for not getting on. But the ambience discouraged it. After the patter of office keyboards and the tantrums of home, I found it calming.

The room was a refuge – Rob's place of exile and now mine. When Jill looked in at eleven – 'Going well? Coffee?' – I felt irritated, as though the room were mine now and anyone else barred from entry.

Had Jill sprayed it with air freshener? Rob's apple-and-woodsmoke musk had almost gone. Even with the blinds down, in the half-dark, it didn't feel ghostly. Occasionally sadness overwhelmed me, nonetheless, set off by the sight of Rob's handwriting (familiar from letters and cards he'd sent me) or objects he'd held (the pens, the spectacles, the glass ornament with an imprint of his hand) or descending from nowhere, abstract, untethered, but real for all that. I wondered if it wasn't Rob I was grieving for but my father – belatedly, by association, five and a half years on. I'd been in Frankfurt, at the Book Fair, when Marie phoned with the news, my mother (unaware I was away) having failed to reach me at the office. He'd been clearing leaves in the garden after lunch. My mother, napping, didn't notice that the leaf blower had stopped. And was slow, when she woke, to spot him lying on the lawn. It would have made no difference, the hospital said. The heart attack had killed him instantly, though the paramedics worked on him for twenty minutes where he fell ('You should have seen all the syringes they left behind,' my mother said) and there'd been further attempts in the ambulance and A&E. I got the message too late to fly back that night, but caught the first plane to Heathrow next morning. The body was in the mortuary by then. I didn't think of asking to see it. Perhaps I'd have felt better if I had. But my priority was consoling my mother. And within days of the funeral Marie went into labour with Jack and my energies were focused on that. Friends said it must be comforting: after the death of a parent, the birth of a child. I was too strung out and sleepless to tell. Now, sitting in Rob's room, my dad's death finally registered, like a message in a bottle reaching shore years later. Perhaps I'd avoided looking at his corpse out of fear of seeing failure there. He'd retired reluctantly, imagining the school would fall apart without him and half expecting to be summoned back. When it prospered in his absence and the colleagues he'd thought of as friends stopped calling, he went downhill, gloomily marooned in an armchair. Cryptic crosswords were his only hobby. He'd little or nothing to say when I visited. But I had loved my dad and resented Rob's memorabilia for hijacking my grief.

I didn't delude myself that sitting in his chair would bring me closer to Rob, let alone that he was haunting me. But it was impossible not to think about him or to forget how often he'd talked about death. Two conversations stuck out, the first of them from decades back, perhaps as early as our time in Brandon.

'I hate the thought of dying young,' he said, and he can only have been in his thirties then, 'because of all I'll never live to see.'

'Who says you'll die young?'

'*Everyone* today will die young, even if they live to be a hundred. A hundred and fifty will become the norm. Then two hundred. OK, we know about Swift's Struldbrugs. There's no point extending life if all it means is a protracted old age. But by the end of the next century the scientists will have cracked that. People will still be teenagers in their sixties, with acres of time for all the experiences we can't cram in. We keep being told what a lucky generation we are, but we're not.'

The second conversation came during one of our Soho lunches, about a famous writer who'd just died.

'In two years his work will be forgotten,' Rob said. 'His life hasn't been interesting enough.'

'You once told me that being alive on the page is all that matters.'

'So I did. So it is. But to most readers, a boring life means a boring oeuvre. You should learn from my mistakes, Matt. Live out loud, Zola said. My poems might have been better if my life had been more adventurous.'

'Stop talking as if it's over.'

'It might as well be. No one under forty has heard of me. I'm not big news.'

'How many writers are?'

'I should have been cleverer at managing my career.'

'You've won prizes.'

'The odd one.'

'And you're highly respected.'

'Killer word, isn't it? I've had the establishment pat on the back. But readers? True readers? From outside the coterie? I've never had those.'

'You've never tried.'

'More fool me. My only hope is that people will come round to me after I'm dead.'

I can't date the first conversation, but I know the second took place in November 2013, because I have the email Rob sent shortly afterwards, which refers to it. Luckily, I keep all my emails, or our office provider does. And on the train back to London, having left Jill's at 2.30 with about half the contents of the first crate annotated, I did a word search on my iPhone and tracked it down.

'Here's the Kipling review,' he wrote, 'a little on the long side but I hope you can accommodate it. You'll see I talk about posthumous reputations. I was being flip the other day. Of course it's outrageous that writers should live on in the public mind only because they've had exciting lives. Wordsworth had it right: "if their [poets'] work be good, they contain within themselves all that is necessary to their being comprehended and relished". I enjoy biographies. But I don't approve of them – nor of letters and journals being made public. It would be like our email exchanges being hacked into. That's all biography is – a form of hacking.

'Enough pomp from Pope. As you'll have guessed, I've begun to fret about the reception of my next collection (now due in March, by the way), which is no less private, occluded and (yes) "formalist" than its predecessors. What's he hiding, the reviewers will say, why doesn't he tell us straight? Well, fuck 'em.'

There he was, at fifty-eight, already issuing implicit instructions to the literary executor he had yet to appoint. His Kipling review had more in the same vein – a dismissal of life writing. Leonie called it 'rambly'. It turned out to be his last for us.

*

'You have to admire Rob,' I said to Marie that night, while watching television. After the spaciousness of his study, the living room felt small and cluttered. The sofa, too, which we'd got cheap.

'Why?'

'For putting his faith in posterity.'

'Posterity. Hah!'

There wasn't anything good on. The choice had been between a celebrity chef and a documentary about complete strangers getting married. We'd tossed for it and I won. Marie doesn't like losing. I'd have done better not to mention Rob.

'You're like one of those rich Americans who have their bodies preserved,' she said. 'What's the point? Cryonic suspension, poetic immortality: they're a fantasy. People die. And the stuff they do in life dies too.'

'Great literature has an afterlife.'

'It's that Christian upbringing of yours. Be a good person and you'll go to heaven. Be a good writer and the future will redeem you. Except that you'll be oblivious to your redemption. You'll be dead. You won't know.'

I folded my hands together, in a gesture of prayer, as though suing for peace. The young woman in the documentary was buying a wedding dress. She chose one that emphasised her cleavage. Whoever he is, her mother said, he's going to like that.

'Don't you want to be remembered after you die?' I said, putting my arm round Marie.

'By my children. And a few friends.'

'Rob didn't have kids. His poems will be his only legacy.'

'I understand that,' she said. 'It's you I don't get. You've all your life ahead. If you're going to write a book, why not write one that appeals to people now? Surely the great writers – Shakespeare and Dickens and so on – *were* popular in their own lifetime?'

'There's also Kafka or Gerard Manley Hopkins, who –'

'But they're the exceptions, right? On the whole, most writers who survive were successes in their lifetime. And most writers who were failures in their lifetime *don't* survive.'

The husband-to-be in the documentary was standing at the aisle. Oh my God, he kept saying, terrified by what he was about to do. When his bride arrived, in a white dress with a deep cleavage, he said it again, in a different tone.

'Rob wasn't a failure,' I said.

'No, but at this rate he'll make you one. Looking after him is stopping you getting on with your own writing.'

'He's not stopping me,' I said. 'Life is. The job, the kids, marriage.'

'Thanks a bunch. How do *I* stop you?'

'It's not anything you do. It'd be the same whoever I was married to.'

The bride and groom were saying their vows, tearful relatives behind them.

'You'd rather live on your own?' Marie said.

'I'd have more time.'

'More time and no life.'

'I wouldn't be torn in different directions. I'd be single-minded. Like Rob. Rob didn't compromise his vision.'

'Rob was an arsehole. His idea of vision was looking at himself in the mirror.'

The couple in the documentary were getting acquainted over champagne in their honeymoon bedroom.

'OK,' I said, giving in. 'Shall we switch channels?'

*

Jill was friendlier when I turned up for my third visit. There was still no welcome kiss but she allowed me to stay the full day. In fact, it was me who thought of leaving early. After the indolence of the previous week, I worked hard. By three, all the items in the first crate had been itemised: six notebooks, with handwritten drafts for the thirty-four poems in Rob's first collection, *Homeboy*; dozens of typed sheets, with further drafts and revisions; a statement supplied to the Poetry Book Society, which had chosen *Homeboy* as one of its recommendations for the autumn; letters from his then editor, Charles, with various queries, and copies of Rob's replies; exchanges with his New York editor about the American edition of the book and, some years later, with his German, Swedish and Italian translators; four draft cover designs, three draft blurbs, two sets of proofs; and photocopies of the eleven poems that Rob omitted from

Homeboy, but had published in magazines before it came out (they weren't especially good poems, but they would help fill out a Collected). It was dull curatorial grind. I'd hoped to find a journal, but could see no sign.

I did make one discovery. While dipping into one of the later crates – to relieve my boredom – I came across a poem, 'Pigtail', that had briefly landed Rob in trouble.

> The crime scene was a rented Bangkok bedroom.
> Or had I no choice, left to roam like a wolf
> After midnight, unused to such freedom,
> Dope-hazed and half-pissed? I'd guess she was twelve.
> I'll be gentle, I said, untying the bow
> Of her pigtail before my hands slithered
> Down to the nub and perforation below.
> Has she forgotten? Blanked it out? Or did
> My actions scarcely matter when each night
> Other punters did the same? Let me take the rap.
> I like to think I'm almost human, but I'm not.
> She was innocent and I fucked her up.

The poem had appeared in a special 'Sexuality and Gender' issue of a small magazine: Rob said he sent it as a favour to the editor, a former student of his. He quickly regretted the poem, as 'melodramatic and metrically inept', but the editor failed to send proofs and next thing the magazine had gone to press. The story would have ended there, but for a Luton schoolteacher using the poem as a starting point for a sixth-form debate on sex tourism. The church-going mother of one of the pupils spotted the photocopy and complained to the head teacher: was such material suitable for teenagers? Dissatisfied by the head's lukewarm response, she went to the local paper, which ran a story ('On page 3, appropriately enough,' Rob said). The story was then picked up by the national press, first as a news item, then on the op-ed pages: at what age, columnists asked, should children be expected to discuss issues such as paedophilia? How convincing was the apology offered by the sex offender in the poem? Had he – had the poet – honestly faced up to the horrific nature of the 'actions' described, i.e. child rape? Rob declined several invitations to respond, including one from me (I was working for an online magazine at the time): 'Just read the poem,' he said. He was sanguine when we talked about it later – all water off a duck's back, he said. But a couple of the writers quoted defending the use of the text in school were dismiss- ive of it as poetry, and Rob didn't include it in his subsequent collection, despite the fact (something he told me at the time, which I promptly forgot about) that he'd revised it.

The revision was there in the crate, paperclipped to the first version, along with several more drafts (including variants on the perforation image such as 'narrow as the slit in a ballot box'), before the poem ended up not as a fictional confession about a rape in Bangkok but as an autobiographical vignette – the memory of a sexually exploratory episode from Rob's teens, during a holiday in the Med. If anything the second version was more melodramatic than the original: though both he and the girl had been 'kids', Rob accused himself of committing a 'crime', if only because she was the more 'innocent'. I didn't go for either poem, but was struck by how he retained the structure (three quatrains rhyming abab), and many of the same images, while making the narrative more authentic. A scholar might make something of that.

Not all my time was wasted, then. And I worked hard, as I say. But if I'm honest – more honest than I could be with Jill or even Marie – not all that work was on Rob's archive. After failing to get on with it for months, years even, I found myself jotting down ideas and phrases for my novel. Perhaps it was the silence that inspired me. Or the fact of sitting in Rob's chair. Or the invitingly empty notebook I'd brought, very few pages of which were needed to make my inventory. At any rate, some of the ideas I'd been struggling with took shape, or rather the voice I needed became audible. It wasn't Rob's voice. But his presence, or lived absence, was inspiring. He'd found the perfect place to write, and by making me his executor had made it possible for me to write there too. The house was a sanctum and the street a haven, empty of its residents – middle-class professionals – from morning till evening. The lack of kindred spirits didn't matter to Rob. He'd talked himself out in Brandon. The hands-on stuff was all that counted and you did that alone. By the time I packed up that day, I'd four pages of notes towards my novel.

Jill wasn't in the house when I came down to say goodbye. I went out the back door, past the terrace, bird feeder and fish pond, and found her by the raised beds down the end of the garden. Trowel in hand, she was kneeling in the earth next to a set of tall bamboo canes tied together like a wigwam. She looked flustered to see me, as though I'd caught her in the nude.

'Impressive,' I said, pointing at the red flowers on the canes.

'Runner beans. I've mangetout, spinach and courgettes growing, too.'

'Do you do it all yourself?'

'Since Robbie, yes.'

'Did he help out, then?'

She laughed. '*I* helped *him*.'

'You mean he liked gardening?'

'Did he never tell you? When he wasn't writing, this is where he came. The veg patch. I told him he should call his next book that.' She laughed again. 'He had bonfires here, too,' she said, nodding at a metal brazier.

'What did he burn?'

'Twigs. Leaves. Newspapers. Some of his writing, too. I don't know what exactly – stuff he didn't want to keep. Ash was good for the soil, he said. He'd no interest in growing flowers, though. He left them to me.'

'Well, you do a great job,' I said.

'How's it going?' she said, ignoring the compliment, or unwilling to forgive me for the last time we'd talked about the garden. 'How much longer will you need?'

'I'm done for today.'

'In all. To sort everything out.'

'I'm only on the first crate,' I said. 'There are five more. Going through them is taking longer than I thought.'

'So you'll need to come again?'

'If I'm going to make a proper job of it.'

'You must, obviously, but . . .'

'Unless you'd prefer me to take everything away.'

'No.'

'Or gave me a key, so I'd not be intruding on your days off.'

'Let's go on as we are. I'll keep Fridays free in future.'

'Not just alternate ones?'

'Every Friday for the next couple of months. Then you'll have finished.'

'With any luck.'

7

At the end of my MFA I returned to England and moved back in with my parents. Despite the praise I got for the novel I'd been working on, I knew it was no good and scrapped it (unlike Rob, who'd have kept them for future scholars, I also threw away all my workbooks). Wasted words, you could say, but I'd learned something, if only to distrust well-meaning encouragement. To begin with, my parents were pleased to have me back. But as the weeks became months they began to grumble: why did I never get up before midday? When was I going to get a job? etc. To placate them, I made myself useful, walking the dog, going to the shops, cooking dinner, whatever was required. After Brandon, the rural isolation felt oppressive: the empty fields, big skies and bitter winds. Occasionally, I'd meet old schoolmates down the pub or go to the cinema in Norwich; I even briefly hooked up with a former girlfriend. But the priority – so I told everyone, including myself – was the novel. A 1,000-word-a-day routine would see it done pretty quickly, I thought. Routine's not my strong point, however. There were always distractions, some (such as job applications) unavoidable, others (such as computer games) self-imposed. The novel went nowhere much, but eventually, nine months on, a friend from uni found me some subbing shifts on a listings magazine. When I left home to share a house in Hackney with him and six other guys in their twenties, a meagre 20,000 words went with me.

Rob stayed in touch after my departure: occasional post-cards would find their way to East Anglia and I'd send gossipy, grumbling replies. He still talked about moving back to the UK and of placing his poems with a London publisher. But I didn't expect it to happen. As an iconoclast with an English accent at a lowly American university, he had some kudos. In the wider world he'd be nothing. So when he wrote to say he'd found a place to live in London, I was surprised, to say the least. It was several months before he summoned me (it really did feel like a summons) to a pub in Tufnell Park. I ought to have recognised him; it had been only two years. But I was halfway through a pint of Guinness at the bar before the man in the suit at the corner table looked up from his paper.

'Where's the beard gone?' I asked after we'd hugged.

'It was getting too grey.'

'And what's with the suit?'

'London's not Brandon,' he said. 'I don't want to look like a lumberjack. This feels more comfortable.'

By 'this' he meant not just the suit and shaved chin, but the white shirt and Oxford brogues.

He'd got some teaching at Birkbeck.

'Just an evening a week,' he said. 'More than enough.'

'If you can live off that . . .'

'I've saved a bit. And my mother's helping. I feel bad, but she can afford it. She's living on her own in a five-bedroom house, for God's sake. It's time she downsized.'

From the pub we went on to a meal in a Turkish restaurant, then back to his flat. It was a large basement conversion with two bedrooms and a rear patio. He used the second bedroom as his study and, to avoid the risk of visitors ('especially my mother'), had removed the bed. The floor-to-ceiling bookshelves were crammed with volumes shipped back from Brandon ('It cost a small fortune'); a cork board hung in the only remaining wall space, with six postcards from the National Portrait Gallery pinned to it – Shakespeare, Milton, Pope, Coleridge, Eliot and Auden ('the only English poets who come up to scratch'). His desk was tidy, the living room sparely furnished (leather sofa, Navajo rug), the pine table in the kitchen well scrubbed. It seemed very grown up: the domain of someone dedicated to his own idea of himself. My ambitions seemed paltry in comparison – since beginning regular subbing shifts I'd done little or no work on the novel. Even if I'd wanted to, the house where I was living (overpopulated, noisy and chaotic) would have made it impossible.

'So,' I said, several whiskies in, 'you couldn't stand Brandon without me.'

'I wanted to get back to Europe.'

'*Europe?* Spoken like an American.'

'London's OK for now. One day I'll move to Italy or France.'

It was something he'd say repeatedly over the next few years. And he did travel abroad now and then – British Council trips, a week-long workshop at the Shakespeare & Co bookstore in Paris, a two-month residency in Rome. Europe remained an important idea for him. Its writers and artists seeped into his work. But he didn't stray far or for long. And when he finally moved it wasn't to France or Italy but to Hadingfield, half an hour from where he grew up.

He'd written enough poems for a collection, he said, and now he was back would start trying publishers ('It's a good moment – British poetry's in need of a new voice'). It sounded like hubris to me; no one here had heard of him. But I hid my doubts while he laid out his plans.

126

'Are you seeing anyone?' he said, eventually.

'I was. Not now.'

'Don't you miss it?'

'The sex?'

'The falling in love.'

'Yes,' I said, 'but then the excitement fades and you discover you're not right for each other.'

'The killer is when you're still in love but she isn't. I had that once. As you know.'

'Did you ever hear any more?'

'About Corinne? Nah. I thought of trying to contact her before I left the States. But how would I? And there'd have been no point.'

'You're over her, then?'

'Did I say that?'

'What a pair of sad gits we are.'

'It all feeds the writing,' he said.

*

His poems began to appear in journals. And within months, to my amazement (and envy), he got some reviewing work, too. Editors liked his fearlessness: he was the new kid on the block, cudgel in hand, ready to take on the old guys. 'It helps that I don't know anyone,' he said. 'Once you're friends with other writers you're sunk' (I was unpublished and didn't count). But writers can't make a living without contacts. And though he continued claiming not to know anyone, people got to know him – editors, publishers, radio producers. 'I'm enjoying my fifteen minutes,' he said, stressing his lack of credentials – failed PhD student, second-rate academic, wannabe poet. 'They'll soon tire of me.'

One evening he phoned with big news. Neither of us had mobiles in those days and I had to be dragged from a football match on television to take the call. The bareness of the hallway created an echo and it was difficult to hear above the noise of my housemates. 'Humbold's been executed,' I thought Rob said, and had to get him to repeat it – I'd no idea who Humbold was or why his execution was so important. Finally I got the point. *Homeboy* had been accepted; Rob's first collection had found a publisher. A bottle of champagne was on ice. Would I come round to celebrate? I'd rather have stayed and watched the match; I didn't fancy hearing him gloat. But what are friends for? I put on my coat and headed for the Tube.

Luckily, the gloating wasn't excessive. It turned out he'd been trying to find a publisher for over a year; that the collection had been turned down at least half a dozen times; that many individual poems he'd written had also been rejected by journals. In his triumph, he seemed to exult in previous failures, and brought out a folder of rejection letters, most couched in faint praise until the inevitable 'but' ('admirable formal control but', 'intelligent and surprising but'), though the one he took most pleasure in, to the point of reading it aloud in a pompously academic Ivy League drawl, came from a small magazine in Boston and skipped the faint praise entirely ('your quaintly English reliance on traditional metre and rhyme betrays a wilful ignorance of, or disregard for, the postmodernist aesthetic to which this journal is proudly allied'). To send his work to a magazine like that showed how desperate he'd become, Rob said. Only now that he had found a home for his collection could he own up to the 'kickings' he'd had in the past.

If *kickings* wasn't the word, he probably said *beatings* or *knifings*. The language of victimhood was a routine with Rob: enemies were always out to get him. He could afford to talk that way because it was untrue, as any listener would tell him. I was the listener that evening. Fuck the rejections, I said, you're having a book out. I'd been delegated to do his gloating for him.

A knock on the door interrupted us; then a female voice and my first sight of Jill. She was renting the flat above Rob's, on the ground floor, and though they'd barely exchanged a word till now he'd left a note inviting her round. Sorry to be so late, she said, she'd only just got in. She was wearing a long woollen cardigan and looked cold, though it was June. She looked tired too – her fjord-blue eyes were rimmed with red and she was runny-nosed. Her face was round and white and heavy, like a dinner plate in a fancy restaurant, and her lips moved when Rob spoke, mouthing his words half a second after he'd said them, as though struggling to understand. I'd have guessed she was older than him (though when they met some years later, Marie spotted at once that she was younger). Her body was slim but somehow unlived-in, and her hair sensibly short. She sat straight-backed, while he poured her a glass of champagne, and dutifully toasted his success. But she drank only that one glass, even after he'd opened a second bottle, and though she asked a question or two about the kind of poetry he 'went in for', her interest was no more than polite: she didn't read modern poetry, she said, it had been ruined for her at school. She and Rob talked about the landlord and the other tenants, and which local shops and restaurants to avoid. When I asked her what she did for a living she said I didn't want to know, it was boring, her only skills involved numbers, not words, and even those skills were limited; if she'd any talent she'd be working in the City, earning zillions, rather than wasting her life in the charity sector – not that the charity she worked for wasn't doing vital work, on the contrary, helping the elderly was as important as helping children, but the workers on the ground were the ones who mattered, not the fundraisers or publicists or the likes of her, Jill, whose job was to balance the books and whose time was spent at her desk, in front of a screen, not cooking for old people or keeping them company or wiping their bottoms. With Rob, self-deprecation was a performance in inverted vanity, but with Jill it seemed alarmingly genuine and I remember thinking: when someone does herself down like this, is there a risk she'll do herself in?

When I said I was off, Jill stood up and said she must be going too, and Rob, rather than protest, ushered us out, with a peck on the cheek for Jill and a hug for me.

'What did you think of my neighbour?' he asked next time we met.

'She seemed very quiet.'

'What's that mean? Mousy?'

'Nervous. Rather down on herself.'

'She's had a rough time – a marriage she's running away from. But there's something steely there, too. Something tough.'

I remembered how he had talked about Corinne: Jill was nothing like my picture of her, but both had tricky former partners.

'Where's the ex living?'

'No idea.'

'Why did they break up?'

'She doesn't talk about it.'

I could tell he found Jill interesting: with her melancholy and his victimhood, they made a good match. But I wouldn't have guessed there was anything between them. Probably, at that time, there wasn't. It was two years before I saw her again.

8

My visits to Jill fell into a rhythm. I'd arrive at ten and work on the crates for an hour or two, listing the contents in my notebook. Then I'd break off and make notes towards my own novel, or sometimes just sit, enjoying the silence, half dozing, or dipping into one of Rob's books, the margins of which he'd filled with 'brilliant' or 'bollocks' or '!' or '!!!'. After lunch, I'd knuckle down and spend another hour on the crates before I left. Now my visits were weekly, Jill was less jumpy about having me in the house. At 11.30 she'd come up with a coffee ('I was making one anyway'), but I insisted on bringing sandwiches from home. I felt sneaky using Rob's room to do my own work. But he'd always said that when the writing is flowing you should go with it, and, though more a trickle than a flow, it was as much as I'd managed in years. Perhaps he'd even foreseen this, knowing how I'd appreciate the quiet of his room. 'Don't worry about my stuff,' I imagined him saying. 'Keep going with yours. I can wait a while – posterity won't shut up shop.' At other times, though, I'd hear him getting on at me. 'Some executor you are! I know scholars who'd kill for the chance you've been given and all you do is arse about.' Seated though I was, I didn't take it sitting down: 'Oh, you'd rather have someone like Aaron Fortune, would you? He'd sort your papers out all right. I can see his monograph now: *The Evolution of a Formalist: A Critical Survey of Robert Pope's Unpublished Drafts.* That'll bring in the crowds.' 'At least he'd make an effort. Which is more than you're doing. You're a louse on the locks of literature, Matt.' 'Shut your mouth, Dead Man. I've found the voice of a narrator for my novel and I need to listen to it. You didn't listen enough – your poems were deaf to any voices but your own. I'm making amends for your failure.' That riled him. '*My* failure? You arrogant shit. Your sec-ond-rate prose has nothing to do with me.' Our dialogues weren't always adversarial. I'd congratulate him on an image he'd used or query a cancelled word or ask him where he was when he wrote such-and-such a line. Or, if I was feeling nostalgic, I'd ask him if he remembered the evening we walked out of a dire production of *Godot* or the weekend we had at that lakeside cabin north of Brandon – and if he did remember, why none of this had made it into his poems. These imaginary conversations weren't only consoling but spurred me on to write more in my notebook.

If she'd known how I was spending my time, Marie would have accused me of abusing Jill's trust. And I was pushing my luck with Leonie, who'd given me Fridays off 'for a limited period' that might expire any moment. Still, even allowing for my procrastination, collating Rob's papers wouldn't take long. Louis occasionally nagged me about progress, but Lexy – who I'd emailed months back to let her know about my appointment – hadn't even been in touch. I emailed her again to say I was working steadily and had found a few uncollected poems from Rob's early career. But she wasn't interested enough to ask to see them. It was new work she and Louis would want. Anything Rob might have been working on in his final months. Late style.

I'd also had an email from Aaron Fortune, whose interest was the same as theirs. He'd heard that I was acting as Rob's liter-ary executor and wondered if I'd discovered any material left behind after 'Pope's untimely death last year'. As the 'principal elucidator' of Rob's work, he'd appreciate being kept in the loop: I should feel free to send him photocopies, he said, and in return he'd give me his informed opinion on provenance, etc. ('I understand you're not yourself a scholar, so may find my input of some assistance'). I pictured him as a sallow septuagenarian in a black gown, whose hopes of making a name for himself were rapidly fading and who clung to Rob as a last resort, despite the indifference of his colleagues in Adelaide, let alone the students, who would treat his annual lecture on Rob ('some unknown British guy') as an excuse to send in sick notes and head to the beach. It must be hard for Aaron. But he was pushy and deserved a brisk reply. It was true I'd been delegated to look through Rob's papers, I told him, but I wasn't at liberty to discuss any finds with him, let alone send copies of manuscripts, at this stage. In other words, I was the one whom Rob appointed, so fuck off.

By the last Friday of May I'd finished with the first two crates. It was a sunny afternoon and my own writing had stalled, so I wasn't in the best of moods. I thought of leaving early, but instead, on impulse, I opened the third crate to see how much was in there. The *Martello Sonnets* were regarded as Rob's masterpiece, after all, the collection in which he'd found his 'true', 'pan-European' style. Built as a defence against Napoleonic invasion, the Martello towers along the south coast became (in Rob's title sequence) a set of quirky fun palaces, their vistas outward-looking not xenophobic. Rob had rented one from the Landmark Trust for his forty-fifth birthday. The first of his sonnets celebrated the occasion: 'Huge waves were smashing the jetty/but no hint of them invaded our party/as we danced to the beat of Boney M.' I'd been there and couldn't remember any dancing. But I may have left before it started. These were the empty years before Marie, and I had come alone.

The *Martello Sonnets* crate was more tidily arranged than the first two, with far less dross to wade through. Apologies, Rob, I thought, smiling to myself, I know the earlier poems aren't dross, but even you might feel a little weary, a little unenthused, at spending your time like this, shuffling through papers, in the service of someone else. I'm not just someone, he came back, I'm *me*. Sure, but imagine how impatient you'd be if the roles were switched, and it was you serving *my* cause. As far as I can see, Matt, the only person you're serving is yourself. Fair point, but my lack of progress that day was making me grumpy and while scrabbling through the crate I continued to berate him. You're so predictable, Rob, I said. Here it is again, all in order, the notebooks, the typed drafts, the toing and froing with your editor. It's not an executor you need it's a clerk, a drudge, an automaton. If only you'd made the job more interesting by throwing in the odd surprise . . .

Which is when he did. Wedged between two notebooks I found a slim brown folder. UNP1 it said on the front. Inside were half a dozen or so poems, handwritten in pencil on lined sheets of paper. I could see at once they weren't from the *Martello Sonnets*. At last! A find! Thank you, Rob, I said (aloud this time), though whether thanks were due I soon came to doubt.

Love and War

'Hey, poet! You want a theme? Take that!'

Obama, Osama, 9/11, 7/7, Helmand Province, Guantánamo Bay . . .
I was all set to write the epic of the twenty-first century,
tapping it out on a shiny new laptop, when you came in
and put the hex on me. Herb tea? you asked. I'll have coffee, I said,
proper coffee not decaf, and off you went with a shrug.
Homs, I typed, to spite you, *Saddam, Assad, Arab spring*.
But the keypad had a mind of its own: put *Putin*
and it morphed to *Cupid*, type in *Libya* and it came out *love*.
I knew it was you doing this: I could hear you humming

as the kettle boiled and *refugee crisis* turned to *urgent kisses*.
'Problem?' you said, bringing the coffee. 'A little blocked today?
After those whiskies last night, I'm not surprised.'
Then you kissed me and looped both arms around my neck.
'No poem can stop an election being rigged,' you said,
'or a terrorist planting a bomb. Write about love.
About sex. About us. Get it all down in intimate detail.
And drop the pompous tone – you're not a vicar.'
I felt like a shore crab stranded at low tide. There was the world,
the planet, the crashing ocean of war, and there was me,
in my rockpool, trapped and strangely enthralled.

Shower

You'd use a pencil to pin up your hair,
so when we stood together under the rose
your nape was left exposed for me to kiss,
my hands brimming over as I cupped your breasts,
then going with the flow, down and inside to where
you were streaming, as though water could pour
upwards, not that the wetness was all yours.

It was one of those showers that runs cold
when someone next door turns on a tap, then scalds
as the heat comes back. But we treasured its force:
if I pecked at your ear, tiny pearls would trip
off my tongue, like beads from a broken necklace.
The power took my breath away, or you did,
reaching behind to soap me hard, both of us

in a lather, your body tipping forward
till your palms lay flat against the tiles, me
holding you steady at the hip, so that our slippy
to-and-fro didn't fling us headfirst or sideways
through the plastic curtain, and we remained within
the beam, like books under a reading lamp, flood-
lit by the brilliance boring down.

And even when limescale blocked the showerhead
and the pillar became a weeping willow,

we hid like fugitives under its spread,
fused and lubricious and in flood, the water
falling in spokes, the shower like an umbrella
in reverse, blessing us with its downpour,
keeping us wet to save us from the world.

Swim

No third party is going to share my goods . . .

Who took these photos of you in the sea –
hugging yourself in the shallows;
your arms raised in surrender as a wave breaks;
your tiny head in the blue-brown vastness?
You say you were visiting home,
that your father was trying out his new camera,
that if you'd wanted to impress a lover
you'd not have worn those goggles or that cap.
But how do I know you're telling the truth?
You hate me being jealous, but you'd also hate it if I weren't,
so I confess I'm green with envy of the waves
licking your neck and the sand under your feet
and the man who held out a towel for you
as you ran up the beach. Who *was* the man?
You really expect me to believe it was your dad?

Hair

It grew luxuriantly, down to below her hips

How would I feel if she lost her hair?
she asks. We're in bed, the lights off,
the garden silent, a hot summer night.
Five minutes back, not for the first time,
a hank of it got trapped as we made love
and she cried out in frustration and pain.

I get sick of it, she says. It's a pain.
I'm forever brushing knots from my hair.
But it veils me like a hijab and I love
how it flows over my skin. Chop it off

and I'd feel so *ordinary*. Last time
it was short I looked terrible . . . The night

sticks to our bodies and a night
train in the cutting stirs a windowpane.
We've had these talks before, the last time
only a week ago. I stroke her face, knowing hair
isn't the point. She's asking will I go off
her when she ages, as she must; will my love

withstand her getting sick; is it a love
she can rely on? She has these night-
mares now and then, where I run off
with a younger woman or she's in pain
from cancer or stress makes her hair
fall out. I push a strand away. That time

in Venice, I say (it must have been winter-time,
the duckboards were out) – remember, love?
We'd just the weekend and had to hare
round the churches and galleries. At night
we took a water taxi and drank champagne,
no Bellinis, in Harry's Bar, then slipped off

early to the hotel and took our clothes off
and lay there like this, in a kind of no time,
our bodies glowing, immune to all pain.
I can see it now: the sheets, our lovemaking, the shimmer of the night-
lights on the water – but I can't picture your hair.

Cutting your hair off won't lessen my love.
It's tenacious and timeless, like the night.
Hush, now – no more pain. You are not your hair.

Cut Lip

*Saudi Arabia's Interior Ministry says a Yemeni man convicted of robbery has
had his right hand cut off, the first such punishment carried out in the kingdom
this year . . .*

Is it true they cut robbers' hands off in Saudi Arabia?

Then put me on a plane there. I mugged my girl.
She has no bruises or black eyes to show for it,
but her lip is split where her teeth bit when I pushed her.

She'd come home late and wouldn't tell me where she'd been.
The more I pressed, the less she'd say, till I lost patience
and seized both wrists to shake some sense in her, catching her chin
as I did – which was how it happened, a bead of blood on her bottom
   lip.

Till last night all I'd given her was love bites. Now she flinches
when I come near. They should put me in the stocks ('There he is,
the bastard who hurt his girl!'), put my eyes out with a brooch,
or fly me to Jeddah to have my hands cut off.

Posterity

I'm in love, I said, several odes ago.
But that's to simplify. Our love's hush-hush.
I can't go tell it to the mountain
or whisper it like Midas in the reeds.

Why these poems, then, so open and intimate?
Because they're written for your eyes only,
not to be published till we've stopped loving
(sorry, typo: *living*), maybe not even then.

The woman in the sea, the girl with long hair,
the bed, the shower, the books –
it's the story of what happened to us
but only you, my love, will know it's you.

What the fuck? These weren't Rob's kind of poem. Not
that they altogether lacked his celebrated formalism. But
where was the impersonality, the elusiveness, the ambiguity?
The word 'I' screamed from every stanza. UNP1 the folder
said. UNPUBLISHED, I took that to mean. But what if it meant
UNPUBLISHABLE? UNPRINTABLE? Or UN-POPE-LIKE, poems

he'd discarded as uncharacteristic or second-rate? And why the 1? Were there more – 2, 3 and 4 – to come? None of the poems was dated. The folder they were in had been deposited in the *Martello Sonnets* crate, as though poems dating from that time. But the references to historical events suggested they must have been written recently. And the tone was so intimate: all but one were addressed to a 'you'. Why would someone whose poems had been described as 'hermetic' suddenly allow himself to appear naked? Ted Hughes had done something similar in the *Birthday Letters*. But Hughes was suffering from cancer and wanted to get the poems out before he died, whereas Rob had gone suddenly, unexpectedly, with no time for a last grand gesture. Even if there had been time, he wouldn't have been so unguarded. What's your greatest fear? I'd once asked him. Transparency, he replied.

The poems were neatly handwritten, as though final copies. I remembered Rob, in Brandon, telling me how he wrote out copies of poems by Robert Frost (one of the few American poets he liked) in the hope Frost's inspiration might rub off. Maybe these poems were of that kind: work by an unknown master, or a master unknown to me. Still, supposing these were Rob's poems, what did they say? That he had loved Jill passionately. That she was a refuge to him. That they had an exciting sex life. That he felt possessive of her. That she sometimes felt insecure. That he once accidentally cut her lip during an argument and felt terrible about it. That she had told him to write honestly, about love and sex. That he had followed her instructions and memorialised her in the process.

Connubial love, then. A celebration of uxoriousness. With acknowledgement that a close relationship could also involve hurt and upset. How good were the poems? I'd have to read them again before I could judge. They were certainly direct.

I was still exulting in the fact that I had finally *found* something when Jill walked in.

'How's it going?' she said.

The door was half open, so I ought to have heard her coming up the stairs. But perhaps she'd come up some time ago. Her light step on thick carpet allowed her to move around the house undetected. For all I knew she might have glanced in the room several times before. Here she was now, anyway, with a glass of water in one hand and a plate of shortbread biscuits in the other.

'I thought you might like these.'

'That's kind. I meant to be off by now, but I got immersed.'

I was sitting in Rob's chair, with a plastic crate on the floor beside me and the UNP1 file in my lap. The chair was a better place for me to be seen than on the daybed, and looking busy was better than lolling about, but Jill had a look of disapproval nonetheless. She ought to have been used to me by now. But only Rob ever sat in that chair; only Rob ever *should* sit in it.

'What are those?' she said, nodding at the plastic crate and the contents lying on the floor

'It's his third collection,' I said. 'All the notes he took and drafts he wrote.'

I felt thankful that she'd asked me about the crate rather than the folder, the contents of which I'd seen enough of to want to hide from her, at least for now. Embarrassed, I closed the folder as casually as possible, laying it face down on the desk.

'Would anyone really be interested?' she said.

'Yes. To see how the poems evolved.'

'It seems mad to me. Surely the final versions are all that matter.'

'Not to scholars. They want to see what sort of feelings and occasions underlie a poem; what sparked it off; the first stumbling lines and phrases; the way he pulled it all together.'

She shrugged and smiled, as though to say: I'm baffled, but proud that my husband's poetry should exert such interest. The reaction was encouraging: she'd begun to see the point of selling the papers. The care with which she stepped round them seemed to prove it.

'Thanks,' I said, standing up to take the glass of water and plate of biscuits from her and turning round to gaze out the window in the hope she'd do the same rather than ask about the folder.

'The garden's looking nice again,' I said.

*

She was busy in the kitchen when I left that day. 'I'll let myself out,' I shouted, glad to get away without having to speak to her again. The new light she'd been shown in embarrassed me: the nakedness, intimacy and desire. She'd surprised me the other week, playing football with the kids. But nothing had prepared me for this. Had I got the wrong impression of her from the start?

9

A week before his first book of poems came out, the *Independent* carried a full-page interview with Rob. I remember seeing someone flick through it on the Tube and then buying a copy from the newsagent's when I got off, just to be sure I hadn't imagined it. It was unheard of for a poet, let alone a debutant poet, to be granted such space. But Rob, so the interviewer claimed, was 'the coming man of British poetry', a 'major talent' who'd 'burst on the scene fully formed' after 'spending his twenties and thirties perfecting his craft'. The accompanying photo showed Rob glaring fiercely into the lens. His ferocity was 'legendary', so the piece said, referring to his 'caustic reviews, in which no living writer is spared'. The collection, it concluded, was a 'shoo-in for awards. You'll be hearing a lot more about Robert Pope in the years ahead.'

When I called Rob to congratulate him, he pretended to dismiss the piece: 'She misquoted two of the poems and garbled everything I said.' But he didn't take issue with the fulsome praise.

That interview set the tone. The reviews were fulsome, too. It was his presentation of small-town Britain that made him unique, critics said. As well as his sensitivity to the surrounding countryside, he'd a gift for observing urban spaces — avenues with lime trees, yellowbrick terraces, steel-shuttered corner shops, dogshit-slimy parks, lonely bus shelters, overgrown ponds, and wooden benches plaqued with local names. 'What we hear isn't the voice of a single poet,' one reviewer wrote, 'but the rhythm of a whole community, a collective *urbs*, our nation as it is today.' He was praised for a lack of nostalgia on the one hand and, on the other, for his use of traditional verse forms; though new to the scene, it was as if he'd been around forever. Already he had a label: 'the small-town muse'. Since he'd grown up in a village, had lived for some years in America and was now based in London, I found the label ironic, and to his credit so did he. Just as long as they don't call me a Middle Englander, he said.

His publication party was in a gallery off Queen Square. I'd been expecting something modest – it was only a poetry collection, after all – but had to fight my way in past writers I recognised from photographs, not all of them poets. I took some fizz from the drinks tray and looked in vain for Rob. Did I write poetry? a woman in a turquoise dress asked, looking over my shoulder. The clinkety-clink of a wine glass brought us to order. Rob's editor, Charles Durrant, introduced himself. He was proud of his poetry list, he said, but no collection made him prouder than Rob's, 'perhaps the most important I've published in twenty years'. Rob shyly hung his head. '*Perhaps?*' I could imagine him thinking. 'Why so mealy-mouthed?'

By the time I got to speak to him, the crowd was thinning out. I assumed the woman at his elbow was from the publicity department.

'Clarice works for the *FT*,' he said introducing us.

'On the travel pages. But I'm here because I'm family.'

'And there I was thinking you'd come for me,' Rob said.

Her hand touched his sleeve. They'd clearly met before. When Charles came up to sweep them off to dinner, Rob took me aside.

'Sorry,' he said, 'the party was expensive; they won't stretch to a meal as well.'

'No worries. Are you and Clarice . . .?'

'She's Charles's daughter.'

'Ah.'

'And young enough to be mine.'

'Even so,' I said.

'Yes, yeah – poet's laurels, *droit de seigneur*, perk of the job. I wish.' Charles was beckoning him. 'Yep, coming!'

It became a pattern. Whenever I ran into him at launches or parties, there'd be a woman with him and he'd introduce us, and I'd infer they were having a relationship, then next time he'd be with someone else. I shouldn't exaggerate. Perhaps it happened only four or five times. And whenever we met at his flat (which bore no signs of joint occupation), he'd deny involvement with anyone: 'The odd fling, that's all. Since Corinne, there's been nothing serious. Once bitten, twice shy. I just prefer being with women – present company excepted.' One night, more drunk than usual, he recalled 'the childishly pink, unusually elongated' nipples of a woman he'd slept with. But he didn't tell me her name. And the context wasn't the boastful recital of a conquest but a discussion of aesthetics: why female bodies are inherently more beautiful than male bodies, and the human form is more inspiring than landscapes, and physical sensation as valid a measure of beauty as intellectual appreciation. We still had such discussions in those days. They only stopped when he married Jill.

*

It would be unfair to say that everything else stopped then, too. Even before they married, we met less regularly. He took to cancelling at the last minute. The cancellations sometimes came as a relief: not only was I now full-time on the listings magazine, I'd begun to make progress on my novel. But in lonelier moments I resented being dropped. Now he'd made his mark, I'd become the junior partner again – protégé and underling. We still got on when we did meet. He was more guarded in speaking about his life, but encouraged me to talk about mine. And if we went our separate ways before midnight, rather than drinking through the small hours, it showed we were becoming more sensible. It didn't matter. It's how it was. I had my life and he had his. All the same . . .

For months he didn't tell me that he'd moved from the flat. That he was living with Jill, now divorced, in Parson's Green. That they were already making plans to buy a house together.

He didn't even tell me they were getting married. It came out after the event, at the dinner for his second collection. His publishers could afford it this time; the first book had done well. There were about ten of us present: Rob, Jill, Charles (but not his daughter), a couple of literary editors and their partners, and two women from the publicity department. No poets (Rob liked to think there *were* no other poets, except dead ones) and no critics (ditto). I remember the shock of what he was wearing that night: not the suit (which he always wore) but the bow tie. It was large, with red and white spots and looked like a pastiche of something, what I couldn't tell. Rob's line, as with the suit, was that he felt 'comfortable' in it. True or not, it marked him out and became a label: Robert Pope, the Bow-Tie Poet. The formalist tag first appeared around that time. This was what a formalist poet looked like.

The other shock that night was to find Jill sitting next to him. I'd not seen her since that time at his flat over two years before and thought she must be standing in for someone (a mistake reinforced by him talking far more to the person on his left than to her). And unlike Marie, who would have spotted it at once, I didn't notice the wedding ring. Her eyes should have told me: the blue in them was deeper, warmer, more Mediterranean than Nordic. It was as though some weight had been lifted and the woman underneath – smart, attractive, independent – had broken free. The round plate of her face seemed to glow. Rob looked happy, too: vindicated in having seen her hidden qualities and vindicated by the reception of his new book, *Mayday*, which had already had good reviews. ('To distance himself from the Middle Englandism associated with his first collection,' one of them read, 'Pope has become a complex technician – his is an Eliotic extinction of personality in the service of formal precision.') When Charles stood up to toast Rob for his 'quick work', he meant the new collection. Rob picked up on the phrase in his reply. He'd been a quick worker in another respect, he said: a week ago he'd proposed to Jill and this morning, at Kensington register office, they'd become husband and wife. He made her stand up for a kiss. Invited to respond, she blushed and said the dress she'd married in – the one she was wearing – had been chosen by Robbie (she was already calling him that, I now realise), who'd insisted on the colour blue. He'd also insisted they marry in secret – no fuss, no confetti, no best man – which suited her. I caught Rob looking sheepishly at me as she sat down. The sheepish look was there again later when he plonked himself next to me.

'I wanted it to be a surprise,' he said.

'It's that all right.'

'If I'd had a best man, then of course . . .'

'I had the speech all worked out. The day we met. The years of friendship. How you were always there when I was having a rough time . . .'

'Which was when you decided I must be bad luck. Yeah, yeah.'

'Jill looks great,' I said.

'Doesn't she just.'

'Where's the honeymoon?'

'I'm too busy with readings. She might come for a night when I'm in Cheltenham. That'll be all. She's done this before, remember.'

'Were she and her ex together long?'

He laughed. 'Are you worried we won't last?'

'Do you know why they broke up?'

'What is this, Matt, the Spanish Inquisition?'

He stood up to say goodbye to someone. I left soon after. A fine mist haloed the streetlights in Soho Square. I understood already that the nature of our friendship had changed. However close we remained, however candidly I spoke to him about my life, certain aspects of his (Jill, love, marriage) were not to be broached again.

10

'God, it's hot,' Jill said in the kitchen. She was wearing a light cotton dress with tiny blue flowers. Her shoulders were bare and the line above her upper lip was moist. 'I don't know how you can work in this. Do say if you need to cool off with a shower.'

'I'm fine,' I said, blushing at the thought of the poem about her and Rob having sex in the shower.

'How's it going? Have you come across any surprises?'

It was my first visit since discovering the UNP1 folder, which I'd been wondering how to bring up. Now her question gave me an opening – though I could tell from her tone that she expected the answer to be no.

'As a matter of fact, yes. Half a dozen or so unpublished poems. Recent, by the look of it. Lexy will be very pleased.'

Be positive, I told myself, hoping that a show of enthusiasm would carry her along. Possessive though she was about Rob's papers as objects or relics, the words themselves might not greatly matter to her.

'What kind of poems?'

'Various kinds,' I lied. This wasn't going to be easy. 'Love poems mostly.'

'That *is* a surprise.'

'They're quite direct. Candid. Erotic, even.'

'Doesn't sound like Robbie.'

'No, that's what I thought. But poets develop. He seemed to be working out a new way to write. For instance, there's a poem where he remembers you going to Venice together.'

'I think he once went, for the British Council, and I've always wanted to go, but we never did.'

'Really? Maybe he chose Venice for the rhyme scheme. It's a complex poem, a sestina. He talks about you having long hair.'

She laughed. 'I used to, as a student. Right down to my waist.'

'There's another poem based on a photo of you.'

'Doing what?'

'Swimming. He's looking at an old photo of you and wondering who took it.'

'I suppose there must be one. I can't remember.'

'If there isn't, it's poetic licence. The swimmer's you, but in disguise.'

'You've lost me,' she said. 'How can you call it a candid poem if it uses disguises?'

'I agree. It's confusing. But the poems are quite something. Lexy will be excited, as I say. Louis, too.'

'I'd like to read them before they do.'

'Sure. When I've finished working through the crates, I'll show you everything. I'm hoping there'll be more.'

'As long as you don't take anything away.'

'It'll all stay here. As we agreed.'

'And I wouldn't want poems being published that reflect badly on Robbie.'

'Absolutely. None of us would.'

Who's she to judge what might reflect badly on him? I thought, as I went back to work. She doesn't even read poetry. The crates were more interesting since I'd found that hidden folder. Surely there must be an UNP2. Maybe a 3, 4, 5 and 6 as well.

But there were no more surprises in the third crate. Nor, when I rushed through it, in the fourth. The work was all slog. With no love poems to lighten the load. Before I left, I looked at the precious folder again – then buried it where Jill couldn't find it.

*

'Of course she said that,' Marie shouted from the bathroom. 'If you'd written love poems for me, I'd want to read them before any strangers did.'

'Louis and Lexy aren't strangers. She knows them both.'

'All the same. You'd think Rob would have shown her. Love poems? It's not loving to use Jill as material and not even tell her.'

'He may have been saving them up as a surprise. For their diamond wedding anniversary, say.'

'Yeah, right.'

Marie likes to take a bath last thing; she gets back pains, perhaps stress-related or perhaps to do with giving birth three times, and finds a hot soak relaxing. She came through, rose-tinted, and sat on the bed, a towel tucked over her breasts and a run of water-beads on each shoulder.

'Are they any good?' she said.

'I find it hard to judge.'

'If they were masterpieces, you'd know.'

'Masterpieces aren't always recognised at first . . .'

'Sweet Jesus,' she said, suddenly Irish. 'You must have formed an impression.'

'I like them. But I don't know what Louis will think. I emailed him copies yesterday.'

'I thought Jill wouldn't let you to take anything away.'

'I took photos with my iPad. When she was in the garden. Then made documents of them when I got home.'

'Bloody hell, Matt. That's really bad. What will she say when she finds out?'

'She won't. I've sworn Louis to secrecy. OK, it was sneaky. But what choice did I have? Legally, I can remove anything I choose. But I don't want to alienate her.'

'If it helps, I'll give you my opinion.'

'Hypocrite! You object to me making copies, but now you want to read them.'

'Eventually. After Jill's read them.'

'I'll consider it,' I said.

'You'd better,' she said, flapping the towel at me as she slipped it off, 'Mr Keeper of the Flame.'

She slid in beside me, her body hot and damp. Like a wet flame, I thought, sleep's logic overcoming me.

*

Louis didn't get back to me for over a week. He pleaded busyness and a trip to the States, but I could tell he was lukewarm.

'There aren't enough for a collection,' he said. 'And it won't make much of a splash. Poet writes a few vaguely sexy love poems to his wife. Big deal. We need more.'

'I've still a couple of crates to look through. It's not promising, but you never know.'

'What about his computer?'

'He either handwrote or used a typewriter.'

'Or hidden under his mattress?'

'Ha ha.'

'How's Jill been?'

'Tricky to start with. Then co-operative. Now nervous about what's in the poems.'

'You're sure they're about her? That last one made me wonder: "it's the story of what happened to us/but only you, my love, will know it's you." Why will only she know, when we all know they're married?'

'He's having it both ways – writing about Jill, but keeping her name out of it. She becomes a kind of Everywoman.'

'Not the Other Woman?'

'Who would that be?'

'You're right,' he said. 'I'd better get on. Let me know if you find anything else.'

'Meanwhile . . .'

'Meanwhile, understood, if Jill gets in touch I'm not to tell her I've seen the poems.'

*

My mum phoned every Sunday at six, though lately she had taken to phoning on other days as well, for no particular reason, it seemed, except to complain that the news everywhere was so depressing – terror attacks, war in Syria, refugees. For once she was upbeat. Did you read about the tiger and the goat? she said. The goat was put in the tiger's cage in a Russian zoo. It was meant to be lunch, but the two of them made friends. The goat even sleeps in the tiger's bed. Lovely story, Mum, I said, if true. I read it in the *Mail*, she said. You don't want to believe everything you read in the *Mail*, I said.

Later I looked online and found the story on various websites, all with the same details: the brave goat, the unvoracious tiger, their unlikely friendship. I could see why it appealed to Mum. Like the tiger, she felt lonely and imprisoned: how wonderful it would be if someone could turn up and change that. I read it differently, as a story destined to end badly, with Jill the tiger and me the goat. At first, I'd found her scary. Then she'd seemed friendlier. Now she was suspicious of me and showing her teeth. If I wasn't careful she'd have me for lunch.

*

It was June by now and quiet on the paper, with the silly season under way. I tried to stay engaged, especially with circulation falling and jobs under threat. But since starting work on Rob's archive, my concentration was poor. I'd reach the last sentence of a fiction review I was supposed to be subbing and have no memory of having read it – like a driver wondering where the last ten miles had gone. Even mid-conversation with somebody, I'd find my mind wandering. If the books pages had been less of a backwater, I might not have drifted so easily. But when you're staring at a green screen, with the gentle pit-pat of keyboards the only sound, it's easy to float off.

Luckily, occasional dramas broke in to bring me back, and within a few days there were two. The first involved the news desk. How would I like to go to Italy to interview Elena Ferrante? they asked. Like everyone else I'd been reading her. And I could see it would be quite a coup: the first ever in-person interview with a writer whose identity had so far been a secret. For a moment I even had fantasies that she or her publishers had specially chosen me, having read something I'd written, my novel even, which persuaded them I was the right man for the job. But it turned out no interview was on offer: that what the news desk had in mind was for me to snoop around and 'solve the mystery of the ageing recluse'. I took the idea to Leonie, who a few years before had stopped them sending a stringer to Alabama to flush out Harper Lee. She agreed the idea was naff and that I might waste weeks getting nowhere, but said that if I fancied it I should go. I told her I didn't. That the truth behind Ferrante's fiction didn't really interest me. That I'd my own theory of what she'd experienced and what she'd made up, and I didn't want the facts getting in the way. Fair enough, she said, but I could see she was disappointed, if only because of the pressure she was under to sex-up our books coverage. The episode left me feeling insecure.

The bigger drama involved the arts desk, with whom we share most of the Review. Notionally we've an agreed allocation of space, but since the paper fluctuates in size, according to the number of adverts, there's a weekly squabble over who gets how much. When the ads are arts- or books-specific, it makes life simpler, but the reader offer ads are floaters and that's where battles rage. The row this time was over an offer for a deckchair, which clearly belonged in a different section altogether, but – with apologies for the last-minute foisting and the promise of more space next week – the ads department insisted one of us take. Deckchairs were for reading, Michael, the arts editor (my age, but already white-haired) said. Ah, but deckchairs were also for listening to music in, Leonie said. It was all quite jokey at first but both refused to budge.

'Do you really need that column of crime shorts?' Michael said.

'We've held it over for three fucking weeks already,' Leonie said. 'Why do you need a fucking interview with a dancer as well as a fucking review of the new *Swan Lake*?'

'Because he's the hottest act in town, with a big show opening next month, and it's a fucking exclusive.'

'Next month? Why run it this week, then?'

'Because someone else will do a feature on him by next.'

'I thought you said it was a fucking exclusive.'

'Yes, and a sight more fucking exclusive than a batch of fucking crime fiction reviews no one will read anyway.'

So it went on, degenerating by the minute, until the ads manager came up with a compromise, to which Leonie and Michael grudgingly agreed: if we took the deckchair, the smaller ad for the new Orson Welles biography could move to Arts. I was used to these rows, if not on such a scale, but the new assistant arts editor, Emma, who'd arrived only a couple of weeks before, looked shell-shocked. I ran into her in the queue at the local Pret that lunchtime. She waited till I'd got my chicken tikka wrap.

'Heavy stuff,' she said.

'You'll get used to it.'

'It was like watching *Timon of Athens*.'

'From the front stalls.'

'With blood and spit landing on you.'

We walked back together, laughing and complicit. And whenever we came across each other for the rest of that week – at the coffee machine, say, or by the water cooler – we'd exchange an ironic smile and raise-of-eyebrows: how ridiculous our bosses were! You'd never catch us losing our cool over six hundred words of Review space! Leonie would have called me disloyal if she'd known. And though Marie had been urging me to find new friends, she might not have approved of one who was young and female. Still, it was good to have an ally about the place.

*

My next two visits to Jill yielded little of interest. Despite what I'd said to Louis, I felt hopeful there was more and worked hard to find it, setting aside the notes I'd made towards my novel while I went through the remaining crates. The one unexpected item was a pair of brown folders. The first was marked LETTERS: SENT. Whereas the folder in Rob's desk contained letters and cards sent to him, these were printed copies of his replies, their tone untypically gracious and modest. The second, much fatter file was marked LETTERS: UNSENT. Mostly they were drafts of letters to newspapers. Poets should stay out of politics, he always said, but he'd obviously struggled to keep his mouth shut. There was one letter to the *Guardian* condemning the invasion of Iraq; another about climate change and the perils of ignoring it; and a third, written just weeks before he died, about a monument he'd seen on the East Coast in memory of thirty-two Dutchmen who kayaked to England during the Second World War, only eight of whom survived ('I hope one day there'll be similar monuments to the refugees who've perished in recent months while making similarly desperate journeys'). At the bottom of each he'd typed UNSENT, preserving his image as a poet who refused to express his opinion on anything other than poetry.

There were some private letters, too, addressed to people who'd crossed him in some way, including one to a theatre producer he'd talked to at a party about adapting a play by Terence ('I wasn't talking about Rattigan, you deaf cunt, I was referring to the Roman dramatist, 195–159 BC') and another to Marcus Downe, who'd reviewed Rob's last book for us – I scanned it to see whether he'd included me in his diatribe, but he hadn't. These, too, were letters he'd dashed off, then thought better of. Like Moses Herzog, I thought, in Saul Bellow's novel, who composes letters by the hundred.

UNSENT: I could imagine it as the title of a book. But Rob had asked for his letters to be destroyed. There was nothing for me here.

To my relief, Jill seemed less wary again and insisted that I break for lunch. She'd made quiche and salad rather than sandwiches and, without asking, poured me a glass of white wine.

'So,' she said, 'any more discoveries?'

I shook my head. 'It looks like that's the lot,' I said, through a mouthful of lettuce.

'I'm looking forward to reading the love poems. Robbie wasn't good at showing love in public. I think his friends wondered what he saw in me. And people at work wondered what I saw in him. What's he *do* all day? one of them used to say. No job, sitting on his bum, leaching off you. One or two knew he was famous, but the others . . .' She laughed. 'What they forget is what a mess I was after my marriage broke up – you did know I'd been married before?'

'Rob told me.'

'I was very low. Could see no point in going on with life. Till Robbie saved me. Not like in a fairy story – the dashing hero and the imprisoned princess. But he did rescue me. And in return I gave him a home, love, the freedom to get on with his work. I'd have given him children, too, if I could. Sorry, it's hard to talk about.'

'Please don't feel –'

'I had a miscarriage at fourteen weeks. Rob was devastated. Me too, of course. We considered IVF. But I was forty by then and we left it at that.'

'I'm sorry. He never mentioned it.'

'He wouldn't. Even we didn't talk about it. He went off the rails for a while. Drinking too much, coming in all hours, et cetera.' She screwed the lid back on the wine bottle. 'It's the one time I failed him. I was suffering too much myself to comfort him. He was better once we moved down here. Are you done?'

She stood up and cleared the plates while I sat there. The idea of Rob wanting children was hard to take in. There was so much more to him – and to his marriage – than I'd known.

Back upstairs, I put away the two letters folders I'd been looking at and brought out the last few notebooks. There were endless drafts in them for the poems that became Rob's last collection – drafts he wrote afresh every time he changed a word or even a comma. Painstaking or blocked? I'd leave that for others. There was nothing in them for me.

Or so it seemed. One of the notebooks was a different size, A4, and spiral-bound. Halfway through, several pages had been ripped out; tiny, torn-off fragments clung to the looping wire. It wasn't like Rob to remove anything. Or leave the evidence of doing so. Why this once? What had been there? I counted the remaining pages: 73. How many had been taken out: 11? 23? 47? There were no clues in the poems on either side; one was set in a graveyard and the other a reworking of the parable of Lot's wife. Whatever the reason for his action – impatience, anger, embarrassment at an especially inept first draft – perhaps Rob couldn't stand seeing what was there. Or couldn't stand the idea of anyone else seeing it. Unless it was Jill who'd ripped out the pages – now that she knew Rob had written poems about her, had she begun going through his papers and come across one she didn't care for? It didn't seem likely: to her, his room was still a shrine. Whoever removed it, what *had* been there? And what was it Rob had burned in those bonfires Jill had spoken of, down the garden? It was frustrating to think I'd never know.

Replacing that notebook, I turned to the next one. Tucked inside, at the back, were half a dozen or so lined sheets in Rob's handwriting. They'd been folded in four so they didn't protrude. The top sheet was blank, except for three letters and a single digit: UNP2.

Adultery

His watch by the bed, her hair on the pillow,
the guilt-assuaging bottle of Chablis.

Transactions

When sex gives equal enjoyment to both partners, why should she sell it, he pay?

We're old-fashioned about it: it's me who pays for the room,
while your contribution is you. It's enough. *You're* enough.
But I worry what it says about us. You've a job, a house, a car,
countless assets besides your body, yet I'm the one footing the bill.
Maybe it's shyness: you're embarrassed to book in at Reception.
Or fear: what if your husband saw your credit card statement?
But I think it's because you're *romantic*: you like to pretend
there's no transaction involved. So I arrive before you do
(as I try not to later, in bed) and the business is taken care of,
and the rest is pleasure with no strings. Ovid grumbles
that his lover keeps asking for presents. You never do.
In fact, it's me who comes away with gifts – not just the memory
of you in bed, but the books you bring, the kind I'd write if I could,
in which the hero and heroine never go to cheap hotels, all we see
is the love they make and the light pouring from their bodies.

Emails

Remember me while you're away! (2.11)

Were I more organised, would I have kept all the emails you sent
while on holiday – the descriptions of galleries, fishing ports,

walks round city walls, or the views from your villa or hotel?
They're never just travelogues. You write of things no one but you
would have noticed, or if they did wouldn't bother to recall:
the woman whose sun hat blew off, the Russian oligarch with hairy
   wrists,
the changing red of the roof tiles in Florence as the sun went down.
The only blank spot is him. But I can't help filling out the picture –
there he is buying you drinks or lying in wait while you finish in the
   bathroom.
That's the reason I've deleted all the emails. It's bad enough
having to think of him at all and even worse when you're away.

To a Cuckold

Miles, mate, you don't know me, and if you did you wouldn't like
   me,
and if you knew what I get up to with your missus you'd like me even
   less.
But honest, I'm doing you a favour. Haven't you noticed how sweet
and attentive she's become, how she sings when cooking supper
and never complains when you spend Sundays at the golf course?
She's lost weight, too, and looks younger. Why be jealous? It's me
   who endures
her guilt and remorse, whereas with you she's happily uxorious.
The key to a good marriage is adultery, you see: every husband needs
   a louse
to warm the bed for him, every union a bastard like me. So when you
   find out
and come looking for me, don't bring a knife, bring a thank-you
   present.
The day she stops betraying you is the day your problems begin.

Two

No man could possibly fall in love / With two girls at once

Why can't a man love two women at once?
We're brought up to love two parents.
And no mother stops at one child

160

In case her love for it should die with a second.
I don't love strawberries any less
Because I also love grapes.

So can a woman love two men at once?
Of course. Same rule applies.
As the poet says, love is accommodating,
It makes room. If there's no threat
That your love for me will lessen,
You can love whoever you choose.

Before They Met

Afterwards, drinking tea, their backs against
The headboard, the lights still off,
He asks about the others, before him,
'Not that the numbers matter or who they were,
I'm just curious to know all about you.'

She's shy, sipping her lapsang to play for time,
And protests that it's ancient history
And anyway very dull, not like *his* past.
They laugh, as though the subject's been dropped,
But when he persists, since it's no big deal,

She offers him Tom, the first boy she kissed,
Then Rick, the first to touch her breasts,
Then Harry, 'The first I had proper sex with,
If you can call it that.' 'And you were how old?'
'Sixteen.' 'That's young.' 'Is it? When did you first ...?'

'Forget about me. How old was this Harry?'
'Twenty.' 'Bloody cradle-snatcher,' he laughs,
and kisses her again, and strokes her hair.
'So you started at sixteen,' he resumes,
'You must have clocked up quite a few by now.'

'I thought you said we weren't doing numbers.'
'No, but *roughly* how many would you say?'
'This is daft. Can you remember all *your* lovers?
Even the one-night stands?' 'So you've had those?'

She sips more tea. 'You're cross-examining me.

'I don't like where it's going, but OK then:
Fifty.' 'Fifty!' 'No, two hundred.' 'What!' 'Or twelve,
Was it? Or maybe just two.' 'You're fucking with me.'
'All that counts is that I'm with you now.
We love each other. At least I thought we did . . .

Now I wonder.' 'I wonder, too,' he shouts,
leaning over and grabbing her wrists
and forcing her head back on the pillow
as the darkness tightens inside her,
and the digits mount on the alarm clock

and she knows as sure as death that they've no future.

11

An internal email came from Emma, asking if we could have a quick drink after work: 'I'm in need of some advice.' I'd noticed her looking glum around the office and assumed she was having problems with Michael; she wouldn't be the first. OK, I replied: it was a Thursday, press day, when Marie's used to me getting home late, and an extra half-hour would make no difference. I suggested The Plough, one of the few pubs nearby where journalists are rarely to be seen: if Emma was upset, it'd be best to go somewhere quiet. I emailed her again as I was leaving and said I'd see her there, but she caught me in the lobby, so we left the building together. I hoped no one seeing us would get the wrong idea.

The pub was crowded. We stood outside, me with a Guinness, she with a rum and Coke, the sort of drink I associate with teenagers. With her milky skin, Emma looked like a teenager, though she can't have been much under thirty, having worked on various magazines before joining the paper. In which case she was only a few years younger than Marie, though in terms of maturity it could have been decades.

'So?' I asked, after the preliminaries of office gossip. 'You've been looking a bit down.'

'That's my work face. My ex-boyfriend used to say I look suicidal when I'm concentrating.' She laughed. 'It's sweet of you to worry about me. If I came to work with a noose round my neck, Michael wouldn't notice.'

'You wanted some advice?'

She was keen to do some writing for the paper, she said, and wondered if I had any tips. She'd asked Michael several times – there were low-profile spots to fill whenever the regulars were away (TV previews, exhibition round-ups, fringe theatre shorts, etc.), but he always fobbed her off.

'I wrote half the student paper when I was at York.'

'What kind of stuff?' I said.

'Anything. Everything. News features. Op-ed columns. But mostly arts and books. More books than arts, in fact. I was chair of the Poetry Society and used to interview the authors that came.'

'Did you ever have Rob Pope?'

'Who?'

'Robert Pope. A friend of mine. He died recently.'

'Oh, Robert *Pope*. The Bow-Tie Poet, right? I think we tried to get him but the dates didn't work. People said he was difficult to deal with. Were you close?'

'Ish. He was quite a bit older than me.'

'Obviously,' she laughed, nudging my arm. 'I'm more into fiction these days. The innovative stuff. Ed McKeane sort of thing. Same again? Let me get them this time.' She stood up. 'He's got a book of stories coming out soon. No doubt you've already lined up a review.'

I could see where this was going, but the Guinness had neutralised my defences. Emma wasn't like the usual hacks who come wheedling round. She was smart, well read and looking for a break. Why not? I'd been in the same position once. It's tough when you're young. And at that moment, gawky, bamboo-limbed, spilling our drinks as she came back, Emma seemed very young.

I told her how the paper had been when I first joined. A lot had changed since then, I said – in my life as well as the job. A needier person might have made more of my quip (when admitting I was married) that 'wedding ring' is an anagram of 'grim ending'. Emma didn't; she even worked out that they weren't anagrams. I said that I'd speak to Leonie and if a suitable book came along maybe she could do it for us. In-house reviewers are useful, because they don't have to be paid. Not that I put it like that to Emma. We parted with a hug and a promise to do it again sometime. It was ten by the time I got home.

There was no reason to feel guilty: if a guy can't have a drink after work now and then ... But when I found myself telling Marie I'd been out with colleagues, plural, I realised I did. For the first time in years, home seemed flat and Marie drably middle-aged.

I knew that Rob's poems were mixed up with this, but it took me a while to work out why. My main feeling on reading the new batch was one of betrayal – betrayal of me as well as Jill. Though he'd been less open with me since marrying, he'd given no hint of being involved with anyone. And when he made me his executor he hadn't warned me what I would find. If the poems were made public, reviewers would doubtless call his confessionalism 'brave'. But wasn't it cowardly to write candid poems then hide them in a drawer? And cowardly to leave the fate of your work in the hands of others? The love affair, so the poems suggested, had been clandestine. But he knew that once I read them, the secret would be out. In theory I was free to publish the poems without consulting Jill. But that was absurd. She'd already said she'd like to read the earlier poems I'd found and I could hardly not show her these. What a mess. Marie was right. I'd spent too many years in thrall to Rob. The adjectives that people used about him – single-minded, uncompromising –

no longer seemed to fit. I felt angry and taken for granted. He'd landed me in the shit.

What sort of affair had it been? Not, by the sound of it, a casual one. It had gone on for some time. There'd been regular visits to a hotel. And – assuming the man in the last poem was Rob – he'd been driven to extremes of jealousy. Most telling of all, he'd confessed to loving two women at once. The last time I saw Jill, she'd spoken of Rob 'going off the rails' after her miscarriage. Had an affair been part of that? Or could it date back to a time before, when he'd been involved with a married woman but was still single? Could Jill herself (not yet divorced when they first met) be the woman in question? Or could it be Corinne? He'd talked about going to a motel with her – 'h', 'm', what was the difference? The affair had been the source of suffering as well as pleasure: of pain, envy and mistrust. But there was nothing to suggest he regretted it. Or that anyone in the same position should feel guilty. The mood wasn't mournful or apologetic. It was buoyant.

After my evening with Emma, the buoyancy felt like a challenge or even a reproach – an invitation to me to reappraise my life, my marriage, my sexuality. You'll never catch me looking at another woman, I'd often told Marie. And when she did (how can anyone *not* look?), she used it as a pretext for a renewal of vows. On one occasion (we were in a restaurant) she accused me of ogling a woman at a nearby table. Sexual appraisal, she called it. No, aesthetic appreciation, I replied. Even if I did fancy another woman I wouldn't do anything about it, I said. Why not? she said. It would be a step into the unknown, I said. All you're saying is you're too scared, she said, you need to do better than that. It'd destroy your trust in me, I said. Still not good enough, she said. It would hurt you, I said, and I couldn't bear that. Better, she said, but still inadequate. I would never sleep with anyone else, I said, because I love you. OK, she said, that'll have to do. Her own take was different: since marrying and having kids, she didn't *want* to fuck anyone else. Moreover, she'd never behave in the manner of people she despised, meaning (though at that point she'd no idea how he *had* behaved) people like Rob. She intended to reassure me, though in some ways I'd have felt better if she *had* been like Rob. Or rather, since of course I'd have felt worse, I'd have felt reassured to know that it was normal to imagine having sex with someone other than your partner. Marie denied having such fantasies, whereas I had them all the time. Faithful sounded a good thing to be. But was a faithful husband – or *this* faithful husband – merely lacking in imagination? Or someone without the initiative to make the imaginary real?

I was only Rob's executor, not the focus of his ambitions. It was paranoid to think he'd set out to mess with my head. On the other hand, knowing me as he did, he must have foreseen that the poems would have an effect. That they'd unsettle and arouse me. That while making love to Marie, I'd imagine I was with someone else – Emma, Leonie, the barmaid at the squash club, the girl with the nose-ring in the local Pret. You should have told me, I imagined telling him. Told you what? Told me you'd written poems about an affair. And told me who she was.

I hadn't known the confessional Rob of the poems. *That* Rob was a new person. So was Rob the gardener, Rob the dog-owner, Rob the almost-parent, Rob the settled suburbanite. The old Rob was fading. I now had several of him in my head.

*

It occurred to me that I *had* known this latest Rob – or that he'd once hinted at his existence. It would have been over ten years ago, before he moved to Hadingfield. We were gossiping

about a government minister who'd been done over in the tabloids for having an affair.

'Don't they just love that word *cheat*?' he said.

'What do you call it?'

'Cheat's what people do playing cards. It's nothing to do with
passion.'

'He's a Tory shit,' I said. 'I don't know why you're defending
him.'

'I'm trying to do justice to the offence. We're talking treach-
ery, tragedy, three or more people's lives wrecked.'

'Yeah, yeah, love's the ruin of people – you once told me
that. You also said that by remembering the past we can avoid
repeating it.'

'I used to think that. But I was wrong. Remembering the
past doesn't stop us repeating it. The only difference is we *know*
we're repeating it. We even *watch* ourselves.'

'When you say "we" . . .?'

'I'm talking in general,' he said, and changed the subject.

In general? No, he'd been talking about himself. He'd fallen
in love. And feared that ruin would follow. Or that ruin had
already come.

*

'What did I tell you?' Louis said. 'He had another woman.'

'Assuming the poems are autobiographical.'

'Of course they're fucking autobiographical.'

With the first batch, Louis had been slow to respond. This
time he was on the phone within an hour.

'Even if they are,' I said, trying to convince myself, 'the affair
might have predated Jill.'

'Except that he talks about sending emails. And he married
Jill before he ever sent emails.'

'It's true. No getting round it.'

'I know magazine editors who'll be keen to take them,' he said. 'Unless you want to run them in your Review section.'

'The will says we should aim at a collection.'

'There aren't enough. We'd need thirty for that.'

'Jill hasn't seen them yet,' I said.

'What's it matter? If I get a good offer, she won't object.'

I'd always known Louis was an odd mixture: old-school man of letters on the one hand, new-school wheeler-dealer on the other. I was surprised by his tone, even so.

'The money doesn't interest her,' I said. 'That was never the point.'

'It'll make a good story.'

'Posthumously published poems about an unknown woman – I can't see it, Louis.'

'I'm the agent here, Matt – trust me.'

'OK, but hold your horses. I've not quite finished looking yet.'

12

I had promised Jill I would be finished by the summer. And even with the time I'd squandered on my own writing, rather than collating Rob's, it still looked possible: a couple more visits should be enough. But Marie was now back at work part-time and I had to miss the next Friday to stay home looking after Mabel, who had a chest infection. Then Leonie took her annual fortnight in early July, which meant me missing two more. In theory that still left several more Fridays before our holiday in mid-August – Lanzarote, this time – until a cock-up on the books pages intervened.

In itself, it was a harmless mistake: the photos of two authors being reviewed together were transposed. That the captions were also transposed, with contrasting one-word verdicts ('brilliant', 'lifeless') appearing below the wrong author, made the mistake more embarrassing, but these things happen. Our pictures editor spotted the error after we'd gone to press and we changed it for the online edition. No big deal, I thought, until Leonie returned on the Monday.

'That picture and caption fuck-up . . .'

'I'm sorry,' I said,

'"Lifeless", the caption said.'

'When it should have said "brilliant", I know.'

'"Lifeless", when, as the review pointed out, the author died two years ago.'

'Shit, I didn't spot that.'

'I'm being bombarded by emails from his agent. The family think it was meant as some kind of sick joke.'

'I hope you've told them it wasn't your fault.'

'I'm the books editor, Matt. I have to take responsibility.'

'Not if you're away.'

'If the staff I employ fuck up, it's down to me. Even if the photos had been right, I thought we agreed to avoid negative captions. "Lifeless", for fuck's sake.'

I'd known Leonie lose her temper with others, but never with me. She was stony for the rest of the day, most of which she spent in the book cupboard not even pretending to consult me about commissions. At five she suggested a coffee in the basement canteen. Since the coffee there is even worse than the coffee from the machine on our floor, I knew coffee wasn't the point.

We sat alone at a corner table, out of earshot of other journalists.

'Forget the captions,' Leonie said. 'There's something else we need to discuss. The paper's about to announce a voluntary redundancy scheme.'

'Right.'

'I've always said I can't afford to lose anyone. There's only you and me full-time, plus Chris with his three days and Gina with her two on the web pages. Other sections are better staffed. But they also have more page traffic. It's a struggle making the case.'

'Are you saying I should take redundancy?'

'The terms aren't bad. A month's salary for every year worked, plus two more.'

'I like working here.'

'That's what I thought you'd say.'

'But you still think I should apply?'

'You need to be aware of the rumblings. Other papers have more or less dropped their books sections. It's not gone unnoticed upstairs. If ours are going to survive, we need to be more dynamic. More news-sensitive. More visited online. Your fuck-up wasn't mentioned at conference. But someone said how dull the pages were.'

'As in lifeless?'

She smiled.

'Let's be honest, since you started taking Fridays off, you've been coasting. You even passed on that Elena Ferrante idea – OK, it wasn't your kind of piece, but you could have made something of it. If you're not committed to the paper, it's hard for me to fight your corner.'

'I am committed. If you'd like me to give up my Rob Pope work, I will.'

'Just put him on the back-burner for a while.'

'No problem. I've nearly finished anyway. What about my holiday – should I cancel it?'

'Don't be daft. No one's going to sack you while you're away.'

'That's how it usually happens.'

'Not on my watch. Before you go, we'll sit down and plan some big features for the autumn. Then when you're back and things settle down, you can finish your executor business.'

'Sure. I appreciate all the days off you've given me.'

She punched me on the arm, to indicate we were friends again.

'How's it going? You've obviously been having an exciting time.'

*

'Leonie's right,' Marie said. 'It's not just your job you nearly lost, it's –'

'Not that again.'

'If I'd been in charge it wouldn't have happened.'

'Nothing happened.'

'It almost did.'

It wasn't as close as she implied. The previous Saturday I'd taken the kids out to the park. On the way back the boys were clamouring to visit the newsagent's, to buy sweets, which meant crossing the road. A single-decker bus had halted fifty yards off. It pulled out as we set off, so we stopped at the bollard halfway. Or rather three of us did – Noah, who'd been holding Jack's hand, let go and made a dash for the far side. The bus was still some way off. But the driver parped his horn and – while pausing at the bollard to let us cross – opened his window and shouted, 'What the fuck you doing, mate?' I shouted in turn when we were safely on the pavement, not at him but at the boys – Jack for not holding tighter and Noah for ignoring the road safety rules we'd been teaching him since the age of two. I refused to buy them sweets. Both were in tears all the way home – Mabel, too, in solidarity. I downplayed the episode to Marie, omitting the shout from the bus driver. It was Jack who gave the game away later, after she heard him muttering *whatthefuckyadoingmate, whatthefuckyadoingmate* in the back garden. Now I was guilty of nearly getting my kids run over *and* of exposing them to profanities. I'd taken my eye off the ball. As with work, so at home.

'Even when you're here, you're somewhere else,' Marie said. 'Do you know whose name you muttered in your sleep last night? Rob's. You're obsessed with him. Jealous, even.'

'The poor man's dead. How can I be jealous?'

'Jealous of the freedom he had when alive. The freedom to write about his affairs. The freedom to *have* affairs.'

Sticking to her principle that Jill should read them first, Marie hadn't seen the poems. But I'd told her what was in the second batch. She wasn't surprised, she said. She'd never trusted Rob. He wasn't an obvious womaniser, but there'd always been something . . .

'Predatory?'

'All men are predators. No, worse than that, something pervy – an old man perving over a younger woman –'

'The poems aren't like that. And Rob wasn't old.'

'– while making out he's some tremendous stud. And in the meantime treating Jill like dirt.'

'OK, I hear you. You never liked Rob.'

'My dislike for him in life is nothing compared to what I feel about him now. To you he's a literary giant, Robert Pope, superhero. To me he's a piece of shit.'

We'd always bickered. Lately the squabbles had escalated to noisy rows. On one occasion Marie threw a Lego brick at me, hardly a lethal weapon, but it caught the tip of my nose and I made quite a show of the pain. We'd been arguing about tidiness. I hated seeing mess when I got home and resented being the one to tidy up. I do everything else round the house, Marie said, stop being so OCD. The issue wasn't untidiness. It wasn't even Rob. It was what his poems were doing to me. The internal mess. The unravelling. I'd become a stranger to every-one – my wife, my kids, my boss. And to myself.

In the past I'd always left work in time to put the kids to bed. But now I lingered over copy that could have waited till morning. And when I got home I drank too much and fell asleep in front of the television. Once in bed, I struggled to get off again. I was used to sleepless nights, but not to me, rather than the kids, being the cause. As for sex, it only seemed to happen when Marie took the lead – another source of friction between us.

'You know there's no one but you, Marie,' I told her. But even that wasn't quite true. The one-off trip to the pub with Emma had turned into a weekly routine. It was innocent enough – no holding hands or smooching – until the evening I talked about Rob and the poems I'd discovered, and read a couple out loud to her. Are you serenading me? she laughed. Just seeking your opinion, I said. *The thrill of the illicit*, she said, I like the alliteration but not what he's saying – surely if you love someone, you want to be open about it, not sneak around. He was married, I said. Maybe he shouldn't have been, she said, he obviously found it a constraint; I know I would too, unless it was open. Do open marriages ever work? I said. They could, she said, we're all polyamorous, aren't we? Are we? I said. There's nothing wrong with having more than one lover, she said, as long as everyone's cool with it. Maybe that works when you're young and single, I said, it's more difficult once you have kids. I wouldn't know, she said. And people are possessive, even without kids, I said. That's stupid, she said, it's dog-in-the-manger, no one owns anyone, the important thing is to be happy and have fun. I looked at her hand lying on the table: purple nail polish, soft blue veins, no rings. For a moment I was tempted to take it. Then the hand moved to her glass. God, she said, knocking her wine back, I hope you didn't think I . . . God no, I said, equally embarrassed, I hope you didn't think *I* . . . Look at the time, she said. You're right, I said, better be off.

We were colleagues. Just talking, nothing more. But there'd been that moment. And there was another at the Tube, a hug that went on longer than etiquette required. I felt euphoric. The walk home might have sobered me, but it didn't. The night was silky blue beyond the streetlamps. A yellow moon rested on the skyline. I had a new person in my life and the universe seemed to expand a little.

The lights were off downstairs. Marie must be asleep: good. I poured myself a glass of water.

'Where the fuck have you been?' she said, as I crept into the bedroom.

'Having a drink after work.'

She turned the bedside light on and stared at me from the pillow. 'It's gone midnight. You didn't say you were going to be late. Didn't you get my texts?'

'Sorry, my phone's flat. Why, what's happened?'

'Nothing. It's what's happening to you. Pissed again and out late again. While I'm stuck here on my own. Don't tell me everyone else was there till closing time. I bet the ones with kids and partners went home hours ago. Who were you with?'

'No one you know.'

'Try me.'

'There's this new person on Arts —'

'Person?'

'Girl. Woman. Emma. She wanted my advice.'

'And it took you till midnight to give it?'

'It's why we went for a drink the first time.'

'You mean it's been several times?' I nodded. 'I see. Is she single?' I nodded again. 'And young, no doubt. A married man in his forties out with a young single woman — how's it look to your colleagues?'

'No one has seen us.'

'Ah, you go somewhere discreet. This gets worse and worse.'

'Nothing's happened. I've not even kissed her.'

'If it's so innocent, why didn't you tell me about her before?'

'Normally I would have but —'

'You've been under stress, you're having a midlife crisis, it's the pressure of working on Rob's poems — bullshit, you're not a child, Matt, take responsibility for once.'

She was sitting bolt upright by now, eyes blazing, more animated than I'd seen her in ages. I began to unbutton my shirt.

'Don't think you're joining me in bed,' she said. 'You can sleep downstairs on the sofa. There's a duvet and two pillows in the airing cupboard.'

'Come on, Marie, there's no need for this.'

'Go. I don't want you here.'

'You're enjoying this, aren't you?'

'Oh, yeah, sure. I've just discovered that my husband and the father of my kids has been sneaking around with another woman. If you were me, would you find that fun? Just fuck off downstairs. We'll talk about this tomorrow. I'll take the day off work. You can do the same.'

'Leonie needs me there . . .'

'You'll phone her first thing and say you're ill. I'm the priority here, Matt. Not your job, not Leonie, not your girlfriend.'

'She's not my –'

'Just go.'

Downstairs, on the sofa, my earlier euphoria was slow to wear off. I get defensive when criticised. And half pissed, as I was, Marie's criticisms seemed petty to me. I thought of Emma: 'We're all polyamorous, aren't we?' And I thought of Rob: 'Why can't a man love two women at once?' If I wasn't unfaithful to her – not physically – surely Marie couldn't begrudge me the odd evening out. It wasn't as if I planned to leave her. I still felt hard done by, even after hearing sobs from upstairs; I'd never known Marie to cry, but it didn't sound like one of the children. At some point I must have dropped off. By dawn, with my back hurting and a hangover kicking in, my self-righteousness had receded. I barely knew Emma; if I'd reached for her hand in the pub or tried to kiss her outside the Tube, she'd probably have batted me away. I felt foolish – all the more so when Jack appeared.

'Why are you sleeping on the sofa, Daddy?'

'I got home late and didn't want to wake Mummy.'

Did he believe me? Maybe. In front of the children, Marie pretended nothing had happened. But once the boys were at school, and Mabel with the childminder, she resumed her attack. 'That's your word for it,' she said. 'What I'm actually doing is finding out if we've a future.'

I'd like to claim that we resolved things there and then. I did apologise, repeatedly. But I was slow to see the damage I'd done. The fear that Marie might not love me any more – as she withdrew, went cold, turned her back on me in bed – was terrifying. If we broke up, she'd be fine without me. Whereas I'd be lost. 'You fucking fool,' I mouthed to myself in the bathroom mirror one night. I scowled at what I saw: a pale, panicky, craven, ugly, prematurely balding, middle-aged non-entity. 'What kind of idiot risks losing his wife in pursuit of a young woman (be honest, you did pursue her) who has no real interest in you anyway? You deserve everything you get.'

What I got was a blow to the face. Or rather, what my reflection got was a blow to the face and what I got, as the mirror shattered, was four bruised knuckles and a bleeding hand. I didn't need stitches. And the mirror was easy to replace. But the violence was a turning point of sorts. Not that Marie was impressed by what she called my amateur dramatics. But she could see my guilt and distress were genuine. And as I regaled her with promises to get back on track – to concentrate on her, the children, the job that paid the bills – she softened a little. We'll see how things go on holiday, she said.

As for Rob, I resolved to be more pragmatic: to wrap up my duties in the autumn, sell the archive and be free of any further hassle. No more obsessing about the poems: that was my promise to myself. And when an email came from Aaron Fortune I passed the test. He was planning to come over to

Britain next year, he said: would the papers be in order for him to look at by then? A month before I'd have been obstructive: No way, man, keep your nose out and stop badgering me, the poems are my property not yours. Now I simply ignored him. The reply remained in the drafts file in my head – UNSENT.

*

People are snooty about Lanzarote – the middle classes, that is. But with its hundred-odd volcanoes, and post-apocalyptic landscape of whorly black lava fields, it's a place worth seeing – even if that summer, with three small children, I saw little beyond our hotel. The package was half-board, which left a gap around lunchtime, one we filled with fruit, cheese and bread rolls (smuggled out at breakfast), crisps and lemonade (bought at the nearby supermarket) and ice creams (from the snack bar on the beach). Slim bodies lay toasting by the pool. I'd have lain there too, but to bag a sunbed you had to be up at dawn. I spent my time teaching Jack to swim. He was happy floating on his back, but would panic – and make a drama of the panic – when his head went under. For a week he stuck to his aids (armbands, float, noodle). You're doing great, I said, let's see if you can manage without them. But he lost his nerve when he tried – swallowed a mouthful, wailed, screamed, accused me of trying to drown him, climbed out and sulked under a blue towel. You're being over-protective, Marie told me, your anxiety is feeding his. Go on then, I said, *you* try, and she did. With me beside him, he'd foundered. With her at a tactful distance, he swam to the far side of the pool.

'Ironic, isn't it?' I said, in bed that night.

'What?'

'You calling me over-protective. When all I've heard from you lately is that I'm not protective enough.'

179

'Of the kids?'

'And Jill.'

'Jesus Christ,' she said, once she twigged, 'you're meant to be having a break. Yes, I think you should care more about Jill's feelings and less about Rob's fucking poems. But we're on holiday. Forget all that.'

And I did try to forget. Swam in the pool umpteen times a day. Jogged each morning. Played table tennis and snakes and ladders with the boys. Made love to Marie (who, by the end of two weeks, seemed ready to forgive me). Still Rob kept intruding. One afternoon I sat with Mabel on a grassy area away from the pool, where if she fell (her walking was still unsteady) she wouldn't scrape her hands and knees. I'd brought the latest Ed McKeane to read, hoping not to like it. Mabel wrested it from me, gnawing the cover and tearing the pages before tossing it away. I was heartened by her critical discrimination. Rob had always said that women were more sensitive readers than men ('It's from books they learn their empathy') and Mabel proved the case.

I thought of Rob again when Jack, up late one evening, turned poetic while sitting on the toilet. When I dream, he said, I'm not there, it's not me, it's not even my life.

And then there was Noah, analysing films he'd seen (*The Jungle Book, The Lion King*) in terms of how mean or kind the characters were. Some baddies were capable of good, he decided. A child of four wrestling with ethics – as I would have to if and when it came to publishing the poems.

*

My mother didn't join us in Lanzarote. She thought it would be too hot. And though I knew it wouldn't, compared to Majorca, I didn't dissuade her. I needed a break. With her there, I wouldn't have had one.

Once home, restored, I was consumed with guilt and arranged to see her the following weekend. The five-hour round trip was boring for the kids, but we aimed to do it every couple of months. Marie's parents were harder to get to, and she usually visited them on her own, taking a flight from London City to Belfast. I think she missed them more than she liked to admit, which made her extra diligent in ensuring I saw plenty of Mum. It helped that the two of them liked each other. My mother's grandfather had come from Ireland, which predisposed her to Marie, even though Marie had barely visited the Republic and had been steadily losing her Belfast accent.

Conditions were perfect: bright skies, low sun behind us, an early start. Leaving the house, I showed the boys a beautiful spider's web strung between our wheelie bins, like a lace doily hanging out to dry. Then, at the end of our street, Jack spotted a woman in a black plastic mac with white dots walking a Dalmatian, and shouted 'Snap!' and for different reasons we all laughed: Marie and I at the absurdity of people who dressed their dogs to look like them or vice versa; the boys to soften us up and put us in a good mood, so they could renew their campaign to have a new pet (dog, cat, gerbil, another hamster, any would do); Mabel, because the rest of us were laughing and, as she'd recently discovered, laughter was something you could share, unlike her brothers' toys, which, despite our recriminations, they'd snatch from her if she touched them, because – they said – a girl couldn't be trusted not to break them, a claim which Marie fiercely disputed while reminding them that they, too, had smashed up toys when they were her age and that gender had nothing to do with it. The boys had been bemused by the length and vigour of her lecture. But she was right, of course. She always is.

From the A406 we took the M11, then the A14. Mabel was asleep by then, and the boys, with headphones on, were staring at their seat-back DVD screens, so for once Marie and I could talk. She was wondering about doing an extra day at the clinic, now Mabel was older, and talked about her plans for the autumn. Then she asked about mine and, though Rob was meant to be taboo, I couldn't avoid him: Jill had been on the phone, wondering when I'd be visiting again, and Louis had been pushing to publish the poems I'd found, ideally on Leonie's pages.

'I hate the position Rob's put you in,' Marie said. 'It shouldn't be you having to decide whether to publish.'

'There's no decision involved. It's stipulated in his will. The only issue is when and where.'

'You'll regret it. When the shit hits the fan, you'll be the fan.'

'Did Mummy say a rude word?' Jack said, removing his headphones.

'Big ears. Go back to your DVD.'

A field of solar panels flashed by, their tablets tilted upwards in sun worship. I prefer fields with crops: wheat, barley, even oilseed rape. But the panels had a strange beauty, each with its hieroglyphic markings and all facing the same way, like an OCD version of Stonehenge.

'There's one consolation' Marie said. 'However bad it will be for Jill to read the poems, it'd be worse if she and Rob had children. Imagine ours discovering you had another life. Their dad becoming this new person: Dad the stranger, Dad the imposter, Dad the cheat. If Rob and Jill had had kids, you'd have to lock the poems away for another fifty or sixty years. At least with Jill it'll only be twenty or thirty.'

'I'm not going to lock them away.'

'You ought to – you'd be doing right by the living instead of indulging the dead.'

After the A14, the rest of the journey was by B-roads. The untrimmed hedges made some of them single-track. Occasional scarecrows hung about the fields, like rustic parodies of the crucifixion. My parents had moved to the village a couple of years before they retired, my dad from teaching, my mum from thirty years as a librarian. We'd lived in Norwich throughout my childhood, but they liked the idea of village life and for a time they'd been happy, till my father got depressed, then ill. He was in his late seventies by then; 'a good innings' he said when I visited him after the diagnosis of lung cancer, which he'd insisted on being told, and accepted with surprising calm, despite the injustice (he'd never smoked) and the inevitable outcome – an earlier than expected dismissal from life and my mother left alone at the crease. At first, she'd coped well with widowhood, filling her days with bridge, flower arranging and cups of tea at the day centre, but then she'd fallen and broken her hip, after which her mobility wasn't the same. To her credit, she never grumbled. There were worse things than needing a stick to get around, and being unable to drive and having carers come in twice a day.

Her house was up a gravel drive. I tooted the horn before I parked, to give her time to get to the door, then rang the bell in case she hadn't heard. Jack and Noah milled about the front step, pushing each other to be first in line, while Marie held Mabel, who was crying because she'd just woken. 'See what you can count to before Granny answers,' I told the boys, and they'd reached fifty-three before we heard the familiar sounds from inside: a voice saying 'Just a minute', the rattle of a chain, a key turning in a lock. Then the door swung back to reveal her, stick in hand, ghost-haired, shorter by a foot than I remembered. The boys ran forwards to be hugged – 'Careful!' – then scooted past her to the kitchen, where they knew she'd have put out orange juice and biscuits, while we stood greeting her in the hall.

'How've you been, Mum?'

'All right.'

'Still taking the pills for your angina?'

'Don't fuss.'

'Carers turning up on time?'

'Glenys's car broke down the other day. They had to send a new girl. Very young she was. With piercings.'

'How's the bridge?'

'I haven't played this week. Aren't you a sweetie?'

The last was said to Mabel, who Marie had pushed forward for a kiss. She shied away from it, squirming in Marie's arms and crying with new vigour, which amused rather than upset my mum, whose policy with grandchildren is to spoil them: have another drink, try one of these chocolates, gosh, how clever/kind/polite/grown up/good-looking you are. 'Naughty' wasn't a word in her vocabulary. When they behaved badly, she pretended to ignore it. Yet she'd been the sterner parent when I was a child.

From the kitchen – Mum with her stick, Marie carrying Mabel, me bearing a tray with three coffees – we moved into the living room, where the boys had already unearthed the box Mum kept for their visits. It was full of board games I remembered from childhood, plus stuff she'd picked up since at fetes and car boot sales: jigsaw puzzles, teddy bears, Sylvanian Families, plastic farm animals. It was always the Lego the boys went to first: Noah struggled with the smaller pieces, but Jack was adept. While Mum gossiped about her neighbours, none of whom I knew, Marie sat breastfeeding Mabel, a process she – Marie – seemed embarrassed by, because of the presence of my mother, who hadn't breastfed me and who'd once expressed surprise when Marie was *still* breastfeeding Jack at ten months. At eighteen months, Mabel was now well on to solids but not fully weaned. Dummies couldn't compete; only breasts pacified her. The devil would be given a nipple and morph into an angel. The magic worked even in front of my mother. Once sated, Mabel got down on the floor with her brothers.

I loved my mum, but to be honest these trips bored me silly: the sitting around, the same-as-last-time dialogue, the wildness of the boys as their sugar levels rose and they rushed about, breaking ornaments or spilling drinks on the blue oval Chinese rug. Mum didn't have the Internet and the village was in a poor reception area, so I couldn't even pick up emails – NO SERVICE my iPhone said when I slipped out to try (furtively, knowing Marie would think it rude). She coped much better than I did, but looked relieved when it was time to go out for lunch. We'd thought of bringing our own (Mum was no longer capable of making it), but it was good to escape the house for a while: good for us but also for Mum, who liked to visit places while she could, knowing what lay ahead for her unless a sudden illness nipped in first: after the walking stick, the Zimmer frame; after the Zimmer frame, the wheelchair; after the wheelchair, the hoist; after the hoist, bedsores, pneumonia and oblivion.

'OK, Mum?' I said, settling her in the front seat, while Marie sat between the boys with Mabel in her arms (four in the back was illegal, but the roads were empty and everyone was strapped in). I drove to The Star & Garter, in the next village, rather than The Bull, in Mum's, hoping the food might be better. I was able to park right outside – even ground, no slippery patches on the tarmac, and only one step to climb. But the 'family room' beyond the bar was gloomy, and the food, when it came, a disappointment: my fish pie was all potato, the boys' burgers were overcooked ('Why can't we go to McDonald's?'), and the only highchair in the place had a crack across the tray, which Marie thought so unhygienic that she sat Mabel in her lap, a position Mabel enjoyed until she lunged forward and banged her head on the corner of the table. I felt like crying, too. We all did. Except Mum, who said her tuna salad tasted delicious, even though she left half of it uneaten.

She wanted dessert, nevertheless, and so did the boys, and with the time it took for her tiramisu to come and their vanilla ice creams and Marie's Earl Grey, and visits to the Gents and Ladies, and the bill to pay, and everyone to be crammed in the car, it was four before we got back to Mum's. I suggested we sat outside, by the pond, and fetched the white plastic chairs and floral cushions from the toolshed. While the boys kicked a football, and Marie and Mum inspected the flower-beds to see what new plants had been put in by the gardener (a widowed ex-policeman called Harold who charged an implausi- bly-low-by-London-standards £10 an hour), I walked Mabel on my shoes across the grass, her giggles as we shuffled forward competing with the shouts of her brothers and the murmurs of the two women and (loudest of all) the cawing of the rooks in the trees down the end of Mum's drive, and yet it felt peaceful, far more so than Wood Green, and for half an hour, before we finally sat in the plastic chairs, and tea, juice and chocolate digestives were served, visiting my mum seemed not just a good thing to do, a duty of care and filial obligation, but a source of happiness, for us as well as her, to the extent that the moment of departure, which I warded off till almost six and tried to soften by reassuring Mum (truthfully) that we'd be back again soon, felt so infinitely sad that there were tears in my eyes as we waved goodbye and Marie (her turn at the wheel) manoeuvred us gently away down the drive and on to the darkening lane.

13

It was October before I made it back to Jill's. My seventh
visit. Or was it the eighth? I'd lost track. The house looked
the same as it always had, and so did Jill. But my missionary
fervour had gone. The job at the paper was my priority now
and things had been going well there. The special feature on
flash fiction I'd commissioned for the Review (the first idea
I'd come up with in months) had had a big online response.
I'd also written a couple of book reviews. As for Emma, we
exchanged smiles when we passed each other, but there were
no more clandestine trips to the pub. I felt myself again.
Whatever interest I still had in the archive was business-like,
not obsessive. By the end of the day, if I kept going, the
plastic crates would be fully itemised. I would give the unpublished poems to Jill and let a decent interval elapse while she
absorbed the contents.

She waved me through and upstairs. Low sun was frazzling
the room. I pulled the blinds down and retrieved the poems
from their hiding place. All were in order, as I left them. Then
I opened the last crate, which I'd rushed through once before,
but set about double-checking, just in case. Notebooks, folders,
cancelled drafts: it was the usual dull fare. No joy – which
to me *was* joy: no more discoveries to complicate my work.
I imagined Rob whispering in my ear: 'Feeling pleased with

yourself, are you?' 'And why not?' I replied. 'I've done all you asked.' 'Really?' he came back. 'The archive's not been sold, the poems haven't been published, people will soon forget I ever existed.' 'I'm getting there,' I said. 'I'd have been quicker if you'd made things easier for me, instead of hiding stuff away.' 'I know you like a challenge.' 'Up to a point. I can think of better ways to spend my time than sifting through the papers of a corpse.' Saying 'corpse' was a mistake. Any reference to him being dead made him angry. But it had been a while since we talked and the word slipped out. 'I'd be less of a corpse if you did your work properly,' he said. 'It was always all about you, wasn't it, Matt? You selfish git. I should never have appointed you.' Now I was the angry one: '*Me*, selfish? You forget there's a world out there, with other people in it. *Living* people,' I said. 'I'm not here to defend myself,' he said. 'You're not here at all,' I said. 'Then why are you talking to me?' he said. 'I wish I weren't,' I said. '*I* wish you weren't,' he said, 'your conversation skills are pathetic.'

I laughed. We were winding each other up. It was just like old times.

I was kneeling on the floor as we spoke, with a printout from a natural history website in my hand. The printout had a photo of a hoopoe, with a description of its plumage, breeding patterns and habitat. I remembered Rob's childhood scrap-book, the one I'd looked at on my first visit, and how for a time he'd pasted photos of birds in it, a phase he'd quickly outgrown. As far as I knew, no poem of his referred to a hoopoe. But perhaps he'd planned one and the website print-out was part of his research. You old hypocrite, I thought, smiling at the memory of him dismissing the Internet as 'a passing fad, like fax machines'. For all his fogeyism, he knew his way around the web. Any reviews he did for us came as attachments. And then there were his personal emails, albeit few in number and stiff in tone (he couldn't bring himself to begin them 'Hi') . . .

I stood up. Christ, I should have thought of it months ago. Yes, Hadingfield must have its internet cafés, like everywhere else. But hadn't Rob told me that he never left the house all day apart from a walk to buy a paper? And hadn't Jill confirmed it (albeit with a Labrador and second walk added in)? In which case, he must have used a computer at home. On which there might be stuff I ought to see.

When I steeled myself to ask Jill, she seemed surprised I hadn't asked before.

'Didn't I say? The laptop's in the spare bedroom. If I bring work home, that's where I do it from.'

'You shared a laptop?'

'No, I have a desktop. Sorry, I should have given you a tour of the house when you first came.'

'So the laptop is Rob's?'

'Yes.'

'But he kept it in the spare bedroom?'

'I took it in there after he died, to close his email account. The provider talked me through what I needed to do. They've set procedures when someone dies.'

His emails might have been worth preserving, but never mind. Poems were my only concern.

'I'm curious what he left on the laptop,' I said.

'I doubt there'll be poems. He handwrote them first, then typed them out on his Olivetti. But have a look if you like.'

'Thanks, that'd be good.'

'Next time you come. You're obviously busy with other stuff today.'

'Today's fine. I'm pretty much done otherwise.'

'The laptop won't be charged up.'

She was stalling again, to no purpose. Self-defeatingly, even, since the longer it took me to finish, the more time I'd have to spend at the house. Perhaps she'd begun to *like* me coming. But her manner didn't suggest so. More likely, she wanted to look at the laptop before I did, to check if there was anything private there (diaries, letters, jottings) and then delete it – that's if she hadn't deleted it already. I wished I'd known about the laptop earlier. Her antennae were up. The trust we'd built before the summer had evaporated.

I idled away the next hour and refused her lunchtime sandwiches, with the excuse that I felt unwell and was thinking of leaving early. She hovered by the desk while I pretended to be busy. What about the unpublished poems? she asked. Once I'd looked at the laptop, I'd have completed my searches, I said, and she could have them. She turned on her heel and left the room. So be it. If I had to wait till next time, she could wait, too. I wasn't going to give in.

She reappeared carrying the laptop. It was fully charged, she said: would I like to look at it before I left?

*

I logged on (no password required). It was a MacBook, an older model than the one I had at home, but otherwise much the same. The big difference was the screen: mine was cluttered with folders; Rob's had only four: REVIEWS, BUSINESS, LETTERS and KILTER, the last an abbreviation of the title of his last collection, *Out of Kilter* (he'd come up with the title after spending a fortnight in St Keverne, in Cornwall, in whose parish there'd once been a hamlet called Kilter). As I scanned the folders, any excitement soon wore off. All the stuff was stuff I'd seen before, in his filing cabinet and desk.

I clicked on the wastepaper basket in the bottom corner of the screen, to see what he – or Jill perhaps – had deleted. It was empty. I clicked on Safari and entered Gmail, hoping Rob's account might come up automatically, as my Gmail account does, but nothing happened – Jill's attempt to close it had obviously worked. There was nothing in Dropbox or Downloads. A hopeless quest, I decided.

Before handing back the laptop to Jill, I clicked on REVIEWS again and – more from nostalgia than anything else – opened a document called APPEAL: it was the last review he had written for us, and began with a quote from a Kipling poem of that title:

> And for the little, little span
> The dead are borne in mind,
> Seek not to question other than
> The books I leave behind.

Rob had used the piece to sound off against literary biography. It was long, two thousand words or so, and we'd cut it, to his annoyance. I read through it again to remind myself what had been there before we did. According to the page count at the bottom of the screen, the document ran to twenty-five pages. That couldn't be right: we hadn't cut it *that* heavily. I scrolled ahead. The review ended on page 4. At the top of page 5 I read UNP3.

Fuck – a large batch of new poems! I started reading through and paused on one called 'Predatory', a word that had come up during an argument with Marie. 'In bed they could be anyone,' I read, then became conscious of Jill, standing by my shoulder.

Even by her ghostlike standards, it was quite an achievement to materialise so suddenly.

'Looks like you've found something,' she said.

'Yes.'

'More love poems?'

'Not sure yet.'

'The printer's in the spare bedroom. If you print them out, I can read them with the others.'

'Right. Yes.'

If she wasn't actually standing with her hands on her hips, that's how it felt.

'Unless you're rushing and want to leave it to me to print them.'

'That's fine. I'll do it now.'

She took me along the corridor. The spare bedroom couldn't have been sparer – an implausibly narrow single bed, a wooden chair, a desk with a phone, computer and printer, and a shelf full of office folders. She showed me how the printer worked and hovered nearby. Then her mobile phone went off. She stepped outside to take the call.

In her absence, I printed out two sets. Knowing how she felt about anything leaving the house, I considered hiding the second set. But these were printouts, not original manuscripts. And I was tired of playing games.

'All done?' she said, returning.

'Yep. This lot's for you.'

'How many more poems did you find?'

'Quite a few.'

'You don't seem very excited.'

'I've not read most of them yet. I've made copies to take away. The handwritten poems I found before are in a folder on

Rob's desk. I've taken photos of them on my iPad. So we'll both have a complete set to read.'

'As long as the originals stay here.'

'I should warn you,' I said, like a TV news presenter prefacing some violent footage, 'you might find some of them upsetting.'

'Why?'

The innocence of the question, her earnest look, the risk that anything I said would make it worse – it was all too much. I bottled it.

'They'll make you revisit the past. And I know how much you miss him.'

She shrugged. 'Maybe they'll console me. When will you be back again?'

'I'm not sure. Apart from finding a buyer for the archive, I've done all I can here.'

'But we'll need to discuss what to do about the poems.'

What's to discuss? I resisted saying. Louis and I are Rob's executors, not you.

'I'm pretty busy at work,' I said.

'Come on a weekend,' she said. 'Bring Marie and the kids. Now you've finished, things will be more relaxed.'

In the hall downstairs, for the first time ever, she kissed me on the cheek: now my occupation of Rob's room was over, she could afford to be affectionate.

'When you began I wondered how serious you were – whether you'd just cut and run. But you've worked really hard, Matt. And I'm grateful. I know Robbie would be grateful, too.'

'All I want is to respect his wishes.'

'Don't worry about the poems upsetting me. I know what Robbie was like. I'm sure it'll be fine.'

'That's good to hear,' I said, wondering once again if I'd underestimated her.

*

Siesta

May my siestas often turn out that way! (1.5)

An afternoon in the old colony, during monsoon season.
The roads were under water, but the rickshaw-man surfed through.
We sat in the kitchen, gossiping over tea and biscotti,
while rain barrelled down beyond the blinds. The light was
   dusk-light,
less for songbirds than for bats, but with a glow through the slats
that printed lines across our faces, black on white, white on black.

I'd come with a queasy stomach and a migraine,
so she suggested I lie down in her bedroom. It felt cool in there,
on the divan, under the rotor of the ceiling fan,
while kids played in the street and rain rat-tat-tatted on the glass.

At some point she came through and asked was I feeling better
and did I mind if she siesta'd too? She lay on her side behind me,
her hand on my hip, her breathing deep and steady, as if she'd
   dropped off,
until the hand moved down a bit – all this and what followed
without a word spoken, just the chop-chop of the fan,
the swish of her underthings, and the whap-whap of naked flesh.

Sometimes I find the memory hard to credit, as if I'd stolen it
from a porn mag, but then the shutters come back and the slats
across her body and the rain rat-tat-tatting on the glass.

Predatory

i
For the hunter, pursuit is all . . . (2.9a)

'When will I see you again?'
they'd ask, some minutes after.

But for me the thrill had gone.
All I wanted was to be alone,
savouring our time together,
which – as I tried to explain
(though they didn't seem to hear) –
was impossible with them there.

ii

. . . when I'm sick of the whole business,
some kink in my wretched nature drives me back (2.9b)

Then the reverie would fade
and I'd need to share my solitude.
You're gorgeous, I'd say,
and mean it, but in bed
they could be anyone
and once it was done
I'd be out of there, pronto.
Bastard, they'd go,
but aren't we all on a journey
to discover ourselves,
and never mind
the guff about finding
our other halves.

Private v Public

There appeared before me Elegy . . . Behind her stalked barnstorming
Tragedy (3.1)

It's a man's favourite dream or worst nightmare,
Two women fighting over him in public.
There I was in Caffè Nero, with Eleanor,
Going over the draft of a new poem,
When in off Oxford Street walked Tania,
Both beautiful in their own way –
Eleanor blue-eyed, high-cheekboned, short-haired,
Her voice rising at the end of sentences,
Tania tall and intense with an Amnesty badge
Pinned to her blouse and black leather boots –

Each, till then, unaware of the other's existence.
I was torn between confessing and running away,
When Tania snatched the poem from my hands
And over the hiss of the espresso machine
Read it aloud in a mocking voice.
'Call this love poetry?' she said, reaching the end.
'I daresay *she* thinks it is. Huh, I've read
Better verses printed on Valentine's cards.
Are your horizons no wider than a double bed?
Don't you read the news? 500 shot dead in Cairo.
Famine in Somalia. The polar icecaps melting.
Poverty and homelessness like never before.
You should be writing about things that matter
Not the sex you hope to get by flattering
The tits off some slag you met five minutes since.
Here's your key back. You're welcome to him, love.'
She turned – then Eleanor spoke. 'Pompous bitch.
Because he's stopped writing *you* love poems,
You think you can rubbish the whole genre.
Catullus? Dante? Petrarch? Shakespeare?
You can't call their poems Valentine's slush.
True, *his* are no good. That's why I'm here –
As his tutor, trying to help him improve.
Did he tell you he signed up for mentoring?
Nah – no more than he told me about you:
According to his poems, he's been living
Like a monk while waiting for the woman
Of his dreams to come along and now she has,
A woman with blue eyes who writes poetry,
Only he's too shy to tell her what he feels . . .
Well, I'm not so daft as to fall for *that* line,
And anyway I'm married with two kids.
Slag, did you say? You owe me an apology.'
Tania stood there speechless, eyes as sharp
As the pin holding her Amnesty badge,
While Eleanor clenched her fists ready for more.
'Ladies, ladies,' I said, like a UN delegate
Urging warring factions to call a ceasefire,

'Can't we talk about this calmly over coffee?'
It seemed my diplomacy had worked,
Because Tania muttered 'Sorry' and sat down,
And Eleanor, touching her arm, said 'Sorry' too.
While I stood at the counter waiting for our order,
I fantasised about them becoming friends
And the threesome we'd have that night,
But while the froth rose in the metal jug
They somehow slipped past me into the street
And were lost among crowds of shoppers
Like wood nymphs disappearing between trees.

Friends

Venus, goddess, please blow my innocent perjury out to sea (2.8)

I can't help loving your friends. Sally, Brigitte,
Daphne, Cindy – not all at once, but each has been to bed
With me. If you knew, you'd call me indiscriminate.
But would you want me to sleep with someone you hate?
In sticking to your mates I'm paying tribute
To your good taste. Not once have I heard them deprecate
Your looks or bitch about your latest coat.
They know their place, too – don't try to compete
With you in my affections or set out
To see us divorced. If you're ever in doubt
How loyal and devoted they are, forget it.
No truer friends exist throughout the planet.

Fruit

Why cheat the laden vine when grapes are ripening . . .? (2.14)

She called one day, asking to meet
Outside her appointed time.
'I've some news,' she said. 'Nothing terrible,
Just something you should know.'

We met near a park in Wandsworth –
her car and mine in adjoining spaces –

and sat on the grassy slope
as the sun fell into Barnes.

Nothing terrible? It was the worst.
I'd been so careful
To keep a clean sheet. Now this.
What could have gone wrong?

I'd sometimes felt her coil scratching,
Like a paperclip or loose wire,
But perhaps she'd hoiked it out.
We were growing fruit

And she wanted me to rejoice,
To tell her I loved her
And would be with her always,
Not to look (as I must have) scared.

I took her hand and squeezed it.
She had a pink gingham dress
And a rash on her legs
From the spiky summer grass.

'You don't want it, do you?' she said.
'It's a shock, that's all.'
'How would you feel if I went ahead?'
'I don't know,' I said.

A mosquito was circling her ankle
And I slapped it dead.
'Ouch.' 'I was trying to help.'
'You're no help at all,' she said.

It was dark by the time we parted,
Agreeing to think things over,
Our cars turning away from each other
At the bottom of a hill.

She phoned two days later.
'I've made a date at the clinic.
I don't want you with me.
I just need a cheque.'

Blood money, she called it
The night of the weepy call
And the threatened leap
From Vauxhall Bridge.

Later she moved away
But I still get Christmas cards
With baby Jesus haloed on the front
And her name in red pen inside.

Elegiac

Though flint itself will perish, poetry lives (1.15)

These women I've written about – were they just bodies to me?
Had I no interest in their thoughts and feelings? Didn't I love
    them?
Of course, while I was with them. But then I went back to my life,
my room, my writing (my writing about them!) and I loved that
    more.
If I'd been free to be with them, they'd not have loved me as much.
If I'd loved them more, I wouldn't have been free to write.
It wasn't a deal we shook hands on, but for a time it suited us

and afterwards there were no hard feelings: they found a new man,
and I had my writing, not erotic now but elegiac.

Yes, I loved those women. But remembering, I love them more.

14

I sat up late that night reading the poems – not just the latest batch, but the handwritten ones from earlier. The new ones were numbered: 1.3, 2.11, 3.4 and so on. A few of the previous ones had numbers too, but until now I'd paid them no attention. The numbers seemed random; the poems didn't come in order. Had Rob been working on a sequence, but failed to bring it to completion? The numbers suggested he must have had a structure in mind, arranged in three parts. But there was no obvious narrative or through-line. Typical of a novelist to look for one, I could imagine him chiding me, but the numbers invited it. These weren't fragments – they progressed, or promised to. Did he expect me to find the right arrangement? His will left minimal instructions. Even those were contradictory.

Some of the poems had epigraphs, too. I've only a rudimentary knowledge of English poetry and didn't recognise them. Were they from the same author? Or by several different authors? Some were so fragmentary that it seemed pointless to include them. Very few were *bons mots*. Shouldn't epigraphs be epigrammatic? Obviously Rob didn't think so.

Since his death, I'd had to assimilate a series of surprises and accept how little I knew him. But nothing had prepared me for this. If they weren't made up, what did the poems say about him? That he'd had affairs with numerous women, including

Jill's friends. That he'd got one of his lovers pregnant. That he regarded intimacy as a threat and stability as a bore. That sex formed a depressing cycle in his life – pursuit/conquest/disillusion/solitude/pursuit. That he was happier recalling affairs in words, than having them in the flesh. That he was liar, roué, hypocrite and solipsist – a piece of shit, as Marie put it.

At one of our lunches he'd speculated whether he'd have been a greater poet if he'd *lived more boldly*. Were the poems an attempt to show he had? Or proof of cowardice – of a secret life he hadn't had the courage to disclose? In later years he had felt sidelined by a younger generation of poets, whom he didn't rate (and probably hadn't read). Were these poems his attempt to clamber back into the limelight? I remembered him gloomily quoting Robert Frost at one of our lunches: 'No memory of having starred/Atones for later disregard.' Perhaps he'd have published the poems had he lived longer. But it didn't look that way: he'd scattered and secreted them for me to come across after his death. A lazier executor might have missed them. But he knew me well enough to know I'd make an effort. I might have worked faster, but I'd done as he asked. Matt the disciple. Matt the poodle. His trusted sidekick and pet.

'Shockingly belated' was how he'd once described his first sexual experiences, in his early twenties. Was that why the poems were so priapic, because he'd never got over his youthful excitement at getting laid? The poems he'd written at the time had been terrible, he said, but perhaps he returned to them many years later. They didn't read like the experiences of a young man, but they might have begun that way. Or could the poems be about relationships he'd had in the States, not just with Corinne (whom he loved) but with other women? Then again, if the 'you' he described betraying was Jill, the infidelities must date from later, and that seemed more likely. Whether Jill or a lover, the 'you' in the earlier poems had been the object of tenderness. The tone here was different: cold, cynical, rapacious. The women weren't addressed but discarded – a series of shes, some named, others not, with whom he'd had it off.

Like it or not, like *them* or not, we now had enough poems for a collection. Knowing the stir they'd create, Louis would want to push ahead at once. Jill might object, but she hadn't the power to stop us and if she understood what was at stake – the posthumous discovery of new work by a leading poet – she might give the book her blessing, whatever her private doubts. There was that thing she'd said in the hallway, too: that I needn't worry, she knew what Rob was like. I was feeling optimistic. Marie would have warned me not to be. But I hadn't yet shown her the latest poems, nor emailed them to Louis. For now I was keeping them to myself.

*

When I remember the following weekend I think of things unrelated to my reason for remembering it.

I remember the mist that came and went, shutting us in, then seeming to clear – the white cotton turning a satin blue – then flooding back again. The sun was a silver coin behind a layer of tracing paper.

I remember an aeroplane crashed somewhere, killing all passengers and crew, and people speculating that it had been shot down by Islamic State militants.

I remember a boat full of refugees capsizing off the island of Samos, and bodies washing up.

I remember a post-match press interview with José Mourinho, whose Chelsea team were suffering a run of defeats, and how he refused to answer questions, just kept saying, 'I have nothing, nothing to say.'

I remember we drove in early to the Royal Academy, knowing there was no congestion charge on a Sunday and that we could park for free nearby. Marie and I were both keen to see the Ai Weiwei exhibition, which, because it consisted of large constructions and installations, we thought the boys might find more interesting than paintings – and they did, though their real fascination was with the photos of Ai Weiwei himself, whose beard and twinkly eyes reminded them of a Chinese wizard in one of their books, despite the fact that there were also images of him in handcuffs being interrogated by angry policemen and soldiers.

I remember coming away with a sense of dismay that the oppressive China depicted by Ai Weiwei was the same China with whom our government was busy negotiating a major trade agreement.

I remember a politely spoken, lightly bearded man in his fifties ringing our doorbell to ask about the chair sitting on the pavement, a large, handsome wingback fireside armchair that had come from my mother and which we were fond of but had no room for in the house and (as I explained to the man) had left out the night before in the hope that someone would take it away, as had happened with previous items such as a shower screen and fire-grate. The man said he'd recently taken up upholstery and thought the chair, once worked on, would sit well in his living room. Do please have it, I said, and thanked him for asking permission (which no one had on the previous occasions) and wished him well.

I remember going to the supermarket – Waitrose for once, not Lidl – and buying fresh pesto, and trying it out on the boys, with rigatoni and parmesan, a partial success in that they ate most of their pasta, a partial failure in that they said they preferred spag bol.

I remember Noah resisting being put to bed, which was unusual for him and which I attributed to three possible sources: the Ai Weiwei show, the unfamiliar pasta or the upset in the back garden, as dusk fell, when we played Donkey with the tennis ball and he was the first to be out (with me on Donk and Jack on Don).

I remember sitting down to watch *The Hunt* on BBC1, not a detective thriller but a nature documentary, notable for the focus on wildebeest as the victims both of dog packs (on savannah grasslands) and crocodiles (at a waterhole), with the usual denouement of bloody innards and bone-chomping.

I remember the phone ringing just as *The Hunt* began its final phase, the now-requisite techy-epilogue to such documentaries showing how the cameramen got the money shot, which Marie likes to watch and I don't.

I remember thinking that it's late for whoever it is to call, I hope nothing has happened to Mum or anyone in Marie's family.

It hadn't. It was Jill.

'I hope it's OK to phone,' she said. 'I never know when people go to bed.'

'We're still up.'

'Especially if they have young children.'

'It's fine, Jill. We always watch the ten o'clock news.'

'Only – if you're free to talk – I've been reading the poems. And I thought I'd better call now rather than wait.'

'Fair enough.'

'I don't like them. I don't like them at all. They give the wrong impression of Robbie. A bad impression. All that sex for a start, in such intimate detail. It's like pornography.'

'Erotica, I think he would call it.'

'Is there a difference?'

'Erotica's subtle.'

'Whereas porn is for wankers. Isn't that all you're saying?'

'No,' I said, too surprised and unsettled by her idiom to be articulate. 'I think it's more than that. It's –'

'Whatever it is, you can't publish. It's not Robbie's sort of poetry.'

Hadn't she told me she wasn't much interested in his poetry? Now here she was coming on like an expert.

'I don't believe he had the experiences the poems describe,' she said.

'I'm sure you're right,' I said, to placate her. 'It's what poets do. They speak in the first person, but the voice is sometimes another person's, not their own.'

'Even so, people will think they're about Robbie. That he spent all his time having sex with different women.'

'Until he met you.'

'The poems don't say that.'

'It's how he sets up the sequence. You're there at his desk at the start and you tell him: Feel free to write whatever you like.'

'He always did that anyway. Me bring him a coffee when he's trying to write a poem about war or politics on his laptop? It never happened. None of it did. And he comes across as such a liar, whereas people always said how honest he was. He can't have been in his right mind when he wrote those poems. That's why he didn't publish them. You can't either, or you'll destroy his reputation.'

'Modify it, not destroy.'

'OK, then: you'll destroy me. I have good memories of Robbie. I hate the idea of a bunch of voyeuristic strangers getting off on his porny fantasies.'

'I understand how you feel . . .'

'Do you?'

'But I think you're misreading the poems,' I said.

'It's how others will read them.'

'You're being over-dramatic.'

'I'm being realistic.'

'I'm sorry you're upset, Jill, but I'm sure when you've calmed down —'

'I'm perfectly calm. I'm just telling you what I think.'

'— when you've had a chance to reflect and read the poems again —'

'I don't need to read them again. I know what I think and nothing's going to change my mind.'

Marie was in bed by the time I finished the call. But she'd overheard.

'What did you expect?' she said. 'I told you.'

*

Knowing Jill might phone him, I emailed the poems to Louis next morning. An automated message came back to say he was out of the office for a few days and wouldn't be reading emails until he returned. The delay gave me some breathing space. There'd be an onslaught once he looked at the new poems, and I needed time to work out what I felt.

Talking to Marie is how I usually do that and on Monday we had a quiet night in. We'd recently put ourselves on the 5:2 diet. Mondays and Thursdays were our fasting days.

'I've had an epiphany,' I said, as she doled out the rocket and watercress salad with grated parmesan and pomegranate seeds – the final two hundred calories of our meagre allowance.

'Bully for you,' she said, flinging the serving spoon into the sink. Because she adhered to it more strictly than I did, she found the 5:2 regime testing.

'Jill probably knew all along that Rob had affairs. That's why she's kicking up: not from the shock of the new, but the familiarity of the repressed. The poems are making her relive what she's been trying to forget. It's like a double blow.'

'*Triple*,' Marie said, 'supposing you're right. First, he's serially unfaithful. Then his poems rub her face in it. And in between he dies on her. That's three kinds of trauma.'

'It would explain why she was so obstructive when I started looking through his papers. She was afraid of what I'd find.'

'Then why didn't she look before you did? It was months before you got involved.'

'Maybe she did look. Who knows how much was there originally: there could have been love letters, diary entries, journals, all sorts, which she then destroyed. But the poems were so well hidden she didn't find them.'

'Whether she already knew about his affairs makes no difference. It's the idea of other people knowing that she can't stand.'

'But she can't stop us publishing. That'd be denying him his rights as an author.'

'His right to write smut. I've read the poems now, remember.' She had, over the weekend, more than once, with expressions of sympathy for Jill and renewed outrage at Rob for having written them. 'They're one long fuckfest.'

'Jesus, you're grumpy. Don't be such a prude.'

'I see Jill's point, that's all.'

'Thank God, tomorrow's Tuesday,' I said, nodding at her watercress.

'Piss off,' Marie said, slamming her fork down and disappearing to watch television. She was full-stretch on the sofa when I went through, leaving no room for me to join her.

Later, naked, before brushing our teeth, we weighed ourselves. I'd not lost anything, but Marie was lighter than the previous week. She didn't say so – we still weren't speaking – but I could tell from her face in the mirror. And once in bed, burrowing down, she let me know that we were friends again.

'You didn't deserve that,' she said, afterwards, 'but I'll not have you calling me a prude.'

*

Jill phoned again on the Tuesday evening.

'Sorry about the other night,' she began.

'No need to apologise,' I said, relieved: perhaps we wouldn't have to do battle after all.

'It was late and I was upset and expressed myself badly.'

'It's fine. I understand.'

'You probably think I'm priggish.'

'Not at all.'

'Now I've read the poems again, I realise it wasn't so much the sex that upset me, it was the morphine poem. About his mother.'

'Which one's that?'

'He talks about her dementia.'

'I must have missed it.'

'You can't have. It's the worst. However difficult their relationship, Robbie loved his mother. He'd never have done what the poem says.'

'Done what?'

'Killed her. Go and read it. Then you'll see why it can't be published.'

*

Morph

i.m. E.R.P., 12.09.07

She might have had a year of being less —
her breath a wisp, her eyes a chalky mist,
her hands too weak to tug the sheet up to her chin —
and me content to leave her swinging in

the playground she'd gone back to since dementia
kicked in, but for the thing I heard her utter
as I sat beside her bed, *Push Dad, higher Dad,*
words she whispered so intently I obeyed,
unscrewing the bottle and filling the spoon
like the parent she took me for. *Go on,*
I said, *down the hatch,* spoonful after spoonful,
till her mouth gaped open with the thrill
of soaring upwards, and she was happy
at last, and so, to have pushed her there, was I.

Why had I skipped past the poem before? In part because I'd not understood it. In part because I was too absorbed in the sex poems. And in part because of where Rob had placed it, halfway through the latest batch. ('With a collection, you have to start strongly and finish strongly,' he once told me. 'Readers lose their concentration in the middle.') Now I had it in front of me, some of the imagery came back: the bedsheet, the medicine bottle, the swing. He'd even pencilled in a dedication. His mother was called Elizabeth. I couldn't remember exactly when she died, but 2007 sounded right.

Could he have killed her? As far as I knew he'd nothing to gain from his mother's death. The flat she owned after downsizing had already been sold to pay the fees for the nursing home and little of the money remained; he wasn't that hard up anyway, thanks to Jill's salary and his own occasional earnings. The only gain would have been his mother's: relief from pain; an easeful exit from a life she no longer thought worth living. So I reasoned, supposing the poem was true. But I also excused it on the opposite grounds, that he must have made it up. If his mother had been *at home*, perhaps he could have given her morphine. But *in a home*, could he really have got away with it? The scenario must be imaginary. The setting suggested as much; the imagery was of Rob and his mother alone together in a domestic space, not in a crowded institution.

On the other hand, to write poetry about killing your mother was in itself dark and disturbed. The matricide might have been invented, but to imagine it in surgical detail, committing it on paper as though it were real and framing it in a rhyme scheme, suggested a brutality in Rob I'd not have expected, but, after the discoveries of recent months, I was now quite ready to believe. I felt sick even thinking about it. Had I ever imagined killing my mother? Not since I was thirteen and then only for about ten seconds after she'd stopped me going to a Hallowe'en party where she knew there would be alcohol. I'd often felt bored, irritated and exasperated by her. But I'd never willed her to die. Were she doubly incontinent, demented and terminally ill, the day might come. Even so: to *write* about it; to have the steel, ice, courage, mercilessness, call it what you will – that was beyond me. Maybe you needed those qualities to be a great writer. Good for Rob, that he had them. I knew my limits.

I thought of my mother standing on the step and waving us off when we'd last visited: walking stick, blue dress, stockinged legs, floppy cardigan with a red stain (tomato ketchup? blood? I ought to have asked, or wiped it off, but she'd once been so elegant and proud of her appearance, and alerting her to it would have upset her). The sadness I felt was a trinity of sadness: nostalgia for who she'd been, pity for what she'd become, fear of a future when she'd not be there. It was different for Rob. He might have been justified in wishing his mother dead, whether from compassion or because she'd mistreated him in some way – bullied, abused, neglected, emotionally manipulated, whatever. Anything was possible. But on the few occasions he'd talked about her, there'd been nothing to suggest she was a monster. When I'd had lunch with him not long after she died (peacefully, from pneumonia he said), he wasn't especially emotional, but nor did he seem cold. And when he described her death as 'overdue' and 'a relief' he was only saying what I've heard other friends say after the death of an elderly parent; even his worst enemy wouldn't have called it sinister. Still, his composure that day *had* been unnerving. I remember asking what it felt like to be an orphan (my father's death was still a way off) and how he replied by paraphrasing John Donne: 'I see no reason for tear-floods or sigh-tempests.' Great title, he added, 'A Valediction: Forbidding Mourning'.

In private he might have shed tears. But with me he played the hard man. Levity was our ethos. On the rare occasions we got serious, all displays of emotion were banned.

*

Louis and I spoke on the Wednesday.

'Yes, Jill called me,' he said. 'Don't worry, I've known this kind of reaction before, with memoirs and biographies. Everyone's in favour of candour, except when it's them the author's being candid about. The poor woman's in shock. And it may take a while to wear off. But she'll come round.'

'Did she talk to you about "Morph"? That's the poem she objects to most.'

'Remind me. The one about a swing and a little girl? Or was it a boat? I couldn't get my head round it.'

'It shows Rob dosing his mother up with morphine. He pushes her to a happy place and her mouth gapes open.'

'I thought that meant she was sleeping peacefully.'

'Jill read it as euthanasia. She's more upset by it than by the philandering.'

'She has her pride – of course she'd say that.'

'But maybe she's right that publishing it would be damaging.'

'Not at all. Anyone with an elderly parent or relative with Alzheimer's will identify with it. Paul Morel does the same to his mother in *Sons and Lovers*, when she's terminally ill.'

'But in the poem Rob's mother *isn't* terminally ill. It's not clear she's even in pain. "She might have had a year," he says, yet he happily speeds her on her way. He actually uses that word – "happy". Happy to have killed her.'

'Who's to say it's true?' Louis said.

'He dedicates the poem to E.R.P. Elizabeth Rose Pope. And puts a date on it. Which I'm pretty sure will be the date she died.'

'It's a brave poem to write, then. Tough, but also loving and humane. Of course it should be published. If Rob's dead and his mother's dead, who's affected? It's not like the police are going to get involved.'

'The press might.'

'You're the press, Matt.'

'I've no control over our news pages, let alone other papers'.'

'Controversy's always good for sales.'

'Rob would want the book to find its own way.'

'That's not how it works these days. Never was, probably. We'll just have to keep talking to Jill.'

'*You'll* have to. I don't think she'll listen to me.'

*

Later that week, Marie and I treated ourselves to a babysitter and a night out – first a film, *45 Years*, then a meal at a Japanese restaurant. We were unlucky with the table, the only available one being near the door; Siberian winds blew in every time someone opened it. With its bleak landscapes and wan colours, the film had been depressing to watch, but was good to talk about afterwards. The couple in it, Geoff and Kate, are a week away from celebrating their forty-fifth wedding anniversary when a letter arrives informing Geoff that the perfectly preserved body of his one-time fiancée has been found in the Alps, where she slipped into a crevasse half a century ago. The extent to which Geoff loved her slowly emerges, casting a blight on the anniversary party and, in the last shot of the film, throwing into question whether the marriage can survive.

'Great acting,' I said, dipping raw tuna on sticky rice into wasabi, 'but the plot-hinge is so flimsy. Didn't you want to shake her? Of course he's upset, being reminded of his fiancée and how she died.'

'You're missing the point,' Marie said. 'His reaction makes Kate see how random it is that they've ended up together.'

'All relationships are random. You and I love each other – but if things had turned out differently we might have loved other people.'

'Once you're a parent it stops being random. But Kate and Geoff haven't had children. Nothing will survive them when they die.'

'But she knew about his past. He told her.'

'He didn't tell her they were having a baby.'

'A baby?' I said.

'Didn't you spot that? Kate sees it when she's looking at the old slides that Geoff has kept in the attic. His fiancée was pregnant. That changes everything.'

'Still, she died. And Kate has spent forty-five years with Geoff. Why's she so jealous of something that happened before he met her?'

'Because what's past isn't past any more. A terrible secret emerges and ruins her life. Ring any bells?'

The waitress brought us green tea. I hate green tea, but they didn't serve alcohol.

'OK, OK, I see where this is going,' I said. 'But it's different with Jill.'

'Is it?'

'Rob's dead, for one thing.'

'So? The poems will change her feelings about their marriage.'

'There are no photos, no facts, no pregnancy.'

'If the poems are true, there was a pregnancy. Think of Jill having to read that. A woman aborting Rob's child. Whereas Jill wanted a child but suffered a miscarriage.'

'Who knows if the abortion really happened. A poem is only words,' I said.

'*Only*? You once told me words are sacred.'

'That was before I started working for a newspaper.'

'What's that thing Stephen Fry says? Sticks and stones may hurt my bones, but words will always hurt me. He's right. Especially with words in a poem, coming from the heart.'

'You don't give in easily, do you?'

'Not when I'm winning the argument.'

'Shut your face and eat your sushi,' I said, smiling. Her eyes widened in mock outrage. 'Joke.'

15

The entrance was between two gateposts and down a gravel drive. If I'd not had flu and been told to take the week off, I'd never have gone. But by the Friday I was feeling better. And the bonus of a free day – Marie at work, the boys at school and nursery, Mabel with the childminder – made it irresistible, despite the risks. If Jill had shown signs of budging, I might have gone to see her. But according to Louis, she remained inflexible. Even he seemed a little cowed by her. There was no more talk of getting the poems out. Give it time, he said, which wasn't like him.

I pulled up in front of the house, Victorian by the look of it, originally home to a prosperous industrialist, perhaps, or high court judge. The number of cars surprised me. The prestigious makes, too (BMWs, Audis, even a Bentley): surely the staff couldn't afford cars like these. They must belong to visitors, I decided, but it was only midday and I'd read on the website that visiting hours were from 2 to 6 p.m. – it was why I'd come early, ahead of the crowds. Perhaps there'd been a relaxation of the rules. I took the last parking space, next to a privet hedge, and walked across to the front door. I'd no idea how I was going to manage once inside.

My neck was stiff, as though I'd swum too many lengths. I'd done the journey in under two hours, no mean feat from north

London, even if it had meant doing ninety on the A23. It felt like an adventure, the rashest trip I'd ever undertaken. 'Don't be crazy,' Marie would have said if I'd consulted her, which was why I hadn't: as far as she knew I'd gone to the office, rather than driving down to Sussex. Of course, I didn't normally take the car to work, but I'd be back before her (she had her evening Pilates class) and unless things went badly she need never know where I'd gone or how quickly I'd got there.

The front door was up three stone steps. To the right of them was a concrete wheelchair ramp – more utilised than the steps, I imagined. I pushed the door open. A small reception desk, with a bell and visitors' book, guarded access from the hallway to the corridor beyond. I signed a name, rang and waited. A couple of women in light blue uniforms entered and exited distant doorways. Then a woman in a dark suit appeared.

'Can I help?'

'I was hoping to speak to the head of the home.'

'Mrs Thomas? Our director?'

'If she's the person.'

'Is it about a relative?'

'Yes.'

'We do have a long waiting list, I'm afraid.'

'That's not a problem,' I said, saving my fire.

'She's in a meeting at present. There's tea and coffee in the sitting room. Just sign your name here . . .'

'I already have.'

'Ah yes. Take a seat then, Mr Pope. She won't be long.'

I stuck a Kenco capsule in the machine, added milk from one of the little cartons, and sat in a wicker chair. The room had the blandness of a doctor's or dentist's waiting room: chairs, magazines, a large noticeboard with photos of all the staff and their designations. The chef and gardener were men, all the rest (nurses, physios, entertainments officer, etc.) women. Mrs Thomas had a place all to herself at the top. She looked formidable.

How often had Rob come here? I wondered. Though nearer to Hadingfield than to Parsons Green, it was no easy journey: he didn't drive and would have had to take two trains and a taxi. I'd no idea how long his mother had been here. Two years? Five? All I remembered was him saying that after selling the family home, and briefly living in a flat close to him, she'd become incapable of looking after herself, and he'd moved her to a nursing home near Carforth: she still pined for the old village, and the home was one she knew, because she'd visited former neighbours there. It had been easy for me to find on Google; there were no others in the area. I could imagine Rob sitting here, while staff prepared her to come down. Or did he barge straight into her room? God forbid I ever end up in such a place, he used to say. But it seemed pleasant enough: spacious, friendly and – in the waiting room at least – free of any whiff of incontinence. If the moment came, and she didn't (or couldn't) object, I'd not hesitate to place my mother somewhere similar.

I sat there long enough to put names to the nurses who passed through wheeling their charges towards the dining room. The smell of stew in canteen metal made me feel hungry. I was about to make myself a second coffee when Mrs Thomas swept in.

'Mr Pope?'

'Simon, please.'

We shook hands.

'How can I help?'

'It's about my mother. Is there somewhere quiet we can talk?'

She laughed. 'Yes, there's a lot of through-traffic here, I'm afraid. Lunch is our residents' main meal, you see, and wherever possible we bring them down. Come with me.'

The room she took me to overlooked the garden – it was more a conference room than an office. We sat up one end of the large oval table.

'I believe you're looking for a home for your mother. Can I take some details?'

'Actually, no. I mean, yes, you can, but that's not what I came about. My mother's dead.'

'I'm very sorry.'

'No need to be. This was some time ago.'

'I'm afraid I don't . . .'

'I'm explaining myself badly. My mother was a resident here. Perhaps before your time as a director.'

'I've been here since 2006.'

'During your time then, just. She died in 2007. Perhaps you remember her?'

'We do have a lot of residents and sadly most aren't with us for long. What was her name?'

'Elizabeth Pope.'

'Lizzie! Of course. She was a great favourite with the staff. Loved to sit in the garden when the sun was out. Always appreciative when we had someone from the Women's Institute come in to demonstrate flower arranging, say. She liked to borrow books from our library, though I often wondered how much she was getting from them, given her dementia. As I recall, that's why the family . . .'

She paused. *I* was family. But she'd never seen me before.

'My brother Robert took care of everything,' I said. 'I was living in Australia at the time. I came back for the funeral, but I never had the chance to visit her here.'

'Your brother – isn't he a writer?'

'He was, yes. Tallish, dark hair.'

'I'm afraid I can't picture him,' she said, deaf to the 'was'. 'I do remember going to your mother's funeral, though. I don't

218

get to many, but she was one of my first residents to pass away. In Carforth, wasn't it?'

'That's right. Quite a small occasion.'

'That's usually the way, if they reach a good age. I suppose you and I must have spoken. Forgive me – I don't remember.'

'Nor me,' I said, growing into the part. 'It was a strange day. The family home had been sold some time before and she'd lost touch with most of her friends. I was living abroad, as I say, so I never visited her here.'

'Well, I can assure you, Mr Pope –'

'Simon.'

'I can assure you she was very well cared for, Simon. You're not the first person to come here long after their loved one has gone, wanting to see where they spent their last years or months. Families are so far-flung these days and the grieving process takes time. Do feel free to look round the garden. Lizzie was very fond of it, as I say. Was there anything else?'

'Just one thing. I wondered about the manner of my mother's death.'

The smile evaporated.

'Whether it was peaceful, you mean? Whether she suffered?'

'Yes, partly that.'

She seemed to relax. 'She died here rather than in hospital, I remember that much. That's how it usually is, if the family has agreed to DNR.'

'DNR?'

'Do Not Resuscitate – if it's clear the resident's quality of life is poor and they're gravely ill. When it's reached that point, we think it's cruel to subject them to invasive procedures. Much better for them to pass away here, among family or staff they know, rather than in a hospital, among strangers.'

'And do you ease their passing?'

'I wouldn't put it like that. When a doctor has been consulted and advises us that a resident won't recover, we help to make them comfortable.'

'By withdrawing food and water?'

'When it's clear there's no hope.'

'And by administering morphine?'

'Morphine or an equivalent. In strictly regulated doses.'

'I always understood she died of pneumonia.'

'Yes, that's often the stated cause on death certificates.'

'But not the real cause?'

'Yes, real, but shorthand. There may be other underlying causes. Haven't you talked to your brother about all this?'

'My brother died eighteen months ago.'

'I'm sorry, you should have said. Poor man. My condolences. But didn't he discuss your mother's death when you were over for the funeral?'

'He found it too difficult,' I said, which seemed a better lie than saying we were estranged. 'Before she went, he worried about how much pain she was in. I sometimes wondered' – I smiled, so she could take it as a joke if she wished – 'if he'd overdosed her with morphine while no one was looking.'

'It's a natural reaction to want to ease a loved one's pain,' Mrs Thomas said, letting me know she understood I wasn't accusing anybody. 'But we have to act within the current law and ensure relatives do the same. We can't leave morphine lying about. A qualified nurse comes round with the trolley three times a day. Only she has access to drugs.'

'That's good to know,' I said. 'Mum's death hit my brother hard and I wanted to reassure myself that . . .'

'That she had died peacefully, in the right way. Of course. And she did. You have nothing to worry about.'

If I'd been pushier, I'd have asked to see the visitors' book for 2007, so I knew exactly when Rob came in those last days of his mother's life; and to speak to the nurses and doctors who'd looked after her, in case they'd noticed anything suspicious. But I knew I'd get nowhere. There was nowhere to get.

'Now,' she said, standing up, 'would you like me to check which room she was in, so you can have a look at it? It may take a little while, but –'

'It's fine, I ought to get off,' I said, as she held the door open for me.

We walked a few paces along the corridor.

'Actually, the rooms are all pretty much the same, apart from the views,' she said, pausing by an open doorway. I peered in, at her behest: hospital bed, wardrobe, desk, armchair, bedside cabinet, table on rollers, television high on the wall. 'Lily will be a hundred next year,' she whispered, nodding at the ghost-like figure in the bed. Her mouth gaped open, but she was sleeping, not dead. For a moment I was back in Rob's poem. There he was, in the chair by his mother's bed, taking notes.

'I'll leave you to look round the garden,' Mrs Thomas said, down in the hall. 'Make sure to stop by the pond. Our patients love to watch the fish.'

'It's been a real help,' I said, resisting the word 'closure', but hoping my handshake would convey a sense of finality, for both of us. If she looked at her records, she'd soon discover that Rob was an only son, and with security camera footage and some googling the trail might lead to me. It had seemed a risk worth taking: to establish that Rob hadn't killed his mother. If I knew that he'd fictionalised himself as a murderer, it was easier to believe, or argue, that his Don Juan-ising was invented too. Though I still couldn't be sure, after today I felt more confident – happier to give him the benefit of the doubt. A useful trip, then. But I wasn't going to hang about and risk my own fiction being unmasked. The garden was large – lawns, pagoda, weeping willow over a large pond – but my tour perfunctory. Within five minutes I was through the gateposts and on my way.

Despite some heavy Friday traffic, the journey back was a breeze. I'd even time for a cup of tea at home before collecting the children. Over supper, I decided to come clean with Marie. How could I not? After the showdown in the summer, I'd made a pact to be open with her. It was just as well I did come clean – with the arrival of the penalty notice a few days later (three points off my licence and a £250 fine for speeding), she'd have found out anyway. She was angry about the speeding, but less so about the stunt I'd pulled. In fact, she seemed almost impressed. Not that she shared my belief that Rob had now been exonerated. 'If he thought he'd get a poem out of it,' she said, 'he'd not have hesitated to kill his mother – that's the kind of man he was.' But if the trip had finally cured me of my 'obsession' with Rob (and I assured her it had), my masquerade was forgivable. Anything to get him out of my system.

16

Jill had to be faced. In some ways the pressure was off me, with Louis no longer gung-ho. But I'd promised to go back at some point and the issue of publication couldn't wait forever. Rob had left a will and I felt duty-bound to honour it. After the visit to the nursing home, I was more confident of winning Jill round. Not that I'd tell her about my trip; she'd be outraged. But it had strengthened my hand.

She kissed me when I arrived, which I took to be a good sign. The luxury chocolate biscuits she brought out were similarly promising. We faced each other across the kitchen table, just as we'd done on my first visit. Then she'd been a general laying out her battle plan. Now came the peace negotiations. The poems sat between us, like treaties waiting to be signed.

I made the obvious points. That Rob was an important poet. That everything he wrote was of interest to his admirers. That his will instructed Louis and me, as executors, to put together a posthumous collection. That the use of the first-person pronoun didn't necessarily mean the poems were autobiographical. That some were almost certainly made up. That others might be *hommages* to poets Rob admired and which critics more widely read in poetry than I would recognise. That the reference to Rob's mother (supposing it was his mother) being 'happy at last' after Rob (supposing it was Rob) has given her morphine (supposing it was morphine) might mean she was peacefully asleep and/or free from pain, not dead. That poems thrive on ambiguity and metaphor. That she was taking Rob's too literally. That ordinary readers wouldn't infer from them what she had inferred. That they would enrich his oeuvre and enhance his reputation.

'The best of them are love poems written for you,' I said.

'A few maybe. But that doesn't make me feel any better. What we did and said to each other in private isn't a matter for anyone else. Here, look,' she said, pulling out a poem called 'Posterity', '"written for your eyes only,/not to be published".'

'But his will says the opposite: that he wants his unpublished poems to come out as a book.'

'There are scenes he's recreated I find too painful to read,' she said, not listening.

'Which?'

She shook her head.

'Just one example.'

'Between ourselves?' she said.

I nodded.

'You know that poem about a man and woman lying in bed? And he asks her how many lovers she's had before him? And he becomes angry and violent?'

'It didn't sound like Rob.'

'It wasn't. It was my ex-husband. Our marriage only lasted a year. Mainly for the reasons the poem describes. There's another poem about a man giving a woman a split lip: that would have been him, not Robbie. If you publish those poems, he'll recognise himself. He took the break-up very badly. And he's still around.'

'So Rob didn't change the details?'

'They're all there, exactly as I told him — even the bit about me drinking lapsang tea. He uses things I said to him in other poems, too. Take that one about the shower. I was cleaning my teeth one night while he was in the shower and I noticed the drops bouncing against the glass screen were lit up in some way. Look, you're swimming in pearls, I shouted at him. OK, it wouldn't take a genius to come up with that, but I hate the way he used it in another context. You do understand my objections?'

'Of course. But as Rob's executor –'

'And another thing,' Jill said, still not listening, 'you made copies of the poems to show other people.'

'Only Louis, as joint executor. No one else has read them.'

Apart from Marie, I might have said, because she's my wife and there are no secrets between us. But if Jill knew that, she'd ask what Marie thought of them and I'd have to admit that Marie was on her side.

'He has them in his office. Where God knows who might come across them.'

'Louis knows they're confidential.'

'What's to stop him making more copies? I don't know who to trust any more.'

'You can trust me, Jill.'

'I used to think so.'

It was as if she was trying to batter me into submission. Or ease me into it. The anger of that first phone call had gone. The chilliness, too. She kept reminding me how she'd come round to the idea of selling Rob's papers. Since she'd given way on that, could I not do the same over the poems? 'Robbie's sex poems', she called them – there was no more mention of morphine.

'You say you want to do your best by him,' she said. 'Then don't publish. And don't punish the woman he loved.'

The woman he loved. As if only she could lay claim to that title. Either she'd known about Rob's affairs but he'd convinced her the women meant nothing to him. Or now that the shock of finding

out had worn off, she'd convinced herself of it. If she really believed
he had loved only her, she'd nothing to be jealous of; maybe in time
she would see that. But for now she was adamant. Over my dead
body was her line. She even hinted that she meant it literally.

'If the poems ever come out, I don't know what I'll do to
myself.'

'Come on, Jill, don't say that.'

'I'm being honest. I've always struggled with depression. And
it's been worse since Robbie died. It wouldn't take much to tip
me over.'

As I left, she backtracked ('Forget what I said earlier about
... you know'). But the dart had been planted. She'd let me
know how much was at stake.

*

On the way home, I remembered a conversation I'd once had
with Rob. Pre-Jill, it must have been, pre-Hadingfield anyway,
when we were still seeing a lot of each other. The place was a
café in Frith Street. For once he'd arrived ahead of me. It was
the only time I ever saw him with a glossy magazine.

'Cat or dog?' he said.

'Dog,' I said. 'Why?'

'It's a personality test. Light or dark?'

'Light.'

'Meat or fish?'

'Fish.'

'Lennon or McCartney?'

'McCartney.'

'Interesting,' he said. 'All your answers are the opposite of
mine. Apparently, you're affable, generous but lacking in will-
power. Whereas I'm a right bastard. One more. Life or art?'

'I'm amazed they ask that.'

'I'm the one asking.'

'Life.'

'Wrong again. I'll get the coffees.'

'So,' I said, when he returned with our cappuccinos, 'if a house is burning down and it's a choice between saving a Michelangelo or one of the tenants –'

'Oh, that old conundrum.'

'Say an eighty-year-old with cancer.'

'Easy. The Michelangelo.'

'What about a healthy sixty-year-old?'

'They'd have had their best years by then.'

'A forty-year-old mother of two? A teenager? A child?'

'I might weaken, out of sentimentality,' he said, 'but I like to think not.'

He was fond of playing devil's advocate. That's what I assumed he was doing that day. If he'd been as brutal as he pretended, Jill would never have stayed with him – she'd left her first husband, after all. But some of the poems were brutal. She could live with them if they stayed private, just about. Should they be published, though . . .? The threat was there, and I didn't take it lightly.

*

'It's emotional blackmail,' Louis said, when I phoned him that evening. 'She's using every means possible to stop us. I'm sorry she feels as she does, but it's time to get on. I sent the poems to Lexy this morning. I'm going to push for a decent advance and an early pub date.'

'Fuck. I told Jill that only you and I have seen the poems.'

'She needs to get real. They can't stay a secret forever.'

'It's Louis who needs to get real,' Marie said, when I got off the phone. She'd muted the volume on the television to listen in. Now she turned it up again. 'They *should* stay a secret.'

227

'If Jill could accept they're fiction . . .'

'He still betrayed her in his imagination.'

'We all imagine doing terrible things. In dreams, for instance.'

'Dreams don't count. We're not responsible for them.'

'But that's what literature is – a kind of dreaming.'

The ten o'clock news began, with shots of refugees at a barbed-wire border post – shouting, weeping, begging for food and drink.

'Books have an effect on whoever reads them,' Marie said. 'Like watching this stuff has an effect. Or hearing Mabel cry has an effect.' She reached for the remote again and turned the volume down for confirmation; yes, the cries were coming from upstairs, not Lesbos. 'Your turn.'

I trooped upstairs, still arguing with her in my head. Surely art belonged to the kingdom of inconsequence, where anything could and should be said: no limits, no censorship, no come-back. Or was that naïve? For Marie – and for Jill – art was as real as a human cry. There it was, craving your attention, breaking your heart.

*

Aaron Fortune emailed again. Give him his due, he was persistent. He could now confirm that he'd be visiting England in the spring, he said. Though he took the point that, as a literary executor, I couldn't entrust 'any old academic' with Rob's papers, he could assure me of his discretion and integrity. Perhaps we could meet? The email was more plaintive than pushy. I deleted it, all the same.

On the paper, we ran a review of Chris Kraus's reissued novel *I Love Dick* that made me go out and buy a copy (something no self-respecting literary editor – bombarded by proofs and freebies – would normally do). It's about Kraus and her husband Sylvère's joint obsession with a fellow intellectual called

Dick to whom they write a series of letters and with whom Kraus has sex a few times. The letters are the basis of the book, part-memoir, part-novel, part-theoretical essay. On the penultimate page, the stalked and enigmatic Dick (thought to be based on the English sociologist and cultural historian Dick Hebdidge) expresses his discomfort to Sylvère about being 'used' as material: 'I still enjoy your company and conversation when we meet, and believe, as you do, that Kris [*sic*] has talent as a writer. I can only reiterate what I have said before whenever the topic has been raised in conversation with you or Chris: that I do not share your conviction that my right to privacy has to be sacrificed for the sake of that talent.'

I wasn't looking for a connection, but there it was. *I do not share your conviction that my right to privacy has to be sacrificed for the sake of that talent.* It could have been Jill.

*

'He comes over as an arsehole,' Lexy said.

Orange light bathed her face. Behind her, to the west, the slow-moving pods of the London Eye were pulling the sun down with them.

'Do narrators have to be likeable?' I said.

'Not in novels. But poets *are* their narrators. When Hardy or Heaney describe some experience, we know it happened to them. We trust them, we warm to them, we let them take us by the hand. Whereas Rob – well, I won't take his hand because I don't know where it's been. Or rather, I won't because I do.'

'So you're against publishing the poems?' I said, more combatively than I meant.

'Did I say that? I know you two were friends. But if I can't give an honest appraisal without you freaking out this isn't going to work. Shall we have another glass? Mine's Vouvray.'

The bar was crowded. I could see her texting or emailing while I waited. Her yellow plastic raincoat was draped on my chair. Five minutes in, and I already felt worn out. Lexy always had that effect. While she streaked ahead, you lumbered in her wake. And by the time you caught up, she'd moved on again, like the runner in a Zeno paradox. It was a talent for making you feel stupid.

She'd suggested the South Bank because she was going to a concert: a large glass of white and a half-hour tussle with me would set her up nicely for Philip Glass or Steve Reich or whatever she was due to hear. Actually, two large glasses. And yet she fully expected to stay awake through the concert. If it were me, I'd be asleep within five minutes.

'He crowds his women out,' she said, as I put her glass on the table. 'He serenades them in order to suppress them. He pushes them under, then pretends to know how they're feeling. Take that last poem, the one where he looks back on all the relationships he's had. How does it go? "For a time it suited us both and afterwards there were no hard feelings," something like that. Really? In every case? How convenient for him – easy-come, easy-go, a mutual shrug of acceptance and no regrets. I'd like to know how the women feel. I'd like to know what happens to them after he's fucked them, got bored and moved on. They've no agency.'

'So you dislike the poems?'

'You're not listening, Matt. I dislike what they tell me about Rob. That's a different matter.'

'I thought you just said that unless the persona behind the poems is attractive, the poems fail.'

'Rob's only work as an expression of unreconstructed male sexuality. Daft analogy maybe, but they remind me of Picasso's paintings of himself as a bull, with his female model or muse alongside. Only, the women in Picasso's paintings are present, however distorted. We can see them. Those in Rob's poems are invisible.'

'To protect their identities,' I said. 'He's sparing with his physical descriptions so they won't be recognised.'

'We never hear them, either. They don't speak. He silences them.'

'Come on, Lexy. There are lines where they do speak.'

She raised an eyebrow, before taking a drink.

'Yes, and what do they say? Nothing memorable. Nothing assertive. They whine and wheedle. Or else melt with love for the shit who's about to betray them.'

'You really don't like the poems, do you?' I said.

'You're like a stuck record, Matt. Whether I like them isn't the point. I'm his editor. I've got to do what's in the interests of my publishing house.'

'Financially?'

'Poetry doesn't make money.'

'What, then?'

'The issue is whether Rob is still a good name to have on our list. Whether he's a fit with what we're trying to achieve.'

'Rob never fitted in.'

'I'm not talking about conformity. I'm talking about quality. Do these last poems meet the standards we expect – that *he* expected?'

'And? Do they?'

'Shit, look at the time,' Lexy said. 'I need to get to the concert.'

'I'll walk across with you,' I said, draining my glass.

Outside, the light was fading. Unseen birds were chittering from the concrete. I felt grumpy – toyed with and outplayed.

'It's too early to decide anything,' she said. 'I'm really busy with our spring list just now. Once things are quieter, I'll sit down with the poems and we can talk again. There's a lot to consider.'

'Including Jill – we haven't talked about her,' I said.

'Next time.'

'You know what a state she's in.'

'Understandably. She told me.'

'She knows you're reading the poems?'

'Of course,' Lexy said. 'I called her the moment Louis sent them to me.'

'And she's OK about it?'

'She hates the thought of *anyone* reading them. But she knows I wouldn't do anything without consulting her. Here we are – I'd better go in.'

Against the backdrop of the grey concrete, her plastic raincoat glowed like a flame.

'What's the concert?' I said.

'Stravinsky and Stockhausen. Incidentally, Jill doesn't seem to have spotted the incest poem. Just as well. That would harden her opposition even more.'

'The incest poem?'

'You know, the one describing Rob and his sister being left alone in a villa. He's rubbing her with suncream and one thing leads to another.'

'I didn't think it was about his sister. Does it say that?'

'You know how Rob usually begins his lines with lower case. In that poem he doesn't.'

'I don't understand.'

'I've got to go,' she said, kissing me on both cheeks. 'Have a look when you get home.'

*

232

The crime scene was a villa on the Med.
Or had we no choice, two kids left alone
All day, sun-dazed, unused to such freedom, half-
Naked and half-pissed? Your shoulders were red.
Gently, you said, as I slicked you with lotion,
Eking out the bottle as my hands slithered
Lightly down under, to the untouched whiteness
And nub . . .
                    We've never talked about it
Since. Have you forgotten? Blanked it out?
Or has the memory been the cause of all your grief?
Reason tells me we were blameless, but remorse
Rips reason into shreds. Let me take the rap.
You were innocent. Sorry if I fucked you up.

Lexy was right. The first letters of each line spelled it out. What were the chances of his having a girlfriend who had the same name as his sister and with whom he'd spent a foreign holiday in his teens? And if there had been another Angela, why would what happened be such a big deal – enough to justify words like 'guilt', 'remorse' and 'crime'? enough to prompt a craven apology decades later? Rob had rarely talked about Angela, and then mostly disparagingly: my bonkers sister, he called her. I knew she'd spent time in psychiatric units both in the UK and Australia, in the latter case after breaking up with the boyfriend she had followed there. (Was the phrase 'down under' in the poem intentionally ambiguous?) The poem was a revision of his one about the paedophile in Bangkok; in this version there were two kids in it, rather than one. Sexually exploratory activity in young siblings isn't unusual and the poem stopped short of describing penetration; Rob had told me he was still a virgin when he went to university. Still, I didn't much fancy drawing anyone's attention to the poem, let alone having to defend it on the grounds that he'd merely fingered his sister rather than fucked her.

Had it really happened – any more than him giving his mother morphine or forcing one of his mistresses to have an abortion? What if the salacious detail was pure invention? No one could check the facts. The subjects of the poems were anonymous or disguised and would probably never read them. There'd be no comeback – no one to dispute Rob's version of the truth. And he'd not be around even if there were. It felt like an elaborate tease. The apology to his sister was an acrostic; even the more direct poems involved puzzles of some kind. He'd set me a series of tests. Was I resourceful enough to discover the texts he'd squirrelled away? Clever enough to decode them? And resolute enough to go public with them, despite opposition from others and my own doubts? I remembered the time, in Brandon, when he'd made me promise to come to his seminar, without telling me where it was. I'd had to find my way to his department, make enquiries and outflank the secretary acting as gatekeeper. That, too, had been a test – of my loyalty, perseverance and capacity for keeping promises. Now he was testing me from the grave.

17

The weather stayed mild all autumn. A wind blew from the south-west, bringing record temperatures and a series of storms – Abigail, Barney, Clodagh, Desmond, Eva . . . Thousands of migrants came with them. Those not risking boat journeys to Greece walked the long way round, some lucking it into Germany, others halted at borders en route. We watched them on the news, begging for food, water, money, blankets, common humanity. Their clothes were thin and their noses ran while we basked in unseasonable warmth. The six raspberry bushes in our back garden were still fruiting in December, while the daffodils in next door's front were already out.

One Saturday I took the boys to a children's matinee at the National Theatre, while Marie sat with Mabel in the foyer. 'How was it?' she asked when we came out. 'The usual toddler fare, lots of sex and violence,' I said, only half joking. There'd been a scene in which a bear ate a rabbit (the blood represented by a scarf of red wool), though the boys seemed untroubled by it, to the point of being slightly bored. The play was an adaptation of a book and I'd been hoping they'd beg me to buy a copy afterwards – no such luck. They livened up when we walked past the Christmas market stalls. A man with a beard was producing giant soap bubbles from a pair of bellows and encouraged the boys to chase them. No longer confined by theatre etiquette, they ran, jumped and screamed along the Thames-side path.

The long countdown to Christmas included a visit to Santa at a theme park (Marie had booked ahead to avoid queues); the school nativity play (Noah was a shepherd and Jack a wise man); and the daily ritual of the advent calendar, the doors of which they took turns to open, finding a chocolate hidden in each, with Marie insisting that Mabel have her share, to the resentment of the boys, who knew that meant less for them, if not (their maths skills didn't extend to division) by exactly how many chocolates. We bought a tree – a non-drop seven-footer – from the local Homebase and set it up in a corner of the living room. Disentangling the fairy lights took hours and when I plugged them in I found they didn't work, which meant another trip to Homebase, where, defying Marie and the boys, who wanted coloured lights that blinked on and off, I bought plain white ones that didn't. The house opposite – a riot of elves, reindeer, sleighs and Santas – was colour enough for the whole street. And next door had a string of flashing blue LEDs draped over its bushes and railings, like a posse of emergency service vehicles. I understood the need to offset the long nights with a pagan orgy of light. But I hated the garishness. 'If it weren't for the kids,' I told Marie, 'I'd go abroad.' 'Don't be such a Scrooge,' she said, 'your mother's coming and she *loves* Christmas.' Did she? Had she ever? The only Christmas childhood memory I had was of her tearfully chucking away some burnt mince pies.

Marie had talked of inviting Jill around. But she'd doubtless be going to her brother's. And now that she'd come to see me as an enemy – the man threatening to bring shame on Rob – she'd surely have refused, no matter how fond of Marie and the boys. I thought of her constantly in terms that varied from mild irritation (a stone in the shoe) to serious pain (a knife in the chest). I felt sorry for her, nonetheless: she'd done nothing to deserve this. How had she and Rob spent their Christmases? I wondered. Did they listen to the Queen at 3 p.m.? Put presents under the tree? Did they even have a tree? This would be her second Christmas without him: a difficult time, though maybe there were worse ones – his birthday, *her* birthday, their wedding anniversary.

*

Jill phoned me early in January – at ten on a Sunday evening. The angry call she'd made back in October had also come late on a Sunday. This time she didn't apologise.

'Have you seen the *Sunday Times*?'

I usually get it, along with the *Observer*, if only to check out rival books pages, but we'd spent the weekend ferrying the boys around – Jack to football, Noah to swimming, both of them to birthday parties – and I hadn't bought either.

'Books section. Big piece about the titles to watch out for in the year ahead. If you haven't seen it, let me read you the last paragraph. Blah blah, here it is ... "Meanwhile there's the prospect of a posthumous collection from Robert Pope called *The Compulsions of Love* – a breakout book, so rumour has it, that shows the famously formalist Bow-Tie Poet in a daring new light. I can hardly wait." I being the journalist, not me. What the fuck's going on?'

It was the first time I'd ever heard Jill say 'fuck'. Though it didn't sound as if she'd been drinking, I didn't rule it out.

'I've no idea,' I said. 'It's news to me.'

'They even have a title.'

'We've never discussed a title.'

'You and I haven't discussed it. But you've obviously discussed it with Louis and Lexy.'

'Nope. Not guilty, Jill.'

'I can't believe this is happening.'

'Nothing's happening. Lexy has read the poems, but as far as I know that's all. She hasn't edited them, there's no publication date and nothing has gone into production. I've seen the publishers' catalogue for the next six months – there's nothing about Rob in it.'

'But the tittle-tattle has begun. It's exactly what I feared. We had an agreement to keep the poems secret.'

'I'm sure there's a simple explanation.'

'I did a lot of thinking over Christmas, and read the poems again, and thought we might reach a compromise – with a pamphlet say – so you could do your duty, while holding some poems back.'

'It's an idea . . .'

I was going to say 'but', but she got hers in first.

'But it's too late for that. I've already spoken to a lawyer. If you try to publish even one of the poems, I'll fight you all the way. You may be Robbie's executor, but I have rights too.'

*

'She does, it's true,' Petra Wainright said. 'The law places a high value on freedom of speech. But the right to disclosure isn't absolute. There's sometimes a duty to treat information as confidential. The likely effect of publication is relevant too. Which is why you're here, I guess.'

'Here' was a fourth-floor meeting room adjoining the board-room: octagonal table, chrome and leather chairs, bottled water, swirly abstract painting on the wall. I'd never been up there before: any meetings involving Editorial take place on the second floor, just along from where we sit. The fourth-floor meeting room was for outside clients – advertisers, sponsors,

238

printers, distributors and so on. Perhaps litigants as well, since Petra seemed at home there, unscrewing the lid of the silver flask on the side table and pouring us both a coffee.

'Black?'

'With milk, please.'

Coffee would be good; I'd come in early, after a broken night (Mabel was teething again). Petra passed me the steaming cup.

'Publication could be an issue if your friend had a difficult relationship with his wife and intended the poems to hurt her.'

'I'm sure he didn't,' I said. 'As far as I know they got on perfectly well.'

'Trouble is, the law takes a complex view of intention. If he knew his wife might suffer by reading the contents, some judges might think that sufficient culpability. Absence of actual ill will is not a defence. If a defendant wilfully abuses a plaintiff's right to legal protection, if he's negligent and acts without caring whether he causes harm or not, he may be liable.'

'That's pretty worrying.'

I'd never met Petra before; there'd been no reason to; authors and agents may grumble about book reviews, but they don't tend to sue. But if it was true that Jill had spoken to a lawyer (and she'd told Lexy and Louis the same), I needed to know where we stood. Petra had been recommended to me as sharper and less stuffy than our other lawyers. Her career path might be as conventional as theirs (private school, Oxbridge, law conversion, training contract, qualification as a solicitor), but this was her first job. The black trousers and grey cardigan were an attempt at gravitas. But she looked about sixteen.

'The key concept is recklessness,' she said. 'In other words, indifference to the likely consequences where there's a risk of harm. The relevant case, if you're interested, is *Wilkinson* v

Downton in 1897. I looked it up after getting your email. Mr Downton thought he'd amuse the clientele of the Albion pub in Limehouse by telling the landlord's wife, Mrs Wilkinson, that her husband had fractured his leg in an accident on his way back from the races and had sent a message asking for her help to get him home. It was only a joke, but the shock caused her to have a nervous breakdown. She and her husband sued Downton. Their case was that he should have anticipated the effect of his story – that even if he'd not intended to cause harm, he'd behaved recklessly. A bit like those Australian radio hosts who called the hospital where the Duchess of Cambridge was having her baby and pretended to be the Queen – the nurse who answered fell for it and there was a tremendous hoo-ha at the security breach, as a result of which the nurse, ashamed at having been so gullible, committed suicide.'

'I don't see what any of that has to do with a book of poems.'

She smiled. 'I knew you'd say that. But it does. *Wilkinson* v *Downton* was the relevant tort in that recent Rhodes case – you know, the pianist whose ex-wife sought an injunction on a memoir he'd written detailing the abuse he suffered as a child. She claimed that if their autistic son read it he'd be distressed. I've got the judgment here for you. The first set of judges found in her favour. Then the appeal court overturned the injunction. Their view was that it would be an inappropriate restriction on freedom of expression. That publication of a book shouldn't be stopped simply because another person might suffer psychological harm from reading it.'

'That's reassuring.'

'Yes. There's no general law prohibiting the publication of material that will distress another person. So long as it's not libellous, of course.'

'But if the contents are disputed? If they're lies?'

'If they're lies about another person, then you're into the area of defamation. That's not the case here, is it?'

'I don't think so. The people in the poems aren't given real names. And any lies or inventions are about the poet himself.'

'In any case, I doubt truth is a meaningful concept in relation to poems. Or am I being thick? I don't get much time for poetry.'

'Me neither. But my friend's wife – widow, that is – feels the scenarios in the poems have been fabricated. She also objects to the poems being sexually graphic.'

'I don't know how a judge would define graphic. But unless it's obscene, writers can use whatever language most effectively gets their message across. Vivid description isn't an issue.'

'But intrusion into the privacy of others is.'

'Yes. It's the difference between Articles 10 and 8 of the Human Rights Act. On the one hand, there's the legitimate interest of writers in telling their story to the public and the corresponding interest of the public in hearing it. On the other hand, there's the right of those being written about to personal safety, protection and privacy. I've photocopied the judgment in another case, from 2006. A Canadian folk singer successfully stopped the UK publication of a book by a friend and former employee, on the grounds that it contained confidential personal information that she'd no right to disclose. Here, take it with you.' Our fingers brushed as she passed the photocopy. Her hands were white marble – as small as Emma's, but colder. 'There've been several comparable cases involving celebrities since – more a problem for the tabloids than for this paper, but the issue sometimes comes up. Your friend's wife isn't famous, is she?'

'No.'

'And the poems aren't obscene?'

'Candid, yes. Obscene, no.'

'Except that she claims they're untrue, you say. In the Rhodes case, Lord Neuberger said it would make no difference if the experiences described in the memoir were invented. He came down on the side of free speech, which includes, so he said (I've got it here), "not only the inoffensive but the irritating, the contentious, the eccentric, the heretical, the unwelcome". Then he quotes someone saying that "the freedom only to speak inoffensively is not worth having".'

'So if Rob's wife does bring a case —'

'Rob's the name of your friend?'

'Robert Pope. You may have heard of him.' She shook her head. 'From what you're saying, if she brings a case and it comes before judges like those in the Rhodes case, she's not going to win.'

'If she goes to any half-decent law firm, it won't even come to court. Given the substantial costs involved, she'll be advised not to pursue it. But there are some unscrupulous lawyers out there.'

'On balance, though . . .'

'On balance, I doubt she'd succeed. She can pursue one of two arguments. First that publication would cause her distress, and second, that publication would infringe her right to privacy. Most judges will feel that the right of an author to publish his work overrides both of those.'

'There's one further argument she might use: that he didn't intend the poems to be published.'

'Really? What grounds does she have?'

'I found them among his papers after his death. It's not clear what he intended.'

'Interesting. But it's not a matter for the law at this stage. It's up to his executors to make a judgement. Is that just you?'

'Me and his agent.'

She drained her coffee and looked at her watch. 'I hope that's been of some use. I doubt your friend's widow could succeed in stopping publication. It might be worth your talking to her, though, to avoid any unpleasantness.'

'Oh, I've talked to her many times. But there's no obvious compromise.'

'Well, let me know if I can do any more.'

We stood up and shook hands.

'What sort of man was he, Robert Pope?' she said, opening the door.

'Strange mixture. Great company when I first knew him. Rather gloomy and disappointed later on.'

'But a good writer? An important writer?'

'Yes.'

'The appearance of whose poems is arguably in the public interest?'

'Insofar as poetry is ever in the public interest, yes.'

'Then it sounds like a case of publish and be damned. I bet you never thought you'd hear a lawyer say that. But that's what it comes down to. Nice meeting you, Matt. Good luck.'

*

I read the Canadian folk singer stuff during my lunch break. Niema Ash had written a memoir about her former friend and employer Loreena McKennitt. Over a longish career, McKennitt had always protected her privacy with (in Ash's words) 'the iron safeguard of a chastity belt'. The one exception came when her fiancé died in a boating accident; afterwards, Loreena became involved with a charity promoting nautical safety and would sometimes get personal for the sake of the cause. On every other aspect of her life – including her health, diet and domestic arrangements – she was abnormally sensitive. Probably *no* book would have been acceptable to her. That a supposed friend should write one enraged her. She hated the descriptions of her grief after her fiancé died. She hated the suggestion that she was mean with money. She even hated Niema's description of her cottage. The judge took her side on this: 'It is intrusive and distressing for Ms McKennitt's household minutiae to be exposed to curious eyes,' he said, arguing that to describe a person's home – the décor, the layout, the state of cleanliness, the behaviour of the occupants – was 'almost as objectionable as spying into the home with a long-distance lens and publishing the resulting photographs'.

'Confidence' was a word that kept coming up – as in duty, breach and betrayal of. 'That the confidence was a shared confidence,' the judgment read, 'which only one of the parties wishes to preserve does not extinguish the other party's right to have that confidence respected.' Shared confidence: a contentious issue. Did the women in Rob's poems know that they'd be written about? How would they feel seeing themselves in print? Would they even recognise themselves? It wasn't like a servant dissing a former employer. In Rob's mind, he was eulogising them. All the same. They might feel, as McKennitt had, that they'd been spied on, if not with a long-distance lens, then with a secret camera – the eye, or 'I', of a poet.

I googled other cases where an invasion of privacy was at stake. *Woodward* v *Hutching* (1977), where a former press agent to Tom Jones wrote salaciously about him for a tabloid. *Von Hannover* v *Germany* (1999), in which Caroline, Princess of Hanover (daughter of Prince Rainier), was granted an injunction to stop the German press publishing photos of her children, but failed to prevent them publishing photos of her, even when she was going about her daily business rather than fulfilling public duties.

Beckham & Another v *News Group Newspapers Ltd* (2005), when the Beckhams tried to stifle allegations from their former nanny that their marriage was in trouble. *A* v *B plc* (2002), in which a married Premiership footballer sought to suppress a story about him having sex with two women. The outcomes varied and the cases had limited application to Jill. More relevant, and worrying, was the original judgment in the Rhodes case, granting an injunction to his ex-wife on the grounds that Rhodes had been 'reckless about causing ... psychiatric injury' to their vulnerable son. Jill wasn't a child, but with the help of a good lawyer she could be presented as vulnerable: a betrayed wife and grieving widow. The Rhodes judgment had eventually been overturned, and the book was duly published. But not before its author had been forced to spend tens of thousands, maybe hundreds of thousands, on lawyers' fees.

It was something I hadn't considered before: the possibility that Louis and I, as executors, might have to spend money fighting for publication. Whose money? There was none in the estate for us, and though Louis's agency doubtless made a handsome profit, he was only one of several partners. Would the others consent for agency money to be spent in that way? On an author who'd earned them little or nothing? It seemed highly unlikely.

*

'Some guy dropped off a book for you,' Marie said, when I got home that evening. 'I've left it by the bed.'

'What kind of guy?'

'Youngish. With a beard. Said he met you at that party at the Brothertons'.'

The Brothertons live three doors away – they have a boy the same age as Noah and had asked us round for drinks one evening. An account manager for an ad company was among the other guests, a languid man in a blue shirt who perked up when I described my job. 'I'm a bit of a writer myself,' he said, and asked what the chances were of getting a book of poems reviewed on our pages. Remote, I told him: if he wanted to develop his skills, he should join a writing group. Oh, he wasn't a beginner, he said, he'd just had a collection privately published – perhaps I'd like to see it. I had smiled vaguely in reply, disinclined to be rude, but remembering the example that Rob had set when 'pestered' (his word) by would-be poets. I'd been standing next to him after a reading when a nervous young man came up and presented him with a large typescript. Rob smiled, nodded and looked delighted to be given it – then, as the young man wandered off, put a finger to his lips ('Shh') and dropped it in the nearest waste bin.

The vagueness of my smile hadn't done the trick. Here were the poems, two copies of them, in fact: *Spring Blooms for Alice* by Daniel Farquhar (the Brothertons must have given him my address). 'To Matt', he'd written on the title page of one copy; 'For review', read a note inside the other. The cover featured a photo of snow-topped hills and the poems were neatly laid out over sixty-four pages. DF Press, it said inside. Daniel had made a decent job of it; even the paper was good quality. Self-publishing wasn't an option I'd ever considered. For my next book, if and when it got written, maybe I ought to. Though he'd have hated the idea, it might come to that with Rob, too.

I skimmed through my copy after putting Jack to bed. Give Daniel his due: not all the line-breaks were random. But it was plodding, amateurish stuff, all azure skies, falling rose petals and heartbreak.

Marie joined me after watching the news.

'What do you think?' she said, undressing.

'Nice-looking book. Pity about the contents.'

'That's harsh. I was reading it earlier. Whoever Alice is he really loves her, you can tell.'

'You can tell because he keeps telling you. Not because the poems are any good.'

'Some are quite moving. The one about hearing the blackbird the day after they broke up, for example.'

'Birdsong as a symbol of hope. How original.'

'You didn't used to be such a literary snob, Matt.'

'I'm being honest.'

'So's Daniel. It's what people look for in writing: sincerity. That's what I hate about you-know-who. He's so busy showing off there's no emotion.'

'There's desire in Rob's poems, there's nostalgia . . .'

'But not love.' She grabbed the book from me. 'Here, look: *When I took your hand/to help you in the boat/that day I thought we'd stay/together and afloat/not that you'd slip like a ghost bride/from my side/and drift through the current and away.*' She shut the book and stashed it on her side of the bed.

'The rhythm's clunky and the rhymes are facile.'

'But the feeling comes through.'

'There's no comparison,' I said, as she turned off her bedside light. 'Rob's poems are accomplished. These are crude.'

'*Rob's* are crude. He can't get over having a willy and looking for vaginas to stick it in.'

'But the forms he uses – sestinas, sonnets, rhyming couplets –'

'Fuck form,' she said, turning over, 'I need some sleep.'

18

Winter slipped into spring, but deadlock remained. I was caught in the middle: between Rob, who'd left instructions, and Jill, who disputed whether we were following them; between Louis, pushing to get a collection together, and Lexy, reluctant to commit; between Articles 8 and 10 of the Human Rights Act; between Marie's allegiance to a wronged woman and Aaron Fortune's to scholarship. Whatever the outcome, someone would be unhappy.

I emailed Lexy, to see how things stood, and she invited me to her office. Though notionally open-plan, it was arranged as a series of cubicles, with shelves, filing cabinets and potted plants deployed to create privacy. Lexy's cubicle was by the window, overlooking a gloomy street. She seemed more relaxed than when we'd last met. Because she didn't feel so embattled? Or because she behaved differently at work? I searched for Rob's books on her shelves and found them – six slim volumes – tucked between fat novels and glossy art history books. Lexy's tastes were diverse: though she mostly looked after novels and poetry, she published non-fiction too. A balanced portfolio, Louis would have called it. I wouldn't have minded her as my editor. In a short time, she'd assembled an impressive list.

'I talked to Jill again yesterday,' she said.

'Any luck?' I said.

'She's still adamant.'

'On privacy grounds?'

'I think it's more basic,' she said. 'Rob hurt her. She wants to hurt him back. I thought she was softening – till the *Sunday Times* item appeared.'

'Yes, that was bad. How did it happen?'

'It can only have been Louis. No one in my office has seen the poems, let alone discussed a title.'

'You think he gossiped to someone?'

'Knowing Louis, it will have been calculated. Present it as a fait accompli, make Jill think it's going to happen anyway, and she'll crumble – that's what he hoped.'

'Instead of which ...'

'Exactly.'

'I talked to one of our lawyers at the paper,' I said. 'In her view, there's little chance of Jill getting an injunction.'

'Probably not.'

'So we could just press ahead. As Rob instructed in his will. We do have an obligation.'

'You and Louis may have. I don't. For me the only issue is the quality of the poems.'

'And?'

She grimaced. 'They're so unlike Rob. Everything he published had dignity. These don't. They're noisy and in-your-face. Depressingly hetero-normative, too – that kind of rampant masculinity feels so tired these days.'

'People will be interested, though. Rob's a big name.'

'Was. Big-*ish*. We don't want to make him look smaller.'

'Are you saying Louis and I should go to another publisher?'

She shook her head, whether as a no or from impatience I couldn't tell.

'Something else came up when I spoke to Jill,' she said. 'Remind me where you found the poems.'

I sighed. I'd been through this with Louis. What did it matter anyway?

'The first batch on loose sheets of paper, inside a folder. The second tucked into the back of a notebook. The rest on his laptop.'

'Where on the laptop?'

'Appended to a book review he'd done.'

'That's what I thought. Jill's disputing the status of the poems. She says that putting them where he did was his way of binning them.'

'He wasn't binning them, he was hiding them from her.'

'Everything he intended for publication was always typed out and put in his desk, she says, and you didn't find anything in his desk.'

'Because he didn't want her finding the poems and destroying them.' I don't often get angry, but my voice must have been raised because I could see people looking over at us. 'When posthumous work by a major author is discovered, it's usually good news,' I said, lowering it. 'We shouldn't have to fight about this.'

'I agree,' said Lexy. 'But might it be worth you going back and checking what's in the desk?'

'It was the first place I looked. There's nothing there. Even if there had been, Jill would have destroyed it by now.'

'Well, let's keep talking,' she said, standing up to signal the opposite: enough chat. 'I'm sure we'll sort this out eventually. But by the way, you're wrong.' She handed me a book from her shelves. 'When an author dies there often *is* a fight.'

'What's this?'

'We published it last year. Everyone knows the story. But this'll refresh your memory.'

'Which story exactly?' I said, as she walked me along the corridor to the lift.

'The burning of Byron's memoirs,' she said.

The lift pinged open. 'Sixth floor,' a French female voice said.

'Read the last chapter,' Lexy said. 'You'll find it germane.'

*

If I knew the story at all, I'd forgotten it. How within days of the news of Byron's death in Missolonghi reaching London, six men gathered in a room in Albemarle Street to discuss what to do with his memoirs. The three key players were his publisher John Murray (whose house it was), his friend John Hobhouse (politician and pamphleteer) and the Irish poet Thomas Moore, to whom Byron had given the memoirs some years before. Hobhouse was for destroying them at once: he deeply resented Byron entrusting them to Moore rather than himself, and, though he hadn't read them, he'd heard they were obscene – for the sake of Byron's reputation, and to spare the feelings of his half-sister Augusta and estranged wife Annabella, they must never see the light of day. Moore disagreed. He'd not only read them, but had arranged for a second copy to be made (the original having become dog-eared after passing through so many hands); they were far less offensive than rumour suggested, he said. Murray sided with Hobhouse: he'd made a handsome profit from publishing Byron's poems over the years, but had also had a deal of trouble because of them (threats, libel suits, angry complaints) and feared the memoirs would bring more. In the middle of discussing a possible compromise – to preserve the manuscripts, but lock them away for many years – an argument broke out over who *owned* the memoirs. Though Moore had sold them to Murray, a clause in the contract allowed him to buy them back – so he thought, until Hobhouse and Murray pointed out that the clause only held good while Byron was alive. Outflanked, Moore began to lose heart. And when Murray's son appeared, by prior arrangement, to help with the burning of the manuscripts, his protests went unheeded. Within minutes, both the original and the fair copy were ash.

It was easy to imagine the scene. The two Murrays, father and son, feeding thick sheaves of paper to the coals. Moore keeping his distance from the blaze, as though Byron himself were being cremated. Hobhouse keeping his as well, from a fear of being implicated in the process he had set in train. Soft grey flakes unloosening and smoke shushing up the chimney into the air of London, a long grey plume slowly dispersing and who knows what revelations fading with it as the men in the room shake hands to reassure themselves they've done the right thing . . .

In my dream that night it was Rob's poetry in the grate as I descended the chimney like Santa Claus, gathering all the soot flakes as I went, and rescuing the ashes from the grate, until the smouldering fragments were sheets of paper again – a triumphant feat of reconstitution, except that the pages were all blank.

*

I phoned Louis the next day to brief him on my meeting with Lexy, expecting him to be even angrier than I was: how many more obstacles could Jill put in our way?

'There's nothing in the will about him putting finished copies in his desk,' I said.

'No, but she's obviously put the wind up Lexy.'

'"I'm sure we'll sort this out eventually," she said. Eventually! Eventually's no good for us. Eventually might mean after Jill's death and that could be another thirty years. We want to get the poems out now, while people have still heard of Rob.'

I sounded more like Louis than Louis did. It was he who'd become the tentative one.

'We could approach other publishers,' he said. 'That's our fallback position. But Lexy holds the rights to all his earlier stuff. It could get very messy. I'd rather stick with her if we can. We just need to persuade her that she won't face a legal hassle. Which might take a bit of time.'

'Is there nothing else we can do?'

'There's the archive to sell. Where've you got to with that?'

'The inventory's finished. It's a matter of approaching some universities.'

We talked about which ones might be interested – London? Sussex? Brandon? – and what sort of money to expect. An author represented by one of Louis's partners had just sold her archive for half a million. But she was a best-selling novelist.

'Is it worth going to Jill's again?' Louis said, before we finished. 'There could be something you've missed.'

'There isn't. I've been through everything.'

'Go anyway. One last trip.'

'I don't see the point,' I said.

I hung up, feeling angrier with Louis than I had with Lexy. Since that *Sunday Times* leak (had it been him?) he'd lost his chutzpah. Or grown weary of fighting Jill. Or – given how busy he was with his *living* authors – had decided that Rob was low priority. It seemed I was on my own.

19

I wrote to a couple of universities about the archive. But weeks went by and neither replied. Then another email came from Aaron Fortune, asking if I'd seen his previous ones: he had just arrived from Adelaide, on sabbatical, and was hoping to meet me, ideally at Rob's house, so he could 'get a feel for the topographical backdrop to his later oeuvre'. He fully understood that – this was the phrase that got me thinking – 'the papers are under lock and key'. Still, we were both admirers of Rob and, even if he couldn't see the archive, a meeting might be of 'mutual benefit'.

I replied at once. Yes, the archive was still embargoed, I told him, but as it happened we were now looking for potential buyers. Might his university have an interest? If so, I'd be prepared to show him a sample of the materials I had found.

I doubted he'd have any influence on his university's acquisitions policy. But he was desperate to get sight of Rob's papers and, as I guessed he would, he emailed back claiming he did.

Jill was amenable when I rang, if only to underline her willingness to compromise: since she'd given in on selling the archive, we should give up the idea of a posthumous volume.

We agreed a date and I emailed her address to Aaron. He'd be travelling from London by train, he replied: perhaps we could go together? I'd other commitments, I lied, and would meet him at the house at midday.

*

The morning began badly. My socks have coloured stripes with the days of the week on them, but I couldn't find a matching pair, and superstition makes me reluctant to wear odd ones.

'I've run out of days,' I said.

'Sounds ominous,' Marie said.

I settled on a combination of 'Monday' and 'Thursday', and went downstairs to make a coffee. But the pods for the machine had run out and the grains in the instant jar were a solid purple mass.

Outside a gale was blowing; it was more like January than May. I hurried the boys towards school – hoods up and laden with backpacks, they looked like climbers setting out from base camp. I, too, had a backpack, empty but for two novels and a screwdriver. At Charing Cross, there were major delays. Power lines down at Gillingham, someone said. I didn't get to Jill's till gone eleven, an hour later than planned.

She was wearing jeans, looked half a stone lighter and had tied her hair in a teenage ponytail. Before Aaron arrives I need to double-check that Rob's papers are in order, I told her, hoping to get to his room unhindered. But she insisted on coming with me, and hung around making conversation while I brought out the crates from the cupboard. How were the kids? How was Marie? Had we any holiday plans? Was my job at the paper going well? What did I think of the current referendum campaign? Had she mentioned that she was now working only three days a week? . . . As I knelt there on the floor, dully flicking through sheets and notebooks, I kept my back turned to the desk. If she suspected anything, she'd never leave.

It didn't look as if she'd leave anyway. At 11.40 she was still there, anxiously monitoring me.

'Just to be clear,' I said, 'I'll only be showing Aaron these crates – not the unpublished stuff.'

'Good.'

'If he knows I've found some new poems he'll want to see them. And if he gets wind of any dispute between us, he'll start asking questions. So I'm not going to say a word.'

She seemed reassured.

'I'll hang the washing out before he comes,' she said. 'Will you excuse me a minute?'

A minute wouldn't be long enough. But five should do.

I stood by the window until she appeared below, carrying a blue plastic clothes basket. On reflection, the screwdriver seemed too crude a tool. I opened the stationery drawer instead, and retrieved Rob's paperknife: stainless steel, solid-handled, with a tapering, serrated blade. Chances were the top right-hand drawer would be empty, or as full of dross as the other drawers, but I had to try. I pushed the knife in the lock and turned: nothing. I twiddled the blade about: nothing. I tugged the brass handle, while twiddling and turning: still nothing. I bent down and peered into the narrow crack between the top of the drawer and the bottom of the desk lid, shining the light of my mobile in for a better view. The flat brass plate of the lock was faintly visible, but nothing protruded from it vertically. Maybe the drawer *wasn't* locked, just jammed, like the one in the old chest we have at home, bought from a flea market, which won't open properly because the wood has expanded. I stood up and looked out. The thin green wires of the rotary washing line were filling out with pillowcases and sheets; Jill's clothes basket was almost empty. I grabbed the handle of the drawer and wrenched: side to side, back and

256

forth, up and down. The top edge was where it seemed to be sticking. To push the paperknife into the slit between desk and drawer risked splintering the wood. Jill would notice if it did. But what the hell . . .?

I stuck the knife in, wiggled the drawer, jiggled the blade, and pulled, hard. The drawer came free with a loud crack, the momentum throwing me backwards on to the floor. I lay there with the drawer in my lap, laughing at the absurdity, before standing up to check on Jill: she was pegging out a last tea towel; she hadn't heard a thing.

There was a single fawn-brown folder in the drawer. It had a white label on the front, with UNPFINAL written in black marker pen, and fifty typed A4 sheets inside. I stuck it in my backpack and returned the drawer to its hollow. How long since Rob had last opened it? The front of the desk was undamaged. But the drawer had left a groove where I'd pulled it through, and the tongue of the lock was slightly raised, not tucked inside the plate. So the drawer *had* been locked. And the key thrown away or hidden somewhere. Which showed the lengths to which Rob had gone to conceal the folder.

'Are you all set?' Jill said, stepping through the door. 'Your chap should be here any minute.'

*

I got the train back with Aaron. He was forty-something, not a septuagenarian, and wore a chunky ring on his little finger, with the letter 'A' on it: A for Aaron, A for Archivist. Large, loud and breezily self-confident, he was the antithesis of the grubbing scholar I'd imagined – so forceful, in fact, that he probably *could* have persuaded his university to acquire Rob's papers. But now he'd been to the house, he was honest enough to admit that its only archive collection – and that a small one

– was of little-known Australian novelists. And I couldn't help feeling that his interest in Rob's notebooks and drafts – which I'd delicately brought to him from the crates, like a white-gloved curator handling pages of the Gutenberg Bible, as he sat at Rob's desk – was less than zealous. He showed more interest in the room, house, garden and Jill. And once on the train he bombarded me with questions: when had I first met Rob? How well did I know Jill? Had his death come as a surprise? I began to wonder if he had a biography in mind, rather than a critical monograph.

At Charing Cross he suggested a drink, but I made my excuses ('I've three kids to get home to', 'My sympathies, mate') and caught the Tube. It was a relief to get away from him. Both at the house and on the train I'd been acutely conscious of the folder in my backpack. My paranoid fantasies included Jill body- and bag-searching me as I left, and Aaron switching the folder to his backpack while I fetched us teas from the train's buffet bar. Only when I got home did I dare undo the zip and confirm the folder was there.

The fifty sheets didn't contain fifty new poems. There were only three I'd not seen before. But all had numbers and epigraphs, forming a sequence. And the three put a new com-plexion on the rest.

Prologue

'And now an urgent SOS message –
Will Publius Ovidius Naso,
Otherwise known as the poet Ovid,
Last seen before his exile to Tomis,
And thought to be travelling in Africa,
Please return immediately to Rome,
Where his banishment has been revoked
And his wife is dangerously ill.'

I didn't listen. I knew it was a trick.
That Augustus or whoever had succeeded him
Would insist my exile was permanent.
That a reception committee would be waiting,
With shackles, if I dared show up.
That my wife had probably remarried by now
Or – weren't such messages a code for this? –
Was already lying in the morgue.

They'd got it wrong in any case. Africa?
I was in London, and had been for aeons.
The new technologies were bewildering at first
But you adjust. I've travelled widely in my time –
In other times, too – and there's little to choose
Between one epoch and the next.
Drink, politics, violence and traffic:
That's all it comes down to in the end.

Oh, and sex. I'm famous for knowing about sex,
The poet exiled for writing erotica.
But here's the thing (more shameful to admit
Than it was to publish the poems):
The affairs, the mistresses, the jealous passions
Incited by Corinne – I made it all up.
The only sex I had was with my wife
And there was little enough of that.

In London, too, I lived like a celibate,
Wasting away in a one-bedroom flat.
Then that SOS came and I went a little crazy.
Why hold back any longer, if my wife was dead?
Softening my speech with Latin vowels
And hiding my grey with Grecian,
I practised the art of seduction at last,
Two thousand years after I'd taught it.

And I was writing again. Or re-writing.
The *Amores Revisited*. The *Amores Revised*.
A new story, and a true one, but with the old story
Like a palimpsest below. Sometimes I'd show

One to my latest lover. But most were taboo.
I knew they'd hurt her. And hurt the other women, too.
In life, I was gentle; in the poems, brutal.
I tried to edit, to make myself nicer, but it didn't work.

The time has come to publish, nonetheless.
The medics assure me I'm good for another millennium
But my bones ache, my memory's going,
And I'm not the man I used to be in the sack.
Oh, I still make the occasional conquest.
But my love life will soon be over
And I want to get it out there in public,
To save myself from oblivion while I can.

So here are the poems: my SOS message.
If they get me in trouble so be it – after Rome
I'm used to that. The narrator isn't me exactly
But he's a version, a metamorphosis.
Ovid is dead. Long live the new Ovid!
I'll understand if you don't care for him
But he's the man I seem to be stuck with
And his story is the only one I know.

Porn

this fickle obsession (3.11)

There was always the Internet to gorge on.
Daytime meant work, and I worked like a Trojan,
but at six I'd pour a drink and go online.

Watch a bitch take a load! Hear the screams of a slut getting her
ass destroyed! See a milf with big tits meet the cock doctor!
It was like going to executions in the amphitheatre.

Sex is supposed to mean desire, but how could I feel it
when the girl on the screen, however exquisite,
had a cock down her throat that was a damn sight

bigger than mine? Gagged, chained and corseted,
slapped about the face while doubly penetrated,
the women were lambs to the slaughter, paid

to feign euphoria even when some brute was pissing
on them. Whatever turns you on, yeah, but who could find this
    exciting?
I thought Caligula had plumbed the depths till I watched fisting.

Still, I too had a favourite website, www.classicalbeauties.
com, featuring goddesses like Juno and Venus
with only their breasts naked and a silky gown hiding the mons
    Veneris.

They were all mine to imagine. And not a single penis.

Soft

There we lay in bed, embracing, and all to no purpose (3.7)

Once I was Zeus, with his Leda.
Now I sit watching birds, at the bird feeder.
Don't tell me it's normal – I don't want to know.
Where the fuck did my libido go?
My prick used to be a relay baton,
Firm in all the hands it passed between.
I was a god, a wolf in swan's clothing.
Until last night. Now I'm nothing.

There we were, under the duvet.
She couldn't have been more lovely.
But when the time came, I couldn't get it up.
Stage fright? All that wine we'd supped?
I lay there imagining the years stretch out –
Bridge, cocoa, the stairlift – while she kept at it
To no end. Taking pity, I thanked her for her time,
Put my clothes on and skedaddled home.

Now I sit here in my backyard,
Watching the water ice over, the earth get hard,
And tits and finches flock to the bird feeder –
How the mighty are fallen, eh, Leda.

20

We don't get to use Harriet Roque very often. But if there's a new version of the *Odyssey* or *Aeneid*, say, or a book about Sophocles or Plato, we're straight on to her: she's the best classicist around – lively, accessible, critically astute. It's amazing how she finds time to do journalism, along with writing books, running a university department and bringing up her four kids, but she sees it as part of her mission to save the ancient world. At the Essex comprehensive she attended in the 1980s, Latin and Greek were still on the syllabus; now she says they're taught only at public schools. Even universities are closing down their Classics departments.

My email gave her the background without naming names: the poems were by a friend of mine, who for complicated reasons had to remain anonymous. 'A *friend*, eh,' she said. 'Bung them in the post. I've a train journey to Edinburgh coming up. They'll help me pass the time.'

She emailed the following week.

'I'm doing a thing at the BBC tomorrow – could we meet near there?'

I waited in Starbucks, just down from Portland Place, while she pre-recorded a talk for Radio 3 ('twenty minutes on *Medea*, to fill a concert interval'). When she arrived – blobby mascara, bright red lipstick, lilac coat, straggly hair – she wouldn't sit down, saying she needed some air and that no respectable person would use Starbucks anyway. We walked north to the Marylebone Road and across into Regent's Park, where, somewhere beyond the Outer Circle, we found a bench, though we didn't sit there for long because Harriet wanted to skirt the zoo and hear the wolves, before passing the boating lake and the building where she'd once talked at an academic conference, all of which we did and none of which halted her monologue, which she punctuated with apologies ('Sorry if this is boring', 'Forgive me for going on'), needless ones, since I was riveted.

'How much do you know about Ovid?' she'd begun.

'Very little.'

'Brief synopsis. Born in 43 BC. A provincial from Sulmo, in what's now the Abruzzi – that's important, I think: he was sent to Rome as a teenager, but he came from elsewhere and at some level he never really understood how things operated in the capital. Not that his family was poor: they were well-to-do, with good connections, and his father had great hopes for him – a training in law and a career at the Forum was the expected path. But Ovid was rebellious. And from an early age, to his father's dismay, a dabbler in poetry. He married his first wife at sixteen, or even younger. Who she was we don't know, but he later described her as "useless and worthless". By the time he was eighteen the marriage was over and he went off travelling for two years. It's tempting to think that some of the emotions he describes in his love poems – passion, jealousy, suspicion that his Corinna is having an affair – stem from that first relationship. He was an innocent. So, perhaps, was she.

'When Ovid returned from his travels his father expected him to knuckle down. For a while he seems to have tried. But to be a senator or person of consequence in Rome you needed military as well as legal training, and he stopped short of that.

Quite a few of his poems cheekily present lovers as the *real* soldiers, because of the wounds they receive. The day job he had in his twenties – minor admin work, at a guess – left him plenty of time to write. The first edition of the *Amores* came out around 15 BC, when he was twenty-eight – in five volumes rather than the three in the second edition some years later, which is all we now have. It's intriguing to think what kind of poems he dropped – juvenilia? Or poems he thought too risky? We'll never know.

'But we do know he married again, probably round the time the *Amores* came out, doubtless under pressure from his father, who'd have been pushing for an heir. His wife died soon after, probably in childbirth. The child was a girl.

'So Ovid was single once more. He'd had ten years of being a man about town, between his first two marriages, and now he was back, with further opportunity for affairs and to make use of them in the books he published – *The Art of Love*, *Cures for Love*, and the revised *Amores*. He was part of a thriving literary culture – Virgil, Horace, Propertius, etc. And he had a nice life – a place in town and a villa in the countryside, three miles outside Rome. He liked to write while sitting in his orchard. And he wrote steadily, at a rate of five hundred lines a year. As Rome's favourite poet, he enjoyed many privileges. There was no suggestion of notoriety or of the emperor being offended by his verse. Even his dad seems to have come round to him.'

Small children went by us every few minutes, asleep in pushchairs, tottering in reins, running ahead of their carers – mostly nannies, by the look of it, mobile phones pressed to their cheeks as they chatted to friends while monitoring their charges ('Do not pick up, Esther, it is dirty'). Marie will be collecting the boys from school, I thought.

'Is anything known about Ovid's mother?' I said. 'And what he thought of her?'

'No. Nor what she thought of him. Perhaps she approved of his promiscuity – *Go on, my son.* Some mothers are like that. Shall I continue?'

'Of course.'

'In his mid-forties Ovid married again, for a third and final time: his new wife – previously married, perhaps widowed – came with a daughter. The marriage seems to have been happy. It also made Ovid even more productive. The books he went on to publish – including the *Metamorphoses* – were the work of an upright citizen, a middle-aged man not a young stud. Feted, lauded, at the peak of his powers, he could look forward to a comfortable old age. Then, disaster! A summons to appear before the Emperor Augustus. Ovid was in Elba at the time. It's possible he knew there was trouble coming and had gone there to lie low, hoping it would blow over. Augustus was no Caligula, but everyone knew he could be harsh. Even so, when Ovid appeared before him he probably expected no more than an angry dressing-down. Instead, he was banished for life. There doesn't seem to have been a public trial. Augustus himself would have acted as judge. He didn't need witnesses or a jury to decide that Ovid was guilty.'

'Guilty of what?'

'No one really knows. The only evidence comes from the letters he wrote in exile, pleading for clemency, which suggest two reasons: either his poetry had given offence or he'd committed an error or indiscretion – not a crime but a blunder. He blames a former friend called Ibis for drawing Augustus's attention to the *Ars amatoria*, *The Art of Love*. But Augustus would have known about the poems anyway. And Ovid had so many potential enemies – men whose wives or mistresses or daughters he'd slept with, or who were jealous of his fame – that any number of informers could have been responsible. The surprise was the timing. Augustus's campaign against licentious behaviour had begun many years before – ethical cleansing, you could call it. But sanctions were rarely invoked and Augustus himself was hardly beyond reproach: there were rumours of incest and pederasty, and of how his wife Livia – whom he'd married after stealing her from a friend – brought him virgins to deflower. Moreover, *The Art of Love* had been out for ten years. Why ban it from Rome's public libraries now? And exile its author for life?

'One trigger might have been the shame Augustus felt because of the two Julias, his daughter and granddaughter. He'd been devoted to the first Julia, carefully supervising her upbringing and arranging her three marriages (the first two husbands died) with the imperial succession in mind. But she became notoriously promiscuous and after separating from her third husband, Tiberius, Augustus arrested her for treason and adultery. Some years later, for the same offence, he exiled her daughter. That was in AD 8, around the same time that he exiled Ovid.

'Does the timing mean that Ovid was sexually involved with the second Julia? Was his crime witnessing one of her liaisons, but failing to report it? Or did he witness some indiscretion by Augustus himself – catching him *in flagrante*, with a woman or boy or with his daughter or granddaughter, and then blabbing about it? All have been suggested.

'He might also have been complicit in some plot against Augustus. Plots were certainly afoot, and while claiming he was innocent – he would, wouldn't he? – the "error" that had led to his downfall could have been his proximity to people Augustus had come to distrust, with political expediency rather than moral outrage the cause of his punishment. Maybe he simply

266

ended up in the wrong place at the wrong time. Whatever the reason, he was banished for life.

'The place of exile couldn't have been better calculated to break his spirit: Tomis, near the mouth of the Danube, on the Black Sea – an outpost of empire, the Roman equivalent of being sent to Siberia. The form of exile imposed on him, *relegatio*, allowed him to keep his property. But his family remained in Rome, while in Tomis he'd neither friends nor readers. He spent the rest of his life trying to get back – pleading for pardon, writing begging letters, toadying to whoever might help. His *Tristia* is full of self-abasement. He names all the other poets who wrote risqué verse yet escaped censure. He moans about the weather, the brackish water, the biting cold, the lack of vineyards and orchards. He lists his illnesses: fever, insomnia, delirium. He worries he can't write any more – yet writes and writes. And he longs for Rome, desperate to return to the society he'd once satirised.

'Augustus's death in AD 14 brought no reprieve. Ovid died in exile, at the age of sixty, around four years later.

'That's the background. You should read the famous mini-autobiography in Book 4, Letter 10 of the *Tristia*. In terms of the poems you sent – I am coming to them, promise – there are a couple of questions to think about. One is why anyone today would want to translate the *Amores*. Many of them are misogynistic. Women as sex objects. And Ovid as a precursor to Henry Miller, full of strategies for getting laid. As though women are dupes or dopes, who have to be tricked into having sex. I exaggerate, but not much. Without knowing your friend, I don't know why he would take this on.

'The other question is this: did Ovid really have the experiences he describes? What if he was actually a faithful husband and his mistress Corinna a fiction? And what if instead of stealing wives from husbands, he was merely stealing tropes from fellow poets – not violating moral codes but adhering to literary convention? Some scholars have argued as much. And there's a good basis for it. "My Muse is wanton," he says in his *Tristia*, "but my life is chaste." Catullus said something similar: "the true poet should be chaste himself/but his poems need not be" – Ovid may have nicked that line. He was working in a well-established tradition. Whether or not the poems are auto-biographical, they're playful about the difference between truth and fiction. My own theory is that the hurt Ovid suffered in his first marriage made him determined never to be hurt again. Which left him two options: either to fuck lots of women but not get emotionally involved, or to be celibate. Either way, my guess is that he wasn't the cynical seducer he pretends to be.

'So, forty-nine poems from the *Amores* survive – fifty-one if you count the two with a second section. Your friend has arranged them in a different order, while also adding a Pro-logue: there's Ovid, still alive two thousand years on and living in London, when he receives a message summoning him back to Rome, fears it's a trick, decides his wife must be dead, and finally gets round to having lots of sex, not having had much when he was married and having been celibate since he went into exile. It's a way of implying that what follows can't be trusted – that it might not be true, or as he says in another poem that he's writing only at the bidding of his wife. All the Ovidian elements are there: pashes, crushes, the exchange of secret messages, and a lot of adultery. But you wonder if they're just a literary exercise.'

'Strictly speaking, they're not translations, then?'

'Not even loosely speaking.' She laughed. 'I'm being unfair. A few of his efforts follow the originals quite closely. The row between Elegy and Tragedy, for instance, which he sets in Caffè

Nero. Or take the so-called siesta poem. It's one of Ovid's most famous, and your friend sticks to the same scenario: a shuttered bedroom on a hot afternoon and the joys of lovemaking. But in his version, it's the woman who takes the initiative, not the man. And there are other poems where he just uses a phrase or image and ends up with a poem that's nothing like Ovid. Perhaps those ones *are* autobiographical. Your friend seems to get through a lot of women, but keeps coming back to a particular "you". Or maybe several. I couldn't tell. Do you know if he has any Latin?'

'He studied it at school, I think.'

'Probably not beyond O level, at a guess. It looks to me as if he worked from other translations.'

'It's possible.'

We'd paused by a horse chestnut tree where a woman and her small daughter were feeding a squirrel. The daughter stood motionless and silent, and held the nuts out nervously. I imagined how Noah (about the same age) would be in her place – shouting, jumping up and down, having to be restrained from chasing the squirrel away.

'So this *friend*,' Harriet said. 'Come on, Matt, there's no need to be shy. The best of the poems aren't bad. What's worrying you – what scholars will say or what your wife will?'

'They're not mine, I swear. Like I said, the man who wrote them was a friend.'

'*Was* a friend? You mean you fell out? It gets more intriguing all the time.'

'He died. I'm acting as his literary executor.'

It takes a lot for Harriet to stop talking, but for ten seconds she did.

'I'm sorry,' she said, touching my arm, 'I feel bad now.'

'I'd tell you more, but there are legal issues.'

'Has anyone else read the poems?'

'Only his agent, who's my co-executor. And the editor at his publishing house. And his widow.'

'Ah, the widow.'

'Yeah, it's tricky.'

'Well, at least you know what I think.'

'Do I?'

'They're spin-offs or remakes, not literal renderings. If you do publish them, you should avoid calling them translations.'

'They're worth bringing out, though?'

'You know me. Anything to stimulate an interest in the Classics! Get a poet to look at them, too. That might help persuade whoever's stopping you.'

'Did I say someone was stopping me?'

'Of course not. Wherever did I get that idea?'

*

I read the *Amores* on my Kindle that night, in Peter Green's Penguin translation, with Rob's version alongside for comparison – *Ovid's Amores Revisited*, he called it on the title page. As Harriet said, Rob sometimes stayed true to Ovid and sometimes veered away. The departures were telling. Where Ovid complains about his lover going through with an abortion, Rob feels relief; where Ovid delights in presenting his lover with a ring, Rob fears it'll give the wrong signal. Still, the mode was similar, with the poems addressed to an intimate 'you' or extolling a sequence of 'she's. The inconsistencies were consistent, too: romantic idealism one minute, cynical libertinism the next. I wasn't writing Rob's biography, but between the lines I could make out a Life. A late introduction to sex. First love, in Tennessee, for Corinne, ending in disappointment, from which he never recovered. Various short-lived relationships, either in pursuit of the One or from a hunger to experience the Many. Marriage to Jill, whom he might or might not have loved passionately, but on whom he could depend. An affair or series of affairs. Till his libido failed, at a time when his popularity as a poet was dwindling, and he set down a record of his life and loves, including a final poem confessing to impotence (unable to perform in bed, he performed in poems instead). It wasn't just that he'd needed the *Amores* to give his own story a shape. At some level he thought he *was* Ovid. Ovid redivivus. The over-identification was mad. But Rob had sometimes described himself as 'slightly off my trolley (unlike my sister, who's completely bonkers)' and he'd got odder in later years.

A feeling that he'd been driven out of London was another aspect of his identification with Ovid. In the Penguin edition of the *Tristia*, again in Peter Green's translation, I found the lines Harriet had mentioned about Ovid's banishment: 'It was two offences undid me, a poem and an error' (II. 207), 'my exile's cause/was not a crime, but an error' (IV. 10. 90–91). Rob had chosen to leave the capital, rather than being forced, but I remembered him moaning about the privations of Hadingfield: there were no good restaurants, the neighbours were nosy, he had constant colds and headaches, the only pubs were the kind where everyone stops talking when you walk in. From the way he went on, you'd think he was living in the Outer Hebrides, not an hour's train ride from London. The tone was jokey, but the language wasn't. He'd been *exiled*, he said, *forced out, expelled, outlawed, hounded from office*, to eke out his days, forgotten, in the sticks.

On the face of it, he'd written or done nothing to offend the establishment. But there'd been kerfuffles. The 'Bangkok paedophile' poem; his 'snooty' dismissal of the Poet Laureateship as a post that 'wrenched an inherently private art into a public display of royal arse-licking'; his 'vicious attack' on creative writing programmes as 'scams invented by the avaricious, run by the talentless and paid for by the gullible'. There'd also been some unpleasantness when he chaired the judging panel for a big poetry prize and fell out with the other judges, one of whom blabbed to the press about Rob's 'churlishness' and 'negativity' – unimpressed by the standard of the entries, he'd been against awarding the prize at all. The spat made the news pages, where it was treated as a comic example of literary bickering, with Rob ('the Bow-Tie Poet') accused of being 'crusty' and 'out of touch'. The fuss soon died down. But perhaps he'd brooded about it more than I realised, to the point of feeling humiliated and ostracised. If Jill, as I suspected, had been campaigning to move somewhere quieter, it might have been enough to tip the balance.

More likely, though, it was a different 'error' that drove Rob away. A weakness of the flesh, a *coup de foudre*, the kind of mistake he'd made with Corinne and made again many years later – love as a disaster. The poems said as much, if you took them as a log of Rob's life. Then again: could you?

21

'This changes everything,' I emailed Louis and Lexy, the day after seeing Harriet.

'Absolutely,' Louis said.

Lexy was more circumspect: 'Have you told Jill?'

'Not yet,' I replied. 'I was hoping you might.'

'No way. You're Rob's executor. Give me a call when you have.'

It took me a while to get round to it – not just because I failed to summon the courage, but because of the referendum result. No one on the paper had seen it coming and, in the aftermath, every department was under pressure to contribute; even Cookery and Gardening carried features about what to expect, post-Brexit. On the books pages we ran short comment pieces by over a dozen novelists, dramatists and poets, none of whom had voted Brexit and none of whom could explain why anyone would. Had Rob been alive, he'd have been among them. I was pleased he wasn't. *So you're pleased I'm dead, how friendly is that?* he said, resuming our conversation. I know how much Brexit would have upset you, that's all, I said. You were always big on Europe – those Martello poems, for instance, and now the Ovid. *All the more reason to get my work out there,* he said – *what's keeping you?* I need to square it with Jill, I said. My will says nothing

273

about squaring it with my wife, he said. Widow, I said, let's drop this pretence that you're alive. Don't get smart with me, he said, just do your job. Will you promise to stop stalking me when I do? I said. Stalking? he said. Oh, all right, I said. Will you promise to stop *talking*? If that's what you want, he said. It is, I said. Deal, he said.

I'd sent out several more letters about the archive. But only three universities had bothered to reply. One said its library lacked the space to house manuscripts, another that its focus had shifted from paper to digital holdings, a third that its annual acquisitions budget had been spent. The pretext of going through the papers again with a potential buyer would have allowed me to 'happen on' the folder I'd found. But none had come forward. Now I'd have to bite the bullet and tell Jill the truth.

And I did. More or less. The definitive version of his poems had been in his desk all along, I told her, but somehow I had missed it. I didn't own up to forcing the drawer.

'I found them the day Aaron visited,' I said. 'But I couldn't tell you in front of him.'

We were sitting at her kitchen table again, battle lines redrawn, her eyes a chilly lido blue.

'Robbie told me the drawer wouldn't open,' she said.

'I thought so too, but I tried it and it did.'

'Why didn't you leave the poems with me?'

'I needed time to check things out. I wanted to be sure.'

'Sure of what?' she said.

'Sure of the reason these poems are unlike all his others.'

'And?'

'They don't sound like Rob because they're not his. They're versions of Ovid's *Amores*. From the Latin.'

Her laugh was scornful.

'Robbie didn't know any Latin. Not really. Just a few words, from school.'

'He didn't need to. There's a copy of Ovid on his desk, in an English translation. I expect he worked from that.' I slid the folder across the desk. 'Take a look. The epigraphs at the top are from the original Ovid poems. The numbers tell you which one.'

She skimmed through, stopping a few pages in.

'How can this one be a translation of Ovid? It talks about emails.'

I peered across. She was looking at 1.11.

'The original was about a go-between carrying letters,' I said. 'Rob has updated it. He does that again with the poem you thought was based on your ex-husband. Here, see: 3.14. Rob takes two lines from Ovid – 'Each time you confess a liaison it kills me by inches, my reason/Blanks out' – then locates it in a contemporary setting.'

'But why bother?'

'It's what a lot of writers do – take an ancient text and give it new life.'

'Don't patronise me, Matt. You know what I'm getting at. Why bother unless he felt a personal connection?'

'In some cases, yes, he's probably using Ovid as a frame to describe his own experiences – the love poems to you, for instance. But in others, it's a matter of imagination. And of paying homage to a writer he admired.'

She turned over another sheet or two, solemn, baffled, unde- cided whether to feel relief or suspicion, pride in her husband or the victim of a scam.

'I need to look at them all carefully,' she said. 'Who else has read them?'

'Only Louis and Lexy. But they agree with me.'

'Agree what?'

'That we do now have a complete set of poems intended for publication.'

'Originally by Ovid.'

'Yes.'

'But describing things that happened to Robbie.'

'To some degree, yes.'

*

'To *some* degree?' Marie said. 'How does that help? If it were me, I'd be tormented wondering to *what* degree.'

'It is a help. With any she doesn't like she can tell herself they happened to Ovid, not Rob.'

'She's not stupid, Matt. What about her friends? The ones who thought she and Rob were happily married? They'll all assume the worst. Dragging Ovid in won't stop her feeling exposed.'

'She might feel it, but if it came to court she'd never persuade a judge.'

'What makes you think Lexy will publish them? You can't force her.'

'She's his editor.'

'She's also friendly with Jill.'

*

I met Lexy a few days later. She chose the South Bank again, the foyer of the National Theatre this time – she'd tickets for a play at the Lyttleton. Louis was due to join us, but texted to say he'd be late.

'I took the liberty,' she said, pouring from a bottle. 'It's Italian, needless to say.'

'To Ovid,' I said.

'To Ovid. I feel pretty stupid for not having spotted it,' she said.

'Me too.'

'The numbers should have told us. Then again, the numbers were missing on the first batch you found. And the epigraphs weren't obvious. And most of *them* were missing too, till you found the complete version.'

'It would have saved a lot of trouble if I'd found it first.'

'He was obviously covering his tracks,' she said.

'He led us a dance all right. But all's well that –'

'Maybe. Jill called me after you'd been round to see her.'

'And?'

'She still has issues.'

'For fuck's sake. Now we've the Ovid connection, I don't see the problem.'

'As far as she's concerned it's Rob's book. And she's uncomfortable with that.'

'If she wants a fight, fine, we're up for that.'

'*You* might be.'

'You can't just cave in, Lexy.'

'Did I say I was caving in?'

'Then how – ?'

'Here's Louis,' she said.

It was strange to see him in the flesh; all our recent dealings had been by phone and email. I'd forgotten how tall he is and how elegant a dresser: linen suit, silk tie (with elephants on it), Italian shoes.

'Sorry I'm late. They should get on and build that Garden Bridge – I'd have got here much quicker.'

He shook my hand, kissed Lexy, shrugged off his jacket, let his glass be filled and led a new round of toasts. To Ovid. To Rob. To love.

'To freedom,' he added, as if he'd just got out of jail – as if we all had. 'Can we fix a pub date?'

'It's not that easy,' Lexy said. 'I was just telling Matt. As far as Jill's concerned, the Ovid business is a distraction. Rob's would be the name on the cover.'

'Absolutely,' Louis said. 'That's what we want. And with a better title. *Ovid's Amores Revisited* is a dog's dinner.'

'You're missing the point,' I said. 'According to Lexy, Jill's still against us publishing. We're going to have to fight her in court.'

'Not exactly,' Lexy said. 'If you'd just let me finish what I was saying. I think there's a way round it.'

'We're all ears,' Louis said, topping up our glasses and sitting back. But staying silent was impossible. It became a three-way dialogue.

'Here's one possibility,' Lexy said. 'We keep all the poems about an individual woman, i.e. the poems which could be read as being about Jill, even if they aren't. And drop some of the others.'

'Thereby destroying the structure of the book.'

'Rob doesn't follow Ovid's structure. We don't know if he did it deliberately, but in his version Books 1, 2 and 3 are all mixed up.'

'Everything with Rob was deliberate.'

'He also leaves some poems out – either because he didn't have time or couldn't get them to work – which gives us licence to do the same. If he were alive, that's what I'd have advised, as his editor. There'll be more of a narrative in the reduced version. And it's one many people will recognise. The poet has various relationships, then falls in love and writes in celebration of a particular "you". The shape's much clearer. And it's the one Rob seemed to be groping towards. Less is more.'

'So you're cutting the affairs and making him monogamous.'

'Whether the "you" is his wife is open to interpretation.'

'It's still a fudge.'

'The point is to keep the good poems and drop the bad. Those where he brags about how many women he slept with are terrible.'

'Why is it OK for Tracey Emin to name her lovers on her tent, but not for Rob to do it pseudonymously in poems?'

'Because Tracey's subverting gender stereotypes, whereas Rob's perpetuating them. She's surprising, he's predictable.'

'It's a matter of ideology, then?'

'Of aesthetics. They're just not very good poems.'

'So you present him as sweetly uxorious.'

'Even edited, he's pretty unattractive. Less of a lecher, maybe, but still a liar. I'm not saying Jill will be happy. But there'll be less for her to object to. No abortion. No hotel rooms. No porn-watching. And no boasting about sleeping with her friends.'

'What about the poem where he gives his mother morphine?'

'It doesn't belong. There's no basis for it in Ovid. And it's out of key with the rest.'

'And the one about his sister.'

'That too.'

'And the one where he talks about being impotent?'

'Either it's horribly true or horribly untrue – at any rate, Jill's very against that poem.'

'How many does that leave?'

'More than enough for a collection.'

'And the rest?'

'That's up to you two. If it were me, I'd deposit them in the archive. Under embargo.'

'Till Jill dies?'

279

'Or for a specified number of years. You won't be destroying anything, just putting it on hold. If Rob's still being read when the release date arrives, some PhD student will have a field day.'

'It's not what Rob stipulated in his will,' I said.

'Authors don't get all they wish for when alive. Why should they when they're dead?'

Neither of us had an answer to that. And Lexy had a play to get to – the three-minute bell had just gone.

'We'll have to think about it,' I said, standing up.

'Of course.'

'We've not even discussed terms,' Louis said, kissing her.

'That's the easy bit. Call me.'

We left her looking in her handbag for her ticket, and walked west, towards Waterloo Station. A warm wind blew off the Thames.

'Nice tie,' I said. 'Rob had a scarf that was similar.'

'Yes, it was me who put him on to the shop.'

'Really? He told me ... oh, never mind.'

Outside the station, we picked up two *Standard*s. The news was all Brexit news.

'Don't look so glum,' Louis said. 'It's the obvious solution.'

'What, voting Leave?'

'The *book*. As edited by Lexy. She gets a collection she can be proud of, Jill's appeased, and we do our bit by Rob. Yes, we'd prefer to have all the poems out there. But there'll still be more than enough to get people talking. And if the response is good, we'll persuade Lexy to do an expanded version in a year or two. Happy?'

'Put like that,' I said, 'not unhappy.'

22

How long can you work for a newspaper when you're not all that interested in news? For a time, perhaps. But even books are part of a news agenda: there are prizes, festivals, trade fairs, controversies, along with the pressure to review the big titles before your rivals do. *Ought* you to work for a newspaper when none of this really excites you? I'd managed eight years. More than long enough.

When Leonie took me for a coffee, I guessed what was coming. We'd had a squabble the previous week – according to her, I'd 'over-subbed' the lead review – but I knew from her expression, more pitying than severe, this wasn't about that. Circulation was still in freefall, she said, sitting me down in a corner of the basement café. Jobs had to go and no department, however small, was immune. She'd fought off management for a year, two years if I wanted to know, but now their patience, or their money, had run out. Go today and I'd get an extra three months' salary, on top of the eight for each year worked; spend a week thinking it over, and the offer of extra might disappear. Redundancy was no judgement on me, she said. Staff jobs were becoming a thing of the past. Soon *everyone* in the media would be freelance and many of them writing for nothing. With the deal she'd got me, I needn't worry about earning for the next year. Didn't I crave more time for my own writing? Well then, here was the opportunity.

I cleared my desk that afternoon, after a ten-minute exit interview with HR. Actually, I had no desk, just a workstation. The only clearing was of a shelf in the book cupboard, stacked with titles I'd not got round to reading. Plenty of time for that now.

Marie, when she calmed down, was philosophical. She'd already been thinking of returning to work full-time. The boys were both at school, and if Mabel continued going to the childminder from Wednesday to Friday I'd be free from nine till three for more than half the week. No more excuses about not getting on with my novel, she said. Think of it as a lucky break. Unlooked-for freedom. And a chance to do more with my kids.

It has been ten months and so far it's working out. Now I'm the one in charge of meals, I've become a better cook; like it or not (and they don't, much), the kids get a varied diet from me, not just the pizza and pasta I used to give them. I'm a better dad, too, more adept at coping with demands for another game, an extra biscuit, a later bedtime. And with the time I spend at the school gates or swimming lessons or wheeling Mabel through the park, I've got to know other parents, some of them dads like me. There are more and more of us, it seems, self-employed, job-sharing, working shifts, on zero hours contracts and a few (the unlucky ones) permanently between jobs. I've had some good conversations in the sandpit. And become firm friends with a graphic designer called Marcus, whose daughter is the same age as Mabel. There's also Greg, an architect with three-year-old twins, who has offered to look at our basement (Marie's pushing for an extension). We don't call ourselves househusbands; between nappies and school runs, we're still pursuing careers. But we've become the prime carers, while our partners go to work and out-earn us. My dad would have thought it an affront to his masculinity; I, too, found it difficult at first. Now it feels as though it's always been this way. Do I miss the office? My colleagues? The banter? Hardly at all.

'I wouldn't have the discipline,' people say, when I tell them I'm writing a novel. In the past I didn't have it either, but a dwindling bank account does wonders for concentration. I wish I wrote more quickly. Still, the novel's coming along. I began it in a voice not unlike my mother's, with occasional echoes of Jill – a woman left alone after the death of her husband. But over time the voice has got younger. And the subject matter isn't just (or even at all) the grief of widowhood, but other kinds of loss: loss of love, trust, self, sanity, a reason to live. 'Sounds grim,' Marie said. But there's humour too. And no one could call it laddish.

I hope it'll work and find a publisher, but my heart won't be broken if not. For Rob all that mattered was the writing. But I've a partner, a family, friends, interests other than books. It isn't art that gives life its purpose. One of the last reviews I subbed before leaving the paper had this quote from Proust. 'We accept the thought that in ten years we ourselves, in a hundred years our books, will have ceased to exist,' it ran. 'Eternal duration is promised no more to men's works than to men.' I have that pinned above my desk now. Rather than discouraging me, it spurs me on.

Meanwhile, I've done the odd piece for Leonie to keep my hand in. Book reviews won't pay all the bills, but if I supplement them with features and interviews I'll get by. Even when the money runs out, and I'm hustling for work, there are certain articles I'll never do. Last year an Italian journalist outed the 'real' Elena Ferrante, using leaked financial statements to link her to a Rome-based translator. I could imagine the daily conference at my office: wasn't this the piece we asked whatsisface, Leonie's former assistant, to do? Another fucking missed scoop.

Leonie, I hoped, would defend me. She'd say the paper had standards to keep up and that the Italian journalist had been crucified for his intrusiveness. But might she secretly regret not having pushed me more at the time? Either way, I'm relieved to have got out when I did. I was never the right person for the job. The truth behind Elena Ferrante and her novels doesn't interest me.

And the truth behind Rob and his poems? That *does* interest me, I can't pretend otherwise. But only because I knew him. Or thought I knew him, before discovering that I didn't. Couldn't he have trusted me with his secrets? Did he think I'd give them away? It's not that I feel angry with him. I wasn't his wife. What he got up to with other women – if he got up to anything at all – is immaterial. He wouldn't be the first writer to have a complicated love life, and it's not my place to make moral judgements. Still, I do identify with Jill. Not only did we both experience a sense of betrayal, his poems put us at loggerheads, which caused us both upset and stress.

A respectable lifestyle, a flirtatious Muse: Ovid's description of himself may have been true of Rob, too. It's what Jill believes, or would like to believe, that any flirting was confined to the page, or that what happened off the page, in life, amounted to no more than flirting. Who can say? Only ... About a month ago I had an email from a woman calling herself Belinda (whether her real name I couldn't be sure, since the email address – bendy1654@gmail.com – gave no clue). She'd read somewhere that Rob had a book coming out and had been told (by whom?) that I was his literary executor. As someone who had known Rob, she was curious about the book and wondered if I could give her a call. The number was a mobile number. I called next day. The call went to voicemail but she phoned straight back. 'Is that Matthew?' she said, the first time anyone has called me that in twenty years. Her accent was neutral (regionless, educated, middle class), her tone too guarded to be warm; I'd have guessed she was in her forties. How could I help? I said. She'd like to get hold of Rob's new book, she said – she'd pre-ordered it on Amazon, but wondered if there was a quicker way. You're keen, I laughed. Yes, I've read every line he wrote. Wow, I said, a real fan. Not just a fan, she said – as I told you in my email, I knew him personally. In fact, I came to his funeral. I was there too, I said, maybe we spoke. I didn't stay for the wake, she said, I felt too sad, too shocked, his death was so sudden, he'd so much more to give. Anyway, about his book ... Finished copies would soon be available, I said – should I ask the publisher to send her a copy? That would be good, she said, but in the meantime could I give her an idea of the contents? She'd read that the book was untypical of Rob – 'daringly candid', in fact. Not exactly, I said, the poems were adaptations of poems by Ovid, but you could hear Rob's voice in them. Which Ovid were we talking about, she said, the *Metamorphoses*? No, the *Amores*, I said. Love poems, then? Yes. It was her turn to speak, but she didn't. I plunged on, made anxious by her silence. They're Ovid's experiences as re-imagined by Rob – different in spirit to the rest of his stuff, but still recognisably him. More silence. Can you hear me? I said. I think I've lost you. I'm here, she said, then fell silent again. Give me your address, I said, and I'll see about getting a copy sent. I'll email you, she said, that'd be simpler – thanks for your help.

No email came. I left it a week, then texted to remind her, but when she finally replied – last week – she said didn't want to be a nuisance and since the book would soon be with her from Amazon she might as well wait.

I haven't told Louis about the call. *Cherchez la femme*, he once said, before we suspected there might be several of them. If he knew, he'd be angry with me for not asking more questions: was Belinda just a friend? Or The One? Or one of many? I might have pushed her, but how much would she have owned up to, in a phone call with a stranger? I might get in touch again when she has read the book. But Marie says to leave things be and Marie is always right.

I've reached an accommodation with Rob as well. We no longer talk. I still think of him, of course, but not every day. And if ever I'm tempted to update him on the world he has left behind – war, terror, refugees, Brexit, Trump, Theresa May – I tell myself he wouldn't want to hear, not just because the news is mostly bad, but because his only interest was in pushing me to get the poems out. That's done with now. The book will be published next month. *Love's Alphabet*, we've called it, after much debate (*Postmodern Love, After Ovid* and *The Lyric Libido* were among the discarded alternatives). *Love's Alphabet* by Robert Pope, pure and simple, with no reference in the blurb to the *Amores*. There are numbers and epigraphs above each poem, and anyone who cares to can hunt down the source, but that's as far as it goes. I like to think Rob would approve. It was Lexy who noticed that in his final version of the poems – the one I found in his desk drawer – all the titles were one-word titles, and that each began with a different letter of the alphabet, or rather twenty-six of them did. And she convinced herself, if not me, that Rob had been planning what she called a double-alphabet version of the *Amores*, first A to Z, then Z to A, with his Prologue added to make fifty-two poems in total, 'also the number of weeks in the year'. Numerological tosh, I thought, but Rob was fond of structural patterns of that kind. She has done a little editing, to supplement Rob's final revisions, but there's been no major tidying up: the libertine and lecher are given their voice. I take my hat off to Lexy. Those months of holding Louis and me at bay gave her time to win over Jill, who eventually agreed to there being more poems in the book than any of us expected, including several to which she once objected and probably still hates.

Lexy's powers of persuasion haven't been the only factor. Something in Jill seems to have softened. I've been to visit a couple of times and noticed the change. Her eyes are a warmer blue again, her smiles less forced. When we looked at the drafts for the cover design, we sat together at the kitchen table – alongside each other, not opposite. She even said she was looking forward to publication, 'if only to draw a line under everything'. While I was there, the house phone went – Sorry, she told the caller, flustered, someone's here, could I call you later? The voice was male. It could have been her brother or someone from her charity. But if so why the embarrassment?

Rob's been dead for over three years. If there's someone else in her life, maybe the poems, and how they'll be received, matter less to her than they did.

Leonie has taken ten of the poems and – on condition I write a short intro – has promised a double-page spread. I already know what I'll talk about: Rob's sudden death, our friendship, my visits to the house, the discovery of unpublished poems. I'll refrain from discussing whether they're autobiographical. That's not a cop-out to spare Jill. I won't say, because I don't know. Leonie may push me. But I'm standing firm. Matt the Scruple.

To my surprise, I've also succeeded in selling Rob's archive. Donated might be nearer the mark, given how little it went for, but I'm confident it's found the right home. Not that the University of Chichester ever occurred to me as a potential home, until their archivist got in touch. It turned out Rob had occasionally run workshops there, despite telling me he never ran workshops. And Chichester wasn't far from where he'd grown up. The head of the Literature Department, Corinne Day, is also a fan of his work. Not *that* Corinne, from Tennessee; this one's Scottish. Still, the coincidence of the name helped persuade me we'd found the right fit, and Louis agreed we'd not get a better offer.

Until Jill reminded me, I'd almost forgotten the other obligation placed on me in Rob's will: to destroy any '*journals, letters and unfinished drafts*'. It was easy to forget, because I'd found almost nothing of that kind. In his last years, Rob had had occasional bonfires, Jill said. It's also possible, despite her assurances to the contrary, that she destroyed whatever journals he'd left. If there were none, why did he refer to them in his will? No unfinished drafts were left, either. All that did remain were the letters: the ones he'd received; the ones he'd sent and kept copies of; the ones he'd drafted but not sent. It seemed a pity to destroy them, but his instructions were clear.

We didn't discuss this in front of the archivist from Chichester (a gloomy young man called Eugene) when he came to remove the crates. But after we'd finished loading them in his van and he'd driven off, I took the three folders with Rob's letters down the garden. The weather was implausibly warm for late October, the trees turning gold, stray leaves scattered about the flowerbeds and lawn. Jill followed me with a box of matches. In her pink padded jacket and lime-green boots she looked frolicsome rather than sombre, spring-like not autumnal. The bottom of the metal brazier was lined with ashes and charred twigs. I tipped them out on to the compost heap and began stuffing letters in, making twists so they'd burn more easily. Let me help, Jill said, and pulled out a letter from the RECEIVED file, pausing to read it aloud – 'Dear Mr Pope, as a great admirer of your verses could you please give me feedback on the enclosed epic?' – before scrunching it up and dropping it in the brazier. Following suit, I read out a letter from the SENT file: 'Dear Melanie, my only creative writing rule is: ignore everything you've ever been told.' Laughing, Jill took over: 'Dear Rob (if I may), we are looking for a patron for our Preserve the Cormorant campaign and wonder if ...' I topped that with an UNSENT: 'Dear Laurence, I don't normally object to kind reviews, but yours was so inane I feel I must protest ...' We took it in turns, our laughter growing louder, as though we were hearing Rob in person, the man we both loved in our different ways, who'd divided us in death, but enriched us when alive. There we were, on the same side, next to the rim of the brazier. I'd a sudden impulse to hug Jill and think I would have done, but at that moment she stepped away, hunching over the match-box, striking a light, then holding it to a twist of paper. The flames quickly caught, the paper browning and blackening, small yellow buds flickering, then large red tongues, a hearty blaze we stoked by chucking on more letters, not in single twists now but thick sheaves, the fire – quicker than we were – leaving no time for further recitals, each of us hurling in great wads of paper (some pages typed, others handwritten) until the last of the letters had been consumed and we threw the cardboard folders in for good measure, holding our hands out for warmth as dusk fell chill around us and Rob's words went up in smoke, thin grey flags spilling out into the darkness while the fire died down, my mood (I can't speak for Jill) both jubilant and sad, the pair of us transfixed by the embers, till all that remained was ash and we turned without a word towards the house, leaving Rob behind, his letters destroyed, but his name preserved both in an archive and in a soon-to-be-published work, all of which (the sifting and the selling, the disseminating and the destroying) was as his will had specified and, whether his reputation rose or sank as a result, was in accordance with the duties imposed on me as executor – duties which, in good conscience, to the best of my ability, I had faithfully carried out.

Love's Alphabet

ROBERT POPE

My morals, believe me, are quite distinct from my verses –
a respectable life-style, a flirtatious Muse –
and the larger part of my writings is mendacious, fictive,
assumes the licence its author denies himself.

Ovid, *Tristia* (II. 353–6)

Contents

Anon

None but you shall be sung in my verses (2.17)

I'm in love, no getting round it.
But our love's hush-hush.
I can't go tell it to the mountain
or whisper it like Midas in the reeds.

Why these poems, then?
Because they're written just for you,
not to be published till we've stopped loving
(sorry, typo: *living*), maybe not even then.

The woman in the shower,
the bed, the books, the hotel room –
it's the story of us
but only you will know it's you.

Bed

May my siestas often turn out that way! (1.5)

A house-call in the old colony, during monsoon season.
We sat in the kitchen, gossiping over gin and tonic,
while rain barrelled down beyond the blinds. The light was dusk-light,
less for songbirds than for bats, but with a glow through the slats
that printed lines across our faces, black on white, white on black.

I'd come with a queasy stomach and a migraine,
so she suggested I lie down in her bedroom. It felt cool in there,
on the divan, under the rotor of the ceiling fan,
while kids played in the street and rain rat-tat-tatted on the glass.

At some point she came through and asked was I feeling better
and did I mind if she siesta'd too? She lay on her side behind me,
her hand on my hip, her breathing deep and steady, as if she'd dropped off,
until the hand moved down a bit – all this and what followed
without a word spoken, just the chop of the fan,
the swish of her underthings, and the whap of naked flesh.

Sometimes I find the memory hard to credit, as if I'd stolen it
from a porn mag, but then the shutters come back and the slats
across her body and the rain rat-tat-tatting on the glass.

Couple

A really determined couple is hard to resist (3.3)

His watch on the floor, her hair on the pillow,
the assuaging bottle of Chablis.

Dawn

What's the hurry? All lovers, men and girls, resent your coming... (1.13)

Rosy fingers, lark ascending, gold disc cresting the skyline ...
Give it a rest. Why do you think the curtains are drawn?
Call back in an hour – till then go bother someone else.
Insomniacs, factory guards, nurses on night shift: they'll be glad to see you.
But to us, under the duvet, you're a dentist's lamp, a prison searchlight,
the naked bulb of a torture cell. I reckon you must be single or divorced.
Or if married, unhappily so – harried from bed by your shrewish wife.
Now you're bugging us with noise as well, the wooden sill ticking
like a cicada as it warms. Bully! Clock-watcher! Control freak!
We're hiding out inside each other, the den where it's always night.

Etiquette

... this ritual (3.13)

In any affair, certain rituals must be observed.
At a hotel, for instance, you should dispose of your condom
in one of those miniature serrated milk cartons they provide.
Better that than try to flush it down the toilet
or leave it lying – a baby jellyfish – on the floor.
You paid for the room. There's no law against having sex in it.
And you'll never see the cleaner. But to brandish the evidence
feels immodest – Look what we've been doing! –
and your lover won't be happy, either. It'll stare up at her
when she goes for a pee and what felt fine inside ten minutes since
will now fill her with doubts. Why a condom? she'll think.
Are you fucking someone else? Do you think she's fucking someone else?
Does the idea of having a baby with her appal you *that* much?
She'll get back into bed a different woman – cold, sullen, accusing –
and you can forget the idea of fucking her again till you've spent hours
telling her you love her, and maybe not even then.
The miniature serrated milk carton will spare you this grief.

Frank

Guarding your girl won't help you (3.4)

Frank, mate, you don't know me, and if you did you wouldn't like me,
and if you knew what I get up to with your missus you'd like me even less.
But honest, I'm doing you a favour. Haven't you noticed how sweet
and attentive she's become, how she sings when cooking supper
and never complains when you spend Sundays at the golf course?
She's lost weight, too, and looks younger. Why be jealous? It's me who endures
her rage and remorse, whereas with you she's eager to please.
The key to a good marriage is adultery, you see: every husband needs a louse
to warm the bed for him, every union a bastard like me. So when you find out
and come looking for me, don't bring a knife, bring a thank-you present.
The day she stops betraying you is the day your problems begin.

Gorse

There stood the goddess's grove, dark-shadowed (3.13)

The starlings tossing their nets
are a signal to head home
and though it's dark among the bracken
gas-flames of gorse show the way.

There's no excuse for wandering off
but I want us to be lost or to find
a quiet spot and lose the others.

Here, look, behind this bush.
Shush, or people will hear.

Hair

It grew luxuriantly, down to below her hips (1.14)

How would I feel if she lost her hair?
she asks. We're in bed, the lights off,
the garden silent, a hot summer night.
Five minutes back, not for the first time,
a hank of it got trapped as we made love
and she cried out in frustration and pain.

I get sick of it, she says. It's a pain.
I'm forever brushing knots from my hair.
But it veils my ears and shoulders, and I love
how it flows over my skin. Chop it off
and I'd feel so *ordinary*. Last time
it was short I looked terrible ... The night

sticks to our bodies and a night
train in the cutting stirs a windowpane.
We've had these talks before, the last time
only a week ago. I stroke her face, knowing hair
isn't the point. She's asking will I go off
her when she ages, as she must; will my love

withstand her getting sick; is it a love
she can rely on? She has these night-
mares now and then, where I run off
with a younger woman, or she's in pain
from cancer, or stress makes her hair
fall out. I push a strand away. That time

in Venice, I say (it must have been winter-time,
the duckboards were out) – remember, love?
We'd just the weekend and had to hare
round the churches and galleries. At night
we took a water taxi and drank champagne,
no Bellinis, in Harry's Bar, then slipped off

early to the hotel and took our clothes off,
and lay there like this, in a kind of no time,
our bodies glowing, immune to all pain.
I can see it now: the sheets, our lovemaking, the shimmer of green night-
lights on the water – but I can't picture your hair.

Cutting your hair off won't lessen my love.
It's tenacious and timeless, like the night.
Hush, now – no more pain. You are not your hair.

Illicit

What's allowed is a bore, it's what isn't/That turns me on (2.19)

Ah the thrill of the illicit ... how I miss it. Miss missing you.
Miss the time when you played hard to get.
It's indecent to admit, but when your body was an archive,
open for visits only rarely, then the pleasure of admission
was a triumph, not a dull repeat. Now we fuck whenever we want
I'm bored – it's like eating oysters seven days a week.

Jealousy

Am I always to be on trial against new accusations? (2.7)

The issue was a blonde soprano. Lisa, was it?
Among the songs she performed was a sonnet
I'd written and at a party afterwards she got your goat
for being pushy, flirty, inappropriate.
We argued all the way home to the flat.
'She's not my type,' I said, 'I was only being polite.
We were discussing Mahler.' 'Yeah, right.
I bet you didn't tell her you were married.
It's something you seem to forget.'
'She knows. I'm wearing a ring. And I pointed you out.'
'It didn't stop her trying to get you into bed.'
'I doubt she's interested. Certainly I'm not.'
'Come on – your need to be loved is so desperate
you'd spend the night with any old tart
just to have her brown-nosing your art.'
'She's a singer. All we've done is collaborate.
I've not even kissed her.' 'Maybe not yet.
But you will. And when you do, that'll be that,
me gone and you on your own, without my support.
Is that what you want?' 'Of course not, sweet.'
'Sure?' 'Promise. Word of honour. Cross my heart.'
So we made up, and slipped beneath the sheet,
and buried ourselves in joint regret,
you for venting your suspicions, me for not
admitting they were more than half right.

Knave

Every lover's on active service, my friend (1.9)

'*What a rogue*, I said, towelling myself
dry while he shot off early, *who is it this time*?
Laughing, I headed off with the team
for a pint, never thinking it was my wife.'

Lies

The gods in heaven/Forgive a girl's lies .../We men aren't so lucky (3.3)

You never did lie, as far as I know.
That's what attracted me. Your clear grey eyes.
The way you said things straight out.

We divided things up. I cooked, you ironed.
You made curtains, I put the rubbish out.
You pruned the window box, I told lies.

I lied about things I'd done.
I lied about things I'd not done.
I lied about things I promised I'd do, but didn't.

I lied elaborately, for the pleasure of making things up.
Some of my lies were full-length novels.
I even believed in them myself.

Occasionally you'd catch me lying,
and you'd feel the thing I'd tried to save you from –
hurt, disappointment, anger, mistrust –

and I'd promise never to lie to you again.
Which was a lie, of course.
I soon went back to my lying ways.

In the end, you discovered the facts.
An anonymous letter came, giving chapter and verse.
We were walking by the river when you confronted me,

boring in with those clear grey eyes of yours.
'I've had enough of your lies,' you said.
'I want to be with someone I can trust.'

A barge went by, then a police boat.
The river was turning mauve in the dusk.
I talked about the lies that writers told

but you were having none of it.
'Art's one thing, life's another,' you said.
'Besides, the best writers do tell the truth.'

And so you ended it, by the river,
straight out, as only you could.
And it wasn't just you I lost, but the premise of my art.

Away you floated, you and the premise,
under the bridge and into the darkness,
like two wooden crates on the tide.

Mirror

She knows herself too well, / Gets her haughty ways (I suspect) from her mirror-image (2.17)

She kept looking over my shoulder into the mirror,
straightening her hair, adjusting her smile,
searching her face to see what I was seeing.
This is good, I thought, a sign she wants me back:

once I've settled the bill we'll take a cab back
to hers, and make love, and start seeing
each other again. I searched her face for a smile.
She was looking over my shoulder into the mirror.

Nostalgia

There's no one type of beauty (2.4)

When she trembled it wasn't one string,
but the whole instrument.

Though she deserved my adoration
I lacked the will to see it through.

For her part, she approved of me,
but approval isn't love.

We were like water boatmen
on a pond, cool and adrift.

Eternity was the god
who allowed us little moments.

Over time I forgot her face
and yet these things come back:

a low white moon, a silent bar,
the cry of seals along the shore.

Outsider

O elegy, unbind your hair and weep tears of loss (3.9)

The day of your funeral I was in bed
with someone. The sun was a blade
through the shutters and the heat
made my head explode. I felt like Meursault.
You'd have expected no less of me. Even so.

Paying

When sex gives equal enjoyment to both partners,/Why should she sell it,
he pay? (1.10)

We're old-fashioned about it: it's me who pays,
while your contribution is you. It's enough. *You're* enough.
But I worry what it says about us. You've a house,
a salary, a husband, yet I'm the one footing the bill.
It's not just fear of him seeing your credit card statement
or embarrassment at leaving a tip. You're too romantic
to admit there's money involved. So if we go to a hotel,
I get there first (as I try not to later, in bed) and the business
is taken care of, and the rest is pleasure with no strings.

Ovid's Corinne keeps asking for presents. You never do.
It's me who comes away with gifts – not just memories
but the books you bring, the kind I'd write if I could,
in which the lovers never go to cheap hotels, all we see
is the love they make and the light pouring from their bodies.

Questions

Most adultery (flagrant or not) remains unproven (2.2)

How many security cameras have watched us arrive?
How many receptionists have checked us in?
How many DO NOT DISTURB signs have we hung out outside?
How many sheets have you pulled back to climb in bed?
How many people in the next room have heard our noise?
How many times have you thought 'This should be the last time'?
How many times has it still not been the last time?
How many times have we started to dress, then made love again?
How many room keys have we handed back?
How many security cameras have watched us leave?
How many times did you think of counting? Me neither.

Rules

Impropriety has its special off-limits/Enclave, where every kind of fun is the rule (3.14)

Meetings take place on a regular basis and generally last 3 to 4 hours

Membership is free, but there is a charge for room hire

Activities are intended to provide pleasure; to enhance skills; and to build mutual esteem

Tea, coffee and biscuits are provided, but members needing further refreshments must provide their own

There are suitable toilet and bathroom facilities. A telephone, television and Bible are also supplied

Numbers are limited to two at a time. Guests are not allowed

Discussion of the club with non-members – spouses, parents, children and friends – is strictly forbidden

Membership of other clubs is discouraged and may lead to expulsion

Failure to attend without good reason will lead to members being reprimanded or even suspended

On departure, members are asked to leave quietly and not draw attention to themselves

Shower

Rivers should help young lovers./Rivers know all about love
themselves … (3.6)

You used a pencil to pin up your hair,
so when I stood behind you under the rose
your nape was left exposed for me to kiss,
my hands stretching round to hold your breasts,
then going with the flow, down and inside to where
you were streaming, as though water could pour
upwards, not that the wetness was all yours.

It was one of those showers that runs cold
when someone next door turns on a tap, then scalds
as the heat comes back. But we treasured its force:
if I pecked at your ear, tiny pearls would trip
off my tongue, like beads from a broken necklace.
The power took my breath away, or you did,
reaching behind you to soap me hard, both of us

in a lather, your body tipping forward
till your palms lay flat against the tiles, me
holding you steady at the hip, so that our slippery
to-and-froing didn't fling us headfirst or sideways
through the plastic curtain, and we remained within
the beam, like books under a reading lamp, flood-
lit by the brilliance boring down.

And even when limescale blocked the showerhead
and the pillar became a weeping willow,
we hid like fugitives under its spread,

fused and lubricious and in flood, the water
falling in spokes, the shower like an umbrella
in reverse, blessing us with its downpour,
saving our skins from the desert of the world.

Thanatos

What's wrong with me nowadays, how explain why my mattress/Feels so hard? (1.2)

Tick-tack went the noise in the darkness,
which I thought was my heart on the mattress
or the clock down below in the kitchen
not the carpenter knocking nails in my coffin.

Unwanted

Why cheat the laden vine when grapes are ripening...? (2.14)

She called one day, asking to meet
outside her appointed time.
'I've some news,' she said. 'Nothing terrible,
just something you should know.'

We met near a park –
her car and mine in adjoining spaces –
and sat on the grassy slope
as the sun fell in on London.

Nothing terrible? It was the worst.
I'd been so careful
to keep a clean sheet. Now this.
What could have gone wrong?

I'd sometimes felt her coil scratching,
like a paperclip or loose wire.
But perhaps she'd hoiked it out.
We were growing fruit

and she wanted me to rejoice,
to tell her I loved her
and would be with her always,
not to look (as I must have) scared.

I took her hand and squeezed it.
She had a pink gingham dress
and a rash on her legs
from the spiky summer grass.

'You don't want it, do you?' she said.
'It's a shock, that's all.'
'How would you feel if I went ahead?'
'I don't know,' I said.

A mosquito was circling her ankle
and I slapped it dead.
'Ouch.' 'I was trying to help.'
'You're no help at all,' she said.

It was dark by the time we parted,
agreeing to think things over,
our cars turning away from each other
at the bottom of a hill.

She phoned two days later.
'I've made a date at the clinic.
I don't want you with me.
I just need a cheque.'

Blood money, she called it
the night of the weepy call
and the threatened leap
from Vauxhall Bridge.

Later she moved away
but I still get Christmas cards,
with baby Jesus haloed on the front
and her name in red pen inside.

Vodka

I captured a girl! (2.12)

And then there was Jess, a lesbian so they told me:
black leather, tattoos, an Olympiad of nose- and ear-rings.
We had flown to Murmansk, where it was twenty below
and an icebreaker had carved a narrow channel.
Her job was to mind me, mine to read poems from elsewhere,
like an Arctic convoy bringing relief. After the reading,
the reception, the dinner of grilled sturgeon, a crowd of us
drank vodka in my room, then three, then Jess and me.
We perched on the bed, watching ships follow the thread of moving water,
their lights like the shiny beads on her jumper. 'I'm hot in this,'
she said, pulling it over her head, then turned ('Down the hatch')
to chink glasses, our rims clacking clumsily, like teeth, as we drank
to the moon, the future, the icebreaker ploughing a watery furrow.

Wardrobe

There's magic in poetry, its power/Can pull down the moon (2.1)

The place was a side street near the station,
our room scarcely bigger than the wardrobe,

but a bed with eider pillows had been made
and we lay together in the darkness

rubbing each other's bodies like lamps
till the wardrobe door swung open

and next thing we were in and through the back,
alone on a beach by the Aegean,

thyme blowing from the cliffs
and waves gently lapping our feet,

till the wardrobe door swung shut again
to the noise of trains uncoupling

and the swish of traffic on wet tarmac,
before we left next morning in the rain.

X-rated

... this fickle obsession (3.11)

There was always the Internet to gorge on.
Daytime meant work, and I worked like a Trojan,
but at six I'd pour a drink and turn the screen on.

Watch a bitch take a load! Hear the screams of a slut getting her
ass destroyed! See a milf with big tits meet the cock doctor!
It was like watching executions in the amphitheatre

at Pompeii. Sex is supposed to mean desire, but how could I feel it
when the girl on the screen, however exquisite,
had a cock down her throat that was (a) another man's, and (b) a damn sight

bigger than mine? Gagged, chained and corseted,
slapped about the face while doubly penetrated,
the women were lambs to the slaughter, paid

to feign euphoria even when some brute was pissing
on them. Whatever turns you on, yeah, but who could find this exciting?
I thought Caligula had plumbed the depths till I watched fisting.

Still, I too had a favourite website, www.classicalbeauties.
com, featuring goddesses like Juno and Venus
with their breasts naked and a fig leaf hiding the pubis.

They were all mine to imagine. And not a single penis.

Yo-yo

For the hunter, pursuit is all (2.9)

It was always the same.
After sex they'd ask to see me again
whereas for me the thrill had gone.
All I wanted was to be alone
savouring our time together,
which – as I tried to explain
(though they never seemed to hear) –
was impossible with them there.

Then the reverie would fade
and I'd need to share my solitude.
You're gorgeous, I'd go,
though in bed they could be anyone
and I'd be out of there, pronto.
leaving nothing of myself
and never mind the search for
some elusive other half.

Zero

Though flint itself will perish, poetry lives (1.15)

These women I've written about – were they just bodies to me?
Had I no interest in their thoughts and feelings? Didn't I love them?
Of course, while I was with them. But then I went back to my life,
my room, my writing (my writing about them!) and I loved that more.

If I'd been free to be with them, they'd not have loved me as much.
If I'd loved them more, I'd not have been free to write.
It wasn't a deal we shook hands on, but for a time it suited us

and afterwards there were no hard feelings: they found a new man,
and I had my writing, not erotic now but elegiac.

Yes, I loved those women. But remembering, I love them more.